LIZARD TAILS

Juan Marsé was born in Barcelona in 1933. Following
the publication of his first novel in 1960 he has gone on to
become one of the most respected living authors in Spain.
He has been honoured with many literary prizes.

Juan Marsé

LIZARD TAILS

TRANSLATED FROM THE SPANISH BY
Nick Caistor

VINTAGE

Published by Vintage 2004

2 4 6 8 10 9 7 5 3 1

Copyright © Juan Marsé, 2000 and
© Editorial Lumen S.A., 2000
English translation copyright © Nick Caistor, 2003

Juan Marsé has asserted his right under the Copyright,
Designs and Patents Act, 1988 to be identified as the author
of this work

First published in Great Britain in 2003 by
The Harvill Press

Vintage
Random House, 20 Vauxhall Bridge Road,
London SW1V 2SA

Random House Australia (Pty) Limited
20 Alfred Street, Milsons Point, Sydney
New South Wales 2061, Australia

Random House New Zealand Limited
18 Poland Road, Glenfield,
Auckland 10, New Zealand

Random House (Pty) Limited
Endulini, 5A Jubilee Road, Parktown 2193,
South Africa

The Random House Group Limited Reg. No. 954009
www.randomhouse.co.uk

A CIP catalogue record for this book
is available from the British Library

ISBN 0 09 945517 X

Printed and bound in Great Britain by
Bookmarque Ltd, Croydon, Surrey

I do not understand why it is necessary to spread slander. To damage someone, all that is needed is to speak some truth about them.

NIETZSCHE

The poet is a faker
So good at his act
He even fakes the pain
Of pain he feels in fact.

FERNANDO PESSOA

It is hard to fight with the heart: what is desired
Is paid for with life.

HERACLITUS

Of the tyrant say everything, say more.

JOSÉ MARTÍ

I

Memories of Chispa

"Come on, kid. Spit it out."

My parents conceived me many years ago now, but at that moment I can have been in existence for only three or four months. Everything that happened then takes place as if in a dream frozen in the placenta of memory, a time suspended when public masquerading and private misfortune were the order of the day, a time of abuses and unhappiness, of prisons and chains.

"What's up? Cat got your tongue?" The man's stern, gravelly voice breaks over the head of my brother David, as the two of them stand outside our house. Less than half an hour earlier, a dark thunderstorm crashed over the neighbourhood, and now that the morning is bright and clear again, although the light and the breeze seem to caress skin and eyes, David is feeling so fragile and exposed he would probably have preferred to face this imperious command dressed as Shirley Temple, complete with blond corkscrew curls, dimpled cheeks and his little girl's mischievous voice:

"Beg pardon?"

"I said, cough it up, if you've got anything to tell me about your mother . . ." Thick with unconscious rivalry, the voice gets tangled in its own hoarse desire, but the words are not harshly spoken, in fact carry so little threat that any boy less suspicious than David Bartra would have taken them more as an attempt to win him over than as a challenge.

"Are you trying to annoy me, sahib?"

"What do you know?" the visitor insists. "Tell me, whatever it is. I'm really interested. Go on, I'm listening."

I can see it all as if it were taking place right in front of my eyes. The man is standing outside our door, trenchcoat slung over one shoulder, calmly tapping the end of a cigarette on his thumb, waiting. But David can spot the internal combustion beneath the cool exterior, and even before he has been ordered to speak, has seen in the man's moist, world-weary eyes a fleeting image of the woman who disturbs him so much; so he stays quiet, looking inside his own mind and refusing to say anything about what he can see there. For a brief moment, the pair of them, boy and policeman, stand and separately imagine my mother as she waits for a tram in the same place and with the same posture – leaning against a lamp-post in La Travesera, a book open in her hands, with the same sun beating down on her head, the same dreamy look on her face. And our red-head looks so beautiful as she waits, not really reading or thinking about the page in front of her, concentrating instead on the blue smoke curling up from the cigarette between her fingers, or perhaps on somewhere beyond the smoke, on some sombre recess of the light, an ill-omened dark flutter of wings only she can perceive on this radiant July morning.

"Well?"

Still waiting for my brother to make up his mind, Inspector Galván cups his hand briefly to shelter the flame from a lighter which, half-hidden by his long, darkly veined fingers, David guesses must be gold and engraved. Then, the lit cigarette between his lips, the inspector repeats his question, standing there hands at the level of his midriff, as though ready to suppress any shooting pain in his liver or sudden heartburn. Seeing his hands pale and defenceless like that, it is hard to imagine they ever gripped a gun, or were capable of smashing into the face of someone tied to a chair, but they do look as if they were swift and caring enough to catch a woman about to faint and fall to the pavement. "A woman smoking in public!" a passer-by grumbles, staring at her disapprovingly, but the inspector's hand signals him to calm down and move on, just be on your way, he says. He doesn't fool me pretending to be so meek and mild, David thinks to himself: they're the hands of a man with no feelings, a real son of a bitch. I'm watching you, flat-foot, I've got my tabs on you, you've no idea who you're dealing with.

"What are you waiting for?"

"First show me your badge."

"But you know me. I'm the one who looked after your mother when she collapsed in the street."

"Is that so?"

"Don't try to be clever with me."

This was the opening skirmish in a baleful combat from which neither of them emerged unscathed, although neither started it on purpose: it simply grew out of a file kept somewhere deep in the archives of hatred and betrayal. But that's another story.

"Ah, yes," David says. "You were following her so closely you bumped into her. That's why you were able to catch her under the arms before she fell into the gutter. What a stroke of luck that was, wasn't it?"

"I was there by coincidence."

"Like hell you were."

"Don't waste my time, kid. You said you stopped me to tell me something important about Señora Bartra. So go on, I'm listening."

"I don't know if it's important. But I know it interests you . . ."

"Come on, tell me what it's about."

"Don't shout so loud . . . I've got a hedgeful of chaffinches in my ears . . . but OK, I'll tell you. My mother's found out that Dad was exploring the River Nile with Lieutenant Harry Faversham – that was last week, both of them were disguised as natives of the Shangali tribe. And as you must know – all the cops in the world know it, I'm sure, the Shangali cannot speak because they all had their tongues cut out on orders from the Khalif, that's why they have a mark of fire on their foreheads. Anyway, with the white feathers in their bags and dying of thirst, my father and Lieutenant Faversham must by now be crossing the desert to join up with the Anglo-Egyptian army commanded by Lord Kitchener in its unstoppable advance on Khartoum . . ."

"That'll do, kid. You're getting seriously on my nerves."

"If you don't believe me, why not arrest me?" David brings his wrists together in front of him, and stares down at the ground, still keeping one eye out for the inspector's idle fists, just in case: "Go on, cuff me!"

As he holds out his hands mockingly, the left one is grasping the cut-off tail of a lizard. How much longer can you survive, little tail? Five minutes earlier, David had been staring fascinated at it writhing on a smooth stone in the riverbed of the gully.

"So, what did you want to tell me about your mother?" the inspector persists.

"Listen, shall I tell you the truth? I simply wanted to get a good look at a flatfoot's mug," David says with a smile, thinking that the first time the redhead felt a furtive caress from those hands at the tram stop, the first time she felt his tobacco breath on her neck, and saw his taut mouth and cold eyes close to her, she could have had no idea the guy was following her, or suspect he was a cop: "That was all I wanted, really, to see what kind of a face you'd make when you were being taken for a ride. Does that bother you?"

The inspector stares at him without a word. He shakes his head pityingly.

"So how long is the joke going to last, kid? Don't you think it's time you snapped out of it? I'll have to have a serious talk with your mother."

"She's asleep. But you could ring the bell if you want." He slips the lizard tail into his pocket, and adds: "Allah protect us, sahib. This lizard is poisonous. I'm getting out of here."

"So you didn't have the slightest intention of telling me anything, you brat."

"No, sir. What for? All I wanted to do was gain some time, so my mother could sleep a bit longer. Just a little while longer."

This might not have been their first meeting or their first tussle, but I remember it took place near our house and in the middle of summer, probably just a few days before the afternoon when there was another downpour and David appeared carrying a mangy jet-black dog in his arms, the dirtiest, most decrepit mongrel imaginable.

"Good God!" the red-head exclaims: "Where on earth did you find that poor beast? You can't be thinking of keeping it."

"He's sick, and no-one wants him. He used to belong to Señor Augé, and now he's ours."

"What do you mean, ours?"

"I'll explain," David says, clutching the dog to him while he dreams up what he is going to say. "You know they picked up Señor Augé, and as he lives alone and didn't know who to leave the dog with, he told the caretaker woman that if I happened to pass by . . ."

"That's all we needed! Have you any idea the work it'll give us?" my mother complains, one hand on her belly, checking perhaps that I was curled up fast asleep, and protecting my prenatal dreams against the flea-ridden presence of this skinny bag of bones.

Her tender gaze meets that of the dog.

"Yes he's very old I know and almost blind and half-dead with rheumatism and so on," David says, "but he's very good and obedient, you'll see, Ma, you'll really love him."

"Do me a favour."

The dog, sprawled trembling on the floor between David's feet, gives a huge sigh that gradually turns into panting and ends with a snoring cough that somehow trails off like a cat's miaow.

"Did you hear that?" says David. "Señor Augé said that in another life this dog had been a cat. He's got a cat's soul."

"I can see it can't keep body and soul together, poor thing, whether it's a dog or a cat."

4

"Don't say it so loud, he might hear. He understands everything!"

"Oh, my boy, how little you understand!" Mother says, busily rubbing the dog's fur with a towel. Her gaze as she looks at my brother has a tenderness which unfortunately I was never to experience, but even in my dreams I can perceive the tiny butterfly of emotion fluttering in her voice: "Couldn't you stop and think just once before you do something, my love?"

I couldn't agree more.

I'm not talking to you, runt, David mutters, turning to the wall, head down.

Don't you have a brain? Couldn't you use your noggin a bit before you bring yet another worry to our red-head, with all the problems she has already? A fine present our dear first-born has lumbered us with, and the day before Pa's birthday too. . . !

You're nothing but a greedy tit-sucker, and I'm not going to let you meddle in my business.

"What on earth are you muttering, David?" Mother says, getting an old blanket out of the wardrobe. "Turn round, so I can see you properly."

"I was saying the dog could stay with us, at least until Señor Augé gets home."

"Señor Augé won't be coming home in a long while, if he ever does."

"So what, then? Are we going to leave the poor thing to die in the street, just like that?"

"Don't tell me you're going to cry? I know you. For now, take this towel, dry him properly, and let him lie down over there. Then we'll see."

"We're both very tired," David says, stretching out beside the dog and kissing it on the snout. "We've walked miles, until we almost dropped. Can we shut the window and see if we can sleep a bit on the blanket, can we?"

Only a minute ago, I was floating curled up in my mother's womb, but even in that sticky darkness my eyes could already glimpse the light of this world, and all its deceptive illusions: what I see and what I don't see are one and the same. Now, someone has shut the windows and blinds once more, my cousin Lucía has brought me my glass of milk and the medicine and tucked me in, and my memories are swaying above the void, trying to find somewhere to cling on to, some fresh voice to guide me. Darkness shrouds all I can remember of that house; everything speaks of frustration, of suppressed emotions, of silences at table concealing family disasters, hidden events, heartbreak. I can't find the words, but I can hear voices.

Zapastra!

Holy shit!

Tinker!

Lucía, assmewarapis!

First name and family names!

Víctor Bartra Lángara!

Achtung!

"Good grief, Ma! Is it true what they say, that he managed to escape by throwing himself headfirst down the gully?"

"It didn't happen the way you imagine, David."

"And that he fell into a bramble bush and got a scar like a lightning flash on his face?"

"No, he didn't," the red-head tells him. "Your father slid down the gully on his backside. And unfortunately, he caught on a sharp piece of glass – probably a bit of broken bottle – and it slit his buttock open like a ripe water-melon. That's what happened. Nothing more, nothing less."

Mother's rough red hands are searching among coloured scraps of material in a cardboard box, and David breathes in all the smells. There are starch and bleach, and the windows let in a light like cottonwool. The house I never lived in is more real and tangible to me than this chewed-on pencil I use to scrawl with on the sheet of paper. Disbelieving and disappointed, David repeats:

"Really? He slid down on his arse?"

"That's right."

"Well, but he thumbed his nose at the people chasing him. He left them empty-handed. And it took courage to do that."

"It took a whole bottle of brandy, that's what it took."

David did not see the famous night-time escape, but he more than everyone wanted to establish the exact truth of this episode at least, which is why several years later he told it me in such great detail. Our father is barefoot and his shirt-tails are hanging out – he scarcely had time to get dressed when he leapt out of bed – but it wasn't because he was so terrified at the cops bursting in or the brandy he had drunk which made him slide down the steep bank of the gully, shoes in one hand and bottle of Fundador in the other, even though the situation was so similar to many previous ones the whole neighbourhood had witnessed: that hothead, that layabout Víctor Bartra rushing around at all hours to rouse his drinking pals, to the despair of his poor wife – all right, it might have looked like that, but in this case he wasn't drunk and was not scared shit-less. He skipped out during that confused transition somewhere between night and dawn, out of the back of the house which years before had been not the back but a showy façade and small front garden – you should have seen him sliding barefoot down the gully, trying to avoid the big stones in fig-tree roots,

6

or the dried stumps of cork-oaks, then letting himself slide to the bottom of the ravine in a cloud of red dust, getting to his feet and standing there seething with fury and bitterness, but still in one piece, alert and quick as lightning, according to my brother David, like a scarecrow or a befuddled duck according to my mother, with torn trousers and bloody arse open to the skies.

"And of course, with his bottle intact and himself safe and sound. That is how your beloved father left home. A sorry sight, my boy."

But if I am to do this properly, if the tumult of voices allows me some respite, the story I am proposing to tell really begins when Inspector Galván knocks at the door of our house one day when I am not there.

We live at the top end of the city, in a dead-end street almost at the edge of a gully. Our house has two doors: one of them opens on to the street and the day; the other to the night and the gully, a shallow ravine of red earth with steep, porous sides that crumble almost as soon as you go near. On that particular occasion, I don't know whether the inspector rang the bell at the day-time door, or banged the knocker on the night-time side (a dainty girl's hand firmly grasping a rusty iron ball) but what my brother David heard that midday of sunshine and showers, convinced as he is that the two doors fulfil different, though complementary functions – as he puts it, one of them allows you to hide in the house during the day, the other helps you escape at night – must have been the sound of the door-knocker, which is only logical because the visit took place during the hours of rationing, and if there was no electricity how could the cop have used the bell? So what, there was no way you could have heard it, because you weren't here, there, or anywhere, shrimp, you hadn't poked your nose out yet.

OK, you're right, you lived it, but I imagined it. Don't think you're that far ahead of me on the road to truth, brother.

I'll always be ahead of you, worm.

But I've found a shortcut.

I don't want to argue with you. You confuse me. I don't know where I am.

You're in your mother's room, for example, while she is sewing doll's clothes or trying blouses and boleros on you in front of the mirror, looking at you face on, from the side, and from the back as well no doubt. It's very hot, it's the summer of the bomb on Hiroshima and that's why when you hear the knocking at the door you say to Chispa: be careful, when I open up you move to one side, in case the atomical blast gets in and you're blinded and burnt to a cinder.

7

Anyway, on that occasion it was easy to guess who was at the door, so it was better to take his time before opening it, and David does so, hiding behind his favourite pose – hand on hip in his little girl's disguise, a pretty pink angora jersey, sky-blue pleated skirt, white stockings pulled up to plump, smiling knees and a red Perspex handbag slung from his shoulder. He is also wearing a pair of cheap white plastic sunglasses, bought at a funfair, and a red beret that covers his honey-coloured curls pulled down over one eyebrow.

"If you've come looking for the sahib, he's not at home."

Standing in the doorway, the trenchcoat taut across his broad shoulders, wet hat in one hand and mud on his shoes, Inspector Galván looks at him evenly. His eyes are bright, but his look is sombre. He's not like other cops, even David has to admit that, he's not one of those who conceal their faces behind dark glasses even when the sky is cloudy. The inspector does not seem to mind that people can see his eyes, even read some emotion in them – whether it is resentment or more usually, complete indifference. Nor does he show his badge or mention any search warrant. He does not even try to enter the house.

"Ask your mother to please step outside a moment." Then, with a rougher edge to his voice, but still just as quietly: "Clown."

"The memsahib isn't in either."

"Will she be long?"

"Do you have a search warrant?"

"That's not why I'm here. I repeat: will Señora Bartra be long?"

One of his large trenchcoat pockets bulges suspiciously. That's not where they normally carry their revolvers, David thinks, as behind his ridiculous sunglasses his eyes bore through the rainproof material and the pocket lining: a hip flask full of brandy, a few coins down among the shreds of tobacco and fluff, house keys and the lighter, a counterfeit Dupont hidden behind a much-handled packet of Lucky Strikes – I bet the flatfoot buys cigarettes one by one and fills it up . . .

What I'm describing are facts that I am reconstructing from my memories of secrets and suggestions my brother told me. I do not claim everything is completely accurate, but it is the closest I can get to the truth.

"Can't you hear me?" the inspector persists. "I asked if she was coming back soon."

"I don't know, bwana. I know nothing."

David looks down, anticipating the impatient clearing of the throat and the scornful phlegm that thickens the next question:

"What are you playing at, kid? You'd do better to tell me where your mother has gone."

"Yes, of course." David keeps his gaze on the floor, and says nothing. He smoothes down his skirt, straightens his beret, adjusts the bag strap on his shoulder, and finally adds: "Seeing you're so interested, I'll tell you. She's gone to the maternity clinic for her doctor's check-up, and after that she has a lot of things to do . . . she has to visit Granny Tecla, who had a stroke and is paralysed on one side of her face, then go to the chemist's, and then she wanted to buy a pair of nylons and an evening gown, and she told me that if she had the time she might go and look at a villa with a garden that's for sale over in Tres Torres — don't think for a moment we're going to carry on sub-letting for the rest of our lives in this crappy neighbourhood where everyone's packed in like sardines. Do you know Tres Torres? It's a select place, the best in Barcelona: that's where my mother was born, and her parents before her — they died in an air-raid. In fact by next week we'll have moved, so remember, when you come back it'll be too late, we'll have upped and gone. I'm pretty sure of it."

"I feel sorry for you, kid," the inspector growls, turning his head to one side while David makes his speech, as though he's afraid of being spattered by all this torrent of rubbish. He puts his hand in his pocket and feels the hip flask, but does not take it out. "How long has it been since your father gave you a good hiding?"

"Aha, so now it's the third degree, is it?" David rests one hand on the door jamb, and places the other on his jauntily swaying hip. "Well, seeing you're so concerned, I must confess I haven't seen my father since the night he leapt into the ravine and escaped to the land of the Kubangas."

"Lift your head and look me in the eye," the inspector says.

"To the jungle. Don't tell me you didn't know."

"What crap are you talking about now?"

"About the jungle in *The Real Glory*. That's where he is now."

The policeman heaves a sigh and puts his hat on. He seems about to leave, but hesitates. "Telling lies is in your blood, kid." David lifts first his left knee to pull up his stocking, then the right, balancing on one foot. Then slowly and delicately he returns his hand to his hip like a rare butterfly, and gazes down at the ground once more. The inspector glowers at him.

"Take off those glasses and look me in the face. I want to see your eyes when you talk to me."

"Bwana stay where he is. I've got a stye on my eye the size of a melon."

"I feel sorry for your mother. I bet she spends the whole day just wishing your father would come back and deal with you as you deserve . . ."

"Do you think so?"

"And at the same time praying that Señor Bartra stops drinking and getting himself into scrapes, wherever he might be. I mean," the inspector adds in a very different, more agreeable voice that seems out of character: "wishing that this situation were over and done with. That your father would come back soon. That he would look after you all."

"I don't know, bwana. We don't mention him at home."

"You're trying to tell me you never talk about him? Don't you miss him?"

"No, we never mention him. The red-head won't have it."

"That's a fine way to talk about your mother."

"She doesn't mind." David smiles sweetly and wiggles his hip. "It's a compliment. My dear Daddy always called her that."

He hears a faint groan and looks away for a moment. In his mind's eye he sees his father's bloody arse and the handkerchief pressed tightly against it.

The inspector says nothing for a few seconds.

"So you've nothing to tell me? You must at least know where your father used to work."

"In the intrepid ratcatchers' brigade."

"Don't be such an idiot."

"Cross my heart and hope to die!" David says. "He killed rats in cinemas!"

"I mean before that. Before he was a Municipal Hygiene employee."

"I wouldn't know, bwana. I was very small. I think he was an anaesthetist. Did you know rats can invade cinemas and attack people? Did you know a pair of rats can give birth to 25,000 disgusting babies each year?"

"Haven't you had any news from him at all, after six months?"

"Yes, but news from the year dot, and it was all bad," David stifles a forced yawn, and a sudden urge to shiver in his angora jersey, which is too small for him and shows his navel. "We did get a letter from him, and it turns out he's not where we thought he was . . . I'll tell you. He always said he wanted to go on a long journey to the heart of Africa, from Khartoum to Lake Victoria via the Blue Mountains, but it turns out he changed his plans at the last minute. Day by day he's penetrating deeper into the jungle of Mindanao – do you know where that is, bwana? In the Philippines. And he writes that he has had to disguise himself as a Juramentado to capture Datu and all the traffickers in pigs' hides and elephant tusks. There's more – he says it's a lie that the Juramentados die of fear if they are wrapped in a pig's skin. It's a rotten lie."

The inspector, head tilted back as if afraid he might catch something from David's words, has his eyes half-closed and is apparently dozing.

"Is that all?"

Beneath the delicate, haughty arc of his brows, David's insolent stare shows how suspicious he is of the inspector's cool imperturbability.

"No, bwana. The Juramentados are like horses, they can only be killed by a bullet between the eyes . . . do you know how to shoot like that? In his letter, my father says that rather than let himself be captured by the Kubanga pygmies, he will shoot himself with his repeater rifle. The letter was sent four months ago, so maybe he's already kicked it. The parish priest at Las Ánimas told my mother he's probably already in hell, because that's where all suicides end up, that's what the shitty bastard of a priest told her. He didn't make her cry because the red-head is tough, but he had no right to talk to her that way."

"Finished?"

"Yes, bwana."

Out of his raincoat's bulging pocket, the inspector takes a book roughly covered with newspaper.

"When your mother gets back, give her this from me. She dropped it at the tram stop the other day. I covered it as best I could, because it's a bit torn."

"You didn't do much of a job, did you?" David says, taking the book between two fingers as if it is infected. "Was that the only reason you came? That's a good one."

And whether this and whether that. Whether they have seen her crying, whether she suffers from nerves and is diabetic and smokes like a man, whether she and her son live on ten pesetas a day . . . Well, all that may be true, but listen, you'll never see her complain, even though her back plays her up even worse than mine, and she is so pale, there are days when her face is yellower than this lemon here, but even so, you'll never hear a word from her. She works wonders with old clothes and a needle.

That's right. Señora Bartra is always working. But she's also polite and friendly: she's a tremendous person, and very well-educated.

First name and family names, come on.

They say she was a schoolteacher.

That red-headed seamstress is still young and very attractive.

A woman on her own, who gets by as best she can. Like so many other women today, Rufina.

Does she like coffee? Strange question for a police officer to ask! Who doesn't if they can get it, isn't that right, Puri? But you should see the price of real coffee nowadays. Or are you asking because you think the red-head might be selling it on the black market? She would never do that. There are so many lies going round . . .

But the way she looks so young, that little girl's face she has, with her pale white skin and that carrot-top, I'm not so sure . . .

Don't ask me anything. I don't know a thing, and that's the truth.

The truth? This blasted dead-end is so narrow you couldn't get the truth out of it with a pair of forceps.

What a load of nonsense you talk, Rufina.

One of our friend here's cousins, Emilia, is in jail for receiving goods that might have been stolen. So who knows?

Señora Bartra's husband? A good-for-nothing.

When they come looking for him . . .

Hey, don't insult him, there's no need.

. . . there must be something to it.

The last time I saw him, he tried to fool me. I asked him: Señor Bartra, how's things? And he lit an Ideales, he was holding the packet just like this – excuse me – then shouted out: Long Live Spain! had a sly glance at my backside, and walked off.

Whenever you turn your back on him, the first thing he does is have a good look at your arse.

He spent that whole night hiding in the gully . . .

Half a league, half a league, half a league onwards.

. . . sleeping with one eye open, like tigers do.

And another woman says:

And what about his son? He spends the whole blessed day out in the street, missing school, or hidden down in the gully clutching a knife, or distributing photos of weddings and baptisms. He's the devil's creature, just like his father.

Yes, nothing good will come from that boy.

Then, as if the hot dry wind had silenced them, the voices disappear from the street, only to resurface after siesta time in whispers in shady doorways or apartment block landings, and at suppertime they boil up again amid the greasy smell of porridge and cabbage and fried heaven knows what, and by nightfall they have become a serpent's hiss, like the hissing sound that has lodged itself permanently in David's tormented hearing. All the while, the policeman's hand calmly fingering his lapel, letting them sense his authority, encouraging the voices and fears:

Ask me, sir, don't bother my husband, he knows nothing.

Nor does mine. But he is not against the regime. It's just that he's a bit deaf.

Mine is a member of the Devout Fraternity of the Bearers of the Body of Christ.

And mine has won the Great Cross of the Airforce Order of Merit. He's a strong supporter of the regime, believe me.

Mine's got a bout of scabies. These are hard times, and no mistake.

First name and family names! I want names!

Miró, Zabala, Benito; Raich, Rosalench, Franco; Sospedra, Escola, Martín, César and Bravo.

All of us go to Mass on Sunday, honest to God.

The only thing wrong with my husband is he spits a lot. He spends the whole day hawking up phlegm, everything disgusts him.

One night, the seamstress's husband said he was going out to buy a soft drink, and he hasn't been seen since.

Soft drink, my foot, Paca! What a child you are!

And another voice adds her pennyworth:

He's a drunkard and a bigmouth, like a fairground stall-owner.

A charlatan, a good-for-nothing, adds Señora Carmela. A real specimen.

Something very serious must have happened the last time he showed his face round here. He changed completely overnight.

Lately he was going around like a tramp, his trousers hanging down and always drunk. But that's how Trini likes them, isn't it, love?

Me? What are you saying, sweetheart? I like men who shave properly and dress well, you know that.

Don't tell such fibs, Trini, you could be excommunicated!

If you are interested, one day my husband saw him so drunk he could hardly stand.

I reckon his wife couldn't stand any more from him . . .

Oh, Rufina, you're as deaf as a post!

. . . especially when she was about to miscarry and that rogue was nowhere to be found.

He was a one! He would see a broom with a skirt on and chase it. Isn't that true, Trini my love?

You're asking me? the youngest of them says, as a gust of wind blows her printed skirt up. Her hands are busy with her sewing, so she makes no attempt to smoothe it down, and it goes on billowing round her short, milk-white thighs.

Trini, your skirt.

What's the matter?

Well, I like him, says another woman who's just joined the group. It's obvious he was once a fine-looking man, a real character.

Pull your skirt down, sweetie.

Why bother? Didn't you know we whores don't have legs? We don't have legs or backsides or souls or anything of any worth, a priest told a friend of mine the other day when she went to confession.

They say he hid all night and the next day not far from here, half a league upstream, hidden in the roots of a dried-up fig tree.

His wife refused to take him any food or clothing. She didn't even want to see him. Let the bastard suffer, they say she said.

That's not so, Felisa. Listen to me, Inspector, if you want to know the truth. That poor neighbour of ours – the red-head, we call her – whose husband you're so interested in, for whatever reason, we don't want to get mixed up in politics, but let it be said I always like to co-operate with authority if I get the chance, and I go to Mass too; well anyway, as I was saying, that good woman the seamstress is no saint – nowadays you'll only find saints on altars, let's admit it – but I can tell you she never feels bitter or betrayed by her husband, and I know for certain she's no whore or blackmarketeer or even a Red like some we've all known, no, she's a señora and it shows, however things may be these days, if you catch my meaning . . .

My husband isn't interested in politics. His passion is collecting stamps.

A poor woman who kills herself working. A refined, well-educated person, who always knows her place.

Outside her front door she has a wonderful bed of marguerites.

You can tell she's not from these parts, there's something about her.

Relatives? A sister in Vallcarca, but they don't speak to each other. The sister used to live in a village called La Carroña, in Tarragona province. On her husband's side? Well, her mother-in-law died in a home not long ago, she had suffered a stroke and didn't recognize anyone. Her father-in-law also died, a year ago. They lived in Mataró, he was a fishmonger . . .

A fisherman, Rufina. You'll only confuse the inspector here.

The fisherman never wanted to know about his son, Señor Bartra. It was one of those stories of broken families, unsettled scores, or whatever.

Women left in the lurch. Dead children. Husbands who'll never come home. That's the way things are these days, sir.

Señora Bartra? She must be three months gone, I'd say.

Four at least, Aurelia.

There is more:

I don't like to mention it, but the red-head has had to cope with two miscarriages. Two or three at least.

What a gossip you are, Consuelo!

She loved her man. That's all there is to it.

How stupid we women are, aren't we?

My life is spent going from home to church, church to home, Inspector.

What else? . . . Well, that poor woman rents rooms in the house they live in. And she must be exhausted. At least she can sleep soundly now that donkey of a husband of hers has done a bunk. And us neighbours too. No cloud without a silver lining, is there? And so on and so forth, on and on.

Over the years, my brother had the chance to get a good look at the faces and behaviour of quite a few of the denizens of the Politico-Social Brigade. He concluded that nearly all of them adopt the same crude tactic of trying to scare you, of planting themselves right in front of you and standing there like great big brutes, eyeing you scornfully and lazily for a few seconds before they deign to ask you anything; but that Inspector Galván was very different. He had his own way of standing for long periods on a street corner or in the middle of the road, opposite a building or behind the window of a bar, a very personal knack of staying still and motionless on his two feet, his colourless mouth stretched taut and with those narrow, cold eyes of his; eyes that never changed, whatever horror they witnessed. He looked on everything with the same chilly disdain, whether it was a flower-shop window display or a street drain, the back of someone walking away from him, a balcony or a closed window, not as if he were expecting it to open and someone to appear, more as though he had just said goodbye to that person and had forgotten to tell them something they would have preferred not to hear anyway. Whether he was looking at the foyer of the Delicias or Iberia cinemas, the Camelias market or a pretty girl walking by, questioning a group of gossipy neighbours in the street, or simply staring at a stray dog, he seemed so used to just standing there, so still and with his shoulders slightly hunched, and so cut off from all the noise of life around him, indifferent to the grey drizzle or the scorching sun, that more often than not he looked like someone from another town who had got lost in the neighbourhood, who wasn't worried about it, and was in no hurry to ask directions or anything else. His tall figure and slow, lethargic movements gave the false impression that he might be handicapped in some way, as though he had a muscular impediment or was under a spell, or was immobile by nature.

Who knows whether that day too he followed her from the moment she left the house, or whether he was already waiting on the corner of Calle Escorial to watch her arrive with her palm-leaf shopping basket and stand in the queue at the number 24 tram terminal. To kill time, the red-head lights a cigarette and opens an old, much-loved hardback book, a novel I have with me now, covered with blue paper. She always loved reading, and took advantage of any chance she had to do so: how often has David seen her standing in the kitchen by the tiny electric stove, book open in one hand, wooden spoon in the other, stirring the food and moving her lips at the same time, following the words and the cooking with equal attention, as if both were rituals. And she also liked marking how far she had got with brightly coloured pieces of card, and covering the books the way they taught her to when she was a child in school. Now she stands beneath the riotous shadow of a bougainvillea spilling over a wall by the number 24 terminal, her beautiful red hair drawn up in a bun, wearing her pretty flower dress and her grey rubber sandals, while Inspector Galván watches her from the street corner, head down low and eyes hidden under his hat brim, motionless as ever. He seems surprised, as if this were the first time he had ever seen a woman reading in the street and smoking a cigarette, and pregnant too. Or is he merely doing his job, does he simply want to find out where she is heading, who she is going to meet, and if either of these things has anything to do with our father, wherever he may be? Could it be that he is simply carrying out orders?

The fact is, the cop has started to behave and say things that do not seem to have much to do with his life as a flatfoot. A week after their far from casual meeting in the market, where the red-head often goes for her work, David runs into him again leaving the grocery store, and once again finds himself being closely questioned. This time, after glancing at the provisions David is carrying in his shopping bag, the inspector wants to know if the doctor has told the red-head she must give up the coffee she likes so much.

"Is that the kind of thing cops want to know?" David asks, intrigued. "I had no idea. Well yes, sir, she does like real coffee. And cream and hot fritters. So do I. She says they're cravings. Because all three of us like them, see?"

It's true, she loves coffee, and its aroma often invades the world of her daydreams and her books; even now she believes she can smell it in the pages of the book she's reading, filling the sad Natasha's lonely room. She shuts the book and tucks it under her arm. This is another afternoon, and she is wearing a freshly ironed mauve blouse and a full brown skirt with flat shoes; she is carrying an umbrella over her arm. As she gets on the tram, the book slips from her, without her noticing bounces on the step and against her umbrella, then falls face down on the wet cobblestones. The tram sets off, and its wheel gently nudges the book away from the rail, without crushing it. In days to come the inspector would probably say he ran to warn her, but it's more likely he didn't make the slightest effort – no point running for something which, on reflection, he would prefer to hand back to her in person at her house. But I can see him bending over to pick the book up, I can see him standing there in the middle of the tram tracks, head tilted forward and shoulders hunched, as if hoping for some kind of reward, as he uses his coatsleeve to wipe painstakingly the stained and crumpled page – a man who perhaps has not held a book in months, if not years.

Absorbed in the torn page, his eyes narrowed in order to retain a moment longer the vision of the red-head and the tram moving off down Avenida Lesseps, the inspector reads: *In the last days of December, wearing a black woollen suit, with unkempt locks and hollow, pallid features, Natasha lay on the sofa staring at the door as she rolled and unrolled the end of her belt. She was staring at the spot where he had left her life for ever.*

She has seen him in the distance, and will always keep in her memory the image of the inspector bending down to the cobblestones to recover her book with an almost religious gesture. This is perhaps the first time she feels any affection for this man she hardly knows. She must think that to pick up a dirty, torn book in the street like that, and to wipe it with his sleeve as he does with such meticulous care, shows at least a certain kind-heartedness.

"I repeat: when she gets home, give her this from me. Tell her she dropped it at the number 24 tram stop. I've covered it as best I could."

David's hand reaches out to take the book. He is still leaning in the entrance, and doesn't open the door; his other hand is still fluttering around his waist. Beneath the red beret and his blond curls, he is still staring at the floor. But his attitude is far from submissive. It's more a sly mixture of fantasy and spite.

"Did you cover it? It looks lovely, bwana."

"If it weren't for your mother and not wanting to add to her worries, I'd rip off your ears and pull out your tongue, kid. Do you hear me?"

"Seriously?"

"You bet."

Inspector Galván's tone is level and clipped, not obviously threatening. He does not growl or spit out his words. But in reply David does, as fiercely as he knows how:

"I know you're following my mother. You follow her in the street, hiding so she doesn't see you. You follow her and follow her. Why?"

The inspector thinks for a moment before replying.

"Sometimes one has to do things which might upset people."

"Like shit! Are you following her in case she leads you to my father? Or is there some other reason?"

"Drop it, kid. Look me in the eye. Have you told her about me?"

"No, but I will."

"You won't." The inspector comes closer to David and leans down towards him: "Otherwise, I'll tell her what you let the barber's boy do to you in the Delicias cinema, the fat kid with a squint, what's his name . . . the one who's always going around with a pair of maracas."

David finally lifts his face, but the big cheap sunglasses hide the vengeful flash in his eyes. In turn, the inspector leans a little closer, stares at him fixedly, and adds:

"You know what I mean. Your mother would die of shame. And we don't want that, do we?"

"No."

"So there's nothing more to say, is there?"

"Yes, bwana."

The inspector shakes his head despairingly. He turns to leave, then thinks better of it and comes back to confront David once more.

"What's the matter with you, anyway? Do you really like it, or does he pay you? Is it just a game for you? Why do you do it?"

David considers his response, eyes twinkling behind the glasses.

"I'll tell you something. No-one is ever going to see me with a hand on my backside!"

"What do you mean?"

"They say my father is going about with one hand on his arse the whole time, like a poor beggar, but you can be sure my mother will never have to see me in such a state. And you won't get another word out of me on the subject, however much you question me, bwana."

"I can't remember the name of your friend, that little angel. Bardolet, isn't it?"

"Paulino Bardolet, at your service, the service of God and all the buggering angels. Now what's wrong?"

"You're so foul-mouthed and shameless you leave me speechless, kid. Just listen: I don't want to see you with that Paulino boy again. And I don't want you to tell your mother."

The inspector stands there considering him for a few moments, once again demonstrating that ability of his to stay so stock-still he seems like a block of ice. As he leaves, he reaches out to give David a presumably friendly cuff round the head, but the boy ducks away from it. As he does so, behind him the inspector spots the basset hound dragging itself across the floor, tail between its legs and ears at half-mast.

"Where on earth did that come from?"

"He's mine," David says hurriedly. "The usher at the Delicias gave him to me. I promised to look after him. Anything wrong with that?"

The dog sniffs at David's stockings and gives a cough that seems more like an urge to be sick, revealing its skinny ribcage. The inspector takes a deep breath, as if reluctantly trying to find the strength to say something more.

"It's a stray," he says, turning his head to look down the path that runs along the top of the dried-up riverbed – hoping, David thinks, to see the red-head coming towards him – and then pretends to be interested in the dog, though only to while away time. "A mongrel."

"Yes, bwana. A mongrel. A ragbag."

"A bit old, isn't it? What do you call it?"

"Chispa," David says. "What's the matter, don't you like him? Señor Augé found him abandoned in the foyer of the Delicias. He called him Niebla, because that week they were showing a film called *Random Harvest*. He also thought of calling him Nodo, because whenever he heard the music at the start of the Nodo Newsreel he perked up . . ."

"Good for him . . ."

"The whole world brought to you for your dogs' delight, Señor Augé used to say. What's wrong, don't you like that either?"

"I feel sorry for you, kid."

"Why, bwana? What have I done?"

Chispa, crushed on the floor by age and infirmity, tries to wag his tail, but gives up almost at once, and turns his less rheumy eye on the inspector.

"That creature is more dead than alive."

"You don't understand animals."

"You'd do it a favour if you put it out of its misery."

"What! What did you say?"

"The best thing would be to give it a strychnine pellet."

"Like shit it would! I'm helping him get better!"

"All you're going to do is make it suffer more. What does your mother say?"

"That's none of your business! The dog is mine! And I'm not going to put an end to him because he's old, sick, or whatever my mother might say!"

"OK," the inspector says, turning to go. "Don't forget what I told you . . ."

"And another thing, bwana." David interrupts him again defiantly, perhaps to divert the conversation from the topic of the red-head, to stop the inspector getting anywhere near her even in word or thought: "Why don't you tell me what happened to the hanged man in the Calle Legalidad? What have you got to say about that? You saw him hanging from the rafters like a ragdoll, didn't you?"

"I've heard something about it," growls the inspector.

"Apparently he was being followed. They say he hanged himself because he was tired of hiding."

"Hiding from whom? From what?"

"He left a letter explaining he was doing it because of his wife. I saw him dangling from the rope. His tongue was hanging out, and there were bright scarlet spots on his cheeks like a clown. He signed the letter he left in a very strange way: The Invisible Worm. What do you think that meant?"

The inspector raises his eyebrows and sighs.

"I don't know anything about worms. Adiós. And don't forget to give that to your mother."

"Yes, bwana."

From behind the shield of his plastic sunglasses, David watches him stride away past the grey mounds of earth on the gully edge. A thrust from Lagardère's sword will send you into the next world, flatfoot! He closes the night-time door, picks up Chispa and in his pleated skirt and pretty angora jersey runs through deserted rooms piled with furniture that creaks beneath its ghostly coverings, pushes his way through the green curtain in the corridor and the frosted glass door separating the villa from the doctor's consulting rooms, and reaches the tiny dwelling we sublet from the owners. He flings open the daytime door that leads out into the street, and takes Chispa for a walk so he can have a good sniff at all the piles of droppings other dogs have left and perhaps, who can tell, feel a little less lonely and decrepit. Who can tell?

Ma asked David to wake her at half past three. A few minutes ago she took her swollen feet from the salty water in the bowl, and now she is sleeping her siesta in the wicker armchair. David goes quietly over to her, removes the basin, and wraps her feet in a towel. Before he stands up again, he takes her by the hand to make sure she is fast asleep and then, very gently, hugs her legs and presses his cheek and ear against her stomach. An undone button on her housecoat allows him to caress the warm skin stretched over her navel, and to hear the faint murmur of what sounds like a melody, as if the red-head were singing in her dreams, and as the tune fell through her body, it lodged in her womb. Can you hear me, midget? Even when she's asleep, she has a song on her lips. What do you make of that, microbe, can you hear her heart through her blood? Why is she singing in her dreams, and who is she singing to?

You don't want to know, brother. It's better you don't know.

Why not?

You'd fall flat if you knew.

Is it one of her secrets? Don't turn round like that: answer me, you little leech! David mutters. If you can hear me, tell me something. You, who according to Ma are going to become someone so clever and important one day, what would you do in my place, seeing how that jinx of a con artist copper is pursuing her? Especially after what happened the other day.

I didn't see anything.

He rubbed out the poor guy without so much as a second glance, he sent him to the other world just like that! Everyone on the tram saw it!

Well, I was there, but I didn't see it. Is it so hard for you to understand, ninny? It's precisely because I didn't see it that I can imagine it much better than you. It must have been horrible.

Horrible? It was terrifying! Let me tell you about it. After lunch on Sunday, the red-head told me 'Comb your hair and smarten up a bit, we'll go and visit Granny.' We took the 24, and who would have thought we'd see a murder on a tram journey! That's what it was, cold-blooded murder!

I doubt whether the people standing on the tram platform saw it like that. And don't shout so loud, Ma is asleep.

The thing is, a cop who's crazy over a red-head is capable of anything. He's off his head, loco! But don't forget, a cop is always a cop. So when you've been born and grown up a bit, if you see a cop staring like a calf at a pretty woman, watch out! Because he's probably in love with her and that could be fatal. You should have seen his eyes seeking her out on that crowded tram platform. And then when he saw what the dirty old man was up to, you should have seen how furious he got! I'll tell you. We were on the front platform, and she had her hands round her stomach to protect you from all the people pushing and shoving. She couldn't get inside the tram, and then a scrawny, balding guy came and pushed against her from behind, you know what I mean, and she glared at him and tried to elbow her way into the tram. No-one on the platform seemed to notice what was going on, no-one except Inspector Galván that is. I don't know if the flatfoot got on at the same stop as us or afterwards, but there he was, staring at her from a corner with those owl-eyes of his. He didn't even have to stand on tiptoe, because he's so tall. Anyway, he saw her trying to get away into the aisle, and acted quickly. As cool as you like, without so much as blinking, he stretched out his hand over the heads of all the other passengers, seized the little guy by the throat, and pushed him to the edge of the platform. It looked as if he was going to drop him off the tram – by then it was speeding down the Paseo de Gracia – but the little runt had time to grab the handrail with one hand, and so he hung there, one foot on the tram step, the other dangling in mid-air. Go on, jump, arsehole, I want to see you break your neck! the inspector said, and the other guy cowered there deathly pale, as if afraid of being hit over the head, and he squinted down at the street rushing under the tram wheels, even put one foot down to try it out, the ground tugging at his laceless shoe, and seemed determined to let go, until he drew back at the last minute. Either you jump right now, or I'll take you to the police station, and you'll see what we'll throw at you there, so come on, choose, the cop says, pushing his way down on to the tram step: so the guy tries out the ground once more with the tip of his shoe, testing for the right moment to leap off, waiting for the tram to slow down a little, or for a bend to appear, and all of a sudden he raises his ridiculous head and looks imploringly at the other passengers on the platform. As long as I live I'll never forget the begging look from that poor guy as he pleaded for help, for some sign of sympathy from them, even though he knew no-one would lift a finger to help him because, well, what a dirty old man, pressing himself up against a pregnant mother like that . . . while all this is going on, inside the tram the red-head has managed to find a seat, and she opens her book, preferring not to know what's happening out on the platform. I reckon she never even saw the inspector, didn't even suspect he had followed her. Jump, you son of a bitch, get out of my sight, the cop shouted, this is the last time I'll tell you. By the time the tram driver decided to put the brakes on, perhaps feeling sorry for the guy, it was too late: you should have seen how his hand grasping the rail turned bright purple – it was a dead man's hand. Eyes closed, and with a look of terror on his face, he finally let go. When he hit the ground he tried to run, arms flailing like a puppet on a string, unable to get his balance, hands whirling round like a demented fan. He was going so fast he collided with a plane tree on the Paseo, and bounced off so quickly he fell right under the tram. Its back wheels crushed his ribs, then smashed his face as it dragged him along. You should have heard the hysterical shouts, and the squeal of brakes as the tram pulled up fifty metres further on. The poor guy's body was caught up in a tangle of iron. One of his legs stuck out and was jerking for a few seconds. Blood bubbled from his mouth. Some passers-by came running up to try to help, but you should have seen it, midget, you should have seen how the ragged bundle gave one last shudder then lay there quite still, eyes open and a trickle of blood dripping from the corner of his mouth like this, look, as if he were disgusted by the whole thing. By now the inspector had got off the tram, and he walked up, taking his time, trenchcoat round his shoulders and lighting a cigarette with his fake gold Dupont, very sure of himself, very calm. He took charge of everything immediately and gave orders – call an ambulance, stand back, keep moving. He'll personally see to the transfer of the body, file a report on the incident and inform the family, he is used to dealing with this kind of thing . . . how can anyone be such a bastard?

What is Ma doing all this time? Was she just sitting there by her window?

Yes. She doesn't turn round even once, she doesn't want to see or know anything, she just sits there with the book open on her lap, and although she has heard all the shouting and is aware someone has been killed, she doesn't ask anything or turn her head or raise her eyes from the book, doesn't even dare breathe.

Why is that, brother? Why do you think the red-head showed so little concern?

I knew you were going to ask me that. Don't you see you're not as smart as you think, tadpole, your brain hasn't developed yet, you can't work things out? When are you going to come out of your cave and learn about life, pipsqueak? Have you still not understood that Ma has seen so much misfortune, has suffered so much and seen such terrible things because of the war that nothing can affect her any more? That she feels nothing inside?

Well, I felt something. It was like a snake coiling round my neck.

Natch. She got a bit dizzy. Only to be expected.

It wasn't only that. I know she's ill . . .

Don't try to be clever, squirt! You don't know or see or feel a thing! If you only knew what's waiting for you! Granny says that all of you babies born after they dropped the atomical bomb will have no arsehole and no ears. But I can hear you through Doctor P.J. Rosón-Ansio's ear, because that's like a giant seashell, and see you with my penetrating radioactive megarat eyes, David whispers, his face sliding down the taut, warm skin of his mother's belly.

Then he sits back, still half-asleep and with his cheek burning, does up the button over the hard navel, and stands up. The summer sun is streaming in through the window, it's another scorching afternoon. David studies Ma's beautiful sleeping face as he finishes drying her feet with the towel, then whispers to her:

"Wake up, Ma. It's half past three. Wake up."

II

Fighter Pilot

A dead-end street of beaten cindery earth, gouged by kids playing with knives. Hardly any traffic, and, depending on the time of day, soaked with urine, dirty waste water or soapsuds. This is our street, a street David Bartra will never consider his own. Callejón del Viento, it's known as. Ten or twelve hovels at most, some of them whitewashed, others red brick; all of them one storey only, with outside staircases and flat roofs cluttered with improvised rooms made of wood or building materials: dovecotes, laundries, store-rooms. The street, springing up as if by magic on the poorest slope of the hill, and set apart from the rest of the neighbourhood, becomes a dead end when it turns and heads down in haphazard fashion until it abuts a former doctor's surgery tacked on to a building from the 1920s or 1930s with the airs of a villa. Even now, the tiny scratched door with peeling paint that leads to the rooms the doctor's wife converted into a flat and offered at a reasonable rent still displays the tin plaque with her husband's name and speciality: *Dr. P.J. Rosón-Ansio. Ear, Nose and Throat Specialist.*

Next to the door is a clump of white marguerites that grow several feet high, like a green umbrella sprinkled with snow.

"I understand you sub-let."

The inspector pokes among the flowers, absent-mindedly reading the doctor's plaque.

"Yes, that's right," the red-head says, a note of hostility in her voice, leaning against the door and clearly having no intention of letting him in. "I rent it with the use of kitchen and bathroom included. And those are my marguerites."

"Yours?"

"All mine, Inspector." The kitchen, bathroom and laundry were all she shared with the doctor's widow.

"It seems this used to be the family summer house," the policeman says, looking down and apparently speaking to himself. His words betray a hoarse edge of emotion. He takes a small notebook out of his pocket, reads a page, and goes on: "About ten years ago the doctor and his wife came to live here, and he had the surgery built. Is that right?"

"I don't know," says Ma. "We weren't here then."

The authorities have all the facts, but everyone in the neighbourhood knows them as well: Doctor P.J. Rosón-Ansio was an ear, nose and throat specialist from Cordoba, with anarchist tendencies. In 1933, on the run from justice for an undisclosed matter, he set up his consulting-room in Barcelona, only to disappear without trace during the Civil War. His wife survived him by six years, living on in this house, which in those days had a small garden in front of the main entrance, on the other side of the building.

"Doubtless the doctor," the inspector ventures without much conviction, "bought the house planning to build on another storey and make a proper villa out of it."

Ma makes no effort to hide her lack of interest in this kind of speculation, and says nothing. Inspector Galván flicks through a few more pages of his notebook. A white butterfly flutters erratically around the marguerites, but does not settle. Ma breaks the silence.

"I've got all my papers in order, in case that's why you're here. I'm only a month behind with my rent."

"That's nothing to do with me, Señora."

"Well, what more do you want to know, then? I've got a lot of chores to get through."

The cop is still staring down at his notes. Every time he turns a page, he licks the tip of his finger.

"You must be from the south of Andalusia, from Málaga I should think," he says. "Or am I mistaken?"

Ma is suspicious now: she did not expect this line of questioning. She says nothing for a few moments, then replies:

"After twenty years in Catalonia, I didn't think my accent still showed. My parents were from the Canary Islands, but I was brought up in Coín till I was twelve."

"You see? I have a good ear for these things. My wife was from Algeciras," he adds, and a dark shadow flits across his face. "Do you live alone?"

Mother closes her eyes wearily and says with a sigh:

"Listen, I was already taken in two months ago for questioning at Police Headquarters. I was there for more than eight hours . . ."

"That was before I was put on the case," the inspector says. "Do you live alone?"

"With my children."

"I thought you only had one."

"There are two more." (I'm sure she is thinking: you killed one of them for me in an air-raid, and the other one will be born soon, alive and kicking, I hope.) "If you mean does anyone else live in the villa, the answer's no. It's been empty since the owner died two years ago."

"As I understand it . . ." the inspector begins, then falls silent, as his cold eyes light for a moment on the red-head's bare arms and slender neck, and perhaps on her curly hair. On the surface, his gaze does not even seem curious: something odd in this man's character – professional routine, a coldness in his manner or possibly a habit formed from years of witnessing other people's suffering – has congealed in his face. "As I understand it, you looked after the lady when her husband died."

"Poor woman! She felt so alone. Her daughter lives in Pamplona; she's married to a one-armed pelota player . . ."

Silence. All that can be heard is Chispa, wheezing under the kitchen table. It's not a joke, she adds, he lost his arm in an accident. The inspector turns his head, rubs his broad, pale forehead. He says in a low monotone, again apparently talking to himself:

"So nobody lives in the other half now."

"No," says Ma. "And they still haven't decided what to do with the furniture or with us. One day a man turned up who said he worked for a furniture depository or something, and had come on behalf of Señora Rosón's daughter to take everything away to the warehouse. But he didn't show me any signed authorization, and the court had not said anything about it, so I refused to let him in."

The inspector nods silently. He is probably considering another question, but the red-head is no fool: in order to avoid or put off any explanations on matters she would prefer not to go into – especially anything to do with my father – she suddenly becomes talkative:

"The furniture is all great heavy pieces, I'm sure the daughter won't want them. And it's a bore having the villa empty. It has to be cleaned from time to time, we don't want it overrun with rats. And who do you think does the cleaning? Yours truly here. I'm not obliged to, of course, but then again . . . I'd really like to know what the daughter intends to do with us, her tenants," she goes on, putting an arm round David, who has just appeared in the doorway behind her, his wet hair swathed in a towel that makes him look like Sabu in a turban. "But it doesn't matter, we won't come to any harm, will we, son?" she says, smiling and squeezing his shoulder. "We're not scared, are we? You're not either, are you, pipsqueak, tell us you're not." She strokes her stomach and, under the light summer clothing and her taut skin, I like to think she can feel me giving a kick of approval for her indomitable fighting spirit. David clings tighter to her waist and looks up at the cop with mistrustful eyes. "We don't need anyone else, do we?" she adds, smiling one of her tough, bitter smiles for David's benefit.

"*Oh, velly true*, memsahib."

A boy affectionate with his mother, but otherwise taciturn; lanky, with big honey-coloured eyes; pert, strong buttocks firmly set on a pair of long, delicate, almost feminine legs. That is how David looks at this time. Until a moment ago, the inspector had not paid him much attention: a furtive shadow behind the red-headed woman, confused with the dog and the kitchen table, something flitting past like a phantom, a flash of resentment on his face. Now he glances at him out of the corner of his eye, with a cold, harsh look.

"Although the day we least expect it," Ma complains, following her own train of thought, "the court could throw us into the street."

"Don't say that. Don't you know there are laws to protect people who sub-let?"

"Really?"

"If you like, I can find out."

"Thanks, there's no need. I know what to expect."

Yet in spite of the disdain in her voice, her look betrays a spark of female curiosity as for the first time she weighs up the apparently gentle manners of this gaunt-faced, grey-eyed man, not bad-looking, with an air of grudging tolerance or perhaps boredom, she doesn't know which yet, and standing so stiffly he appears taller than he is. His features seem dangerous, puffy and somehow unhealthy-looking, as if his skin oozed impurities, but overall they convey an air of manly harmony. He speaks slowly, and occasionally – due perhaps to the habit of firing questions he has carefully emptied of cruelty or compassion – his cold monotone takes on a strained quality that seems impersonal though vaguely menacing.

"Did your son give you the book you dropped at the tram stop?"

"Oh, yes, I forgot to thank you . . . What a coincidence you were passing by just at that moment."

Still clasping his mother's waist, David has not yet looked up. He is staring at the spot on the ground the cop has just been rubbing with the sole of his shoe, as if crushing a cigarette butt. Perhaps he has trodden in some of Chispa's shit. The inspector consults his notebook again, and says:

"If you don't mind, I'd like to have a look at the other side of the villa."

"I've already told you, there's no-one there. It's shut up."

"You must have the front door key."

The red-head does not hide her annoyance.

"There's no need. You can get in through here." And she adds, sarcastically: "So you can see for yourself how people live renting a doctor's surgery."

She steps aside, and lets go of David. He quickly slips in front of the policeman with a crooked smile, muttering as he does so:

"Every time I go in this way, my hearing goes crazy. It's the doctor's curse!"

It takes no time at all to visit their tiny rented apartment. It is barely fifty metres square. There is nothing like a hall or parlour: the door leads straight into their living-room, with a rectangular table covered in a check oilcloth, on one side of it the sideboard, on the other, beneath the window with blinds that looks out over the dead-end street, a Nogma sewing-machine, a side-table and two wicker chairs. It is plain that what now is hallway, dining-room and living-room all in one, was once the doctor's waiting-room: still visible on the walls are faded patches and tacks where posters and diplomas used to hang. The same is true of the red-head's bedroom, which is also her sewing-room. It's the largest of the rooms, with enough space at the foot of the double bed for a black chest of drawers and the unpainted wooden bench she uses to lay out her patterns, and a padded basket always full of scraps, scissors, measuring tapes, chalk and cotton bobbins. This is where the doctor saw his patients, and some of the floor-tiles bear the marks of where the torture chair was screwed down. Open your mouth, boy, show me your throat.

"Aaaggh! This is where the doctor used to cut people's tonsils out with a knife," David whispers behind the inspector's back.

The inspector says nothing. The only nice things in that shitty surgery turned into an equally shitty home – to use the description David gave years later in his typically forceful way – are its doors. They have glass panels, decorated with butterflies and lilies; and Ma has made some curtains and hangings for them. But what the policeman's slow, circular gaze is taking in now are not the marks on the floor or the walls, but the double bed with its salmon pink cover, the photos of father and Juanito on the bedside table, the red velvet, heart-shaped pin-cushion stuck with needles on the chalk-marked workbench, the wardrobe and the black chest in the corner.

David slips back until he is pressing against his mother's welcoming belly once more, clings to her and says in a low voice:

"Why don't you ask him to show you his search warrant?"

"These people don't bother with legal formalities, son."

"Get him to show you his badge, at least."

"What for?"

"Tell him to show it you!"

"Ssshhh! . . . Don't you remember what your father used to say: before, the police obeyed the orders of justice, now it's the other way round, it's justice that obeys the orders of the police. Do you understand?"

"I'm sure he's got the written warrant in his pocket this time. Get him to show it you," David insists, his mouth pressed against her stomach, then talking to me in a whisper: You believe me, don't you, little monkey? But I see everything because my eyes have got atomical radiation and can see through walls and doors and even clothes, including a cop's coat folded over his shoulder, his jacket and blue shirt, and that's why I could tell you right now where he keeps the warrant and his gun and if it's loaded and has the safety catch on, and I can even see his brandy hip flask in the other pocket, with the packet of Lucky Strikes and his gold cigarette lighter, a fake Dupont. I can see it all because my atomical gaze bores through everything . . .

"Ssshhh!" Mother draws back to the entrance to her bedroom.

"Will you show me your room, kiddo?" the inspector asks, turning on his heel. All of a sudden he appears ill at ease, moving awkwardly. "I'm sorry to disturb you, Señora."

She responds with a weary twist of her lips.

David's room is the smallest of all, little more than a cupboard which used to be a store for patent medicines and medical equipment. The walls are a grimy green, and the room is windowless apart from a small skylight high up on the west side of the house. The marks left by shelves and damp on the walls look like the remains of a washed-out crossword. The policeman's tired, deceptively threatening eyes flit over David's bed and the wooden clothes rack where his red beret and raincoat are hanging, the wardrobe and the open skylight. They come to a halt on an old, faded world map, like two shrivelled apple halves, stuck to the wall with drawing-pins next to a photo of Joe Louis torn from a newspaper. His trenchcoat neatly hanging round his shoulders, the inspector stands staring at the map and photo. Behind him, her arms folded and trying her best to be patient, the red-head watches him, while at her side David is thinking: well, what kind of a search do you call this? I know your game, flatfoot, you're trying to spend as much time as possible with her, even if it means pretending you're interested in a map from the year dot . . ."

"Would you like me to show you my full colour Universal Atlas, or my collection of the world's greatest heavyweights?" says David. "Would you? Or would you like to see my collection of cards from *The Drums of Fu Manchu?*"

"Thanks, but I don't have the time."

On the broken chair he uses as a bedside table, there is a lamp, a much-handled Edgar Wallace novel, a penknife with mother-of-pearl handle, a dried lizard tail, a box of matches and a Perspex wrist watch with a light-blue dial, and luminous metal hands painted on at an unchanging hour. The objects collected on the broken-legged chair give off an unpleasant sense of silent violence floating in the atmosphere, of some unspoken argument carried on in secret. But the inspector is more interested in the wall, in two of the doctor's old diplomas hanging above the picture of Joe Louis, two paintings my mother put there to hide patches of damp, and above all in Doctor P.J. Rosón-Ansio's ear, an enormous ear framed in a brightly coloured poster, pierced here and there by lines of tiny writing explaining the functions of the interior organs and all their hidden twists and turns.

"Why have you put that there?"

"The plaster's flaking on the wall."

As he turns to leave the room, the inspector almost stumbles into David, who is busy unwrapping the towel from his head. He stretches out a hand to stroke his hair, and says in that thick, expressionless voice of his:

"How are we behaving, kid? Are you helping your mother?"

"Yes, bwana. Did you see how shiny the plaque on the door is? I polish it with bicarbonate and a wet cloth every Saturday, and I go shopping as well, for the coal, our rations and bread, and soft drinks and ice . . . and in the afternoons I work as a photographer's assistant . . ."

"David!" mother interrupts him. "Don't pay him any attention," she tells the inspector.

"Don't worry," he says. "We know each other already, don't we, kid?"

He looks all around him with that apparent lack of interest of his, and eventually focuses his attention on a front cover torn from *Adler* magazine and stuck with tacks to the wall under the skylight opposite the bed. The cover shows an Allied pilot at the moment of capture beside his shot-down plane. It's a propaganda photo, a snapshot taken in daylight. As he looks more closely, the inspector notes the devil-may-care attitude of the young pilot, standing there arms akimbo, his almost imperceptible smile and his defiant, guardedly ironic gaze directed not at the pair of German soldiers pointing their sub-machine-guns at him, but straight at the photographer's lens, at his uncertain future and at the eyes that will now always see him as captive. But his face means nothing to the inspector.

"Who's this? Another boxer, a cinema star?"

"I don't know," says David.

"My son saw the photo in a magazine and fell for it," the red-head says hastily. "He's always cutting out pictures of planes and pilots, he loves them. He's crazy about airmen."

David stares at her in amazement: this is the first lie he has ever heard his mother utter, the first lie that wasn't a joke, and said with a strange sense of urgency in her voice.

"OK, I can't see any reason to do a more thorough search," the inspector says. "Would you mind coming with me to the other side, to the villa?"

David has thrown himself down on the bed, hands behind his head. The fighter pilot stares at him from the opposite wall. His Spitfire went into a spin with its fuselage in flames, David murmurs to himself, but he landed safely. And he remembers what he said one day to Paulino Bardolet in this very room: "What a photo, fatso! One point two-five seconds to capture all the courage of a hero determined to die on his feet!"

As he unbuttons his flies, he can hear the voices of his mother and the cop walking along the corridor.

"You shouldn't let him put those ghastly war pictures on his wall, Señora."

"Children are full of surprises aren't they? Until just recently he had a photo of Donald Duck and cards of the Heroes of the Crusade in the same spot," says Ma, opening the door to the villa, the sound of her ironic voice slowly fading in the distance. "Do you think Donald Duck and our Crusade heroes are more suitable for a boy his age, Inspector?"

"Dead people are never good company."

Lies, it's all lies! David mutters under his breath. You flatfoot swine, how would you know whether the Germans killed him or not?

Mother's patient, cheerful gaze takes in the diamond-shaped tiles on the corridor floor leading to a green velvet curtain that is hanging loose, and beyond it a pair of grey felt slippers left in front of a door, heels together and toes pointing outwards. Widow Rosón never wanted to move them, says Ma jokingly. We've respected her wishes. Follow me, Inspector. It's only for a moment, he mutters perhaps apologetically. How does your son behave outside the home? He seems a very bright kid, he adds, adopting the weary tone of an official who is bored at always having to ask the same kind of question.

Juan is sitting astride the chair, arms dangling over the back, facing David's bed. His head is swathed in bandages, and his torn trousers show one leg severed at the knee, though there are no traces of blood on the splintered bone. His brown scarf and overcoat are still thick with reddish dust from the building that collapsed on top of him one far-off 17th of March, although he is not the age he was then, but seems as old as he would be now, around twenty.

You would be my older brother, David says sorrowfully. What a shame.

It wasn't to be, kid. Don't let it bug you.

You could have taught me all kinds of things about life.

Forget it. My fate was sealed.

What shitty rotten luck!

Well, there was nothing to be done. One fellow tried to pull me out from the rubble and got hold of my leg, but it came off in his hands. I didn't feel a thing.

Did you hear the whistle of the bomb as it was falling?

No, I didn't. I was in the Gran Vía looking at the Coliseum cinema adverts when I heard someone shout: Quickly! Throw yourself on the ground and open your mouth!

Why did they say that?

Because of the shock wave, kid. If you don't open your mouth, you explode inside. So I threw myself on the pavement and opened my mouth as wide as a ladle. But it did no good, Juan concludes, wiping away a trickle of blood from his nose with the back of his hand.

Holy shit, David says, everyone in our family bleeds like stuck pigs.

Others had it worse, you know, says Juan, and as he speaks a fine dust like stucco or marble emerges from his mouth. There were people blown to pieces everywhere, and a short distance from me, the shell of a tram was burning fiercely.

But didn't you hear the bomb?

Why do you go on so much about the bomb, David? I've told you a thousand times, no, I didn't hear it!

Well, so's you know, the whistling of that bomb got into my hearing like a poisonous snake, and it won't go away.

That's too bad, Juan says, scratching the dried blood off his hand. It's a pity, because living here you could have consulted Doctor P.J. Rosón-Ansio, the ear, nose and throat man from Cordoba. But he's kicked it too. Come to think of it, he could have operated on my nose as well.

The ear man from Cordoba, David says dreamily. When I first heard that, I thought he must be a bullfighter . . .

And it's bad luck that Bolshevik doctor friend of Pa's copped it too.

Keep your voice down, and be careful what you're saying, brother.

For a brief moment, their gazes converge on the poster showing this pink appendage, this huge ear pierced by arrows, opening out like a shell to take in everything said in the room and beyond, every sound made in the house – the creaking of a wardrobe or a door, wind rattling the window-panes, rain beating against them, I know what I'm talking about kid, it can hear everything, even Chispa's panting under the kitchen table, or the soft, silent tread of a mouse or a scurrying cockroach, even the scratch of a pencil on a piece of paper . . .

Is it true what the red-head says, that you wanted to be a writer when you grew up?

It wasn't to be.

You were her favourite. She thought you were the best, she put all her hopes in you.

Well, look at me now, a heap of rags. But the one coming after you might have more luck.

That tadpole? Why do you say that?

I know Ma wants him to do well, says Juan, squirming painfully on the chair.

With Pa not at home, he doesn't stand a chance, David replies.

That's where you're wrong, brother. It's precisely the lack of a father that'll make the pipsqueak an artist some day: he'll spend his life imagining him.

D'you know that just now, for the first time in my life, I heard Ma tell a lie?

There's always a first time.

But it's very odd . . . I didn't tear out that photo. It was her!

Get back to her, don't leave her on her own with that man, Juan urges him in a hollow voice. Especially not in the villa, with all those locked rooms and that stink of dead people's clothes and moth-eaten furniture, that smell of camphor seeping under the doors that chokes us whenever we have to go in there to use the bathroom or the kitchen.

There's a distant crash of metal and glass. David sits up on his bed, and as he does so, the Spitfire pilot also gets up behind a barbed-wire fence, next to the fuselage of his crashed plane, and stands with hands on hips.

Do you think he's dead? David asks before he leaves the room. Do you think they gunned him down beside his plane? Or that they took him prisoner and tortured him, then he managed to escape? Do you think the red-head knows something about it . . . ?

Stop inventing things, and go and join her, says Juan, his voice full of dust. I'll go and change my bandages.

I'm going, says David, staring sadly at the severed leg. You ought to replace that bit of bone sticking out and clean it up, brother. And while you're at it, dust yourself off a bit, you look like a ghost. Or don't ghosts bother to brush their clothes?

When, soon afterwards, David catches up with us, the inspector is standing in the middle of the villa's living-room surrounded by furniture, some of it covered in yellowing dustsheets. Mother switches the light on near the doorway, and stands waiting for him, arms folded as if expecting him to leave. Here there is a different colour, a different light, another kind of silence. Everything David sees whenever he comes or goes from the bathroom or the kitchen seems not to exist in time any more, but to be merely part of someone's wayward memory; broken-backed, misplaced pieces of furniture, stiff curtains and torn lace, antiquated, sombre paintings hanging askew on the walls, portraits of dead hares and partridge displayed on tables overflowing with vegetables and fruit. It all seems not only to have been abandoned in haste many years earlier without the slightest regret by the people who lived here, but to have been repudiated and cursed, cast angrily into a wilful state of total neglect.

Behind Mother are the darkened parlour and the front door to the villa, which lets in the midday light. To the right of the red-head, the inspector notices a round table and two orange wicker chairs. He immediately realizes there must have been a set of four of them, and that the other two are in our own living-room. Mother has borrowed them. Alert but silent, the inspector turns round slowly, his crow-like gaze taking in everything: the useless mirrors, the old pendulum clock, the shelves filled with books, the paintings, the table and its two chairs, the empty glass cases. Finally he looks at Mother, with a kind of weary concern.

"You'd live much better here than you do on the other side."

"Yes, of course, paying twice or three times as much as I do now. We can't afford such a luxury," she says, with an impatient sigh: "Through there is the kitchen and a small toilet at the end of the corridor, and down here are the bedrooms and the bathroom, a study and some other rooms. If you want to see . . ."

The policeman shakes his head. He can figure out how big the villa must be, even though it is only one storey, but he does not show the slightest interest in seeing it all. His eyes linger on the corner table. On it lie a pair of leather gloves, a fat brandy glass, and a glass ashtray which has the remains of a cigarette in it, a worm of ash still intact. David follows the cop's gaze, and can still make out the spiral of blue smoke drifting up to the ceiling, and then see the figure of his father with no shoes on and in his shirtsleeves, sitting relaxed and cheerful in one of the wicker chairs, lifting the brandy glass in greeting. The inspector bends over the cigarette ash; as he does so he catches a fleeting, blurred glimpse of my mother's soft, pregnant outline in the spotted leprous surface of an old mirror, while from the far side of the room she conjures up the same image: the cigarette burning down in the ashtray and sending its blue spiral, with its hidden, coiled fury, up towards the ceiling.

"Are you the smoker?"

"Who else would it be?" She puts her hand on her belly. "As for you, little devil, just stop your kicking, will you?"

"What did you say?"

"It wasn't meant for you." Then she opens both sides of the tall, heavy main door. The rusty iron hinges groan. "This is the main entrance. Now we're out in the street, so to speak."

There's a smell of burning wood in the air. The inspector descends what is left of the three front steps, then stands looking at the patch of level ground stretching to the gully's edge, bare earth interrupted here and there by the remains of what once must have been a clump of trees. Immediately in front of him are some blackened rose bushes, the roots of a felled olive tree, and straggly shoots of geraniums and oleander next to the remains of the garden wall. He walks over to the gully, considers how deep it is, and the steepness of its clayey, worn sides. Then he turns round and looks back at the old, south-facing façade of the villa. It is rectangular, and boasts a moss-covered balustrade behind which there must be a rotting flat roof. It has a pretentious air, with ceramic ornaments and a frieze topped by terracotta baskets spilling out fruit and flowers. A ruined porch protects the front door and its iron knocker; shiny Russian ivy covers everything but the two barred windows. It is built of cut stone to a metre high; the rest is red brick, except for the frames round the door and windows, which are also stone.

The red-head exchanges a glance with David which says: just look at him, you can tell from his face what he's thinking – this must be how Víctor Bartra escaped, here's the night door, the threshold of the void and nothingness, the drainage pipe of a criminal past . . .

"So this is where he escaped," the inspector says.

"I've no idea, I was fast asleep." Ma is standing at the top of the three steps, arms folded, and leaning against the door jamb. "Like a log, believe me."

"Do you know someone called Señora Vergés, who was married to a man called Monteys?"

"No," she replies hastily, and the rush of blood reaches me inside her. "Why do you ask?"

The sudden pale look on her face does not escape the inspector's attention. He can see her clenched lips too.

"Aren't you feeling well, Señora?"

"It's nothing. Come here, son." She puts her hand on David's shoulder, and presses her back against the doorframe. "You get used to everything in the end. Whoever would have thought . . ."

"I don't understand," says the inspector.

"It's nothing. Have you finished here? I need to go out."

Hands in his jacket pockets, he stands in front of her without moving, searching her exhausted face.

"I think you should sit down for a while."

"You can think what you like, but I have to get to work."

"OK." His right hand feels for something in his coat pocket – David could have sworn it was the hip flask. "I won't keep you. But there are still a lot of things to clear up. I'll come back another day. Let's see, if I go down here," he goes on, pointing to the track alongside the riverbed, "I guess I'll come out in Avenida Vírgen de Montserrat."

"When you get out of the gully, cross over and you'll soon see the road leading down to Plaza Sanllehy. Mind how you go," Mother says, then ducks back inside the house, head down and apparently suddenly chilled.

"I hope you feel better."

David shuts the door but keeps a close eye on the cop, who is still standing in the middle of the dead garden, now with his back to the house as he consults his notebook before beating a retreat.

Ten minutes later when David takes Chispa out for a pee, the flatfoot is still in the same spot, but is staring at the villa once more. He has just had a drink from the hip flask, and slips it into his back trouser pocket. He rubs his thin, taut lips with the back of his hand, without once taking his eyes from the door.

"Is your mother feeling better?" he says with the rasping, no-nonsense voice of his.

David stares at the trenchcoat folded over his shoulder.

"Yes."

"I should have asked you why you took so long to give her the book. I really don't know what to make of you, kid."

"You can think what you like, bwana. I couldn't care less."

Inspector Galván stands there for a few moments looking hard at the dog, who's wheezing and seems barely able to stand upright. All of a sudden, he pats David on the shoulder, offers him his hand, then turns and strides off along the cindery wasteland by the gully's edge. Unable or unwilling to make himself heard, David mutters under his breath:

"He is the best fighter pilot in the world. And he isn't dead! Get that straight, flatfoot!"

As he watches the inspector disappear, he strokes the tail of a lizard he is keeping in his pocket for Paulino, and remembers: Look, they don't have any blood, he told his friend the first time he cut one off. Instead of blood, they produce this sticky, cold liquid, like the sweat on the cop's hand.

I'll never see my mother's eyes, although I know they are slightly close together, yet that their expression is clear and bright, the same colour as the sky, especially when she is listening to one of David's more or less fantastic explanations, or when she is lost in thought about my father. I also know her skin is very white, and that the shock of red hair she has is a sight to see. That is why, on our street and at the market and in the children's clothes stalls where they know her, everyone calls her the red-head.

In the mid-morning of this distant August month that is turning out to be so hot, and will end up being so remarkably, so dreadfully memorable, the atmosphere is full of foul-smelling atomical sulphur and the ghostly procession of the dead, like toy soldiers, stiff and flayed and lacking noses and eyes. Later, black rainclouds build up, the sky opens, and the stench of burnt hair and charred bones dissolves in the rain. The rain is torrential for a while, but now it is as hot as ever again, and the afternoon light is like a sponge.

In the smoke-filled kitchen, the red-head feels dizzy and scalds her hand with some boiling water. Shortly afterwards, Chispa retches endlessly and finally is sick in the corridor. While Ma is wiping it up with a cloth, kneeling on the tiles and humming, go to sleep, my little baby, a tune that is more catchy than anything on the radio, she suddenly gets another of her migraines and can't see properly, and just then David has to start telling her about the man who hanged himself in a bandstand on Calle Legalidad, he swears that sometimes at night he sees the hanged man, his tongue protruding, wearing pyjamas and felt slippers, he seemed far too respectable a man to commit suicide, always so neat and tidy, this happened two months ago, but David is obsessed with the dead man turning slowly in the wind, rope round his neck, and tongue as big as the sole of a shoe lolling out, until Ma finally shuts him up.

"Not now, my love, forget that poor fellow and help me get up."

"Hup, up you come."

"That's a good boy."

Later on, David is wiping the muck out of Chispa's eyes with a piece of gauze, and whispering ridiculous promises of games and chases to him. Ma is sitting at the table sorting through a plate of lentils with her scalded fingers when she feels dizzy again, and gets the streaks of light in her eyes once more, so she stands up, goes into her bedroom, and lies down. While she waits for the migraine to pass, she talks a while with the photograph of her husband on the bedside table. It's a retouched, posed studio portrait, showing our drunken, charming father in half-profile for posterity, with that seductive grin of his, black hair smoothed back with brilliantine and mouth smiling beneath the trim moustache – a charming, lopsided smile, with a hint of devilry at the corners. I'll never get to see it for real or close up, but I know it's a broad, deceiving smile, or rather, I know it's not exactly his, that the gleaming, perfect teeth do not belong to him; because that triumphant smile, as virile and seductive as any to be seen in films – like Clark Gable's, the one my mother likes best – is in fact a dental prosthesis.

"It can't be true!"

"I read it in a magazine."

There's nothing wrong, Señor Bartra, she is telling him now from the bed, I felt dizzy and I got those glowworms flashing in my eyes again, but don't worry, it's nothing, wherever you may be you can carry on tilting your elbow, and I hope you manage to drown your sorrows in the bottle you took with you, damn you, along with your dentures and your beloved ideals, if you have any left. Don't you worry about me, I'm feeling better already and I'm going to make myself pretty, I'll dry my tears, comb my hair, put some colour on my cheeks and on my lips and I'll go out. Also on the bedside table there's a tinted photo of our brother Juan at school. He is sitting at a desk holding the delicate stem of an ivory pen over an open notebook, with the map of Spain hanging on the wall behind him. He is smiling and looking at us, but this time the red-head doesn't have anything to say to him.

After David has taken Chispa out for a walk, Ma combs her hair, puts on lipstick, and struggles into her rubber boots, although she knows it has stopped raining – the fact is, the boots look better than her shoes, which are so old they need throwing away – and picks up her umbrella. When she emerges into the street, she is surprised by a weak, peevish sun shining through a mass of clouds, and sets off determinedly towards the Avenida. At that moment, through the umbilical cord, I, who am nothing more than an obscure wish in her mind and

David's, and probably not even that in Chispa's last sad desolation, suddenly receive the happy backlash of her indomitable will to live, to overcome all heartaches, deception and scorn, as day by day she strengthens her determination not to be overwhelmed by loneliness and fear, illness or an unwanted pregnancy, poverty, lack of love, or anything else fate might throw at her.

As she leaves the house to visit the doctor, I could swear that if she had been able to, she would willingly have left me there. But who can tell? At that moment I was poised on the threshold of life, but only a step away from death, my back turned to the world, and probably upside down. The tadpole could sense life around him, but only like a brief flame, like flashes of light.

III

Voices in the Gully

If, as they say, he spent the night hiding in the gully, perhaps he left something of his behind, thinks David, a crumpled cigarette packet, or a butt, a few drops of blood or the empty bottle of Fundador . . . Or a piece of paper, a scrap of paper rolled up and stuck inside the bottle – a message. That's it, I bet that'll interest the flatfoot!

Hello there bwana. Good news. I know where my father is.

He watches him arrive, waiting for him in the night-time doorway, squatting on his heels and stroking a handful of sticky lizard tails in his trouser pocket. (Five minutes earlier, down in the gully, he had also been crouched waiting, sharp penknife in hand, staring at the crack in the ground where the lizards peeped out. Hello there, pretty one.)

"Hello there, bwana. Listen to what I've got to tell you . . ."

"I have to talk to your mother."

"I've just found out where Víctor Bartra is."

"Oh, yes? You can tell me later. Now go and warn your mother."

"She's not home. She rushed off to the skating rink as soon as she read this. Would you like to see it? I found it in an empty brandy bottle, next to a pile of Chesterfield cigarette butts – that's the brand my father smokes. Look. It's in code."

"Are you starting your nonsense again?"

"Oh, OK, I thought it would interest you," says David. "At least have a look at it, bwana."

"Why don't you read it for me?"

David unfolds the piece of paper and clears his throat.

"This is what it says. 'A girl out skating fell to the ground, and everyone could see . . . she didn't know how to skate.'"

"Why don't you sing it for me too?"

"It's a coded message!"

"Fine. Is that all?"

"What kind of a cop are you? Don't you smell something in it? The message is in code, even a blind man could see that! I know it's the words of a song that's always on the radio, but it's obvious what my father's trying to say: go to the skating rink at Turó Park, you'll see a girl who doesn't know how to skate fall over, and she'll tell you who you have to get in touch with to hear news from me . . . it all fits, doesn't it? What have you got to say to that, Inspector?"

"All I've got to say is that I feel sorry for your mother."

"The problem is you don't have the sense of smell of a real bloodhound," says David. "I don't know why I'm wasting my time on such a novice, who hasn't the faintest idea . . . What, leaving already? Too bad for you."

Paulino Bardolet, heart of gold, arse of glass, may be his accomplice and confidant, the little fat kid looking for consolation, forever affectionate and forever scared witless, the tireless companion of their musical hunts in the gully, the moaning but grateful recipient of the lizard tails – but his secret night-time friend, the ally of his heroic dreams, the comrade David will never share with anyone, is an RAF pilot whose name he does not know and whose more than likely death – after being caught on camera next to his downed Spitfire in his fabulous leather flying jacket, scarf knotted round his neck and smashed goggles pushed up on his forehead – David has lived through a hundred times. Day and night he's there tacked to his bedroom wall, standing hands on hips staring at the Wehrmacht soldiers pointing their sub-machine-guns at him on an ashen plain destroyed by the Luftwaffe. *Achtung*! It is a wartime photo coloured sky-blue and fruity pink in pastels or chromo, except for the dark patch of smouldering scrap metal, and the pilot's scorched hands posed lightly on his waist, while behind him a thin, dense column of smoke rises from the wreck of his aircraft. Flames can be seen inside the fuselage as it nuzzles the ground, and on its shattered side a phrase in black lettering: THE INVISIBLE WORM. Apart from some smudges on his face and his blackened hands, one of which is holding a pair of still-smoking gloves, the captured pilot appears not only unharmed but completely at ease. His legs are wide open, his feet firmly planted on the ground; he stares at the camera with a cheerful glint in his eye, utterly disdainful of the threat from the German guns.

Aim at my stomach, the pilot is telling his killers. Don't make any holes in my jacket, please.

Achtung!

I bet you've never seen such a fabulous leather jacket, have you?

Hände hoch!

Bugger you, you filthy Boche!

The barber's apprentice runs terrified through the darkest night, cut-throat razor in one hand and shaving brush in the other, in a landscape lit only by lightning flashes.

"I think of him and I fall asleep, and when I'm asleep I call out to him," David says. "And the Paulino of my dreams stops and turns to look at me, the idiot, but he can't see me. He's got the traffic policeman's whistle in his mouth, the fool, his lips are split and his shirt is torn."

"And this coward in your dreams is meant to be me? What are you trying to do, fishface?" Paulino says. "Scare me even more?"

"You could do with getting a good fright in the middle of a storm. Perhaps that would help you make up your mind to die fighting and cut the balls off that arsehole of an uncle of yours once and for all."

"I don't want to talk about my uncle. Shall we go and hunt lizards? I need a lot of tails, at least a dozen. Go on, give me a hand."

"All right," says David. "But you'll never cure your piles with them."

"Why not?"

"Because it has to be worlizard tails."

"Worwhats . . . ?"

"Worlizards from Ibiza. They're another sort of lizard, with green and yellow stomachs, and their tails give off a liquid as black as ink because they like eating old books and magazines and all kinds of manuscripts. One day I saw one in my desk at school in the Parque Güell. It was chewing on a notebook and its tail was all black. Word of honour."

"You're pulling my leg, sweetheart."

"You don't often see them and you have to be able to spot them, but with a bit of luck we'll find one, you'll see. If you boil them with fennel and marguerite leaves they cure piles and warts much better than your ordinary lizard tail. Granny Tecla told me so."

"At the moment that's all we've got," says Paulino. "Are you coming with me or not?"

"I'm telling you to keep your eyes peeled, because when you least expect it a worlizard might dart out from under a stone, and catch you by surprise. If you're not ready, you've had it!"

"Fine, but do you want to help me now or not?" Paulino insists. "Come down into the gully with me, I need more tails. Do it for your father's sake . . ."

"You're so dumb! I couldn't give a damn about my father."

This is not true, of course. David respects his memory, although he would prefer not to have to think of him so often. It so happens that whenever he is least expecting it, he gets fleeting glimpses of him in a way he never before imagined, pursued by his furies and his demons, groping his way up the riverbed, one bloody hand on his backside, the other swinging the bottle. A drunken beggar staggering along the dried-up riverbed. But there's no doubt about it, it is him. Beyond his dishevelled appearance and air of defeat, above his unkempt and furious head, the evening sky lays on its deceiving opalescent splendour with an intensity and depth David has never seen before, and which suddenly pulls the ground from under his feet. He is not surprised to hear all around him the crash of the scrap metal of war, crumpled iron and anxious voices beneath waters that have swept by long ago, and so he pays even closer attention. The slit on his father's buttock leaves a trail of blood on the stones of the riverbed.

Where are you going looking like a tramp?

My belt – where's my belt?

"Who are you talking to?" Paulino wants to know.

"He must be down here somewhere. And you should see how he looks. Shit awful. It's a disaster, Pauli. It's so embarrassing."

Stroking Chispa, his friend Paulino gazes upstream to where market gardens growing lettuces and tomatoes have encroached on the dry riverbed.

"How would you know what he looks like? You're a bit off your rocker, you know that, David," he says, as he quickly drops to his knees in front of a limestone boulder. Before it darts back underneath, a lizard gives him a leaden-eyed stare. "Oh, shit!"

"My head's like a birdcage," David complains, covering his ear. He snaps his mother-of-pearl penknife shut and says: "Let's go home. We can't see anything now anyway, I've got this buzzing in my ears, and Chispa's on his last legs."

He sets off back the way they came, followed by Chispa and Paulino, who closes up his cut-throat razor and puts it in his pocket, muttering his disappointment. Avoiding the gully, they climb the less steep side and walk along the path that runs parallel to the riverbed, until they reach the back of the villa. They sit on the three steps of what had once been its main entrance. Paulino squints anxiously around him until he spots his pair of gaudily painted maracas. A swallow skims the ground with a piercing cry. An atomical mist clings to the dusty shoots of straggling oleanders. Paulino starts to shake the maracas, producing a gentle shuffling sound that underscores his words, giving them

43

rhythm and meaning. The maracas are painted sky-blue, with green and red stripes and bright yellow stars on their handles. Paulino bought them in Los Encantes with the tips he got for helping shave the patients in the Cottolengo.

"Your momma st..ill . . . aint ba..ack fro..oom the do..ooctor . . ."

"Sshh!" David snaps, listening hard for sounds from the riverbed. "Be quiet a moment. I heard something . . ."

"Yess you crazeee kiddo, babee," Paulino sings to the rhythm of his maracas.

"Shut up and listen!"

The cork squeaks in the bottle again, like the squawk of a bird. All charm, Pa is in their living-room staring at Ma's belly, laughing out loud. Then he bends over ceremoniously, mocking and seductive, pressing the wine bottle between his thighs as he struggles purple-faced to remove the cork. As he is pulling with all his might, he belches.

I'm sorry Rosa, my love.

One of these days you'll give yourself a hernia opening bottles like that, Víctor. She is sitting in the armchair, her swollen feet soaking in the basin. You'd do better to use your strength to educate that son of yours and bring some money home.

You'll never go short, I promise you, says Pa. Do you know what my biggest problem is, fearless red-head? It's not the drink, or my ideals, my womanizing or my taste for adventure. My problem is I've only lost one war. When a man's only lost a single war, he's still a long way from finding his dignity . . . Pop! There's your cork.

"Did you hear that?" David asks.

"Don't go on so," Paulino says. "You and those great flapping ears of yours that hear everything."

"Even Chispa here jumped with fright. It sounded like a gunshot," David insists, as the echo comes rolling out again from the foliage of the copse of trees over on the far side of the stream.

For a moment he blocks off his ears to stop the obstinate, incessant buzzing that he always gets when he imagines these scenes: the explosion and its echo reach him even before the finger has squeezed the trigger, because the shot has already been lodged inside his head for a long while. My brother David recklessly appropriates other people's memories as his own, and this vicarious, piercing memory, inherited from Pa and a Grandfather we never knew, includes within it the violent, muddy waters of another era, the waters that dug the gully bed. Anyone who climbs the gentle slope up to the house from the Avenida can see the apparently lifeless trickle of water in the bottom of the gully, the cracked clay earth, the rubbish, a few tail-less lizards and dead roots twisting like snakes; but only David sees the rushing waters which charged through and gouged out the ravine here, only he keeps their frothy echo flooding in through his sick ears, forcing him to stand there terror-struck on the edge of the void, dreaming up tales of hurricanes and watery perils, thick fogs, tempests and shipwrecks.

"It was a shot, I'm sure of it. Someone fired a shot up there by the market gardens."

"Whatever you say," Paulino grunts, staring cross-eyed under the hypnotic spell of the maracas.

Head drooping and sway-backed, Chispa drags himself to the edge of the gully and stands there quivering, knowing he is finished, but perhaps still wanting to enjoy the last rays of the setting sun. Paulino Bardolet stands up and says:

"Listen, Sitting Ear, Red Cloud is off. He has to take his uncle a jar of Floyd massage oil and clean his topee. So farewell."

"What your uncle has to do is stick his shitty traffic policeman's topee up his arse, that's what. Why don't you tell him so?"

Paulino wanders off playing his maracas, and David calls in vain to Chispa. Deaf as a post, or perhaps dreaming of a leap that would end his ills once and for all, the basset hound stands tail between his legs, staring head down into the depths, at the riverbed where the trickle of dirty water curls like a dead snake. Perhaps, thinks David, in his own way Chispa too can hear the fury of the waters that formed this ravine, the cavernous roar and the dark foam that one day tore through the rough clay. It is not as though in reality this gully is so deep or dark, it hides no great dangers and provokes no great romantic passions or memories of suicides or anything of that sort: my brother David is the only one impressed by it. In the past, a ramshackle wooden plank bridge led across it, but all that is left now are a few scars on the sides of the gully, and the odd piece of rotten timber pointing up to the sky. Scrubby plants and bushes have filled the reddish earth like a badly healed wound: brambles, thistles and sharp-pointed agaves. The eastern side, the one nearest our house, is a gentle slope only some ten yards deep, with roots and bushes to hold on to. All that remains of the rushing torrent and collapsing earth that David dreams of is the steep crumbling cliff on the far side, and the almost invisible trickle of water that is home to a variety of discarded objects – a headless doll, shards of broken glass, which gleam in the midday sun. At this time of year, the water gives off a stink of rotting garbage, but in winter this somehow turns into the sweet smell of split water-melons and seaweed, just like that of the fishing nets spread out on the sand outside Granny Tecla's house in Mataró. Some evenings, at sunset, a cloud of reddish dust rises from the bottom of the gully, as if it was on fire; it could be children, or frightened rats. A few metres further downstream, the gully broadens and flattens, and finally peters out on the rocky slope covered in broom that overlooks Avenida Vírgen de Montserrat, which in turn curls its way down towards the Parc de Les Aigües and Guinardó. At evening, the breeze blowing up the narrow ravine brings with it the cheerful tinkle of bicycle bells as they speed down the Avenida, and the voices of men and women leaving work and freewheeling downhill from the top to Horta, the women laughing as they let go of the handlebars to tie their headscarves or smoothe down their skirts, the men teasing them, one hand nonchalantly on their hip.

"Didn't you hear anything either?" says David, kneeling on the ground next to Chispa. "There was a shot upstream. Go up to the house and wait for the redhead to come home."

But the dog prefers to follow him up the riverbed, stumbling on the stones as they climb up and out on to banks dotted with dry ferns and bushes. A few spits of untouched sand lie deathly white like fish bellies alongside the rivulets of water in the middle, water that trickles down from the reed-bed and the irrigated market gardens higher up. David mutters to himself: rats, scorpions, beetles, spiders, lizards, grasshoppers, toads and snakes, one day a huge flood of water will come and sweep you all away . . .

Suddenly, behind him he hears the clink of a bottle as it knocks against stones, and then a voice like broken glass.

I need a clean handkerchief, son. And a belt. And a good patch on my trousers. Our little seamstress is taking her time to come home.

A cloud of vapour smelling strongly of chloroform emerges from his mouth. Eyes half-closed against the light, David peers closely, but can make out only a smiling face whose swollen grey features are hard to distinguish from the polished round stones of the riverbed. Yellow-eyed and with several days' growth of beard, the remains of a Chesterfield dangling from the corner of his mouth and the bottle of brandy under his arm, his father is bending over the muddy water trying to wash a blood-stained handkerchief. The almost empty bottle slides from him and bounces on the stones.

The bottle's almost done for too, more's the pity, Pa says, quickly grabbing it again. He is surrounded by bare tree branches half-buried in the riverbed and bleached by the sun. Chispa arches his back and a squirt of liquid comes out, like a green puree. David sits on a rock, head to one side, and hears himself say:

I can't see you properly, Pa.

You'll have to get used to it. It's more than you deserve anyway.

In my dreams I saw you differently . . .

Well, this is what there is, my boy. Take it or leave it. Open your eyes good and wide. You're not the one who dreams me.

I don't understand.

It doesn't matter. In my dreams, I see a lot of fried eggs, but the only ones I'd really like to eat are the ones Velázquez painted.

David remembers Inspector Galván, who at this very moment is probably posted on some street corner or sitting behind the window of a bar waiting for his mother to go by, but could equally well be sniffing round here somewhere. He bends down and chooses five pointed stones, which he stuffs in his pockets. The tiger's yellow eyes are staring at us, Pa, but we'll get you out of this, you'll see.

That wasn't why I escaped. It wasn't to save my own skin or that of my comrades, or because of any dangerous documents. I didn't get my arse stuck like a pig because I was afraid they'd catch me, he adds in a whisper of a voice. Without standing up, he gives little sideways leaps like a monkey as he looks for some clear water in the murky puddles of the river. He is barefoot, his hair is dishevelled, his shirt hangs out of his trousers, and he is still pressing the handkerchief tight against the gaping wound in his left buttock. None of those are the reasons I abandoned your mother. I did it because I loved her. And still do.

His father's movements remind David of the last lizard Paulino caught in this same spot a few days earlier. He had chopped it in two with his razor, and the two halves, each with two legs on it, had been hopping around and twisting about desperately on a flat rock while he and Pauli looked on to see which bit died first. It was the part with the head. The tail end went on writhing for several seconds in the palm of David's hand. What good did thinking do you, poor little lizard? Who chooses the twists you're making, what brain thinks them, if you haven't got a head any more?

She knows I love her, in spite of everything, Pa adds while he washes the handkerchief in the memory of other waters, in the gushing torrent of another era, other loves. The tear in his trousers reveals how ugly the wound is.

You're bleeding a lot, says David. It'll get infected.

Nonsense. Blood spilt for one's country never gets infected, it's immune to all microbes, because it's already rotten, rotten to the core.

Ma wouldn't like to hear you talk like that.

I'm a defeated man. What else do you expect? A defeated man can't ask for anything more. What a fool I look, with my arse flapping in the wind and bleeding like a stuck pig. I thought I would give everything for my country, everything except my arse . . . speaking of which, that friend Paulino of yours is having a really bad time with his, isn't he? I suppose you know what I mean.

We don't want to talk about it with anyone, David says. He can see his father's false teeth are not in properly; every so often they make a clacking sound. Be careful you don't lose your teeth, he says. And please, don't go any further up the river. You're fine here. Half a league, half a league, half a league onwards, up beyond that skull sticking out of the sand with the hole in its forehead, up there by the market gardens, someone might see you.

They wouldn't recognize me. I've changed a lot recently, my boy. My motto nowadays is: the damned truth will teach you to mistrust everything. Oh and by the way, I've seen that rotten skull with the bullet hole and I reckon it's a goat, he says with a click of the tongue, unable to tell the effect his broken voice has on David. It's a voice which does not aim directly at other people's hearing like a normal one, but first makes a wide detour round David's feverish, proud head, as if to make him dizzy. But David is quite happy this is the way it is.

Ah well, Pa says finally as he stands up straight, holding the handkerchief against his buttock. So what's new, son?

You're bleeding a lot.

Tell me something I don't know, damn it!

What can I say? You were unlucky, that's all.

I got the luck I deserved. I deserved this treacherous stab wound all right. He stands there lost in thought for a moment, an air of resignation on his face as he rolls the cigarette butt from one side of the mouth to the other, then adds: The luck I deserved.

Why do you say that?

Because of something bad I did once, in the name of high ideals, do you know what I'm talking about?

It sounds like a riddle . . .

Well it isn't. With time it will become a sinister riddle (a village priest kneeling in a roadside ditch, an ant crawling over his tonsured head, a finger pointing at the back of his trembling neck, who does the finger belong to?), a nightmare that should give more than one person sleepless nights, but which for the moment troubles only me . . . It might have been the top of a tin of sardines I myself threw into the gully, who knows. That must have been what sliced my backside open.

It wasn't a tin of sardines, David says. It was a sharp piece of a thick bottle sticking up out of the ground, probably a soda siphon.

A bottle of vodka would have been more like it . . .

What does it matter?

48

Well, there has to be some reason for the Social Brigade to say I'm a Bolshevik who is still faithful to his ideals . . . Ha, ha. Anyway, tell me about you and your mother. What are you having for supper today? Lentils?

Boiled spuds.

Fantastic. And what are you up to? Are you working already?

I'm Señor Marimón's assistant, don't you remember? David says, disappointed. Señor Marimón takes photographs for the Cristo Rey church. And at home I work the sewing-machine for Ma sometimes, for simple things. I sew on buttons and pockets for school pinafores and on her doll's clothes, and I iron collars and cuffs. And I also take the stuff down to the market and to the stalls at La Travesera de Gracia.

That's good, son.

David looks closely at his father's hand clutching the bottle.

Your hands will give you away, Pa. Don't you remember they always smelt of ether? And while I think of it, couldn't you anaesthetize your wound so it wouldn't hurt as much? Ma says you were a good anaesthetist when she met you and fell in love with you . . .

Well, I'm not any more. Who needs an anaesthetist nowadays anyway? People live with their mouths and eyes shut, and their ears blocked. Nobody needs me any more. And how is our intrepid red-head getting on? What does she do at home all day?

She sews and sweeps and cleans and washes and irons, David mutters. And smokes and drinks lots of coffee. But above all, she washes and sews, washes and sews.

Rosa Bartra, you're on the slippery slope, Pa says grimly. Aagh, this hurts so much! And tell me, do you remember to go and visit Granny Tecla now and again?

I'm going tomorrow, but Granny won't talk to me. And she's always looking at me out of the corner of her eye. Like that cop does.

Ah, it fucking well hurts! Pa moans as he turns and limps off into the reeds beside the stream, pressing the handkerchief against his buttock. Even though he can't stand properly, the efforts he makes to keep upright and maintain some sort of dignity briefly suggest the tall, well-built figure, the unconquerable vitality David had endowed him with until the day he ran away. He looks over at him sitting on his one good buttock at the river edge, raising the bottle to his mouth again. Knowing what I know now, it's easy for me to imagine David crouching head down over the hot stones of the riverbed, seeing Pa without even wanting to, and hearing him say with that sieved, evaporating voice of his: You still haven't given your mother the book that cop picked up in the street and took the trouble to cover and bring home. That's not right, son.

But I can't stand the guy. He gets on my nerves.

No need to tell me. He tries in vain to light the cigarette butt with damp matches, then gives up. This rotten luck of mine . . . Inspector Galván has got an expensive brand-name lighter, hasn't he?

It's a fake, Pa. It's a fake Dupont. It's worthless. Everything about that guy is an incredible fake: everything he does and says is a lie. Look, he seems decent enough, doesn't he? But one day in Plaza Sanllehy, Paulino Bardolet saw him aim a kick at a poor old pigeon curled up on the ground waiting to die. David stops, thinks a moment, then adds: and the pigeon was blind and lame as well.

I can see you're on a slippery slope too, David Bartra.

But it's the truth!

Of course. But that bit about blind and lame was too much. You didn't need it.

I don't understand.

Let me give you some advice as a foul-mouthed, experienced liar. If you're going to do someone down, don't add details. They always make people suspicious. It's best to invent the whole thing. If it's true like your mother believed before she dropped you into this world that you've got an artist's soul, if that's true, then one day you'll understand what I'm telling you.

It's not me who has an artist's soul, David says in a hurt voice, stroking Chispa's back. You always get it wrong, Pa. It's the kid who's going to be born who is the one with the artist's soul. That's what Ma says. She also said it about poor Juan, don't you remember? She never said it about me.

Well, so what anyway? That's nothing to get upset about. Artists aren't much use these days, whatever your mother might say . . . I have to go now. If ever you come back this way, bring me matches. And a clean handkerchief. Is that dog following you everywhere dragging its belly on the ground yours by any chance?

That's Chispa. He used to belong to Señor Augé. Don't you recognize him? He's mine now.

The poor thing's in worse shape than I am. You should put him out of his misery . . . Don't look at me like that, son. Nowadays they kill them off with strychnine and it doesn't hurt a bit. I read somewhere that the Germans have invented a lethal injection. They inject benzine or God knows what straight into their hearts and do them in painlessly. You should look into it. Now go home and don't worry about me. I dream the most awful dreams, but wake up laughing out loud.

The red-head is tidying the drawers of the chest. David comes into the bedroom peeling a banana that has gone beyond being ripe – its skin is black, and the flesh is mushy and sweet as jam. Grimacing with disgust, David takes a bite at it, then stares quizzically at his mother's rounded belly:

I heard you, you dirty little tadpole.

Aren't you always going around saying you're dying of hunger, brother? Well then, eat up and shut up.

I heard you.

All I said was you shouldn't upset her. Ma buys them like that because they're cheaper, but you should know that the riper they are, the better bananas are for you.

What would you know! All you need to know is that it makes no use your hiding or whispering, I can hear you and see you whenever I feel like it! growls David. I can see you with my powerful radioactive megarat's eyes!

There you go talking to yourself again when the red-head's right beside you, dear elder brother!

She's sick because of you. You suck her blood, you leech.

And you scare her talking to yourself like a crazy kid.

When are you going to pop out of your hole, you shitty weasel?

When she feels well and strong and in good spirits, and Pa is back home, and no flatfoot from the Social Brigade is snooping round here and we're all happy again, and we've forgotten about poverty and hunger and cold and everything . . .

What a lot of nonsense you talk!

OK. Thanks for the chat.

Yeah, I really enjoy chewing the fat with such a stupid embryo.

Thanks for keeping me company, anyway. Sometimes I get anxious in here, thinking about Ma's poor health and all her problems . . .

They're your fault, you know that. You've managed to make her think only about you. Look at her now.

Ma is getting a pair of clean sheets out of the bottom drawer. Then she opens the top one and stands blissfully stroking the blue wool. David swallows the almost liquid banana and mutters: Just look, there she goes stroking your baby clothes again, your woollen hat and your rompers, that's all she thinks about, she's already imagining you growing up, putting cologne on your hair and combing it for you, making a nice parting, tying your scarf round your neck and putting your lunch in your schoolbox . . .

"What are you whispering, David?" Ma says. "Are you talking to the dog?"

"No, nothing, I was just thinking out loud."

"Well, there's something wrong with your throat."

"I can hardly speak . . . aaggh! And it's very sore."

"Don't you go getting tonsillitis. Make sure you gargle with some warm water and bicarbonate . . . Now where are you going? You haven't done your chores yet."

"I'll do them later. I'm going to look for asparagus on the far side of the river, with Pauli."

You're such a liar, brother! There's no asparagus at this time of year!

I meant blackberries, you loathsome foetus, David growls (all at once he hears Paulino's low whistle from the cinema seat next to him: Wow! It's gone as hard as a bar of real chocolate!) I'm going to pick blackberries in the gully. Blackberries is what I meant to say.

That's a lie. You're off to the Delicias with Paulino Bardolet and his maracas.

That's enough, shrimp, or I swear I'll bash your head in as soon as it pokes out into this world . . .

"What's the matter, son? What are you muttering about? You're not trying to gargle with that banana are you?"

"No, I'm just fooling around a bit to make you laugh . . ." he sticks a finger in his mouth and picks out a banana fibre. "We hardly ever see you laugh . . ."

"Well, thanks for the thought, sweetheart. Come on, lend me a hand." With David's help pushing, they manage to shut the heavy chest drawer. "And does that fat little friend of yours, Paulino, still go to school?"

"Of course not. He goes round with his father doing hairdressing. In Asturias he used to look after his grandparents' cows, but he knows lots, because he finished two years' school. He's got an uncle who's a traffic policeman and lets him clean his pistol . . . He wants him to become a Civil Guardsman, but what Paulino would really like to do is play the maracas in a tropical band. He plays them really well. Would you like to hear him some day?"

"Why not?"

"Listen Ma, where are we going to put little Víctor's cot?"

"We haven't got one yet."

"What about mine?"

"You don't think I've still got that, do you? I gave it to a neighbour years ago. Come on, help me make the bed before you go out."

On Saturdays if all the best seats are taken in the Delicias cinema you can find yourself behind a column, and either you get a stiff neck or you have to lean your head on your neighbour's shoulder. No cloud without a silver lining, Paulino Bardolet must think, because more than once he has used this as an excuse to snuggle up to someone. But the trick does not work with David: he is quite happy to sit in the front row down near the toilets.

Sabu is a clever little copper-skinned rogue, the Technicolor is out of this world, and the princess's red lips are just waiting to be kissed. When my time came, I was to learn all this too.

Who are you? the princess says in her garden, while Paulino moves his lips in time with those on the screen, repeating the words with his squeaky voice:

Your slave, says the prince who has escaped from his reflection in the lake.

Where have you come from?

From the far side of time so that we should meet.

How long have you been searching for me? the princess and Paulino whisper as one.

Since the dawn of time.

And now that you have found me, how long will you remain?

Until the end of time. For me now yours is the only beauty in the world.

"It's so moving, isn't it, David?"

"Crap."

"Does the film bore you? Would you like me to guess what you've got in your trouser pockets just by touching on the outside?" Paulino whispers, sliding his hand across in the darkness.

"Not now, Pauli. I've got that ringing in my ears again."

"Go on, let me."

A faint sigh escapes his swollen lips. It's not the first time he's shown up at the Delicias like this, his crossed eyes still staring at the memory of something that haunts him, and blood trickling from his nose, down his top lip to the corner of his mouth and into it. Later on, in the middle of the film, the arrogant Conrad Veidt with his icy sneer also admires the princess's beauty, and professes his love in words which this time do catch David's attention:

. . . your eyes are from Babylon, your brows rival the shining moon of Ramadan, your body is as straight and tall as the letter A . . . he misses the rest because Paulino coughs three times and spits into his handkerchief. He is wheezing like a pair of bellows. David shakes the hot shaven head resting on his shoulder and digs him in the ribs.

"Ow, that hurts!" Paulino says, starting back.

"Still the same old song, you booby?"

"Oh, oh, I think I'm dying!"

"Don't go on so, I hardly touched you."

"Put your hand on my ribs here, under my T-shirt. But gently!"

"I see what you're after!"

"It's not that . . . Can't you feel my broken rib? Just there?"

"I can feel the soft satin little girl skin of yours, you great sissy."

"Why are you laughing at me? I've got a broken tooth as well."

"So what happened, has that butcher of an uncle been beating you again?" whispers David. "You sucker, I told you not to go near his place any more."

"What can I do? My father wants me to shave him every Saturday. That's the way to learn, he says, and just be thankful he isn't scared you'll cut his throat."

"Yes, slit his gizzard. I would have done by now."

"You wouldn't say that if you saw him like I do. With the towel tied under his chin he looks like a dead man stretched out to be shaved (that great big mouth of his opening to the razor when I pinch the end of his nose: a gold tooth, a rotten stench). He lies back with his eyes closed, not saying a word, he doesn't even protest if I slice the top off a spot or nick his skin without meaning to. He goes over to the mirror and sticks little bits of cigarette paper on the cuts; but then he locks the door, puts a record on the gramophone, and calls me all the names under the sun. That's just for starters, because then he grabs me by the hair or the bollocks, here and here, look, and goes on about how I'm sick, that it's the devil's curse, but that anyway he will never mention it at home because it would upset my parents, or so he says." In the darkness, Paulino's voice is thick with mucus and blood. "What you've got is a crime against nature, and I'll beat and kick it out of your body, he says, even if it means killing you . . . Then he forces me to kiss the mermaid tattoo he has, the one with a smile like a disgusting slut, the kind that make you shit yourself just by looking at you . . ."

"A tattoo?" says David. "Where?"

"Where do you think? On his arse. If you could see him (and if you saw his prick, it's got more shit on it than a henhouse pole) every Saturday it's the same story, and most Sundays too, that is when he's not directing the traffic in his white uniform and topee at the Gran Vía–Rambla de Cataluña crossroad . . ."

The same old moans whispered right in his ear, the foxy smell of fear and Paulino's hot breath on his cheek, but none of this stops David gazing up at the dazzling explosion of colour and music beneath the blue Baghdad skies. Now the princess has closed her eyes and is offering her ruby red lips to the treacherous kiss from Conrad Veidt's black mouth, and David feels a sudden warmth in his spine, like a honeyed worm crawling up from backside to brain, and he cannot be sure if this creeping sweetness is due to June Duprez opening her beautiful mouth like a rose of fire, or the trembling, playful hand of his friend, crushed yet again by the brute of an ex-legionnaire. Because Pauli, David thinks, has already seen the film three times and knows it off by heart, so he only pays attention in the scenes where Sabu appears, with his dark hairless chest and his loincloth. Now he is feeling a bit better, he prefers to mess around:

"I bet I can guess what you've got in your trouser pockets."

"Not that again."

"Why not? Go on, let me," and his hand starts feeling the surface. "That's a handkerchief, that's a tin of Juanola pastilles, that's the mother-of-pearl penknife, that's a stick of licorice . . . and this, what's this? Is it a sausage, a little worm?"

"Stop it, you're tickling!"

"And this is where Pili scratched you."

"It was Chispa's nail. That's what I get for wearing short trousers," David complains, exactly as he does all the time to the red-head. How much longer, Ma? You're always telling me how grown up I am, and yet you still make me wear short trousers.

And you'll wear them a good while yet, she tells him, sitting in the wicker chair soaking her swollen feet in a basin full of hot water.

You heard her, brother. A good while yet!

You can shut up, you runt, I wasn't talking to you! David mutters. What are you saying, Ma? I'm fourteen already . . .

For the rest of the summer at least, that way you'll be cooler, she replies, gazing down at her sewing, glasses perched on the end of her nose. Anyway, where would we get the money for long trousers? You could alter a pair of Pa's, suggests David. He only has two pairs, and I don't want to touch them; and besides, it wouldn't work. I'll wear skirts then! Well, we've got more than enough of them, but your brother in here tells me first you should clean all that muck off your knees. That's a lie, it's not muck, it's sand from the river! Are you sure? Of course, don't pay any attention to that greedy dwarf, don't you know he can't say a thing yet anyway?

And don't you know, dunderhead, that as early as four weeks we have a brain and can dream as well, and that our most common dream is of flying?

"And what's this, eh?" Paulino chuckles to himself in the dark cinema. "Could it be Chispa's tail?"

"Don't make fun of my dog."

"All right, I'm sorry."

David is not worried by the increasingly frantic movements of his friend's hand, leaping from one thigh to the other like a weightless spider, or crawling up and resting on his groin. The giant hand of the genie of the bottle deposits Sabu at the temple entrance.

"You're going to miss the best bit," David says in a languid voice, his eyes fixed on the screen. "Sabu is going into the temple of the All-Seeing Goddess."

"Now it's your turn. I bet you can't guess what I've got in my pockets!"

"I'm fed up with all this touching business. It's boring!"

"Please!"

In the end, David changes his mind, because he knows exactly what his friend has got in his pockets: a tube of Bragulat sherbert, a handkerchief covered in snot and dried blood, a bobbin of black cotton, the knife his father gave him, perhaps a cut-off lizard tail, and bits of fluff and fear. Paulino stretches back in his seat and closes his eyes. Through the darkness at an angle, the screen reflects its dazzling light and prophetic dreams on to the audience.

". . . It is said that although Allah has greater wisdom and compassion, there was once a king among kings. This lord of time and people was a great Oppressor, and the earth was like blackest pitch on the faces of his subjects and slaves . . ."

Sabu is listening wide-eyed to the old man's prophecy, but David shuts his to be able to understand better.

". . . and the people cried out: we will seek him out among the clouds. But if our judges are not courageous enough to save us from this tyrant, how can a man of such little importance do so? And the enchanter of the stars replied: Have faith, trust in Allah, and one day in the blue of the sky you will see a young boy, the most insignificant of all, and from the firmament he will destroy the tryant with the arrow of justice."

Just before the end of the film, a man who is nothing but a formless shadowy shape smelling of acetate, comes and stands in the aisle next to David. It's the phantom of Señor Augé, he thinks, because some people say the old cinema usher is in jail, others that he is dying in hospital. The shadow is carrying a torch in one hand, but does not switch it on. In the other he is holding a sealed, very crumpled brown envelope.

"Hide this under your shirt, and don't open it till you get home."

"Is it from Pa?"

"Don't ask any questions, just give it to your mother," says the shadow.

"You're not Señor Augé: who are you?"

"I said, no questions," the shadow insists, before turning on its heel and leaving.

"Who are you talking to?" Paulino Bardolet wants to know.

"Nobody."

IV

Amanda

Granny Tecla sits in a filthy armchair by the side of her bed while Ma brushes her hair. She must have been beautiful once. Now she has thick, strangely lurid pink lips, light-coloured eyes – although the right one is only half-open – thick strands of yellowing hair, and the shadow of a moustache at the corners of her mouth. Her chin is tucked down on her chest, and even though she is smiling, her brow is knitted in a frown, as if she disapproved of her own levity. The right side of her face droops lifelessly, and the eye on that side is lidded like a withered almond shell. Yet despite all this, it is obvious she was beautiful once. The bunch of marguerites Ma brought her lies on the newly made bed.

"They don't give me wine with my meals any more, daughter."

"Don't they?" Ma says. "I'll talk to the nuns."

Her wrinkled hands move restlessly in her lap, as if she were constantly unpicking a knotted piece of line. Ma explained to David that Granny still thought she was mending fishing nets with cotton thread on the beach outside her house in Mataró. There are three other old women in beds similar to hers in this room at the nursing home, but David does not like to look at them. Ma always offers them affectionate words of encouragement when she comes in.

"David, don't stand there saying nothing. Say hello to your grandmother."

"Hello. Here I am, Granny. It's David."

There is no response. He tries again:

"Granny, I've got a dog called Chispa."

Still nothing. He knows his Granny is not in her right mind.

Sometimes she never stops talking; at others, she does not say a word. But always at some point in their visit, usually when Ma is brushing her hair or pinning up her bun, his grandmother suddenly gives a start, as though she had just remembered something.

"Rosa, have you put the cod to soak?"

"Yes, Tecla."

"It needs to be in water at least two days. And without the skin – remember that."

"Without the skin, I won't forget."

The brush flutters in Ma's delicate white hands, making Granny's grey hair shine. Ma has a hairgrip between her teeth, her bare arms move up and down, giving off the fruity perfume of her reddish armpits as she bends over the old woman's head with a patient, dedicated sense of concentration.

"Could you do the bun a bit higher?" Granny says. And almost simultaneously her voice thickens with sadness as she asks an unexpected question: "Where is Amanda, the dangerous one? Hasn't Amanda come today either? What's happened to Amanda, why doesn't she come to see me any more?" She bursts into tears, Ma tries to calm her, but she goes on between sobs: "I've always known how things are, Rosa, but I've kept quiet out of respect. Amanda can tell you."

As far as Ma is aware, there never was anyone called Amanda in the family, in the neighbourhood or among Granny's friends in Mataró. At first, when the nuns looking after her heard her shout the name at night, they had no idea what to do or think, but now they pay no attention. It's useless trying to ask her who this Amanda might be. Her mind must be straying, or it could be the ashes of a distant dream or emotion, perhaps the lingering perfume of a youthful experience or a secret desire. Whatever it may be, Granny's constantly renewed expectations about Amanda fascinate David.

"Please don't cry, Tecla. Look who's come to see you," Ma says as she prepares to cut her fingernails. "Come closer, son, and talk to her."

As he draws nearer his grandmother, he can smell the brackish odour of fishing nets drying in the sun.

"Hello, Granny, it's me, David."

She never acknowledges him. She does not seem to see or hear him: her watery eyes stare straight through him. Standing there, facing this unseeing gaze, David feels ill at ease in his own body, and this is perhaps the first time he is conscious of this discomfort. He takes a couple of steps back and asks his mother:

"Why can't she see me?"

"Of course she can see you. She probably has nothing to say to you, that's all."

"No, Granny doesn't want to see me. I know she doesn't."

"You just have to be patient with her. The poor woman's a bit slow. Try talking to her again, go on."

David steps forward in front of his granny once more, and insists. Hello Granny, it's me, David. Silence is the only reply, and that liquid gaze that does not see him. A few moments later, the grandmother asks the air:

"Do you know the story about the naked Empress?"

"The Emperor," says David. "It was an emperor, Granny."

It is as if she does not hear him. She goes on:

"I was told it when I was a little girl, I can still remember it. In the story, everyone sees the Empress dressed in fine clothes travelling through the streets of a town, and the only one who sees she has no clothes on is a little girl riding a bicycle . . ."

"A little boy," David interrupts her. "And he isn't riding a bicycle. And it isn't a naked empress, Granny, it's an emperor who has no clothes on."

"Who's that?" the old woman wants to know.

"It's your grandson David," Ma smiles sadly as she gently rubs Grandmother's brow and temples with a handkerchief soaked in cologne. "How nice and cool this cologne smells, doesn't it, Tecla?"

"Why on earth were you riding a man's bike like that?" Grandmother asks. "You'll fall and hurt yourself."

And so on, all the time. It's the same during the other visits he makes with his Ma, Granny just gets worse and worse, increasingly out of it, and David feels increasingly uncomfortable and invisible. And each time, after he and his mother have said goodbye and are leaving along the corridor, they hear her voice repeating the refrain: What about Amanda? Why doesn't Amanda come? most likely directed now at the old women she shares her room with, all of them as absent from this world as she is.

Some nights a wind from the gully beats furiously against doors and windows that are never opened now in the house of the ear, nose and throat specialist; it raises groans from hinges and long since rotten wood; it brings echoes from trees and branches that lightning or the encroaching city swept away years earlier; whirling piles of leaves can be heard, together with ships' sirens in the fog, whistles from the four frozen corners of the world. And the sleepless, distant waters that gouged out the gully rush past once more, slowly and silently carrying with them dead eyes and chopped-off hands, plastic arms and legs and doll's clothes, radio sets with their insides hanging out.

David wakes up shouting in bed, and the shout burrows its way into his hearing and will not go away. Moonlight is streaming in through the skylight, bathing Doctor P.J. Rosón-Ansio's giant ear. David raises himself on one elbow, opens his eyes sleepily and looks up at the photo of Joe Louis staring down at him from behind his boxing gloves with his thick black lips.

My ears are a mess too, they're buzzing all the time as well, says Joe Louis. Hang on in there, kid.

Then David consults the huge pink ear with the explanations written round it in neat red script, each one with its arrow pointing to a particular part of the hearing organ. But he cannot find any reference to the sensation he has, no diagnosis for his strange and disturbing pain.

With eyes still half-closed, David sees the specialist from Cordoba come into what used to be his laboratory. He is wearing his white gown, a bullfighter's cap on his head, the small round doctor's mirror on his forehead, and a cape folded over his arm to cover the hole the bull has gored in his stomach.

Is that where the horn went in? David hears himself ask.

What horn are you talking about, the doctor says in the reedy voice of a bullfighter.

The bull's horn.

What bull? The doctor insists, looking down at him now with a stern expression.

Why, the bull that gored you in the ring. You were a bullfighter known as "The Earman" from Cordoba, and a bull gored and killed you in the ring at Badajoz.

Doctor P.J. Rosón-Ansio frowns, and his bushy black eyebrows appear to take flight.

Like hell I was a bullfighter! Are you soft in the head, boy? How can you think that any bullfighter in their right mind would be called "The Earman"! You should show a little more respect. You should know I wasn't killed by a bull goring me.

You weren't? I'm sorry.

What happened was that I was in the Republican army and the Nationalists put me in the Badajoz bullring, made me wear this cape and hat, and then cut off my hands. Then on the 8th of August 1936 an officer under the command of General García Valiño machine-gunned me and several hundred other poor wretches along with me. So fewer jokes and more respect!

With a sudden, furious gesture, the specialist tears off the hat and cape and flings them to the floor. Then he turns the forehead reflector on to David's sleepy astonished face, and asks him:

Have you seen my suede gloves anywhere around?

David is about to reply that the gloves must still be on the side-table in the living-room, and that his father was just about to try them on while he was sitting there drinking a glass of brandy when the cops came looking for him and he only managed to escape by the skin of his teeth, and to add that when Inspector Galván saw them a few days later he thought they must belong to Pa; but he sees how the doctor is quickly hiding the stumps of his arms in his overall pockets, and he feels so sorry for him he prefers not to mention the gloves at all. Standing next to the bed, the doctor presses his arms so hard inside his pockets they almost tear the cloth. He looks down at David with a mixture of affection and curiosity.

Are you going to check my ears at last? David asks him.

Let's see . . .

Give me a proper check, won't you? I'd like to be healthy, as strong as an ox, because there's a lot I have to do in my life, and this blasted buzzing . . .

Hmmm. Let's see. Try to describe the sound – what's it like?

I don't know . . . I imagine it like gas escaping from the open spigot of a gaslamp.

Have you ever heard the sound of gas escaping from a lamp?

Now that you mention it, I don't think I have . . .

So why is that how you imagine it?

Perhaps because I've never heard it. Sometimes I also think of it like the sound of rain falling very softly, at others it sounds like a motorbike far, far away.

Hmmm. And when did you start talking to yourself, boy?

It was after this cricket got inside my head . . .

You know very well it's not a cricket. Tell me exactly what happened to you.

At first it was just like having the sea in my ears, David says, getting excited as he starts to describe it. Like when you put a shell to your ear and you can really hear the sea. I didn't think it was anything, Doctor, I wasn't at all scared. The sea in my ears! But the second time it was worse. I'll tell you. I was with Paulino down in the bottom of the gully where all the rubbish is, and I was holding the two halves of a broken record I had just found: it was "Arrullos de amor" by Rina Celi, and I was sad because we couldn't hear her voice, you know the one where she sings When I hear your voice it sounds just like a lullaby of love, the two pieces fitted together perfectly but there was no way we could stick them back again: Not even with spirit glue? Paulino asked. Not even with Holy Spirit glue, fatso, I said, and it was a real shame because I wanted to give it to my mother as a present, she's always singing that stupid song, and the record looked brand new too . . .

You were telling me about the buzzing in your ears, Doctor P.J. Rosón-Ansio says, chin on his chest and looking at him sternly.

Ah, yes. It's not like Juan Centella's, David explains. I wish it were, then it could warn me of any danger . . .

Get to the point. What happened with the record?

I had to drop it because all of a sudden I felt like an electric shock! I had half of the record in each hand and I could feel the strangulated voice of that singer shooting up my arms and lodging itself in my ears, in some corner of my cochlea, like the one on that pink ear you've got on the wall over there. I dropped both pieces of the damned record and put my hands over my ears. Bloody hell, I shouted, what's all this going on? Has a bee or a cricket got in there? Is it the siren warning of another air-raid? A Spitfire fighter plunging to earth? The whistle of the atomical bomb over Hiroshima? But long before I heard any of those, the whistle of another kind of bomb entered my hearing. When I was little. It was the whistle that bomb made when it hit the ground which was the first to get inside my head, doctor, and it's never gone away. Ever since then, the noises have never stopped. Sometimes it's as if a piece of silk was being torn inside my ears, or like when a wave gently pulls back from a sandy shore. Or the throbbing of a fan. I know all the different sounds by now. Then, later, a cricket got into each ear, or better still, a swarm of bees. And some days it's as if I had a whole birdcage in there, doctor. That's on good days, when the bastard is behaving itself, because on other days there's a change, and everything suddenly gets louder and then it's like a thunderclap, a real nightmare. But I never get that when I'm in the crowd at the Campo de la Calva, or when I'm with the Calle Verdi gang, or at the pictures with Paulino getting on my nerves, or when I'm listening to his maracas or to the radio; and the buzzing hardly ever gets loud when I'm scared it will, or when I'm expecting it to, like with the firecrackers for St John's night, or when I'm on a tram or the metro. I had no idea why until one day I finally understood: my boss who takes photographs of weddings and baptisms was bawling me out for losing some photos, so I went and shut myself in the red silence of the dark-room, and it was there I realized that it's not that the son of a bitch of a cricket is quiet sometimes, what happens is simply that a louder noise drowns him out. That's why I'm so terrified of the silence at night, doctor. Right now for example I'm scared out of my wits. That's why I started talking to myself.

Hmmm. You think you're talking to yourself, but in the majority of cases that does not actually happen, the doctor pronounces. These hearing complaints can fool even the experts. The cause may be in the cervical canal, although I am not someone who believes in diagnoses that are too close to reality. There's an element of mystery in your suffering that we should respect. I'll show you some very easy exercises for your neck and shoulders.

Is it serious, doctor?

It's not hereditary. We might also consider a controlled silence therapy in the tympanic cavity, but that's a complicated process which has not produced very satisfactory results so far . . .

So what have I got, doctor?

There's a poisonous flower growing in your hearing, my boy. There's no known remedy for these noises and buzzing, you have to learn to live with them, to subdue them, to control and deceive them. You have to give them the slip, to confuse them, or they will be the death of you. Pretend you don't hear them. Listen out for other voices calling to you, be alert to other winds, other echoes. Drown the hissing of the snake with another more bearable sound. Because throughout your life, until you die and the lead of nothingness is poured into your ears and you can enjoy an eternity of silence, those noises will go with you, and worm their way into your days and nights like the worms that burrow into the earth beneath the green grass up above. You'll have to defend yourself tooth and nail, my boy. Remember that every time you look at my ear hanging there on the wall. And now, good night.

Inspector Galván's next visit is as strange as it is unexpected, first because it takes place almost at nightfall, and second because he says he is just passing and is in a bit of a hurry, he only wanted to say hello, she's not to worry, he claims as he stands there in front of her, cool as you please and not in the slightest hurry. The two of them meet out on the narrow strip of land between the night-time door and the gully's edge. Ma has just brought in all the washing off the line and is about to carry it inside; she adjusts her bathrobe and watches the inspector draw nearer. As the first long shadows of evening gather, her freshly washed carrot-coloured hair and the white gown stand out clearly, but what was most extraordinary, according to what one of the women neighbours commented later, was the bold way she treated the policeman, something so unusual in such an unassuming, discreet person. She has got the washing basket hitched on one hip, and the inspector offers to carry it for her, but she refuses, and then stands on the three steps and turns back to look at him.

"Do you know how to fold sheets?"

The cop stands staring at her, trying to spot some sign that will give him a clue as to the real meaning behind her question.

"I'm glad you're in such a good mood, Señora . . ."

"Fine, you're glad I'm in a good mood. But can you fold sheets?"

The inspector still stands there silently, interrogating her calmly inquisitive, almost laughing face.

"Of course I can," he says finally. "My mother taught me."

"Well then," she says, bending down with the basket. "You won't mind helping me, will you?" She takes out a sheet, gives the inspector two corners of it, and walks backwards with the other end. "We can talk about the adventures of Señor Bartra some other day, don't you think?"

As they pull on the sheet, it flaps and stretches, then as they fold it, they come closer and closer together until their hands are almost touching. Four times at least. There were four sheets in the basket.

Perhaps it is the strange signs of senile dementia that led him to do it, or perhaps it's just a joke, or who knows, maybe it's even out of a sense of pity – the fact is I'll never know why he does it – but the flashes of daylight that always glint in his honey-blond eyes, the pressure from his soul that exhausted him throughout his short life, his everlasting desire to perfect what was bound to happen by anticipating it with some minor adjustment, a point of emphasis that would make it even more extraordinary, drives him towards the nursing home one Sunday in June last year, to Granny Tecla's bed, a bunch of marguerites in his hand.

"Hello Granny, it's Amanda."

The old woman is lying flat on her back in the bed, and stares up at him for a moment. She closes her eyes and smiles faintly. Then she opens them again, and fixes her gaze on the cut on the boy's knee. She does not say a word.

"Your grandson says you won't talk to him," David remarks.

"I don't have any grandsons. Why didn't you come before to see me?"

"Your grandson says you don't love him."

She cannot take her eyes off the cut on his knee, streaked with iodine.

"You've fallen off your bike. I told you. I warned you."

"It's nothing," David replies. He notices that two of the three women who share the room are not in their beds. "Look, I've brought you some marguerites."

"You've gone and fallen off that dreadful bicycle again, haven't you? Don't lie to me."

David thinks for a moment before he replies.

"Yes, it's true."

"What happened to it?"

"To what?"

"To the bike. To that man's bike you ride!"

David again pauses before replying.

"Oh," he says in the end. "It had a puncture and the saddle got torn, but I've fixed it. Everything's fine, Granny."

"Is it fine for a bike saddle to tear like that?"

"Yes, of course." David thinks quickly, and adds: "The seat and the plate and the pedals or anything else. I managed to jump off in time, but the bike hit some thorn bushes and that's how the saddle was torn."

He adds all this because he has noticed that the more details he gives, the more attention Granny pays to his story.

"You should be more careful, you could have been left with a limp. You take too many risks, Amanda."

"Oh, no, I know how to look after myself."

"Like hell you do! Remember the saying: it's easier to catch a lame man than a lie."

"I think it's the other way round, isn't it?"

"Don't contradict me!" Granny protests, finding it hard to breathe. "These things happen because you ride a bike that isn't meant for you. Because it's a man's bike. You do know you're riding a man's bike, don't you?"

"Yes I do, Granny."

Standing motionless beside her bed, David lets her examine him. For once he does not feel invisible or anonymous or defenceless confronting her gaze, and although he senses his grandmother's death is close and her crumpled face in the hollow of the pillow frightens him, he cannot avoid a strange feeling of completion, a sudden awareness of the future. In fact, his grandmother has been dying for days now, and he would never have thought this was how old people die, chatting, conjuring up and savouring who knew what dreams and memories.

"Come and sit here next to me," she says, touching his face and hair. She takes his hand and adds: "Your hair is very long."

"I've been told that the longer I have it, the less I'll hear the ringing in my ears."

"That's a lie. You've turned into a fine one, and no mistake," says Grandmother, her voice wheedling. "Don't lower your eyes, look at me! Where were you going on your father's bike, sitting on that tall seat and showing what girls ought not to be showing? Tell me."

"I can't remember, Granny."

"Well, I can." A bluish veil draws over her half-closed eye as she goes on:

"There was the sound of a hurdy-gurdy from the other side of the river, or from the end of the street, I don't know which now. At my age, I've forgotten half of what I knew and I make the other half up, or that's what the nuns tell me . . . throughout my life I've been nothing more than a woman who has mended nets drying on the beach. But they weren't torn by dolphins, not likely, it was the propellers of that big plane that crashed into the sea outside our house. That day you were riding your bike to see the organ grinder's music . . ."

"You can't see music, Granny."

"Don't interrupt me! I know what I'm talking about. And another thing: I don't like that blouse you're wearing. You've got the blue one, that's smarter and it's as good as new. Blue is a trustworthy colour, it's the best for times like these, don't you forget it . . . what colour is the bicycle?"

David is fascinated by a black sore on his grandmother's top lip.

"It's red."

"Take my advice, paint it some other colour. You're all right wearing a red beret, because a beret is a beret, but be careful what else you use the colours red and orange for. Yellow – if you paint your bicycle yellow you'll never fall off or hurt yourself, no harm will come your way."

"I know I'll come to no harm," David says with a smile. "I've got atomical legs and heterodyne eyes. I'm a superheterodyne girl, Granny."

"Don't be so cheeky."

It's not a sore on her lip, it's a fly which now decides to take flight. His granny's face turns pale, and from time to time she is racked by hiccups. There are hairs growing out of her ears. Would the sight of these small calamities horrify Amanda or whoever the person might be who is meant to be there, would this fantasy girl wrinkle her nose up at the crumpled folds of Grandmother's nightdress, David wonders, or at the stale smell of her yellowing hair and her cracked skin, since Ma is not there today to rub her neck and forehead with cologne?

"What are you thinking, Amanda?"

"Nothing."

"You're bored."

"No, Granny."

"If you are bored, you can go. But before you do, soak the handkerchief in a few drops of cologne and give it me, would you?"

"Of course. I'll do it, Granny."

I have no way of knowing whether my brother realized at the time that the person visiting Granny Tecla was not him, but his imagination: it was make-believe, a mixture of childish dare-devilry and compassion, the fleeting embodiment of a phantom which started as a game, almost a game of hide-and-seek, matching her wanderings with his own.

On his own initiative and alone, without Ma ever learning about it, David pays two or three more visits to the nursing home dressed as Amanda. He also goes with Ma on Sundays, but on those occasions he feels less than nobody, because when he is there as David, Grandmother still insists on not seeing or hearing him. At the end of May, without ever properly recovering her remaining wits, and just before Inspector Galván comes on the scene, Grandmother has another stroke and dies.

Three days later, while out hunting lizards with Paulino and Chispa, David finds the broken pedals and saddle of a bicycle among the detritus of the riverbed rubbish. It's a pointed, thin saddle from a man's bike, and the leather is badly scratched. The springs and the neck of the saddle are rusty and stain his hands brown, but in spite of the tear, the leather is still shiny and retains its colour of burnished copper.

Let's go back a bit, brother. That page from a magazine you hung on the wall in your room, that photo of the fighter pilot next to his crashed plane, where did it come from, and what's it got to do with Ma?

You ought to know, you disgusting tadpole. Don't you reckon you always go everywhere with her, don't you claim you're always so close to her heart and her secrets, her worries and fears? See how you spend all day sucking the red-head's blood and don't notice a thing? See what a cheat and a liar you are, and how you'll end up a jinx like that cop who's always on our tail?

What I can see now are tiny fires in the darkness. David burning bundles of papers in the rocky riverbed at nightfall. Did Ma tell him to do it? It happened the day before we let the inspector slip in and tour the whole villa, and he saw the photo of the pilot and said, by the way, Señora, if I were you I wouldn't let your son put pictures of war and death on his walls, or words to that effect. Yes, it was Ma who told him to do the burning.

The afternoon of the day before, the red-head cleans out the wardrobe in her room, and then sits on her bed with three shoe boxes stuffed with bundles of letters and postcards, old school notebooks and cuttings from newspapers and magazines, together with a few yellowing oval photographs of grandparents, great-grandparents and other relatives we will never meet. She spends more than two hours patiently looking at and rereading all this, with a weary, melancholy attitude that from time to time becomes defiantly wary: she tears some of them to shreds. Finally she throws everything back into the boxes, forcing the papers in with her fist. There is still a third box, but by now she is really tired and does not even open it. She calls out to David.

"Here, son, take all this outside and burn it."

"What is it? Are you frightened the flatfoot might see it? Do you think it could cause trouble for Pa?"

"What I think is that this house needs a good clean. That's what I think."

Fire consuming papers: it's a recurring image in our family's memory. Granny Tecla burning documents and passbooks and banknotes in her house at Mataró by the seashore, Pa burning books and magazines in the gully, along with folders, identity papers and pamphlets, and Aunt Lola and Uncle Pau doing the same in their house in Vallcarca . . . bonfires in the night, bonfires and grim faces reflected in the diabolic glow. David crouches down, his back to the eastern slope of the gully. He has a box of matches in his hand as he kneels under the twisted, withered roots of a dead fig tree. He has built the torn-up contents of the first two boxes into a pile, and throws on everything from the third one his mother did not even touch. Before striking a match, he picks up a few pieces of lined paper that have blown away, and out of curiosity reads the almost indecipherable remains of words, expressions of desires and emotions torn apart with the paper. There are two different handwritings, one written in blue ink, the other purple: *to see you again . . . endless night . . . that tall and charming airman . . . those kisses . . . the invisible worm . . . only hope . . . to hell with flags and to hell with the country of my soul . . . That flies in the night . . .* It's impossible to read a whole sentence, so David gives up.

Just as he is putting the lighted match to the papers, the usual buzzing in his ears changes to the whine of a fighter plane engine nose-diving out of the sky. When the fire catches, David spots the pilot's haughty look just before he is consumed by the flames; the man is portrayed on what looks like the carefully folded front cover of an illustrated magazine, which is uncurling as the heat reaches it, while a strong smell of fuel spreads through the night air. At the risk of burning his hand, David rescues the picture from the fire, and blows quickly on the singed edges of a leaden sky into which a column of black smoke is rising. The pile of written words is reduced to ashes, but he only has eyes for the Allied pilot standing in front of the burning fuselage of his Spitfire: he gives not the slightest sign that he knows he is about to die, of being injured or cowed, or

69

that he will try to duck and avoid the bullets. His flying jacket is superb. A short ivory cigarette holder dangles from the corner of his mouth, and his hands, nonchalantly resting on his hips, are charred and still smouldering; he is still carrying the big leather gloves he has just pulled off. His gesture and the defiant, calm way he is gazing back at the camera seem to want to distance himself from this wasteland down below, from the sombre world of ruins and desperate violence reflected in the scene of his own capture, these machine-guns about to let rip at his chest. To judge by the tenderly tinted photo, it was taken not long ago. Presumably shot down over French soil – a broken signpost reads *Roubaix 12 km* – and taken by a war photographer at the moment of capture, the pilot is standing next to his crashed plane behind a wire fence, his brand-new flying jacket zipped up and his goggles high on his forehead, looking at the person looking at him with mocking eyes, a blackened face and a smile that is the smile of someone who is still flying, thinks David as he stuffs the photo under his shirt, someone whose plane may have been destroyed, but not his courage or his belief in victory, or his fighting spirit which is still soaring high in the skies, above the clouds and beyond the lightning storms and the artillery, there where the sun always shines . . .

"That was how I found the fighter pilot."

"Shit, how exciting!" Paulino shouts when he is shown the photo. "What amazing things happen to you since you've damaged your Eustachian tubes. Will you let me examine them for you?"

———————

I wouldn't know how to talk about you without talking to you, brother. I find it hard to disentangle your voice from mine, and I succeed only occasionally, at moments when your voice rings out unexpectedly and imperiously, and becomes the only real, urgent way of telling things, because it is the true echo of a time which for both of us now seems forever like an imaginary refuge.

Here he comes again. Over there.

That flatfoot really gets me, says David. He pretends to be dumb, but he's smart all right!

What does Ma say? I could swear she doesn't feel the same, brother. How do you think she sees him?

She sees him as a rather good-looking policeman of around forty, who sometimes behaves as if he were lost and who does not seem particularly happy with what he is doing, a tall, soft-spoken man who now and then tries to be friendly. That's how she sees the flatfoot, according to David. A grim-faced guy, sad and lonely . . . stiff and annoying in manner, and who knows whether he has deaths on his conscience, but at least he's not such a brute as so many of them are, she told me one day, you shouldn't let him scare you.

"Did your blessed mother really say that?" Paulino Bardolet says, shaking his maracas.

"Yes. So I reminded her what had happened on the tram, but she said that was just an unfortunate accident, and that she'd already forgotten it."

"The red-head tries to see the best in everyone."

"She reckoned she'd forgotten it! Grrr . . ."

If you don't want to forget some faces, you have to look askance at them. Replies who, and where? The smoky exhalations of our father in the gully? Granny Tecla giving Ma advice from her death bed? Chester Morris' frog croak or Paul Muni's whisper in the darkness of the Delicias? David's own voice, foreseeing greater dangers?

However that may be, perhaps Inspector Galván's face does not deserve such a harsh, suspicious judgement. But that was how my brother felt from the very first time he saw him standing in the night-time doorway and confronted the blue ice of his eyes and the froth of his voice, a way of speaking that was like salivating, rescued only by a habitual terse hoarseness. Now here he is again, in the middle of the street:

"Hey you, boy. Yes you, mophead. Hold on a minute."

He stands there stiff and unforthcoming, he looks at people with a mixture of condescension and pity and is silent in an offhand way that can seem more threatening than any of his questions: this is the technique the inspector uses to search their anxious faces for any traces of the past, any sign of disloyalty; but whether he discovers these tell-tale signs or not, he does not allow the slightest flicker of emotion to alter his wooden features. Always wearing a baggy brown suit, a pair of worn-out two-tone shoes and with the knot of his black tie loosened beneath his protruding Adam's apple, sometimes fanning himself with his hat, the inspector's aquiline profile peers into bars for clues of Víctor Bartra's alcoholic loud-mouthed presence, which for sure is easy enough to detect, who hasn't seen that wastrel Bartra at this very bar roaring with laughter and knocking back the brandy, and with more than his fair share of swearing, who hasn't heard him openly cursing everything, no I wouldn't be able to tell you, why against this that and the other, but that was some time ago, yes goodbye Inspector, and good luck to you. It was the summer of the Hiroshima bomb, and all morning a sticky drizzle soaked the grey flat roofs and the barren gardens and turned brown all the white sheets spread out on the broom bushes on the far side of the river, all the women in the neighbourhood are chatting about it, just you wait and see, it's bound to change the weather and the atmosphere and the fruit and vegetables, they say it will affect pregnant women too, and girls' menstruation, just look at your dog, my lad, this fine hot rain pricked with light is killing the poor thing, it's eating at his soul and his bones, look at the way he's dragging himself under the table.

"Come out of there and defend yourself, Chispa."

Panting, the basset lets its head droop between its front paws.

"You're wasting your time, son. He hasn't even got the strength to die," Ma says. "He'd be doing me a real favour: you should see the state he leaves the house in, doing his business all over the place, the poor animal."

"Sshh! He'll hear you! Didn't you need to go to the market for clothes? If it stops raining we'll go with you, won't we, Chispa?"

Every day, David washes the dog's eyes with boiled thyme, gives him a spoonful of condensed milk, brushes his coat and whispers little white lies in his ears, how sweet you smell, how good you look today, brave dog, tomorrow we'll go to market and for a run in the Parque Güell, while you're with me you don't have to worry about dying, we're safe here, the atomical bomb's poisonous mushroom cloud will never reach here, or the shock wave that incinerates everyone on the spot, our gully is a great shelter.

"You don't really believe that, do you sweetheart?" says Paulino. "Millions of megarats are already flying through the air and they'll sweep everything away! Not even your dog's shadow will be left! Nothing will happen to me though, because I'm a superheterodyne boy . . ."

"Shut your trap, fatso. Can't you see he can hear you?"

"Jesus, kid, you really do have a heart of gold."

"And you have a china arse, which is going to get well and truly stuffed any day now."

"Shut up, don't say that, tomorrow I have to go and shave Uncle Ramón again."

"You're not going are you? You can't be so dumb."

"I've no choice. Christ, he'll kill me if I don't!"

"You have to escape from that trap, Pauli."

"Yes, but how? Tell me what I should do."

"Cut off his ear with your razor! Stuff his topee up his arse!"

"What a mind you have! Do you know something, sweetie?" Paulino chants, to the rhythm of his maracas: "You follow your yellow-brick road, and I'll follow mine."

"You really are dumb."

My brother David. He has a small face, big round honey-coloured eyes, a soft chin, straw-coloured hair and a heart of gold. He is standing on the corner opposite the market, holding Chispa's lead far more gently than he would hold his own umbilical cord, let alone mine if Ma were forced to ask him to do so in an emergency, God forbid. Paulino has stuffed the maracas down his shirt front like a pair of tits. The dog is panting, sprawled out on the wet pavement. A little further on, standing alert on the kerb, trenchcoat over his shoulder and hands in his trouser pockets, Inspector Galván is watching the women come and go among the rails of cheap children's clothing. The intrepid red-head is one of them. The drizzle has stopped, but the afternoon air is humid and this only increases the stifling heat.

"Look," growls David. "It's him."

"He's staring at your mother with fish eyes."

"Take a good look at his face. It's as if he'd just received a sacred host or something."

"He looks like someone who sells fountain pens and fake watches," Paulino says. This is the first time he has set eyes on him.

"Too right. He spends his time spying on my mother day and night. He follows her round like a poodle. And he's killed a man for her, I saw him."

"Good God!"

I can only see Paulino Bardolet as a kind of small round barrel on legs and with a shaven head, ponderous and affectionate, with a slight squint and white, soapy hands.

"It's written on his face," David says.

"Watch out, he's coming!"

The green trenchcoat that David likes so much, with all kinds of belts, buckles and buttons on it, smells faintly of tobacco.

"Hey you, boy. Yes you, mophead. Hold on a moment."

"What do you want? We've done nothing wrong, sahib."

The cop lights a cigarette with his lighter.

"Don't start your nonsense. Just tell me something."

"Why don't you offer us one, sahib?"

"If you behave."

"Thanks, sahib."

"I didn't say I would give you one."

"No, sahib. At your service, sahib."

"That's enough of that." He stares down at the lighted cigarette between his fingers, as if he suddenly could not recognize either his own hands or the cigarette. "Tell me something . . ."

"Captain Vickers is charging at the head of his troop of lancers towards the hills of Balaklava," says David. "Half a league, half a league, half a league. What more do you want to know?"

"His royal highness Surat Khan," adds Paulino evenly, without the slightest hint of mockery, "the most powerful emir of all the tribes of Suristan, is saved from the claws of a tiger thanks to Captain Vickers' sure shot."

"It's the film they're showing this week at the Delicias," David explains.

"That's enough of your nonsense. I want to ask you something," the inspector says, looking away from them and back at the red-head as she moves around the market on the far side of the street. "Does you mother like coffee?"

"Beg pardon, sahib?"

"Does she drink coffee? Is she allowed to, I mean?"

"You've already asked me that, don't you remember?"

"Well, I'm asking you again."

David stares at him, unsure what to say. The flatfoot must know his mother has health problems and has had high blood pressure, and perhaps he wants to bring her some real coffee. He is still looking at the other side of the street without saying anything, but David can see his lips moving even though he is not speaking, and the tip of his tongue frequently pokes out, as if he is trying to taste or to remove some speck left there. His upper lip is taut and well-defined and has a tiny vertical scar, a dark cleft that lends a scornful twist to the entire mouth. David has still not replied when all of a sudden Chispa, still splayed on the pavement, releases all the air trapped in his stomach or God knows where, and appears to laugh. The air pours out of his mouth like the hiss of a coffee pot, growing fainter and fainter until it ends up as a kind of sad meowing.

"Did you hear that? My dog can meow like cats do. Look at him. Meeoowww . . ."

"I asked you a question."

"And what a question! I told you before, no real cop would ask a question like that . . ."

"So what's the answer?"

"Well, she says the doctor forbade her coffee and sugar. But the fact is that when she's got coffee, she drinks it, and when she doesn't, she drinks chicory, like everyone else. That's all there is to it. Ersatz coffee of course, don't go thinking we're rich or anything. What the memsahib most likes are hot *churros*, cream and things like that, as I've already told you . . . and now, excuse me, but

74

my dog needs a pee . . . no, what are you doing sweetie, you mustn't sniff the sahib flatfoot's shoes like that!"

The dog's howl as the inspector gently prods it away from him with the tip of his shoe is almost inaudible; David's voice as he pulls on the lead rings out loudly above it: Can't you see the poor animal is almost blind? And the distant outline of the red-headed seamstress is soft and pregnant as she carefully examines scraps of material on the market stall. This is my mother, tall, white, exhausted by the heat but still cheerful-looking, wearing her years-old flimsy summer dress, the front edge of the skirt slightly raised, black umbrella folded under her arm, a few red curls escaping from the sides of the mauve scarf tied round her head: all details Inspector Galván's persistent gaze has registered with the precision of a photographic lens by the time David sees him turn on his heel and walk away, while at his feet more foul air seeps out of Chispa as if he were a wineskin.

V

The Red-Head's Lie

A deafening, terrifying noise loops out like a reel in his ears, robbing him of sleep. Stretched out on his bed, hands behind his head and staring up at the ceiling, David summons up different noises and tries to imagine and imitate devastating hurricanes whistling through palm trees bent double beside raging waves, Warsaw being bombed, or the San Francisco earthquake roaring through the Delicias cinema, trying to make sure the sounds are loud enough to drown out the bedlam that fills his head at this time of night. Finally he makes out the sad whine of the Spitfire as it falls to earth, it's a drone that tonight forces itself on him in an even more insistent and angry way than usual. He switches on the reading lamp on the chair, and peers at the wall opposite. The skylight is open, letting in the stifling night and the chirrup of crickets in the gully.

Hello there, friend.

As ever, David starts by admiring his leather flying jacket, goggles and scarf, but soon he is more interested in the pilot's attitude towards death. The airman stands in the midst of the cindered plain, surrounded by the smoking scrap metal of war and also doubtless by bodies; arms akimbo, snow-white cigarette holder clenched between his teeth, his jacket untouched, goggles high up on his fore-head and the earflaps of his helmet hanging down his powerful, muscular neck. Behind him, disrupting the jagged line of the horizon that hints at a ruined coast-line, the column of black smoke goes on rising to the sky from a tangled heap of iron. If any of his squadron colleagues spotted him – always supposing there was someone else from his squadron flying nearby – thinks David, they could swoop down firing their cannon and free the pilot from the two German soldiers hunched tensely over their sub-machine-guns, one on each side of him and only partially visible as they never quite manage to get into the frame, their backs to the photographer. A metallic crash comes from the plane's fuselage, a last lament of metal and defeat. David spells out once more on the side of the cockpit: THE INVISIBLE WORM. The downed fighter pilot tilts his head to one side and half closes his eyes, as if avoiding smoke drifting into his face.

Hello boy, he says more or less.

Haven't they killed you yet?

They are thinking about it. Those Boches are a bit slow. If they take any more time the fuel tank will explode and all three of us will go up in smoke. What do you make of that?

That's good. Kill as you are killed.

These eyes which watch him sleep every night from far-off, devastated regions express confidence and courage in the face of everything, and there is always a spark of devilry in his gaze. Which is strange, because the more David stares at the prisoner, the more convinced he is that the Germans are about to riddle him with bullets. There is a tension about the whole scene that heralds this fatal outcome. That bastard cop was right, he's a dead man. Behind his back, the plane is about to disintegrate.

Last year I saw a plane crash into the sea, mutters David.

Really?

Granny saw it as well, but couldn't believe it, or was too scared to believe it, and so always denied it. But I saw it with my own eyes. It was a B-26 bomber.

The reason there's a wisp of white smoke floating over the pilot's head is because the intense heat has just shattered what remains of the cockpit windshield into a thousand fragments. The tail rudder has come off and is in the process of falling, but has not yet hit the ground. I'm talking about your fighter now, David explains, not the other bomber. I could swear the starboard navigation light is still flashing on and off under this stormy sky. And the white cloud over his head might be because the soldiers have started firing; if that is so, when the smoke clears, you will be dead. Echoing in the distance, as if in a cave, comes the sound of anti-aircraft guns.

The big, charred hands that are resting calmly on his hips, one of them still holding the remains of his leather gloves, remind David of another, still blacker hand – severed and with blackened nails – being pushed to and fro by the waves of white foam near the shoreline on Mataró beach. In this sea steeped with illusory visions, floating outside time, the high tide had been about to deposit the hand on the beach like a fish-pecked bird, before eventually the insistent undertow carried it out to sea. A few moments before David loses sight of it, the severed hand emerges from the water, palm upwards, as if seeking attention or signalling to him. This happened more than a year and a half ago: it all started when he was reading a novel about Bill Barnes, Air Adventurer, as he sat by the nets piled up on the sand, leaning back against the hull of a fishing boat. *But the joy was short-lived, and Cy Hawkins turned pale when he saw Bill's craft hesitate for a moment and then plunge like a mortally wounded bird.* David has been expelled from school two weeks earlier, and Ma still does not know what to do with him. I have not yet even come into consideration: Pa hardly ever sleeps at home, perhaps only once every six months. Here in Mataró, Granddad Mariano is still very ill in bed, and will never get up or climb aboard a fishing boat ever again. He doesn't want to see Pa or hear anything about him. Granny Tecla's mind strays occasionally, but she still has the strength to look after Granddad and the house. They live in a tumbledown fisherman's cottage in Calle San Pedro, right on the beach. Ma often visits them with David, who she sometimes leaves for two or three days so that he can lend a hand or at least keep them company. David says that one fine day the old couple decided to settle here, with their faces to the sea and their backs to the land, and that they only know the names of fishes and the winds, and nothing at all of what is going on in the world, least of all of where Pa is or what he is doing or not doing, because they prefer not to know.

It is Saturday, 29th of March. David wets his thumb and impatiently turns the pages: he needs to be sure as soon as possible that the mutilated, charred hand floating at the sea's edge is not that of Bill Barnes, but belongs to the enraged suicide pilot who has crashed into Bill's plane as he was attempting a risky sea landing, his engine on fire and rudder useless, when all of a sudden the roar of another engine, in the real blue sky, captures his attention. From the dozens of cut-out drawings he has, he immediately recognizes the imposing outline of the bomber as it swoops low over the sea, barely a kilometre from the shore. It is an RAF B-26 Marauder. Tipped over on its starboard side, the plane is circling round a cargo ship heading north. David stands up, scarcely able to believe his eyes. What is a Second World War bomber doing off Mataró? At a certain point he believes he hears a loud explosion, although he could not say whether it comes from the plane or the boat. Painted on the side of the plane's cockpit is the picture of a girl in a swimsuit and the slogan: FOREVER AMANDA. Its engines spluttering as though they are tearing apart, the bomber circles round once again until it is between the sun and David's astonished gaze, and at that moment the sunlight glints on the cockpit window. As it tilts even further over, David clearly sees the pilot's bloody face and his arm hanging lifeless out of the windshield, right above the word AMANDA, the flames and dense black smoke inside the cockpit. Then the plane rises into the air for a few seconds, only to nose-dive into the sea not far from the cargo boat, which continues serenely on its way. Puffs of smoke like red Indian signals rise from the aircraft in the sea, before it slowly sinks.

David looks all round him to see if anyone else has witnessed this marvel. At this time of day, the beach is deserted. Granny Tecla's hand grabs his and drags him off home.

Did you see it, Granny? Did you see the plane go down?

I didn't see anything. And nor did you. Time to go in.

Later on, from the sea wall because he is not allowed to get any closer, he sees the burnt bodies of five crew members stretched out on the sand. The fishermen have pulled them in. Then they are loaded on to an army truck and covered with blankets. The boot of one of the bodies sticks out from under its covering. The body and the foot have been sliced in half. On the breeze he hears the voices of a young NCO and a few fishermen. There's one missing, the officer says, these planes have a crew of six. Are you sure? asks a fisherman. The current must have carried him away. He won't go far. Who knows? a third, older fisherman says, the way a body behaves in the sea is unpredictable. And what do you think of the way that cargo boat captain behaved? the officer asks. He didn't want to know, he did nothing to come to their aid, he just carried on his way . . . Perhaps it was a camouflaged warship, the old fisherman replies.

The Civil Guardsmen order any curious onlookers who come down to the Maritime Parade to move on, there's nothing to see, keep moving, go back home, close your doors and windows and don't say anything about it. Over the following days, not a single paper has any news of the plane that crashed into the sea, and there is nothing on the radio either. People in Mataró are asking questions. Can it be that the Allies are on their way, can it be that things here are going to change? Don't be stupid, listen to the authorities and keep quiet, nothing is happening here. You're the stupid one. Be careful, I've got a cousin who's a corporal in the Arenys militia . . . At nightfall, with his Bill Barnes novel under his arm, David sneaks down to the beach to have a look. A Civil Guardsman comes up to him.

Go home, will you?

Why?

Because it's better that way.

Why is it better, sir?

Because I say so! Be off with you!

David walks back up the beach to the Parade, where another guardsman is drinking water from a fountain, shotgun slung across his back. He is very young, has green eyes and a star-shaped scar that gives his chin a fascinating puckered look. David stands beside him, head down and hands behind his back.

Listen, mister officer, sir, I've got something important to tell you.

Didn't my colleague tell you to get home?

But I saw the plane come down. I saw it.

What are you talking about? There's no plane here.

It's underwater, just near here. It's a . . .

Don't start with your stories. Be off with you!

. . . a B-26 Marauder bomber with six crew and two Pratt-Whitney R-2800-5 Double Wasp radial engines each with 1,850 horsepower, David gabbles quickly, overcome all of a sudden by a strange sense of melancholy. Beneath his feet firmly planted on the Parade he suddenly feels a distant tremor coming from under the sand or from the depths of the sea. The plane was hit, David adds, it must have been bombing Berlin and then crossed half of Europe all shot up and in flames, on one engine and with the six crew dead in the cockpit, and the controls jammed . . .

Be off with you back home if you don't want me to take you to the barracks! the guardsman threatens.

Have they still not found the sixth crewman? Well, I've just seen a charred hand down by the shore.

You must have dreamt it, kid, the guardsman replies, staring at him in silence for a few moments. What did you say you saw? Where did you say it was?

Just over there, on the shore, it was a severed hand, black as soot . . .

OK, that's fine, now go home. And don't let me see you here again, all right? He climbs down on to the beach to join his colleague, and looks back. Be off with you!

Stretched out on a corner of the bed, Chispa stirs and whines, in the grip of another fantasy, perhaps even more ghostly and inexplicable than his own. Drowsily, David strokes his back with his foot, and the dog calms down.

Down on the shore, the two guardsmen exchange a few words and then set off in opposite directions along the beach, shotguns across their backs and peering closely at the gentle waves and the foam licking the sand, trying not to get their boots wet. So what's going on, eh? Why do they deny it, if they're looking for . . .

Granny, did you really not see the English plane crash into the sea? Didn't Granddad see it either?

Nobody saw anything here, and I forbid you to go around talking about any English plane.

Before he falls back to sleep, David stares at the pilot again and can make out behind him, on the wrecked cockpit seat, a long-stemmed rose wrapped in tinfoil, its petals shrivelled by the nearby flames, like a tiny, blood-red fist being consumed by its own anger.

A cloud of reddish dust hangs in the air all afternoon, swirling around at the level of the track flanking the gully. All at once, out of this dust cloud the inspector appears, hands in pockets and stiff as a poker as usual. He walks slowly up to the night-time door where David sits on the three steps and hides the penknife in his belt.

"Sahib, if you give me five cents I'll show you a very strange photo of my father at Montserrat monastery with a candle in his hand, for ten I'll tell you the story about the bomber that crashed into the sea at Mataró, for a wretched peseta I'll tell you which shop my mother is in right now trying on a pair of shoes, which have to be cork-soled because they're better for her feet . . ."

"So she's not at home," says the inspector.

"Today sahib no have luck either."

"If that's all she's gone out for, she'll be back soon."

"Who knows? She took a book with her, the one she lost in the street and you were so kind as to return to her, so perhaps right now she is sitting quietly reading it on a bench somewhere, but heaven knows where . . ."

As the inspector listens to him, he loosens the knot on his tie and puts his foot up on the third step. David notices there is a big bulge in the left-hand jacket pocket.

"If you've brought something for my mother, you can give it to me." He falls silent for a moment, then adds: "I'm sure you've brought something nice to eat for the memsahib, isn't that true?"

The truth doesn't yet exist, but David has already spoken it. I can't find any better way to explain this strange ability my brother has, the sure aim of his malice, the intuitive arrow dipped in the poison of premonitions and sleepless nights that give him this second sight, a sort of extra possibility of seeing what is going to take place. The same thing has happened to him when he is out on the streets with the gang of immigrant kids in the Carmelo neighbourhood: before the stone is even thrown at the street lamp, he sees the shattered fragments of glass on the ground.

Whatever might be causing the bulge in the inspector's pocket – a tin of condensed milk, a couple of cans of sardines in oil, a half-kilo of white sugar –

he stares without speaking as Chispa struggles up and collapses at David's feet, panting and with his tongue lolling out.

"I've got eyes that can pierce walls and the darkest night, sahib, I'm like Garu-Garu the phantom and besides, I've got London's mysterious eyes," David says quickly, seeing him unable to make up his mind. "It's a tin of peaches in syrup."

The inspector is wondering whether he should stay or go. He lights a cigarette with his gold Dupont lighter. The precise flick of his thumb against the flint, the wheel turning and then the clunk! of the lid as it snaps shut, all fascinate David.

"Christ! What a brilliant lighter!"

"Tell your mother I'll come back tomorrow."

"If you don't have any fresh news about my father," David spits out a glob of saliva that gets caked in dust and rolls beside the inspector's foot, "there's no point your coming."

"You just tell her I was here," the inspector says, starting to beat a retreat, then turns back and wags his finger at him: "And be careful how you mix things up. If we keep sight of the truth, we can be friends. OK?"

"Yes, bwana."

David watches him trudge wearily off down the cindery path and disappear once more into the spiral of red dust in the air.

David tiptoes back through the dark, uninhabited side of the house, fleeing his own fear of the creaking furniture, the peeling walls that reek of saltpetre and foreboding, the mirrors and their spotted quicksilver, the mouldy curtains where spiders climb and the tips of shoes poke out, until finally he reaches his room. He knows his mother is in there making the bed or sweeping up, and prepares to play one of his tricks on her. But it is not just her he has in mind:

Hang on to your placenta, you poisonous little frog, because you too are going to get the fright of your life.

Can't you see your nonsense startles her and could make her miscarry?

You cause her even more anxiety and stomach cramps.

As he comes into the room he raises his arms and is about to shout Aaagh! As if he were the Wolf Man: Mister Talbot wants to eat the red-head! Aaagh! But he stops short when he sees her sitting so absorbed by the photo of the airman nailed to the wall. His mother is sitting on the edge of the bed, the broom on the floor and her hands resting on her lap, and there is something about the way her face is tilted sadly, and the way her lips are moving slightly as if she is praying, that confuses and paralyses David. It is not the ever-present fear that she may pass out again, it is the complete immobility of her body, the soundless whispering of her lips, and, above all, the look on her face that goes far beyond simple curiosity to establish a pact with something that, if it really is in what she is contemplating, is much more than the photograph itself and the interest this scene from the war might arouse in her, much more than the wreckage and the desolation of the landscape, the black smoke, ruins and death.

Have you given her a kick again, you disgusting monkey? David mutters to himself.

I haven't moved, brother.

Is she talking to you?

No, not now she isn't.

Well she's singing under her breath to you, like she does when she's sad.

She isn't singing to me.

David gives up. He takes two steps back, clears his throat, and enters the room normally.

"Aren't you feeling well, Ma?"

She starts, as if caught out doing something she should not.

"I was looking at . . ." she pauses, then quickly goes on: "I was thinking how boring it must be to spend all that time on the front of a magazine like that, without being able to move . . . what do you think? Come and give me a kiss, son."

She hugs him and kisses him in return, her eyes still on the fighter pilot. On the bed beside her there is a bundle of dirty clothes. She reaches for the broom and uses it to help herself stand, then hastily picks up a pair of David's shorts and examines them, turning one of the pockets inside out.

"What do you put in your pockets to make them so sticky always, David?"

"Oh, that. That's from the lizard tails. It's not blood, you know, it's something else . . . those creatures don't have a drop of blood."

"Aren't you getting a bit grown-up for games like that?"

"I do it for Pauli . . ."

"And just look at your hands," she says, pointing to the stains on them from the developing fluid. "Look at the state of your nails. Is there no way of getting that yellow off them? And besides," she says, waving her hand in the direction of the photo of the fighter pilot on the wall: "I told you to burn everything. All the papers in the boxes."

"That's what I did. This is the only thing I kept. Does it matter?"

"It would have been better to burn the lot, including the photo."

"Why?"

"Just because. I know what I'm saying, son."

Now David is the one who sits at the end of the bed. He stares at the pilot, wondering if he is doing the right thing when he asks:

"Why did you tell a lie, Ma? Why did you tell the cop it was my photo?"

"I told him that?"

"Have you forgotten already?"

"Well, it was you who saved it from the bonfire, wasn't it? You decided to keep it instead of burning it with all the rest like I told you to."

"But it wasn't my photo. Why did you tell the inspector it was?" David insists. It was in that shoe box filled with papers you gave me to burn, but I had never seen it before, and it wasn't me who put it there, or tore it out of the magazine or anything like that . . ."

"All right, so what?" she says, interrupting him impatiently. "The police don't have to know everything about your father."

"So those were Pa's things in the shoe box?"

"Yes."

"The photo too? Did he cut it out?"

"Your father knew that man."

"Really? He knew an RAF pilot?"

"Yes." Her back turned to David, Ma is still disconsolately examining his threadbare clothes. "Good Heavens, this T-shirt is worn out . . ."

"So is that why you lied to the cop, because you didn't want him to know?"

"Because your father doesn't need any more trouble. He's got more than enough problems with the file they already have on him."

"So Pa and the pilot were friends? How did they get to meet?"

"Oh, didn't I ever tell you about the time your father and his friends used to guide airmen across the border, and when they were in Spain gave them papers so they could reach Lisbon or Gibraltar?"

"Really? Tell me all about it."

"I thought Granny Tecla had explained it all to you when you were staying with her in Mataró last year."

"She was already right out of it, poor Granny."

"Well then, it's for your father to tell you when he comes back home, if he ever does . . . and that's enough questions for now. Go and wash your hands and come and sit down to eat. And it'd be a good idea if you took that photo down from there, your father wouldn't like anyone to see it . . . Are you listening to what I'm telling you, son?"

"Ma, what I'd really like to do is learn languages. That's what I want to do."

A few minutes later, David is in the living- and dining-room sitting in front of a plate of boiled chick peas, when a drop of blood falls into his plate.

"Pa isn't feeling good," he says, rapidly blocking his nostril with his hand. "Right now he's feeling terrible."

"Don't talk such rubbish. Put your head back."

Ma wets a napkin in the water jug.

"He's losing a lot of blood . . ." David insists.

"And you'll lose all of yours if you don't do as I say. Put this on the back of your neck and sit still for a while. And if possible, don't talk either. It's nothing, don't be afraid."

"Who's afraid? Come here, Chispa, brave dog."

David and Chispa joined by the dog's lead as the sun beats down on them, avoiding a swarm of bees as they slowly climb the riverbed treading on thistles and rubbish, slippery stones and sword-shaped spits of sand, with watery voices, premonitions and intuitions all around them. Half a league, half a league, half a league onwards and with their backs to the city, at a spot where the dried-up bed flattens out, is less rocky and has much more sand, and the ground is damp because they are close to the market gardens, David clearly hears a match being struck. He turns and sees him lighting his cigarette butt, perched painfully on a rock, the bottle and match in one hand, in the other the bloody handkerchief pressed against his buttock.

It'll get infected, says David. Why don't you pour a bit of brandy on it?

The brandy is for a different sort of wound. You should know about these things by now, son.

Have you still not found anywhere better to hide?

No, here I am in this den of iniquity, infection and muck, Pa mutters, a seam of rust in his voice.

David thinks as he watches Chispa struggle up to them, tongue hanging out.

Pa, is it true that the body of a pilot in the sea behaves in an unpredictable way?

If you're talking about the body I think you are, I don't know about in the sea, but in our house his behaviour was perfectly predictable. Ask your mother if you don't believe me.

I'm talking about the body of the airman the fishermen couldn't find.

So am I. That's precisely the body I'm talking about too.

As he speaks he is glancing over his shoulder in a wary but disdainful manner, as if listening to some other voice in another place, far beyond David's or his own. He is barefoot, and his shirt-tails are hanging out of his trousers. Like dark snakes twisting in the air, the roots of the dead fig tree protruding from the steep side of the riverbed crown his head.

Ma lied to me, says David.

That dog is for the knacker's yard. You should finish him off.

Don't you start.

Take a look at him. Don't you have a heart, son? Just think a bit.

I think with my heart. And she lied to the cop and me. I swear it's the first time I ever heard her tell a lie. She didn't ask him for his search warrant either, but that's not so important . . .

Your mother never lies, Pa grumbles. But since these days the truth has to creep along the ground, like the muddy trickle of the waters of this river in the morning mists – I see it every day, and there's nothing whatsoever poetic about it, I can tell you – then sometimes we have to use lies to recover our lost dignity. Do you understand what I'm saying?

Ma told the flatfoot I cut the photo of the pilot out of a magazine. But it wasn't me.

It was her, Pa says, emphatically. Her in person.

Was it? Then she's told two lies, because afterwards she said it was you.

Did she really say that? Pa inquires, unfolding the soaking handkerchief and then carefully folding it again and holding it against the wound through the tear in his trousers. This blasted cut won't stop bleeding. If you come back up here when you're more awake, bring me a couple of clean handkerchiefs . . . it was your mother who happened to see the photo on the cover of *Adler* magazine, she was in a police station and she tore it off, put it in her holdall and took it home.

Why did she do that? Was it for you?

For me? I don't get it . . .

She says you knew the airman. Try to remember, Pa.

Our memory is a cemetery, son, the fugitive says mournfully. But anyway, I do remember . . . David had imagined his voice might come from his brandy-filled stomach, and sound like an old alcoholic bum's, but it doesn't; it emerges from his attractive mouth with firm lips, and sounds disarticulated, toneless, thick and rapid and sly. How could I forget Flight Lieutenant Bryan O'Flynn, Pa goes on. He was a tall blond-haired fellow, very friendly and talkative. He had a tattoo on his arm: a heart with a little worm inside it. He was Australian of Irish origin, and smiled out of one side of his mouth in a way that fascinated your mother. He had freckles on his hands and flew a Spitfire.

Eight wing-mounted machine-guns, David says quickly in a single breath, one-seater, can climb to a height of 3,500 metres in four minutes and eight seconds, its service ceiling is 10,000 metres and it has a maximum speed of 587 kilometres per hour, with a load of 2,610 kilos.

Christ, you really know your stuff.

Everybody knows that, Pa.

And who pinned our noble flight lieutenant to the wall in your bedroom, was that you or your mother?

Me. Why do you ask?

He looked interesting to you, did he?

I like his leather flying jacket. But it's not just that . . . He knows they're going to kill him, but he is smiling. What kind of man can smile when he knows he's about to kick it?

They didn't kill him, Pa says, taking another swig from the bottle. He managed to escape.

How do you know?

I always knew the way things were, but I kept quiet out of respect.

Respect for what, Pa?

Respect for my elders. And for women. But you have to be careful. Women are always mixed up in some affair of the heart, so you have to always be on your guard . . . Aaargh, how this blasted cut hurts. Hells bells, when is it going to stop bleeding?

You hardly see us any more, Pa, why?

Because I need to think, son.

You think a lot about Ma, don't you? You're still very much in love with her, aren't you?

Love is for men who don't look back. And I do nothing else but look behind me, staring at this rotten arse of mine . . . But tell me about your mother. How is our red-headed seamstress, what's she up to?

Well as usual she's sewing things for the markets at Camelias and La Travesera. Little ankle-length dresses, pleated skirts, boleros and things like that, clothes for cheap dolls. She uses patterns from the doll factory, but they're useless.

And how's she getting on with the baby she's expecting?

Badly. The foetus never stops talking. One day, I heard it shout out loud.

David covers his ears with his hands, but the buzzing will not go away. He has two squares of dark-brown chocolate in his pocket, which must be melting by now. He picked them up at home in case he met his father, but he would not dare offer him them. It is obvious that is not what he wants. All he wants is to go on drinking.

Chispa is sprawled at his feet; a low groan escapes from his mouth, like a wineskin emitting foul air. A swarm of bees flies over the gully, the buzzing going higher and lower as it constantly forms and re-forms its compulsive symmetry. But as David climbs up with his dog, he is most immediately and persistently aware of a kind of underwater nausea, the feeling of walking beneath the dead waters that one day long ago had rushed through here, scooping out the sides of the gully as they cascaded down from far away, sweeping away trees and mud and dead soldiers. Chispa is exhausted from the heat and tiredness; David is aware of this and bends down to pick him up.

As he straightens up, the dog licks him all over his face, and David turns round, muttering to himself: that killer of a cop should see this, he should see how much he loves me and needs me and how far he is from wanting to die, and my father ought to see it too, if he were sitting here under the roots of the fig tree with his slashed backside, his bloody handkerchief and his bottle. They could see how much he wants to live and how he keeps me company, and how he understands who it is I'm talking to even though he doesn't see them, the way he hears and sees with those gentle eyes of his everything that the flatfoot, the red-head and everyone else cannot see or hear . . .

Be that as it may, that same afternoon David is suddenly filled with doubts about whether Chispa is so keen to live or not when he sees him standing on the very edge of the gully, staring down into the bottom with a despair and longing he has never shown before, really as though the aged dog was weighing up the possibility of ending all his troubles once and for all by throwing himself into the void. But however great their pains and afflictions are, is there room in a mongrel's head for the idea of suicide? A short while before, Chispa had been spreadeagled on the steps of the night-time door, warming his bones in the sun, when all at once he got up and set off, slowly and with bobbing head, straight for the gully. He looked in such a sorry state that the birds on the clothes lines did not even bother to fly off when they saw him. He came to a halt on the very edge of the gully and stretched out his neck. His front paws caused a small land-slide of earth and stones, but he leaned out still further over the empty air. Perhaps when he looked down he wasn't thinking about killing himself, brother, but there's no doubt he was already thinking of the next life. I'm sure of it. How are you supposed to know what a dog is thinking, you booby? You must be dumb!

"What on earth are you muttering, David?" Ma says, seated at her sewing table.

"Nothing. It's just this buzzing in my ears . . . Do you think Chispa might want to kill himself by throwing himself into the gully?"

"Who knows? Once when I was at your Auntie Lola's house in Vallcarca I saw a dog throw itself off the bridge."

"But Chispa is blind," says David, "he doesn't know where he's going. He doesn't know which direction the river is, he can't even find his own way home . . ."

"Maybe, son. But we have to consider the possibility that the poor creature wants to end his own suffering. I think you ought to keep that in mind, when you're so soft on him . . . You know Inspector Galván has offered to help."

"No, no! How is my dog going to want to kill himself or have someone else do it for him! He would have given me a sign!"

Ma sticks her needle in the pin-cushion and straightens up with a painful grimace. But then she smiles.

"That could be, son. But listen, when someone really and truly wants to die, they don't usually tell anyone. And now, could you bring me the basin with water and salt in it?"

With my mottled fists squashed against my eye sockets, still in my foetal position and, if the truth be told, none too keen to push my way out into the bloody splendour of this world, I enjoy watching David lying on his bed and summoning up the therapeutic roar of the Spitfire engine for his tortured hearing. The roof of his darkened room has just lifted off, and high above, the endless blue of the sky appears, with a few fingers of long, rosy-coloured clouds sailing over the fearless, arrogant head of the fighter pilot sitting protected in his cockpit, the collar of his flying jacket turned up, wearing his helmet and goggles, staring at the far horizon with that attractive lopsided smile of his. The plane tips gently over on one wing, and for a moment the sun flashes blindingly on the windshield, then the aircraft wheels majestically and is swallowed by the red and emerald dawn.

Here, down below, outside our house in this dark dead-end street, a black butterfly floating on the air hovers above the bed of marguerites, searching for the secret intimacy of the dew.

He opens the day-time door, his hands all bloody. In the left, he is holding up a gutted rabbit by its back legs. Opposite him on the doorstep, his trenchcoat unbuttoned and his tie slack around his neck, Inspector Galván inspects him coldly.

"Is your mother at home?"

"Today not be your lucky day either, bwana."

"Do you know where she is?"

Looking humbly down at the ground, but with his arm stretched out above his head as though the bloody rabbit is a trophy, or rather as if determined to show the immediate and irrefutable proof of an act of cruelty he is part of, David puts on his best smile.

"You're really out of luck. But I'll tell the memsahib you called. Is there anything more?"

"Just for you to behave, kid. Your mother deserved better."

"My mother . . . have you really not heard . . . ? You ought to know, seeing how you follow her everywhere."

"That's none of your business. Where has she gone?"

"I'll tell you. My mother has had a miscarriage. She fell in the kitchen just as she was about to kill this rabbit. And what with the rain . . ."

"What nonsense are you talking?"

"What you hear, bwana. She was losing a lot of blood when the ambulance took her away. I bet right now they're giving her an emergency operation with transfusions, anaesthetics and a mask. I had to kill the rabbit all by myself, a quick chop to the back of the neck like this, look. There! I do it very well, just one blow, clean and quick and ruthless, Granny Tecla always said you should never feel any pity when you're killing a rabbit. Then I skinned and gutted it."

The inspector stares at him without so much as blinking. The more expressionless half of his face, the one with the silken sheen and drooping features, with a smaller and more piercing steely eye, seems to be affected by a nervous tic. He thinks for a few moments.

"What are we going to do with you, kid?"

"I don't know, bwana. That's up to you."

"You're almost fifteen. What the devil are we going to do with you?"

"You know, I really like your coat? I really do. It's brilliant. If I had a trench-coat like that, I wouldn't take it off even in bed."

His head down as if he were about to charge, while the inspector stands rooted to the spot, David can appreciate from close up the wide lapels and the loops, all the buttons and buckles that he admires so much, and all at once on the green rainproof material he can smell, or perhaps imagine, the scent that the wet pines exude into the gully after it has rained, when he and Pauli, penknife in hand, are waiting in vain for a worlizard to appear.

The inspector takes off his coat, shakes it, and tosses it over his shoulder. Then he stands there again, silent and thoughtful, his hands holding his hat brim in front of his stomach. He seems used to standing like that, staring at people without speaking, as if waiting to see something special in your face, something to do with what you think of a flatfoot from the Social Brigade, or a problem you may have had with something you have done or said. So close to you and yet so far off, so pressing and overwhelming with his watery gaze, and at the same time so apart and so distant that you are never quite sure whether his attitude is meant to conceal the usual threat or instead a secret wish to offer help and protection.

This man is a policeman who occasionally behaves as though he wasn't one, the red-head would say sometime later. And therefore – Pa might have replied – you should trust him even less, sweetheart.

Its stomach slit down the middle, the rabbit has not been completely cleaned, and bloody bits of guts dangle out.

"Would you mind taking that damned rabbit out of my face?" says the inspector.

David bends his head even lower, and pulls back the hand holding the rabbit, but not enough to spare the inspector the sight of the steaming, gouged-out flesh.

"A rag and bone man gives us a miserable five pesetas for each skin. Just because we're poor . . . one day I'm going to get my own back. I know a kid in Carmelo who hunts cats, strangles them and sells them as rabbits."

"Great. Another bright spark."

"Have you heard anything more about the man who hanged himself in Calle Legalidad? Do you know who he was and why he did it? I do – I've got friends in Calle Verdi who know everything . . ."

The inspector points a warning finger to shut him up. He says, betraying no impatience in either gesture or voice:

"I warned you the other day, kid. Do you remember what I said?"

"Yes, bwana. You said I was on a slippery slope," David whispers. "But you were just leaving, weren't you? Or have you brought a search warrant?" Barely looking up, he watches the policeman light a cigarette with his Dupont lighter, clunk! then put it back in his pocket. "Because if you want to search the house again you'll have to be quick, Ma could die at any moment from her miscarriage. Now that I come to think of it, I wouldn't be surprised if the atomical bomb, as my Granny calls it, has something to do with it, because the fact is Ma began to feel bad the same day that photo of the giant mushroom cloud appeared in the newspaper, so it must be the radioactivity. The temperature went up to 10,000 degrees that day. Mr Roig, my friend Jaime's dad, who has a pharmacy and knows a lot about chemistry, says the bomb is like a blast of poisonous air, and when it explodes it throws out a kind of slime like a squashed snail which first of all rises up to the clouds and then falls from the sky in rain, and that it will kill a lot of people all round the world, and the first to go will be those with TB or asthma and bronchitis . . ."

The inspector lets him go on, drawing on his cigarette. He watches his lips move with a look of scornful contempt, but does not seem to be listening. David speaks in an even tone without flinching; he could continue for hours, spinning these yarns one after another. The gutted rabbit still held aloft in his gory fist gives off a persistent warm stench, and the inspector gazes silently in turn at both of them, the blusterer with his head bowed, and the skinned rabbit.

"That's enough. Raise your head. Come on. And look at me, I'm not going to eat you. Did you give your mother from me . . . What's the matter, can't you bring yourself to look at me when I'm talking to you? Look at me!"

"My eyes and my ears hurt, bwana."

"Did you give her the packet of roasted coffee I brought the other day?"

"Yes, bwana."

"What did she say?"

"She said what can that man be thinking, we shouldn't take it, but we could do with it."

The inspector observes him without saying a word, then puts his hat on. A drop of blood falls from the tiny bared teeth of the rabbit and falls between his shoes. The arm holding up the rabbit is growing weary, but the head maintains its elaborate parody of submission and keeps its eyes stubbornly fixed on the ground.

Many years after he himself told me of this encounter, I can still see the mocking, foolhardy gleam of malice in David's look as he stares at the tiles on the floor, a look he kept right up to the moment of his death; I can see the tiny blood-stained teeth of the skinned rabbit waving at the end of his arm like a banner, as Inspector Galván turns on his heel and casts a final sorrowful cold glance at David and his prize.

With tears in his eyes, Paulino Bardolet bursts into the darkened stalls of the cinema and searches for the golden gleam of David's hair among the seats. The film started some time ago.

. . . the massacre of Chucoti was imprinted on the minds of the lancers of the 27th regiment of the Light Brigade like a wound that would never heal.

All of a sudden, a flame breaks out on Olivia de Havilland's gentle face, spreads to devour her huge dark eyes and mouth, and the film vanishes, leaving the Delicias in complete darkness. As soon as he has sat down next to David, swamping him in his smell of tincture of iodine, Paulino's trembling hand reaches for his friend's. David is having none of it.

"You're late," he says.

"My uncle wouldn't let me out."

"Have you been shaving the ex-legionnaire again?"

"Yes, I have to do it every Thursday as well now."

"And you've been playing maid for him again, cleaning his leather kit, his topee and his uniform?"

"What else can I do?" Paulino snivels.

"Your fault, dolt. Then you have to soap his gorilla's gob and shave him . . . and thank him for it. You're such an idiot! You say he lets you do it so you can practise with the razor? My arse! If I were you, I'd give him a good slit across the jugular, and watch him bleed like a pig. That's what I'd do."

"He also lets me strip and clean his pistol and hold it for a while. It's a genuine Star . . . hey, they could at least switch the lights on," Paulino says, stirring in his seat in the darkness, but at that very moment the projection starts up again, and David whispers to him: shut up, I want to see the film, and jabs him in the side. "Aargh, not there, please, I think I've got a broken rib. It really hurts!"

"You're full of bullshit, Pauli."

But soon afterwards he senses the nervous fluttering of his friend's nostrils, his heavy, painful breathing, the livid moistness of his bruised cheeks and swollen lip, and guesses at rather than sees – because he does not dare look directly at him yet – the cut eyebrow and the puffed-up lid almost closing his right eye. By now the screen is giving off a dazzling silver light: it is the vast plain between the hills of Balaklava, and into it charge the lancers of the 27th, rolling out across the nearly empty stalls. The 600 charging into the Valley of Death. Paulino curls up in his seat, trying to avoid David's scrutiny and his reproaches. He whispers:

"It doesn't hurt any more. Don't make fun of me."

In the darkness, David feels for the hand he had rejected earlier, and sits in silence for a while. Captain Vickers is charging at the head of his lancers towards the hills of Balaklava. Half a league . . .

"We're going to your house right now to tell your father."

"Don't even think of it!" says Paulino. "Uncle Ramón would kill me."

"Well, kill him first, the bastard. Stick the razor in his chest and escape to the Montaña Pelada in Parque Güell. Thrust him through with your lance, like that villain Surat Khan!"

Half a league, half a league, half a league. Into the Valley of Death ride the 600.

"It's a great film, isn't it, David?"

"Kill him! Kill him!"

VI

The Spitfire in Flames

Still smiling his faintly mocking smile, Flight Lieutenant Bryan O'Flynn takes his hands from his hips, jumps lithely over the barbed wire fence and sits at the bottom of David's bed. He crosses his legs slowly and elegantly: the yellow parachute tape is still attached to his left thigh.

If I hadn't been in such a mad hurry to tear my gloves off, he complains, looking down at his blackened fingers, I wouldn't have peeled all the skin from my hands.

The heat of this August night does not seem to affect him: he does not take off his leather jacket, or remove the goggles from his forehead, or the cigarette holder. His trousers are torn, but give off a pleasing smell of oil. From close up, he looks very distinguished. Behind him, in what is left of the Spitfire cockpit, something is still whirring in the instrument panel.

My fingernails are brown too, David says with fellow feeling.

It's not the same. You can't imagine how many nails the Luftwaffe has ruined, my bucko.

And my father's got torn trousers too.

It's not the same, boy. It's not.

He had to escape as well, David insists. Just like you. Did you get away from the Germans like that, jumping over the fence and walking calmly away across the ravaged fields of France?

Bueno, it was slightly more complicated than that. Your father can tell you. It was he who set me on the trail back to Biggin Hill, my base. But don't think he did much more than that, apart from making your mother feel bad . . . ask him.

My father left home some time ago.

Did he? Flight Lieutenant O'Flynn raises the goggles higher on his head and goes on: he always did have ants in his pants, your dear father. Well then, you'll have to make up your own mind who is the hero and who is the villain here.

The police are after him, David mutters, his sleepy eyes fixing on the flying jacket moulding the airman's slim body. He senses or dreams of another sticky-sweet smell, of burnt leather or roasted acorns. In his left hand, O'Flynn is clutching his gloves, which are still smouldering.

Why do you have that inscription on the port side of your cockpit: THE INVISIBLE WORM? David wants to know. Do all the Spitfires in your squadron have it? Flight Lieutenant O'Flynn gazes down at his burnt hands and says nothing. David lifts himself up on to one elbow on the pillow, and studies the pilot's silence and cat-like gestures through half-closed eyes. Why didn't you parachute out, Flight Lieutenant?

I thought I could land. And I almost did.

What happened?

In fact, they didn't shoot me down. Sorry to disappoint you, but there was no nose-dive, no spiral of death. But I landed in very difficult conditions, and the plane overturned.

The other day, David remembers after a while, my mother sat on the bed right where you are now, and stared at you for a long time.

Yes, I saw her.

She was looking at you very thoughtfully, as if she was praying . . .

Well, let's just say she was doing something more than that.

What do you mean?

Hmm, *bueno*. The pilot checks himself, then flashes one of his famous lop-sided smiles at David. Right or wrong, it is my life. You must know by now that I am an RAF hero.

So? My father is a hero too. David thinks about it for a moment, then adds in a low voice: Of course, if anybody saw him now . . .

Oh yes, dragging himself around with that ugly wound on his arse, unshaven and barefoot, and drinking all the time, he doesn't exactly look the part.

He'll pull out of it.

Oh, *por supuesto*, he's a resourceful man. But let's not compare the two, shall we? I'm a flying ace. At least, that's what they say . . . Don't you believe me? In the Battle of Britain I came up against Werner Mölders himself, the great Luftwaffe pilot. Don't you believe me?

What most attracts David about the pilot is the way he talks as though he is not really concerned whether he is telling the truth or not. Stretched out by the wall under Doctor P.J. Rosón-Ansio's giant ear, Chispa has also woken up, or dreamt he has woken up, and comes hobbling over to sniff at the pilot's singed trousers smelling of grease. O'Flynn strokes his head.

He's my dog, David says. Do you like him?

Oh, no, *por favor*, don't ask me if I like your hound. What I most want in the world, believe it or not, is not to meet up with my squadron and fly again, but to get back to my home in Chelsea and be reunited with my own dog.

Would you like to take Chispa with you?

Oh please, let's say no more about it. Look, my body's aching all over from the crash, I've lost all the skin from my hands, and I don't much feel like talking – I'm not in the mood, you know, so with your permission I'd like to go and see to my plane, or what's left of it.

It's a Spitfire MK IX, David says, rolling the words round and gently spitting them out of the side of his mouth. A 12-cylinder Rolls Royce Marlin 61 engine, four Browning 7.7mm machine-guns that fire 350 rounds each, two 20mm Hispano cannon, a Rotol four-bladed propeller, armour-plated windshield and sliding hatch.

And now all that's left is a heap of scrap, the Lieutenant says. His smile becomes so broad his face almost disappears in it, then he adds: Well, it is my life. I guess that was what made such an impact on your mother . . .

But it wasn't only that. You have to tell me more.

Me? Who can understand a woman's heart? Well, now I really must go. Good night. He says goodbye, and as he is getting up off the bed, adds: Do you know something? In the cockpit I had three pairs of silk pyjamas I bought in Bordeaux, and I'd like to save them if possible, and a white rose as well . . .

After Flight Lieutenant Bryan O'Flynn has left, Chispa climbs laboriously up on to the bed and snuggles up at David's feet, in the hollow that still bares traces of human warmth, the smell of adventure, or something of the sort. The pilot returns to his place on the devastated plain. His defiant stare across the broad Valley of Death reaches even our distant hill in the captive city.

"Good afternoon, Señora Bartra. Could I see you for a few minutes?"

It is not even three days since his last attempt, but here the cop is again. The weather is still suffocatingly close, although occasionally a gentle drizzle wets the streets and adds to their echoes of submission and abandonment. But there is nothing gentle about the silence haunting every crumbling corner. Standing beside the clump of wet, revived marguerites, his trenchcoat folded over one arm and his rainproof hat in hand, Inspector Galván stares at the door until it opens.

"What do you want?"

"I came this morning, but there was no-one in. It's about your husband."

"Ask away."

The inspector looks up at the grey clouds, and shifts his coat to the other arm.

"It's a good thing it's stopped raining."

"So it seems."

Ma has got one hand behind her back, as if she is about to untie her apron and take it off. But instead of that, she presses the small of her back, and thrusts forward her pregnant stomach. This is the third or fourth time she is going to be questioned, in the same spot and at the same time of day; in response, she shows the same resigned weary look, the same cold forbearance. David is not at home, and she thinks it is better that way. She holds the side of the door with one hand, while the other, placed on her aching stomach, feels me kick.

"Turn round, will you?"

"Beg your pardon?"

"I'm talking to my son. And as for you, lie down or you'll fall over, you bag of bones."

She has lowered her gaze to her swollen ankles, where Chispa's warm muzzle is sniffing out familiar company; the dog sways on its feet, and its black coat is full of knots. The inspector bends down to stroke him.

"Hello there, comrade. Here I am bothering your mistress again. Who I can see can't make up her mind whether or not to put you out of your misery . . ."

"Try convincing my son."

"Nobody can convince that lad of anything," the inspector growls, straightening up again.

Squeezed between the policeman's muddy shoes and Ma's green slippers, Chispa looks asleep standing up. As he lifts his head, the inspector lowers his and points his fingers at him like a gun. The dog collapses to the ground. In the darkened room over the red-head's right shoulder, the inspector can see the two wicker chairs and the table under the window. After a pause, she wipes her hands on her apron, then sighs and closes her eyes.

"I've already told you, I haven't seen or heard from my husband in six months."

"I know. I'd prefer not to have to bother you like this, especially in your condition, but there's an arrest warrant out for him."

"He hasn't done anything wrong."

"I'm not here to judge him, Señora. That's not down to me."

"Listen, Inspector, let's get things straight. You have been kind to us – at least, you haven't been rude or threatened us, and I'm grateful for that . . . but you're wasting your time."

"That's possible. You might not believe it," a faint smile appears on his lips: "but wasting my time is part of the job."

"I don't have that luxury."

The inspector thinks for a while.

"Well, the fact is we ought to get some things clear in this matter . . . so that you know what's going on, above all."

"I don't know what you mean."

"Let's see. Do you know your son's friend, the one with the shaved head who's a bit slow?"

"He comes up here a lot. Why do you ask? What's he got to do with my husband?" While the inspector is searching for an answer, she goes on: "Ah, I get it. You probably thought we were friends of his family, and that Víctor is hiding in their house . . ."

"No, that's not what I was thinking."

"He's the son of the Plaza Sanllehy barber."

"There's no barber shop in Plaza Sanllehy," the inspector says.

The red-head smiles.

"I didn't say there was. You're always so observant, aren't you? Señor Bardolet is a barber who has no shop. He shaves the patients in Padre Alegre's Cottolengo, in the Clínica de la Esperanza, and the men in the old people's home in Calle San Salvador. He's a scared old man who earns a living as best he can and nobody bothers him. He spent two years in jail for reasons you'll know better than me . . ."

"I have no idea why he was in prison, or whether he deserved it or not," the inspector says in his slow, even way, with a faint suggestion of hurt. "I'm not a judge, Señora Bartra, don't confuse me with one." He shakes his head, thinks for a moment and then goes on: "Let's leave it, shall we? Would you like some advice? If you have any means of getting in touch with your husband, and I suppose you do, tell him it would be better if he came forward voluntarily. I'm telling you this in confidence. It'll stand him in good stead. The charges against him don't seem that serious."

"Oh, they aren't, are they? That's a good one!" Ma smiles broadly this time, and her voice is like a caress, a puff of wind. "That's all I needed!"

"Besides," says the inspector, "I hear the government is preparing a decree to pardon all those accused of military revolt."

"So you, a policeman of the regime, don't consider it serious for a man to have ideas contrary to our new state, as you call what we've got now. So what am I to think? Do you mean to say you aren't pursuing my husband precisely because of his ideas? Or don't you think like the rest of them?"

"I'm just carrying out orders, Señora. What I think doesn't matter to anyone."

"Fine. Well at any rate, I have no way of getting in touch with him. I don't know where he is. For the love of God, how else am I supposed to say it? How many times have we gone over this already, Inspector?"

"I've seen your husband's file. Some of the things in it are a joke."

"Some of it must be serious though, or they wouldn't send you here so often . . . or are you doing this off your own bat?"

The inspector does not seem to have heard the question. After a short pause, he says: "The problem as I see it, Señora Bartra, lies in the subversive propaganda he was so busy with at the start of this year. But I don't think all that stuff from five years ago, his smuggling activities across the frontier and the escape network for the Allies, is important any more. The government sees those things differently nowadays."

"Does the file say he was involved in smuggling?"

"Well, that oughtn't to surprise you, a lot of them did," the inspector admits, "as well as a lot worse. We know some who ended up as real criminals, living off the Resistance. I could tell you endless stories."

"You don't know Víctor. What else does his file say?"

"There are a few very confused allegations . . . among them one that your husband took part in a clandestine meeting here in Barcelona, and invented a real cock-and-bull story about it. His statement is a pack of lies, a complete joke, when you read it you don't know whether to laugh or cry. There are about thirty or forty typed and handwritten sheets, full of nonsense."

"Why don't you let me see the file, inspector?"

"I can't, Señora. I don't have the authority."

"Don't tell me you can't. A state official, a police detective like you, someone so efficient and determined, unable to remove a document from Headquarters, from the court, or from wherever? Go on, do me this one favour . . ."

"All you'll do is give yourself more heartache . . ." he stares at her, then adds: "OK, I'll see what I can do. But I can't promise anything."

He switches the coat to his other arm and glances over Ma's shoulder. He would dearly like her to invite him in, of course he would, but she keeps the door half-shut and leans against the jamb in a relaxed and friendly enough way, but one that leaves no room for doubt: you'll go no further than this, at least for today. Behind her, Chispa pads slowly back into the cool freshness of the house, aiming for the table which has on it some scraps of material, a coffee cup, an open book the inspector recognizes, and an ashtray where a cigarette still smoulders. He collapses under it and waits, looking suspiciously at the cop.

"Little lizard, how pretty you are, little lizard. Nature was kind to you when it gave you no blood, little lizard, you haven't got a single drop in your body," Paulino mumbles fervently to himself, caught up in the sound of his own trembling voice as he lies kneeling forward on the edge of a rock, the open cut-throat razor in one hand. His little finger sticks up in the air as he brandishes it with all the easy elegance of a professional barber.

Up above him, a mass of heavy clouds, a mother-of-pearl opening appears, and a shaft of sunlight slants down across the riverbed. The lowest cloud hangs fat and purple-hued over the villa. Hearing the boy's footsteps and his strange muttering, Inspector Galván goes to the edge of the gully and narrows his eyes as he looks down, avoiding a sudden dazzling glint of light, unsure whether it comes from the boy's shaven head or the razor.

"What are you looking for down there, kid?"

"I'm waiting for David Bartra."

"Didn't your father tell you we didn't want to see you round here?"

"I have to give David a message . . ."

"What are you doing with that razor?"

"It's broken, it's only a toy, look," Paulino says, almost choking. "My father threw it away. I only use it to cut off worlizard tails with."

"What on earth are they?"

"They're a rare kind of lizard. They have yellow and green stomachs and sleep a lot . . . Worlizards from Ibiza, they're called. They like eating tomatoes and all kinds of school notebooks."

"What's your name?"

"Paulino Bardolet Balbín, at your's and God's service."

The inspector looks at his watch, glances at the villa, and then turns his attention again to Paulino. But he says nothing. Hands in trouser pockets, it seems he is in no hurry, he is simply passing the time of day.

"What's wrong with your face? Raise your head so I can get a proper look."

"There aren't many worlizards around here . . ."

"Answer me. Who did that to your face?"

"A wasp stung me. Well, two or three of them did . . ."

"You're the nephew of someone who fought in the Spanish Legion, and is now a traffic policeman . . . what's his name? Balbín."

"Yes, sir. Uncle Ramón."

"Then it was a wasp wearing a topee that stung you, was it?"

"All right," says Paulino, "I'll tell you the truth. It was some tinker kids from Carmelo who did it."

"Why would your uncle want to lay into you so hard, kid? Could it be he's trying to straighten you out, because of you know what?"

"I'm not a tell-tale who gets stung for sticking his tongue out."

"Don't play the wise guy with me. You know very well what I'm talking about, idiot."

"I promised David I'd never tell tales . . ."

"And have you never even told your father?"

"At home, it's my uncle who is in charge, not my father. But it's true that some bastard immigrant kids beat me up, Inspector. That's why David and I hunt lizards . . . but don't think we do them any harm, we don't play with them like we used to," Paulino adds with calculated brevity, seeing the cop appears to have lost his concentration again, and is consulting his watch and then looking up at the villa door, "we don't string them up or put them on the tramway lines with their feet cut off, we don't fill their stomachs with vinegar from the little wineskin, or make them smoke . . . we don't do any of those nasty things any more, you know, all we do is cut off their tails. And when we've collected a lot of them, we boil them in water with thyme, petals from white marguerites, three wings from a black butterfly and one from a yellow one, and a silk worm. When you boil all that together you get a fantastic cream for abscesses and bruises, and above all for piles and boils in the armpits. An old man in the Cottolengo gave me the recipe while I was soaping him for a shave. I was so distracted I covered him in the stuff, and my father shouted at me . . . giving shaves in the Cottolengo is no joke, you know, you have to be really good with the brush – all the grand-dads have got twisted faces because they're paralysed or whatever, and never stay still . . ."

"Shouldn't you be at school?" the inspector asks absent-mindedly, glancing up at the villa door. "Tell me something. Have you seen Señora Bartra go out?"

"No, sir."

"I asked you why you don't go to school."

"It's because I'm learning to become a barber. On Sundays I go and shave my uncle and stay to eat, that's what my father wants, for me to learn the trade.

But my uncle wants me to be a Civil Guardsman when I grow up. He's a bachelor, he doesn't have any children . . . he wants to make someone out of me, someone who will serve God and the fatherland."

"And what does your father say to that?"

"He says it's fine."

"Come up here and give me the razor."

"We really do only use it for catching lizards. I swear."

"Do as I say."

Paulino climbs the side of the gully and comes to a halt in front of the inspector. The policeman stares at his puffy closed eye, with its lid as pink and livid as a boil about to burst. He takes the razor from him and examines the blunt edge. As well as the black eye, Paulino has swollen nostrils and is continuously having to swallow a trail of bloody snot.

"Two years ago," the inspector says, closing the razor, "David and you used to go to a municipal school in Parque Güell. Did you ever see his father there?"

"Only once. David was hardly at school, they threw him out almost straight-away."

"Why did they do that?"

"He took his trousers down during the Formation of Our National Spirit lesson. He said they fell down, but I know he did it on purpose . . ."

"So his father went to the school and there was a big argument, is that right?"

"No, sir. It was his mother."

"Señora Bartra?"

"Yes, sir. She threw an inkwell at the headmaster and called him a donkey and an arselicker. So David was out in the street."

"What happened after that?"

"Nothing. Señora Bartra gave David lessons at home, the lucky kid! In summer he had no exams and could go to the beach with his grandparents . . . but since his father's been gone, he's not the same, I don't know what problem he's got in his ears. It's incredible! It's as though he had antennas, really, I reckon they must be at least 500 megawatts strong. If you get into his magnetic field, he can hear it even when you're swallowing saliva, or so he says . . ."

"That's enough," the inspector grunts, opening the razor again. "I don't want to see you round here any more, got it?"

"I'm doing nothing wrong."

"What would you think if I told you to undo them right now?"

"Undo what, sir?"

"Don't play dumb – your flies, of course."

"I don't have any flies on my short trousers, sir."

The inspector coolly tosses the razor from one hand to the other, his eyes smiling as if he were joking.

"What if I told you to take it out to one side then? Do you know what could happen to you? Or would you prefer me to talk to Señora Bartra . . . ? Don't worry, I'm not going to do anything to you. But listen carefully to what I'm saying: you can be sure that if you don't mend your ways, one day someone is going to slice it off for you. Understood?"

Paulino lowers his head.

"Give me my razor back, please."

"Here. Go home and get them to put something on that artichoke of a nose of yours."

"I've got my medicine, sir," Paulino says, swallowing more snot as he scuttles off down the path towards Avenida Vírgen de Montserrat. "I've got my lizard tails."

"I see you haven't lost your taste for cigarettes," the inspector says.

"Or for coffee. Or sugar and white bread. Those of us with no taste for the present regime have got lots of vices"– there is no hiding the harsh edge to the red-head's voice.

"You shouldn't joke about things like that, Señora Bartra."

"There are lots of things I shouldn't do."

"By the way," the inspector says, pulling a blue cellophane package out of his jacket pocket, "I've brought you a bit more coffee. I thought you might like it . . ."

"Why go to so much trouble? I don't think I should take it . . ."

"It's from the police co-op, I get it cheap."

Ma stares at the gift, then at the inspector, and back again at the gift. She is not going to invite him in this afternoon either, though he will get in anyway.

"Go on, take it," the inspector says, all of a sudden averting his gaze in the direction of the gully, as if a voice there had caught his attention. "I have more than sufficient."

She takes the coffee and puts it in her apron pocket.

"The fact is, it's very welcome. Nowadays everything is scarce . . . what about my husband's file?"

"Be patient, I'll see what I can do. Did your son say I was here yesterday, and Saturday as well?"

"No."

"Aha. I think I need to talk to you about that boy. I don't know if you have any idea of the lies and gibberish he talks."

"Well, he has a healthy imagination."

"Imagination? He's a born liar and troublemaker."

"I won't deny he sometimes gets weird or strange ideas. He's had to grow up quickly. He might seem a bit of a madcap like his father, but underneath he isn't like that at all. He lives a solitary life, he talks to loneliness. He's a boy with faith. He's similar to me in many ways."

"Faith? You mean you've taught him to be religious, to go to Mass . . . ?"

"No, not at all. But he has faith in important things. I admit he can be very nervous and moody. He's a very special boy. He was even before he was born. His father didn't want him, you know, he was involved elsewhere, so perhaps that's why I felt as if the child inside me was . . . well, as if he was hiding. I felt as though he wanted to escape and hide. I'm sorry, I don't know why I'm telling you all this."

"Don't apologize. I understand."

"You may not believe this, but even before he was born I knew my son was a sign sent by the heavens, the herald of a lot of things that were going to happen . . ."

"So you believe it's all written in the stars do you, Señora Bartra?"

"Who knows? Does it really interest you?" Before he has the chance to reply, she adds, incongruously: "But children aren't to blame for anything, don't you agree?"

"I could swear there's a fair amount of devilry in that youngster's head, Señora Bartra," the inspector ventures, then adds: "He works for a photographer at the parish church, doesn't he? Someone called Marimón . . ."

"So what? Do you have a file on him as well?"

"All we know is that he was a friend of your husband's. Do you know him well?"

"Enough to entrust my son to him. Why?"

"Someone reported him a year ago. Nothing serious, it seems he took photos for a libertarian pamphlet . . ."

"That's a lie. Señor Marimón takes portrait photos of weddings and baptisms, that's all he's ever done. I've hardly met him, but I know he's a good person . . ."

The inspector thinks for a few moments.

"Anyway, I think you should keep your son on a tight rein. I'm afraid he might do something stupid one of these days."

"Did you say he had devilry in him? Well, I've no intention of getting rid of any of it," says Ma calmly.

"A lady like you shouldn't say things like that . . ."

"A lady like me shouldn't be standing here talking to a policeman. The fact is, I don't know why I am."

"Doesn't he have any girl friends?" the inspector says after a pause, then immediately regrets it. "I mean . . . there must be some girl he likes."

"David? I think he likes a very pretty young girl who often rides her bike near here."

"Who is she?"

"I don't know. I've never seen her."

"Maybe she's another figment of his imagination."

"Why should she be? What a mind you have!"

For a moment it seems as though the inspector is about to say something, but then he lapses into silence once more.

"All I can say," he adds eventually, "is that his mother is killing herself with work. You try to earn a few pesetas working honestly at home. But do you have any idea what that boy of yours does with the clothes you sew . . . ?"

"He's always liked dressing up, if that's what you mean. I used to like it too, play acting, or when it was Carnival time. Now that's prohibited, of course. When he grows up, my son's going to be a performer. And they are different from us, they do strange things. Besides, the poor child suffers terribly with his hearing."

"His friend Paulino told me he talks to himself the whole time."

"David says he can hear voices in his ears . . ."

"And you believe him?"

"Why shouldn't I? I also talk to this child I'm carrying. Why shouldn't I believe David communicates with the noises and voices he hears?" Chispa appears again from the living-room and keels over at their feet, licking one of his hind legs. Inspector Galván turns his face with the strange patient but leaden half-smile he has, and lets out a sigh that ends in an indignant snort.

"My son is very intelligent, Inspector, why are you laughing?"

"No reason."

"That's what I call having faith."

"It's odd to hear someone who doesn't believe in God talk about faith."

"Who says I don't believe in God? I'm sorry, but you're going a bit too far." Then the red-head smiles as she continues: "I wouldn't want you to think I'm a little church mouse either . . . I think you've got me wrong again, Inspector. I'm a wife and mother twenty-four hours a day, I have no choice, but that doesn't mean that when I'm least expecting it, walking down the street for example, when someone I don't know looks at me, I don't start to daydream . . . Can you understand that? No, I suppose you can't," she says smiling again, as if mocking him. "You don't know me."

"I think I know you a little."

"Well anyway, I don't have time to stand here arguing."

The inspector nods.

"Just one more thing before I go," he insists, in the slow, slightly stilted way of his, as if he is putting on the voice and the words he uses, but not the feelings behind them: "I can understand you defending your boy. But I consider it my duty to tell you what happened the other day. That little angel told me with a straight face that you had had a miscarriage. What do you think of that?"

"Did he say that? My goodness."

"And that you'd been rushed off to the maternity ward or to the clinic, I can't remember what he dreamt up."

"He shouldn't have said that. I'll give him a piece of my mind. Anything else?"

"Isn't that enough? That boy tells lies as easily as if he was making *churros* . . ."

"Yes, that was dreadful. But you know, he wasn't too far off the mark. I felt very ill that day and went to the doctor's. I've been feeling dizzy and getting bad headaches. It's true, lately David's been behaving . . . I don't know how to describe it. A couple of months ago he saw a man who hanged himself in a bandstand on Calle Legalidad: he didn't know him at all, but it affected him a lot. Apparently he and his friends had followed the man the day before in Gracia, probably to poke fun at him, they said it was as though he was sleep-walking, and he was crying, the poor man. Well, seeing him dead had a great impact on my son. But you came to talk to me about my husband, trying to find out more about him, and here I go . . . Oohh!"

"What's the matter, Señora Bartra? Don't you feel well?"

Something has happened – whether related to me or not, I can't tell – something more serious than the usual momentary stab of pain or dizzy spell – but I think I can feel, floating for ever in my warm bubble, that there is a disruption to the light and the flow of blood, a change of rhythm in my pregnant mother's body and in the tranquil beat of the afternoon. She is going to faint again. As if sensing it, Chispa gets to his feet and moves away slightly. A sudden rise in the temperature of her amniotic fluid and perhaps another inconsiderate flip by yours truly, force her to grip the edge of the door with both hands. She goes very pale, shuts her eyes and turns her body to one side. The inspector just manages to leap forward and catch her as she falls. He lifts her in his arms, and when she does not react, carries her inside the house. He pushes the door shut with his foot, walks round the living-room table, and gently deposits her on one of the wicker chairs by the side-table. Ma's head lolls on to the back of the chair, her mouth half open and eyes shut. Her red hair is tied up with a black ribbon, the top button of her housecoat is undone, and I can hear her heart beating furiously. I'm sure of all this, and I am still living it, but what I am not so sure about is whether she fainted by the bed of marguerites during their third encounter, or some time later, when Chispa already had a bullet in his head and was rotting where he had been buried in the riverbed, and David was busy plotting his revenge, a time when the cop was coming regularly to the house two or three times a week, always bringing with him some little gift or other, tins of condensed milk, half a kilo of sugar, a bar of chocolate . . .

"Señora Bartra. Señora . . ." the inspector whispers, bending over her with his narrowed eyes and their sad, drooping lids, those sharp features of his that seem half-way between bird of prey and reptile, although this lends him an attractive rather than a shifty or menacing look.

He taps her gently on the cheeks, takes her hand and rubs it vigorously, but she still does not react. He feels her pulse, then places his big, dark hand on her belly. Although presumably he does this with the utmost caution and the best of intentions – I don't want to give in to prejudice, after all this time – I like to think that when he does this I have my head down and am very quiet in my feverish cave, and so this supposedly lovelorn and presumably murderous hand cannot detect any heartbeat or other sign of life. I like to think that even though I could not do anything else, I at least manage to give the cop the slip and even succeed in worrying and scaring him a bit, without having to lift a finger.

Yet he behaves calmly and sensibly, doing all he can to bring her round. He calls her respectfully by her married name, rubs the back of her hand, thinks about giving her a glass of water but remembers the toilet and the kitchen are in the other half of the house, and so opts for a quicker, more radical solution, a drink of the brandy he has in the hip flask in his back trouser pocket. He slips one hand behind her head, and lifts her up to drink from the mouth of the hip flask. Before she can take a sip, the smell of the alcohol makes her open her eyes.

"My God, it's happened again . . ."

"Are you feeling all right now?"

"I think so."

"You gave me a fright."

"It's over now. It was the heat. You shouldn't be frightened, it happens all the time."

"You're very pale. Take a sip of brandy."

"No, not that," she says, smiling as she pushes the hip flask away. She tries to get up, then flops back. "As soon as I feel less dizzy . . ."

"Are you taking any medicine? Do you want me to get it for you?"

"No, no thanks. I'm taking a diuretic, but it's not time for that . . . You can leave if you like. I'm fine now, don't worry."

"If you don't mind, I'll stay with you for a minute."

The red-head says nothing, and lies back in the chair with her eyes closed. After a few moments, she opens them again.

"Don't stand there like that. Sit down. It must have been the baby, he never stops . . . although sometimes he is so still it scares me."

"Shall I get you a glass of water?"

She does not respond, and shuts her eyes again. They are still closed a few moments later when she insists:

"Either sit down or go, will you? Didn't you hear me?"

The inspector sits very stiffly on the wicker chair opposite Ma, who appears to be asleep. And then, let me think about it, brother, then it is true that he feels something more than respect and admiration for her, he sits quietly observing her for some time with a strangely intimate licence, staring at her beautiful smooth brow, her fitful sleep beneath waxy eyelids, her full, suffering mouth, her red curls and her white hands lying limply across her stomach.

Now she is no longer looking at him, I like to think that for a few seconds this man's eyes are searching out in her weary features, in her trusting sleep and in these humble surroundings, this pale imitation of homely warmth she has struggled to re-create in this poor rented dwelling, something his heart lost earlier in his life.

When she opens her eyes again, perhaps expecting to see the policeman's worried anxious look, she sees instead that he is bending over and stroking the dog's back between his feet, although he steals a surreptitious glance at her swollen ankles. The inspector straightens up, picks his hip flask off the table, and stores it in his pocket.

"I'll leave as soon as you assure me you're all right."

"I'm fine. Thank you."

When they took that photo of him looking so insolent, with his legendary shot-down Spitfire and his famous smile, Pa says, the one that hypnotizes you every night from your bedroom wall, Flight Lieutenant Bryan O'Flynn and I had already been through quite a few adventures together.

Of course, that's why you kept the magazine photo. As a souvenir.

I'm telling you, it wasn't me, Pa insists, painfully scratching the hair on his chest with the hand holding the bottle. He does not look any better. He is puffing on an age-old cigarette as he leans against the withered trunk of a chestnut tree as bald and white as an egg. His bare feet are sunk in the wet snake of sand and pebbles. For some reason, probably because of the roaring in his ears, David is convinced that the waters which dug out the gully in another age have been raging through here again. It was your mother, Pa adds. His body and neck are shiny with sweat, but the rest of him is unclear. His white shirt is drying on a nearby rosemary bush. Your mother, our red-headed seamstress, he repeats forlornly.

Why did she do that?

Ask her.

Did Ma know him as well?

No better than I did. Let's just say she had more dealings with him, but she didn't know him any better than me . . . Didn't you bring any clean handkerchiefs? No disinfectant, no bandages or gauze? What on earth were you thinking of, son? You can see the state I'm in, with the bottle nearly finished and my arse open to the skies pouring blood, spilling it generously for a better future and the triumph of our ideals. The same old crap.

Don't say that. You're a hero.

Not exactly. The only real hero is the one who lies about what he's going to do. I never did.

What do you do at night, Pa? Where do you hide? Where do you go?

From the gully to La Carroña and La Carroña to the gully.

But Ma says you aren't there any more. Where are you?

Right now I've no idea where I am. That's what happens when you spend the whole damned time dreaming. Your mother always said you live in a dream, Víctor, you can't face reality any more, that's your problem, the bitter cup you have to drink every day. And I'd reply: well, if I'm dreaming, don't wake me up because I've got a bottle of authentic Baron Rothschild in my hands . . . your mother and I had a lot of fun with my dreams. Now look. In this riverbed there's the stench of a carrion crow so strong it'll knock you over, and that stench is my own dreamer's breath.

You were telling me about the RAF pilot.

That blasted Australian, who said he was Irish and lived in London, was a brave one all right. The Germans shot him down twice over France, the first time in July '41. He landed near the town of Renty, in the Calais region. He was lucky, he set off walking across the devastated fields of France and met up with one of Pat O'Leary's escape team. They gave him medical assistance, clothes and fake papers. He was taken to Paris and from there to Toulouse, where he got in touch with Ponzán Vidal's group to help him cross the Pyrenees by a clandestine route. In those days a lot of prisoners of war who had escaped the Germans managed to reach the Spanish border thanks to the secret networks set up in occupied France. The Gestapo was suspicious because a lot of the pilots who had been shot down couldn't be found, so they had to be very careful. I was involved with that and a lot more besides, but on this side of the Pyrenees. Later on I went over to France and took part directly in the network . . . are you following me? When he reached Toulouse, our pilot had to wait a couple of weeks while they prepared the expedition to Spain with two guides who knew the area and would take him as far as Osseja, in the eastern Pyrenees, together with a Jewish couple and their fifteen-year-old daughter. In Osseja, a young woman took over, and the two guides went back to Toulouse. From there on, according to what O'Flynn told me later, the journey was slow and difficult because the Jewish man could hardly walk. Our airman was carrying a heavy suitcase which he wouldn't let go of for a minute. Finally, they got across the mountains to Ribas de Fresser, then began the descent to an agreed refuge, where I was waiting for them. Still following?

I'm with you, Pa.

My job was to escort them from there, while the girl who had brought them into Spain crossed back to France. We took a coach to Ripoll, and then a train to Barcelona. The Jewish family went their own way, and I put the pilot and his wretched suitcase in a taxi. I left him outside the British Consulate, where they were supposed to provide him with counterfeit papers to take him to Gibraltar or back to London via Lisbon. Sometimes it took two or three days to get the papers, and it was part of my job to find these pilots somewhere to stay in the meantime. I don't know why, but on this particular occasion I hadn't done anything about it. For some reason I never bothered to ask myself, O'Flynn decided to go into the Consulate without the suitcase, so he asked me to look after it at home, and said he would come and fetch it as soon as he had all the proper papers. I gave him our address, and he turned up that night, but still without his identity card . . .

How come I didn't see him?

It was August, when you were in Mataró with your grandparents . . . by this time I could speak more or less acceptable English, so we could understand each other. O'Flynn told me he didn't trust certain people in the Consulate, and preferred to leave the case at home. Top secret. Following all right? says Pa, turning over the handkerchief he is pressing against the wound that shows no sign of healing, which will never heal. Then he feels in his trouser pockets. Damn and blast it, he says, I've run out of cigarettes.

You left one half-smoked in the kitchen ashtray, says David. Shall I go and get it for you?

That's your mother's cigarette, and it's her last. You should notice these things. You need to keep your eyes peeled, son, there are hard times ahead. And now, tell me: what is our intrepid seamstress up to? How is she?

The same every day. And she's not well.

Very gingerly, Ma puts her feet in the basin of water: first the left one, then the right. David has heated the water in the kitchen, poured it into the basin, tossed in a handful of salt, carried it into their living-room, and knelt down to take off Ma's shoes as she sits in her wicker chair.

Some time later, she is alone in the kitchen, patiently wafting the embers of the fire, the other hand holding the cigarette resting on her stomach as she stares into empty space, her eyes fixed on nothing anybody else could see. She leaves the cigarette in the ashtray, lifts her hand to the black ribbons in her red hair, and then rests it on her belly once more. Seen in silhouette against the light in this dark, narrow tunnel of a kitchen, her pregnant face and body, and the dreamy, sad way she has of standing offer me my favourite image of her as she confronts the endless grind of daily poverty; the clearest and most persistent of all the images I have patched together and reconstructed in my memory. Although she cannot see the photo of the pilot smiling as he defies his executioners because it is still tacked to David's wall, for some reason even here in the kitchen he is just as close and cheerfully defiant.

Chick peas, lentils, sweet potatoes, porridge. I can name these things and in memory smell them with the same gratitude and respect as Ma used to caress them with her hands and voice. Salt cod. The old coffee grinder. Lard melting in the frying-pan, and all the other objects with that strange desire of theirs to be camouflaged, their stubborn propensity for being where they should not be: sugar lumps in the chipped pan, lentils in a biscuit tin, sweet potatoes in a zinc bowl, cloves of garlic in a cocoa tin. Remember, brother, the poverty that was our faithful companion all those years, the poverty Ma struggled so courageously with and never protested at, the kind that has a thousand faces and shows itself in a thousand ways, also means this: that in spite of the cleanliness and order she is so quick and eager to bring to everything around her, things never seem to be in their right place, slyly and insidiously they are always occupying one reserved for something else. And yet, even when they are apparently misplaced, randomly scattered in this world of appearances, not one of those objects has lost its identity; on the contrary, they seem even closer to hand and ready for use, just like the charred, blurred image of the fighter pilot, which one day was where it should have been among perhaps the most private and best-kept memories our mother had, and now, long after it has displayed its defiant smile on the cover of a German magazine published in Spanish, suddenly turns up like an old friend in the bedroom of a dreamy adolescent in a distant corner of Guinardó.

National Security Headquarters
Information Section
File on *Víctor Bartra Lángara*.
Dossiers F-7 (17-3-40) and F-8 (2-5-45). Summary for internal use only.

— Born Huesca 4 April 1901. Lived in Mataró to age 12.
— Seminarist and later "server" at the Jesuit College in Calle Caspe (presumably the origin of his violent anti-clericalism).
— Accused of taking part in the kidnapping and murder of parish priest of San Jaime de los Domenys (Tarragona) on 20 July 1936. Not proven.
— Served in the Red army during our war of liberation, as part of the medical brigade (anaesthetist), wounded at the Aragon front.
— At the end of the conflict changed his name and worked in a spinning mill in the Gràcia neighbourhood. Attempted to spread his revolutionary anarchist ideas among the workforce, inciting his workmates against the current regime.
— According to reports by local residents, instigator of Catalan separatist activities under cover of the Fiesta Mayor of Gracia and Guinardó.
— In March 1940, arrested in a department in Calle Conde del Asalto where a clandestine meeting was taking place. Meeting supposedly for sport and health club (in fact probably libertarian). Alleged in his defence that he was there by mistake (see Appendix F-7) as he had gone to the building for a different reason. When questioned, explains error with apparently convincing details.

— Crossed clandestinely into France at the end of 1942. Believed responsible for support missions for French Resistance, such as guiding Allied pilots shot down by the Germans across the border. Thanks to collated information, established that he was linked to a secret British group set up in Marseilles, known as the "Garrow Organization". In Toulouse, lived at 40 Rue Limayrac. Indications that as well as acting as frontier guide, he trafficked in contraband items. Evidence that he gave shelter for several days to an English airman who later returned to his unit via Lisbon using false papers. For this work, the aforementioned received the sum of 2,000 francs per person. When smuggling documents, could charge up to 5,000 francs.

— In libertarian circles known as the author of several pamphlets published by the Spanish CNT union in France.

— In October 1943 tries to establish contact with the so-called "Basque government in exile". The next day, narrowly avoids arrest at a picnic in Las Planas after taking part in a clandestine meeting held with the pretext of a *"costellada"* organized by the so-called "Sindicat d'Espectacles Públics de la CNT", made up of theatre workers, film projectionists and ushers, among whom is his friend and comrade Germán Augé.

— In 1944, on the recommendation of the parish priest of the Capilla Expiatoria de Las Ánimas (Dr Masdexexart) joins the Municipal Hygiene Services for work of disinfection and pest extermination in cinemas and elsewhere. A member of the clandestine CNT Arts and Entertainment Union, his task is to distribute newsletters and subversive propaganda hidden in the sacks used for distribution of film reels.

— Prominent member of the MLR (Moviment Llibertari de Resistència) until February of this year, when he is expelled for insubordination and misuse of "revolutionary funds" as the members' contributions are known.

— Disappears from his house approximately in March of current year.

"If what you want to know," says Ma, "is if I think it's better to live in peace without freedom than to live free but at war, then the answer is no, Inspector."

"I never ask that kind of question."

"Of course not, why would you? That's one of the advantages of living in peace without freedom."

"I've no intention of arguing with you, Señora Bartra, not today. I'll only say one thing. I don't know who wrote this report, but whoever it was, it's obvious your husband made a fool of him."

"Why do you say that?" Ma wants to know.

"Finish reading it, then tell me what you think. The best bit is in the appendix from five years ago, and his statement."

"You mean about him and the contraband? I never believed that nonsense."

"No, I don't mean that. Read it for yourself."

"Have you got a cigarette, Inspector?"

"You shouldn't smoke so much, Señora Bartra."

F-7 (17-3-40)
Víctor Bartra Lángara:

Adult. Health auxiliary. Home address in Guinardó. Poor economic situation. He states that everything is due to a series of coincidences that led to his mistaken arrest. About two weeks ago, he met a certain Madame Carmencita in a bar on Las Ramblas. He does not know her real name. She took him either for a commercial agent or a lawyer, although she never explained why she thought these were his professions. Madame Carmencita introduced him to a young woman by the name of Florita García Nieto, also under arrest. Said Florita showed him a tattoo on her left arm which referred to the brand of American cigarettes called Lucky Strike. Madame Carmencita told him she had thought of an idea that could bring some money both to her friend Florita and to him in his capacity as lawyer, if he was interested. She said this idea involved an American-style advertising campaign on the skin (these were the words used by the defendant) and that several other friends of hers would be happy to display similar tattoos, on even more intimate parts of their bodies which we will not go into at the moment (the defendant's expression) provided that the Lucky Strike agent in Spain paid for them. What did he think of the idea? he said she said. It was then that the defendant said he began to suspect that Madame Carmencita and Florita looked and behaved – in addition to touching him and displaying her emotions far beyond the demands of the polite behaviour appropriate to our noble national temper and the unity of the people and lands of Spain (I am merely transcribing the words used by the defendant) – I repeat, began to suspect that his two companions might have something to do with prostitution and the like, but that he preferred to remain polite and so said that yes, it was an idea. Madame Carmencita told him she had set up a meeting of 20 or 30 interested friends, and asked whether he would like to attend the meeting, which was to take place in an apartment

115

at number 13, Calle Conde del Asalto, where they would be discussing payment and other work-related matters which called for legal advice. Since he was not particularly interested, the defendant said he declined the offer, but that after imbibing several drinks and becoming more intimate with the said Florita García Nieto and her showing him another brand name, this time tattooed on the inside of her thigh (Cerebrino Mandri, the famous pick-me-up) he somewhat impulsively decided to go to the meeting of whores (at this point in his declaration, the defendant states that by now he was under no illusion as to how the two women plied their trade) and offer them advice.

He further states that he went with Florita García Nieto to the meeting arranged in Calle Conde del Asalto, but that he mistook the floor it was being held on, so that the two of them suddenly found themselves in a meeting of alleged unemployed travelling salesmen invited there by a representative of the firm Suco y Hermanos, makers of an "orange juice that cures everything automatically", according to the defendant's statement. Florita left as soon as she realized their mistake, but when the Social Brigade arrived, he was unable to get out because he was sitting in one of the front rows, although those at the back did manage to escape. He states that he cannot believe that the real reason for the meeting was political, and says he was neither invited to it, nor told about it.

Defendant has a police record.

Resolution: suggested fine of 5,000 pesetas.

VII

The Invisible Worm

Squatting on his haunches, David lets the lizard escape, then picks up the severed tail oozing its sticky liquid over the drowsy rocks. He presses the penknife on his knee to shut it, opens his other hand and puts the new tail in his palm next to another one still writhing there. I do not know what harsh sunlight is beating down on the riverbed and the disembodied voices he hears down there. With all the sly tricks of which a river is capable, even though for many years all it has had to show are these crumbling banks and its dried-up bed, the stream conjures up echoes of raging, rushing waters determined to prove they still exist, and to sweep away any useless, discarded object clinging on at a bend, anything not where it should be, like the rebellious blood putrefying on our father's backside.

Where were we, son; where had we got to? he asks, swapping the handkerchief to his other hand, one foot up on a rock. Oh, yes. Four days and nights our lanky, brave friend spent at home waiting for the papers from the Consulate. That's right, it was in the month of August. For four days your mother and I kept him hidden in the house – only to find out later that he had been given all the documents he needed within a few hours of arriving. He didn't tell me that, the rogue. Yes, that's right. I can see him now sitting in the wicker chair by the window opposite your mother, all very right and proper as they drank coffee and chatted to each other. They got on well from the start. They were linked by a strange kind of childish complicity, they spoke a funny mish-mash that had them in stitches the whole time and bored me to tears: they understood each other thanks to an incredible baby-talk that was part gestures and part words that only kids and madmen speak. He would recite poems with that insolent nasal lilt of his, and our red-head, caught as ever between the two worlds of fraternity and fantasy, tried to imitate his romantic cadences and poetic effects, and learn English at the same time. Then they would look at each other and collapse laughing. What do you reckon, David? Don't you think that in such an extraordinary situation, such extraordinary people as them should know their place? I know life is made up of meaningless moments and worthless chat, but *quand même!* Dammit!

What do you mean, Pa?

Learn languages, son. I can remember a poem Flight Lieutenant O'Flynn repeated over and over until your mother had learnt it by heart. At night it was so hot we had to get out of the house, so we sat out on the edge of the gully drinking gin beneath the stars . . . we used to drink until dawn from big blue glasses, I can still smell the sharp scent of the gin and hear the Flight Lieutenant's beautiful voice:

> *O Rose, thou art sick!*
> *The invisible worm*
> *That flies in the night,*
> *In the howling storm,*
> *Has found out thy bed*
> *Of crimson joy,*
> *And his dark secret love*
> *Does thy life destroy.*

What does it mean, Pa?

I've already told you, they spoke a strange language of their own, because your mother didn't know any English, and he had no Spanish. Still, I have to admit he was a very well-educated man . . . before he left with fresh wind in his sails, I asked him what he had in the suitcase that was so heavy. He said it was a piece of equipment from a German submarine, and that he had to hand it over personally in Gibraltar or London. He explained it was made of a very dense, very expensive metal, that it was a cylinder with grooves and numbers at one end and traces of shrapnel or fire at the other. An object of immense scientific and strategic value to the Admiralty.

Did he show it you?

He refused to.

And you believed him?

I seem to remember it was the only time I did.

What happened after that?

He left. And we'll never see you again? I asked him in English. Never is a long time, he replied.

What does that mean?

Dammit, David, study languages! Get your mother to teach you!

But you said Ma couldn't speak English.

Yes, but she learnt a bit, she learnt a bit . . . where were we? Oh, yes. Well, I did all I could for that pilot, I took him in and looked after him while he was waiting for his papers, then he had no problems getting to Gibraltar and from there to England, where he rejoined his squadron. He was given another Sptifire, and in February of the following year, he was shot down again, near Calais this time. The photo of his capture, with blackened face and burnt hands, appeared on the cover of *Adler* magazine in March three years ago – in the edition of the 15th of March 1942 to be precise – the one your mother swiped from the waiting-room in some police station or other, while she was waiting to be questioned . . . some flight the intrepid Bryan O'Flynn has had, from the horizons of gold and emerald where heroes live, to the peeling walls of a tiny room in Guinardó! Well, anyway. By then I had crossed over into France and was working as the contact between Pat O'Leary's network and Ponzán's group. I learnt later that our hero had got help to escape and cross the border into Spain again, then had reached London via Lisbon. His hands had been so badly burnt and crippled he couldn't fly a plane any more, so from then on he worked as a liaison officer in North Africa and during the push into Germany. After that he joined the Special Services, worked for a while with an MI6 agent, and I saw him once in Marseilles with O'Leary's men. I remember he was carrying another enormous suitcase, so I said to him as a joke: What have you got in there, Bryan, the prow of a German battleship? The last I heard of him, a few months after the Normandy landings, was that he was in a bomber that crashed into the sea as it was returning to base in North Africa, most probably following a raid on Germany. It had crossed half Europe with its wings shot up, and not only that – just listen, I'll tell you it exactly as I heard it – apparently the plane flew on with all its crew burnt to cinders in their seats, six bodies and the cockpit on fire, skimming the sea until it crashed and sank . . .

I saw it! David shouts excitedly. I saw it! Nobody believed me, not Granny Tecla or Ma or the Civil Guard, nobody. And they said nothing on the radio or in the papers, but I saw it with my own eyes. It was a B-26 Marauder, and on its fuselage there was the picture of a girl in a swimsuit with the slogan FOREVER AMANDA. What does that mean?

You'll find out when you learn foreign languages.

No-one believed me, but you must, Pa . . .

I do, Pa cuts in, raising the bottle and squinting at it against the sun. Does that make you feel better? We have to unmask the truth! Now listen. We also have to make our red-head feel better by telling her the naked truth, don't we? What could we tell her . . . ? I know. You can tell her the waters of the river have swept away my bottle.

But there isn't any water in the river any more, Pa.

We won't worry about that. I remember the dog Latin a schoolteacher – your beloved mother – was always repeating: *fortis imaginatio generat casum.*

Ma used to say that? What does it mean?

See how important it is to learn languages, dolt?

Its face dented as if by a sudden blow, a celluloid doll pokes out from the tangle of rubbish scattered over the dried-up riverbed, with its twisting ribbon of wet sand that once, long before he was born, had been a place of tranquil, clear waters. Lost in contemplation of the crushed head, and with one of the lizard tails still wriggling in his hand, David wonders when there will be another roaring torrent capable of cancelling out the suffering in his ears and sweeping away everything in its path: all the rubbish, the rotten branches, the mud and drowned animals.

I've never seen water or anything of the sort flowing through here, his father says. Flags and cornets, cassocks and patriotic essences, a lot of that kind of shit, a lot of fanaticism, that's what I've seen. From the very first moment those people handed me this bottle that will never be emptied, and left me lost like this, with no memory, only lies in my own home and in this big mouth of mine. Oh, well. We have to turn the page. What can we tell your mother to lift her spirits . . . ? I've got it. Simply tell her I don't drink any more.

I'll tell her.

You won't forget?

No. Come on, Chispa. Get up.

But tell her as well that now I'm not drinking, every night I dream I am. And tell her that while I am dreaming I'm drinking I really suffer because I know I'm not drinking. Ask her to explain that if she can, she studied to be a schoolteacher.

I'll tell her, Pa.

Get a move on. And let's see when you finally end that dog's calvary. Hand him over to that policeman and let him end his suffering, the poor thing.

You're not in this with all the others are you, Pa . . . ? David says with a sudden parody of sadness that makes his vision fade: he has the two lizard tails in his hand, one of them quiet now, the other still twisting and turning. He closes his fist and screws up his eyes, and in the cloud of dust and the blinding sun, thinks he can still make out the dim outline, the ever filthier and more hunched figure of his father struggling determinedly upstream, firmly clutching the neck of his bottle.

Go home, son. Ma needs you.

"Bwana, for ten cents I'll tell you where the red-head is, and for twenty I'll spill all I know about Víctor Bartra and throw in one of the cards from my Heroes of the Fatherland collection, like the one the traffic policeman gave my friend Paulino Bardolet . . ."

"So she's not at home today either," the inspector cuts him short.

His stolid face does not betray the slightest impatience or annoyance. All around him is the red dust and the rank smell of uprooted trees, that strange odour from the gully that seems always to accompany him.

"This week you no have luck, bwana." David's flashing eyes fix for a moment on the inspector's weary, wrinkled lids, as if hypnotized by their calmness.

"How is she?" the cop says, staring down at his shoes. "Do you know she fainted the other day?"

"It's not the first time."

"Did she tell you where she was going, how long she'd be?"

David shakes his head, not taking his eyes off the inspector. In spite of every-thing, he admires his calm attitude, the way he keeps an unlit cigarette in his mouth, his right hand in his jacket pocket, the economy of each and every one of his gestures. Today he is carrying a blue folder under one arm; the other is in a sling made from a brown polka dot scarf.

"What happened to you? Were you wounded in a shoot-out? Did you come across some villains? Get in a fight with wicked bandits?"

"I asked you how long your mother would be."

"Have you brought news of my father?"

"You'll find out, if she decides to tell you," the inspector says, taking his hand out of his pocket and lighting his Dupont.

"Christ, what a brilliant lighter!" says David. "Can I try it?"

The inspector gives it him. David carefully lights his cigarette, then tries the lighter a couple more times, the tip of his thumb against the golden wheel and the spring of the lid, enjoying the sound of the clunk as it snaps shut. It's fantastic, when I'm grown up I'll have one the same, but a real one. Clunk!

"Well," says the inspector, reclaiming the lighter. "You still haven't answered my question."

"A medical check-up. Who knows how long she'll be. That depends on what Doctor Isamat thinks of my little brother, the one about to appear."

"Tell her I'll be back tomorrow, I've got something that will interest her."

"If I remember, I'll tell her."

The inspector says nothing. He cannot think of anything more to add, and so reluctantly he turns round, although he would like to stay and wait. All at once he sees something over David's shoulder that will allow him to prolong his stay: under the table, the basset hound who according to him should already be dead and buried, struggles to its feet, leaves the blanket it has been lying on, staggers a few paces and then collapses to the floor tiles with creaking bones.

"Can't you get it into your head that the poor animal over there is a real burden to your mother? You wouldn't admit it even when it's on its death bed, would you? You don't want to see it. I know how upset your mother gets to see it in that state. If you won't decide, let someone else do it for you. The most convenient thing would be . . ."

"Yes, I know," David shouts. "I know what you think would be convenient. And I know she is thinking of killing him too, you've talked her into it."

"Your mother and I both think all you're doing is prolonging its agony, simply because you're hot-headed and stubborn. Look at the poor thing, it can hardly breathe . . ."

Chispa totters over and falls at the inspector's feet, his muzzle on one of his shoes. The policeman lifts his leg and fends him off; he does not exactly kick the animal, but even the slow, gentle bending of his leg and the raising of his foot suggest he is controlling a wish to do so. David notices this, and says to himself, look at the bastard, how can he kick a dog he claims is dying? Almost simultaneously he stares at the policeman's hand in the sling, and sees the swelling disappear and the fingers close in a slow deliberate movement as if he were holding a weapon and pulling the trigger. Then, as though in a lightning flash, David sees the mouth of the revolver pressed against his dog's ear, sees it spit the bullet that crashes through his head.

"Yet again," the inspector growls, " and I'm thinking above all of your mother when I say this, I'm asking you to consider it, kid."

"What's it to you anyway? Besides," says David, glancing sadly down at Chispa, "the poor thing will die some day soon, I know, because he's got galloping pneumonia, so he doesn't need anyone else's help . . . he could kick it tomorrow, but he'll do it for himself . . ."

"Don't be so sure. Who knows how long it might last in this state."

"I'll look after him until he dies."

"Don't pretend you have good intentions. If you really cared, you'd worry less about that animal and more about your mother. Why didn't you go to the doctor's with her?" He leans forward towards David and jabs him repeatedly in the chest with the hand in the sling. He continues: "One of these days you and I are going to have a really serious talk. Better start thinking about that."

"I couldn't care less."

"We'll see about that. You ought to know that I'm telling you all this for your own good. Goodbye. Tell your mother I'll be back tomorrow afternoon."

You'll bite the dust, flatfoot, David mutters as he watches him walk off down the street with his springy gait, the half-lazy, half-watchful air there is about the back of his head and his broad shoulders.

In the early morning light, lying curled up beneath a leaden, spectral sky, the sprawling city looks like a crumpled mirage, its defeated shades of grey shimmering by the shore, a battered theatre décor freshly repainted by the same nocturnal angels who patch up our dreams at the break of day. At the same hour, sturdy sparrows settle on the flimsy wires of the washing line at the gully's edge, cleaning themselves of parasites and the black scum of night.

Some time later, Ma comes out of the front door with a basket of washing on her hip. She crosses the ruined garden, walking between rose and oleander bushes she still cultivates nostalgically in her memory, and heads for the gully, where David is sitting with Chispa, his legs dangling over the edge as he talks to himself.

Her attention is caught by wisteria spilling over demolished walls that once enclosed the garden, then she looks once more for David, who is muttering under his breath and swinging his legs as though he were splashing in still water. In friendlier times, the seamstress's boys could have caught a lot of fish here, if not with their father then with their Mataró grandfather, who always had rods and lines.

On the far side of the gully, on the hillside that has not yet been built on, a barefoot young girl wearing what looks like the jacket of her father's striped pyjamas is also laying out her washing. On the broom bushes David can see a yellow skirt with green pockets, a saffron-coloured blouse and two small pairs of pink knickers. The sun emerges from behind the clouds and lights up the yellow broom flowers and the girl's golden hair.

"You'll be late for church," Ma says, a peg between her teeth as she pulls the washed laundry from the basket. "Didn't Señor Marimón tell you he had a wedding this morning?"

"I'm going," David says, watching Chispa try in vain to produce some droppings. "The flatfoot was here yesterday. I forgot to tell you."

"OK."

"He's coming back this afternoon. He was carrying a folder with papers in."

"A folder?"

Yes, a folder and an evil mind, David whispers to himself. Damned pig of a cur of a son of a bitch of a cop.

"I can't hear you, but I know what you're saying. You've really taken against that man, haven't you?"

David stands up.

"Naw. I was arguing with my brother. You do it too."

"I don't argue with him. We get along fine. And don't you think it'd be better to wait until he's actually arrived, before you start squabbling with him?"

"Pa told me one day: learn to watch for what hasn't happened yet, and you'll understand a lot."

"He said that?"

Very clever, Señor Bartra. Listen to this. The red-head is lying on her back on the bed, and holding me up in the air with hands like goldfish, while beside her David looks on astonished, and Paulino is there too, playing his coloured maracas. You've chosen the wrong moment to come into this world, my son, I feel very weak and alone, I've had to stop working, I don't know if I'll have any milk and there are only two dried-out sweet potatoes and a bit of cod to eat at home . . .

Why don't you strangle yourself with your umbilical cord and leave us in peace, you disgusting foetus? mutters David as he walks along the edge of the gully, Chispa's lead hanging round his neck. He is staring across at the blouse and yellow skirt spread out like a tiny ecstatic body on the broom bush. The little girl has already gone. The dog follows on at David's thin, tanned brown heel, sniffing for emotional affinities.

"Wait, we've got to talk about that dog of yours," says Ma, spreading out a sheet. "We have to take a decision."

"I don't want to talk about it. I'm in a hurry."

He leaves Chispa in the house and heads off down the track to the Avenida. Up beyond the gully he crosses to the other side and walks over to the slope where the little girl's washing is drying in the sun. What would you do in my place, microbe? He's got chronic pneumonia, that's all, I'm sure that can be cured, he's not all that old . . . What would you do, would you let them cart him away? I would, I have my feelings, brother. Don't you? What do you know about feelings, if you haven't popped out of the shell yet, you hairy worm poisoning Ma's blood? What Chispa needs is care and compassion. You and your blessed compassion are letting him die in the worst way possible, bit by bit, having a hell of a time. You're massacring him, brother, making a martyr of him with a Chinese torture worse than any of Fu-Manchu's dacoits could dream up. You're worse than that cop who's nosing round the red-head, and that's saying something. Of course I am, you shitty louse. No doubt about it! I'm much worse!

Before he comes out on to the Avenida on his way to Cristo Rey church, David stops for a moment by the broom bush to get a good look at the skirt with green pockets drying on it. It's a girl's short skirt, made from coarse, faded material. A wasp is buzzing round the hem, and one of David's knees starts to tremble. He knows it is a sign of the agitation he feels inside, a sign heralding mischief.

"Oh yes! I'm worse than the plague, I am."

Inspector Galván has rung the bell and stands waiting at the day-time door. He looks thoughtful, and an empty hand is plunged into the bush of marguerites. The other, freed from its bandage and sling, is carrying the blue folder. The door opens, he says a few words, shows the folder, and he is inside.

"I have to thank you for the trouble you took . . ." Ma begins.

"I'm at your service, Señora Bartra."

"Do you mean it?" the red-head says with a smile, one hand on the neck of her housecoat. "Please, sit down."

She herself sits in her wicker chair and without more ado starts to read the dossier, with the folder on her lap and a cigarette smouldering between her fingers. She pays no heed to the inspector, perched awkwardly on the other chair. After a while, though, she stops reading, smiles again, and excuses herself for not looking after him properly. The policeman notices all the bits of coloured sewing thread stuck to her housecoat like tiny snakes. The handle of a pair of scissors is sticking out from one of the coat pockets. There is a coffee service on the side-table, with two small cups and a bowl full of sugar lumps.

"I was so anxious to read this . . ."

"I understand."

"I hope the house smells all right," she comments, glancing down at the newly washed tiles under her feet, and at the dog breathing painfully as he snoozes in his corner. Next to him is a zinc bucket with a floorcloth in it. "I've spent the whole day wiping up the sick from that poor mongrel, you've no idea how my back aches. I've even begun to think seriously about your offer to take him off our hands . . ."

"That would be the best thing to do. Did you talk to your son?"

She does not reply; she is busy again reading the files. The inspector says nothing more, and sits looking at her. Ma's head, with its mass of red hair tied up with black ribbons, tilts attentively over Víctor Bartra's supposed misdeeds. Underneath the folder, her tightly drawn-up knees look as if they are smiling too.

A few minutes later she snaps the file shut, gives one last furious draw on the cigarette, and stubs it out in the ashtray.

"This file and the dossiers are an insult to my husband's intelligence," she says calmly. "To his moral integrity and his ideals. It's a joke."

"Well, to judge by some of the things in his declaration, it's hard to tell who's laughing at whom. But let's forget about that, Señora Bartra. I can understand your wish to defend his ideas . . ."

"Don't get me wrong, Inspector. I defend my husband and respect his ideals, but I'm not his ideological mouthpiece – not his, nor anyone else's; I'm the woman who brings up his children, the seamstress, the cook, the cleaner. Isn't that enough? I suppose like all those on your side you think I must feel defeated and alone, and that because I am having such a hard time I can't possibly still share Víctor's ideals . . ."

"I think you have suffered a lot unjustly, that's what I think."

She hesitates a moment before going on.

"And now you think you can make fun of all that, that's the national watchword, the policy of the steady, alert gaze and calm, virile hands resting on the pommel of your swords, all that paraphernalia and rhetoric. I know the score. Well, listen to this: if it weren't for some of my husband's ideals, I'd say there's nothing to lose in life."

"Don't say that. You know there are lots of things worth fighting for . . ."

"Give me a cigarette, would you?"

"Another one? You've only just put out the last one."

"Yes, but smoke helps clear my mind," she replies tartly. Then she softens her voice, and adds: "I'm sorry, I haven't offered you anything."

At about seven that evening, before it grows dark and with the setting sun lending a scarlet tint to fingernails that are permanently stained yellow by the hypo he uses for developing the photographs, David comes home to find Paulino Bardolet waiting for him by the gully's edge, maracas in hand. Warned by his friend of the inspector's visit, he pushes through the marguerites to peer in at the window. The first thing he sees through the shutters on the side-table is the Dupont lighter, then the pack of Lucky Strikes, the old coffee set with the Chinese figures on it and the bowl filled to overflowing with sugar lumps. Then he notices the inspector sitting uncomfortably on his chair sipping his coffee. His steely eyes are staring over the top of his cup at the red-head. The coffee is both a gift from the house and a gift from the visitor.

"Snug and warm," growls David a few moments later as he gets out his penknife in the gully. "The other day I heard Ma saying that thanks to him she didn't have to drink any more ersatz or chicory. The sugar lumps are a present from him too, he steals them from bars."

"Why didn't you want to go in?" asks Paulino.

David thinks it over in silence. At what point in her conversation did the red-head decide it would be better to respond to this man's attentions, why did she not control her impulse or wish to invite him in and offer him a cup of coffee? Why, I've only just made a pot, inspector, would you like a cup? Sit down, please. How many lumps? Would you be so kind as to offer me an American cigarette? You shouldn't smoke, Señora Bartra, especially in your condition – he says looking apparently absent-mindedly at the top of her frayed housecoat as she finishes pouring him the coffee and sits down, her face reflecting her weariness.

"Don't be so bitter about it," Paulino say, walking a few yards in front of him, producing a gentle rattle on his maracas. "This isn't the first time the flat-foot's slipped into your house."

"No. But this is the first time she's asked him to sit down and have coffee. It's very different."

"Very different," agrees Paulino, following the dried-up riverbed. Suddenly, he gathers the two maracas in one hand and opens his cut-throat razor in the other. He stalks carefully round the bare, hollow trunk of a half-buried holm oak. "It poked its nose out, but I've lost it. Did you see anything?"

"My father's backside dripping blood. That's all I saw."

"We're not going to catch any today, the sun's almost set. Shall we go to the Montaña Pelada? I'll show you the cave where Mianet lives, the tramp with bits of mirror on his shoes . . ."

"OK."

Before they leave, David goes up to the house and crouches under the window. He does not do it to overhear what they are saying: he has a hedgerow full of finches in his ears again. He uses his fingertips stained the colour of blood by the evening light to push the frame inwards, and the window slowly opens. Above the heads of the red-head and the cop, the ancient murmur of the river floods into the house.

"Let's get out of here, fatso."

"What if I tore all these insults to shreds?"

"Go ahead. They're copies," comes the inspector's velvet voice. He has just lit Ma's cigarette, and now does the same with his own. As he leaves the lighter on the table he notices the short white ankle socks the red-head is wearing, with thick cork-soled shoes. "You shouldn't wear shoes like that."

"What's wrong with them?"

"I don't think they're suitable for someone in your condition. You might fall."

She shuts the blue folder and takes a sip of coffee. Eventually, the policeman breaks the awkward silence.

"I knew you wouldn't like it."

"It's a pack of lies."

"Perhaps I should tell you that what's in the folder is not what's most important. I think your husband's problem, one that could cause him difficulties in court, is the open file of other things he's wanted for . . ."

"That's also full of lies, no doubt. What a way to distort reality. Revenge, accusations and calumnies are what count today, as you well know. And just look at the way it's written!"

"You have had a good education, haven't you, Señora Bartra?"

"Why do you ask?"

"Don't get me wrong, I'm not interrogating you," the inspector clarifies hastily, sitting even more upright in the chair. He switches his cigarette to the other hand, smoothes back his hair, stares down at his worn shoes. "I mean that there's something about you, in spite of your Republican past and the ideas you share with your husband . . ."

"I know the rigmarole, inspector, don't bother."

"I'm being serious," he says, trying to sound neutral. "I admire your spirit, Señora Bartra. I don't often meet people like you in my line of work. In fact, I consider it a privilege to have had the opportunity to get to know you and help you as far as I could."

"I don't know why you call it a privilege, and I don't think I want to, but thanks for the compliment anyway. You've just earned yourself another cup of coffee and two lumps of sugar . . . you surprise me, do you know that?" Ma tries to smile as she goes on: "Policemen never used to be like this. I think you cops must have undergone some kind of genetic mutation."

"How am I supposed to take that, Señora Bartra?" the inspector replies. When he gets no reply, he continues: "I know that people are very suspicious of us. I'm used to it, and it doesn't bother me."

"I think it does."

"That depends on who it is."

After this there is another, longer pause. The red-head looks down at the blue folder and strokes it thoughtfully.

"Thanks for letting me read it. Here it is," she says, handing it back. "It's all written in bad faith. You don't know anything about my husband."

"What really happened to that man?" the inspector asks, relaxing a little and allowing the threadbare velvet of his voice to take over. "I've often wondered. How could a man like that allow himself to be destroyed by drink from one day to the next: someone who had fought for his ideals, for his dreams of the future, as you yourself said . . . how did he fall so low?"

"I don't think that's a relevant question, Inspector."

"Perhaps not. I must confess my interest is not solely professional."

"You're asking me for the truth about a private matter. You'll have to make do with the public version, which is: my husband is against this regime. And he's an alcoholic."

"We already know that. It wasn't my intention . . ."

"Fine, now, do you mind if we talk about something else? Let's see. I think you mentioned my studies earlier."

"Yes. I have to complete my report, and there are a few details missing."

"All right then. What would you like to know?"

"During the Republic, you were a schoolteacher. Or for a few months at least, when you were living with your in-laws in Mataró. Then, following the death of your first son, you were ill for a long while, and you had to leave your post. At the end of the war you did not return to teaching."

"I wasn't allowed to."

"You weren't allowed to," the inspector repeats, without the slightest hint of curiosity.

"That's right. I suppose that doesn't surprise you," she says. "We all know people like doctors or lawyers who haven't been able to return to their profession."

"That's true. So what did you do, how did you get by?"

"We were already living here," she says with a sigh. "I went to work in a mill in Calle Escorial."

"The Batlló mill," says the inspector, crushing the packet of Luckies and tossing it into the ashtray.

"I'm still on their payroll," Ma says. "As I've already said, I've been off for three months now. I used to work from six in the morning to two in the afternoon, and my weekly pay was twenty-five pesetas. I looked after two looms. Ah, and first I had to do two years as an apprentice, when I earned fifteen pesetas per week . . . What more can I tell you?"

The inspector has taken out his notebook and, rummaging in his pockets, finally discovers the stub of a pencil scarcely longer than his cigarette butt. Despite this, he does not take any notes.

"You were right to ask for time off," he says in his neutral, tranquil voice. His voice now is breathy, lacking in conviction, though he seems to be searching for it, a voice like smoke. "You need to look after yourself."

"It was doctor's orders, you mustn't think I made it up."

"Of course not, it's obvious just looking at you. You need looking after."

"What more would you like to know? Oh, yes. At home I sew blouses and skirts for girls or for dolls, I don't care which. I've been doing it for a long while now, and I prefer sewing to going back to the factory. That's all, I think," she has picked up the Dupont, and turns it round in her fingers, above her pointed belly, apparently with nothing more to add. She notices the initials M.G. engraved on the lighter, and puts it down again on the table, next to the coffee cup saucer. Then she stares at the crumpled cigarette packet, and he guesses what she is thinking.

"It's empty," he says, and with something approximating a smile, goes on: "And I'm glad for your sake."

The inspector does not seem to have any more questions to ask either, and sits there silently for a moment, drinking his coffee and straightening the folder on the table. As he does so, it pushes the lighter to the table edge, and from there, without either of them noticing, it falls softly and silently on to the folded-up blanket Chispa was lying on until a few minutes earlier. Suddenly the inspector appears to remember something.

"You have a sister, who lived for a long time in a village near Tarragona."

"Lola. She came to Barcelona at least six years ago."

"She doesn't think much of your husband."

"She trembles when she hears his name. She's eight years younger than me, but she was always like an old woman, prejudiced and a religious devotee . . . she has unfortunate ways, but she is a good person."

"I've spoken to her," the inspector says, consulting his notebook. He adds: "She lives in Vallcarca. That's right, her name is Lola."

He still has a vivid image of her, not so much because of her unattractive appearance – a thin woman who seemed to be constantly opening and closing her black velvet bag whose clasp made a metallic noise like a gunshot – but more because of her barely disguised disgust at her sister Rosa for marrying such a worthless rogue. She showed him her Congregation of the Legion of Mary membership card, and told him she knew nothing and did not want to know anything about the man who had made her sister so unhappy, when she thought she was so clever. No sir, I've no idea where that Red might be, and I have no wish to.

"She married a farmer from outside Tarragona. Now he works on the trams," Ma adds. "He's called Pau, and he's a conductor on the number 30 route."

"Are there any relatives still living in that village . . . what's it called?"

"La Carroña."

"That's right, La Carroña. Where all the carrion is."

"It's not so much a village," the red-head says, ignoring his comment, "as one short street. There can't be more than a dozen houses in it. My brother-in-law's brother must still live there. I don't know, Lola and I haven't spoken for years. The fact is, I regret that, not so much for her or for me, but for David. My sister has a daughter the same age as him, perhaps a year younger, and they've got on very well since they were tiny . . . But why are you asking me all this? Don't tell me you think Víctor could be hiding out in La Carroña? Forget it. Even supposing one of the two brothers – and I'm thinking above all of my brother-in-law Pau, who's a bit crazy but a really sweet man – had wanted to hide my husband in his house, there's no way Lola would have allowed it. That's my sister for you! But you lot must already have investigated all this."

"There is a report from the Civil Guard."

Chispa abandons the cool of the tiles and staggers back to his blanket. As he flops on it, his belly fur covers the Dupont. He starts to groan. Lying spread-eagled with his head on the floor, he already appears dead.

"David should be here to take him for a walk," Ma says. The dog lifts his head with so much effort, and there is such a sad expression in his eyes that she thinks he is pleading with her. "Well, I'll take him."

Perhaps because the idea of handing him over to the inspector is already at the back of her mind, she attaches the lead to the dog's collar. I can visualize Chispa's collar as if I had really seen it: it's red and very broad for a dog his size, with little tin stars on it and a golden buckle. The lead is made of light-brown plaited leather.

The inspector picks up his folder and follows Ma and the dog to the other side of the house. It is he who opens the door, and the three of them climb slowly down the three steps to the ruined garden. Yet Ma listens to another comment from the inspector about how she ought to avoid prolonging the poor creature's suffering, but it is not until he is about to leave her that she finally makes up her mind.

"Wait," she says all of a sudden, holding out the lead. "Do you want to take him now? Here, and let's hope I'm doing the right thing. I'll see what I find to say to my son . . . I hope he'll forgive me."

"Tell him a lie," the inspector suggests. "Sometimes a little white lie is necessary, especially if good comes from it."

"I'm not sure if there are necessary lies."

"Leave it to me, Señora Bartra."

Chispa eyes the policeman and tries to bark, but the sound comes out as an asthmatic cough. Then he starts to tremble and paw the ground, doing all he can to resist, because he can scent danger.

"Be quiet," Ma says, turning back to the house with her hands across her stomach. "You go with the inspector, he's a good friend . . . But please, make sure he doesn't suffer," she says, looking back at the policeman.

"They don't suffer. It's all over in a minute."

"Don't describe it to me, please. I don't want to know."

"Just remember it's better for the poor animal. Come on, brave dog, come with me."

"You'll have to be patient with him, he can hardly walk . . . what happens afterwards, where will they bury him?"

"The vet will take care of all that," says the inspector, pulling lightly on the lead. "You go indoors and forget all about it. Do as I say, Señora Bartra."

Trying his best to fall into step with the dog, the inspector leads Chispa away. He pulls on the lead with his hand behind his back; in the other he is still clutching the blue folder.

A few moments later, when Ma glances at them from the doorway, she sees them walking slowly along the cindery path along the gully's edge. Both of them have their heads down, and the two of them appear to be joined together not just by the dog's lead, but by another link as well, no less real for being invisible: they look equally tame and cowed as they pursue their slow, painful walk that they seem like accomplices or comrades-in-arms. The last thing the redhead sees is Chispa lying flat on his stomach, refusing to go on, while the policeman yanks furiously at his lead.

As she closes the door, the inspector turns round and changes the lead and folder from hand to hand. He is finding it hard to conceal his impatience.

By now I am engaged in the pelvis of the story and I can see strange flashes of light, but I am in no hurry. From this bubble still protecting me from the world and its illusions, I hear stealthy footsteps along the corridor in the villa of the dead. It's my brother returning home, full of the premonition he felt that afternoon when he crouched beneath the window to spy on them and heard Inspector Galván's voice as he sat so stiffly opposite Ma, a voice so surprisingly velvety, sitting there so attentively . . . Now she is sewing in her room. As soon as he enters the house, David notices the dull gleam of the Dupont among the folds of the blanket, as if it had just fallen there and was winking at him from the exact spot where his dog should be waiting for him, wagging his tail.

He starts calling out to Chispa, knowing with a terrible certainty he will not get any response. Furtive and reverential at the same time, he bends slowly over the blanket, scoops up the Dupont, and hides it in his pocket.

God knows how long David mourned his dog's death. He had loved him so much, lavished so much care on him to try to alleviate his suffering, stroked him so often and with such affection that the palm of his hand retained an indelible memory of the patches of sparse fur on his back and stomach, of his scrawny ears and his not always cool muzzle, of the cysts and peeling skin. And it was this faithful, bitter memory that was the start of his revenge; perhaps not the direct consequence, but the germ of it, the poisonous seed. Nothing that was to happen to David in his short, intense life, none of his many private misfortunes, his crazy schemes and painful defeats, was as important to him as his dog's unfortunate death; neither the day when, dressed in rigorous mourning, crying and with me in his arms, he was taken in by Aunt Lola, nor years later when he had become a young hooligan and Aunt Lola had to go and fetch him endless times from the police station, not even when Cousin Fátima fell in love with him and he seemed happy, although deep down he still felt completely desperate – none of the many setbacks that marked his destiny, his loneliness and his wildness, had anything like the effect on him that the death of Chispa did.

The swine. The pig. The queer. Butcher bastard. Arsehole cop. I wish they'd stick a live rat up your backside so it could eat your guts.

Stop swearing like that, brother. This afternoon your mother heard you, and she's upset enough as it is . . .

You can shut up, you hairy yam. Just keep swimming round in your fishbowl and don't bother me.

He is cursing in a bend in the gully, crouching over a crack where he and Paulino often find lizards and snakes. Beside him there is a large rock on the surface of which is the clear trace of the grooves of a seashell and the whorl of another. This was because, as he explained to Paulino, a million years earlier, even before this became a river, the sea came right up here and covered everything with its brightly coloured fishes and all kinds of shells. This idea of life totally destroyed by the endless dead waters comforts him for a while. Squatting down by the crack, above and beyond the roar of real crickets or the ones he hears in his ears, he feels as though he is inside a huge shell, listening to the echoes of a rushing river that only exists for him here, a summer murmur of insects and waters from the start of time, when the gully was still a tranquil, crystal clear stream.

Fluffy clouds form over the Montaña Pelada, and as the suns starts to set, flocks of sparrows looking for their night's shelter drop from the sky like dark, heavy curtains unfurling over the twilight splendour.

"My poor Chispa! My poor dog!"

He spends the whole of the first night sobbing beneath the protective shade of Doctor P.J. Rosón-Ansio's huge pink ear, and throughout the next morning he curses and laments under his breath, refusing to speak to anyone. He walks about lungeing at the air, fists bunched in his pockets and head down until midday, when he sits on the steps outside the villa door and for the hundredth time closes his fingers round the inspector's cigarette lighter, and suddenly the tears dry in his eyes. To his surprise, he discovers he does not want to cry any more: he sits and stares at the sheets flapping on the clothes line.

Ma returned from market some time ago with her big sewing bag, and he knows she is busy cooking rice with lentils. She soon comes out to take in the dry washing, and David resumes his muttered curses.

"Still going on about it?" Ma says, pretending she is angry. "I had to do it, son. You would never have allowed him to be taken away."

"Of course not! How did you let him persuade you? How could you hand over my dog for that loud-mouth policeman to take him to the abattoir?"

"Don't speak to me like that, please . . . I don't feel well, son. Will you help me bring in the washing?"

"I can't now. Can't you see I'm thinking?"

"Fine. Carry on thinking, but hurry up."

What are you thinking, brother? You know we all love you, but just look at you! Didn't you hear Ma, or don't you want to get it? She had to decide for you. She was brave, she plucked up her courage, and now she needs you.

You shut up, bloodsucking leech. I don't have to put up with your moaning.

I'll tell you what I think anyway, brother: that piece of poisoned meat was the best way out for Chispa.

Do you know what it's like to die poisoned by a strychnine pellet? Three or four hours of agony, that's what!

OK, but don't say that to Ma, she doesn't need it. Besides, I reckon you're exaggerating.

I know what I'm talking about.

Fine.

And leave me in peace will you, ninny? It's hard to believe you're so stupid!

Fine, thanks a lot.

"Are you coming in or what, son?" Ma says. "If you're going to carry on muttering like that, you'd better go inside and lay the table. That way at least you'll have something to do."

See? She hears you and sympathizes with you. What more do you want, brother? Get up and help her. We have to be a family united in our misfortune . . .

United family my arse! This sentimental louse is a real dummy!

"Get up and go in, David. Right now," says Ma. "Come on."

He stands up, but instead of going into the house he walks over to the clothes line and picks up the washing basket. He stands next to her, and whispers as though he does not want to upset her more:

"Who actually killed him? Did the flatfoot tell you?"

"A vet friend of his."

"I don't believe it. That cop's as fake as his Dupont." He falls silent, then goes on: "And am I allowed to know where they buried him, if anyone took the trouble to bury my poor little Chispa, that is?"

"The inspector buried him himself," she says, trying to calm him. "He didn't tell me where. I'm sure it wasn't down in the gully, so don't go poking around there like you did last night. And stop sniffling. Let time do its work." All at once she takes the peg out of her mouth, leans down and plants a big kiss on David's burning cheek. "And if you want some good advice, don't waste your tears: keep them for more important things. Otherwise you soon won't have any left, and when you're grown up like me and want to cry, you won't be able to. Get that towel, will you, then we're done."

Her busy arms are aloft, the breeze ruffling the red fuzz of her armpits and the back of her neck, when Ma feels the sharp stab of pain she knows so well. All round her, the honeyed air is teeming with insects drunk with the light. The scent of lavender and the clucking of hens are borne on the air, as well as music from a radio on the far side of the river, above the three holm oaks and the rocks, in the new neighbourhood of cheap housing being built, a maze of houses with rabbit hutches and pigeon-lofts on their low flat roofs. The saffron-coloured blouse and other girl's clothing are still drying on the bushes.

"Many years ago on that hill," says David pointing at the far side of the gully, "there used to be a wheatfield with poppies."

"How do you know that, son?"

"I know because I know."

Staring closely at the colours and shapes stirring in the sunlight, David is about to grasp the foretaste of an emotional experience, even though it is still only his intuition.

You'll bite the dust, he mutters.

"What's the matter?" says Ma. "Talking to yourself again?"

"It's your belly rumbling. It's the little monkey kicking inside you, Ma."

"I don't like you calling him a monkey. Come on, time to eat."

As David is climbing the three steps into the house, he suddenly sobs uncontrollably.

"This is where he used to lie for me to treat him . . . he was almost better! You saw him. I used to put tincture of iodine on him every day, and brush his coat. He would wag his tail and stare up at me. He was so happy, even though he couldn't see me . . . Poor Chispa, poor friend! How he would have loved to run through a wheatfield with poppies . . . !"

"Please, son, don't make my life any harder than need be, I've got enough with other people . . . does it seem right to you that you cry more over the death of a dog than your father's problems?"

"That slaughterer of a cop," says David, "he could at least give back the lead and the collar, couldn't he? They're mine!"

"I didn't think of that," Ma says. "I'll mention it to him. If they're not lost, I'm sure he'll give you them back. He's not a bad person. He really isn't, David."

VIII

Real Coffee with Two Sugars

Just as with the memory of personal experiences that had seemed to us indelible, so our memory of things seen with our imagination because we never actually lived them can fade with time, disappear altogether. For an instant, I see them beside the clump of unforgettable, never seen marguerites, then they fade into thin air even as they greet each other politely: Inspector Galván, cigarette in mouth and one hand on the wall, the other in his jacket pocket or brushing his hat brim, stiff and gallant as ever; and our red-head, shoulder pressed against the doorframe, looking out calmly, one hand resting patiently on the apron covering her stomach.

"Oh, it's you again."

"I won't bother you for long. It's very hot. How are you feeling today, Señora Bartra?"

"So-so. This one has had hiccups all day long. He must have swallowed too much water," and she smiles as she adds: "that's something he doesn't get from his father, at least."

"You're in a good mood."

"Didn't you know that when they're in the uterus, babies get thirsty and drink and have hiccups just like you and me? No? Well, now you do."

"Goodness. You really are extraordinary."

She must be asking herself for the umpteenth time whether it's wise to ask him in, and I'd like to be able to tell her, no, don't do it, Ma.

"Sshh, behave yourself . . . I'm talking to my son," she explains, then goes on: "Inspector, you know something about my husband you don't want to tell me."

"What makes you think that?"

"Lots of things. The way you behave with me . . . You know I'm right. Come on, admit it."

It is just the flash of an instant, similar to the way my brother blinks in premonition as he leaves Marimón's dark-room, with stained nails and a raging heart, a long while before he arrives home, and again sees the policeman's hand fiddling with the marguerites, hears the ring on the consulting-room doorbell even before his finger pushes the button, sees Ma coming to open it even before the bell has rung; he hears and sees all this and decides to stay on the other side of the house, between the gully and the night-time door. He feels safe and secure on the edge of the void, on his own or with Paulino and his maracas, so he delays going home as long as he can, because he knows the cop is already inside offering for example two tablets of perfumed soap he has just pulled from his jacket pocket, and a packet of coffee from the other, paying no attention to her protests as she politely refuses the gifts, and saying to her brusquely: take them and don't say a word, Señora Bartra, I know you need these things. Life is very hard . . . The inspector stands there beside the table, tall, bulky, stiff as if he had swallowed a broomstick, staring at Ma as though trying to grasp some mystery in her words or appearance, wanting to be able to agree with her about something important, or perhaps wishing he could hear her say, please, sit down, I've just made some coffee with the last packet you brought . . . You say there's no news? I can't believe that with such an efficient police force as ours, with its famous nose for rooting out dangerous anarcho-trade-unionists and separatist Reds, there's been no progress in this matter, that you're still in the dark.

She brings another cup and saucer from the sideboard, puts them on the table next to hers, then sits down opposite him, hoping to get out of him all he knows about what interests her. She fills his cup, then serves herself a second time.

"You ought to take care how much coffee you drink," the inspector insists. "It's a stimulant. I don't know if I should bring you so much . . ."

"The truth, it's just what I need. There are days when I get up and if I can't have a good cup of coffee I'm useless, my engine won't start, as my son says."

"Yes, it's the same for me."

"Two lumps, isn't it?"

The inspector looks at the red-head's hand above the sugar bowl, and appears to hesitate.

"Two."

"Half a lump for me, the doctor has forbidden me sugar." She takes a sip and returns to the topic that interests her. "So there is no news at all. Not even a lead you've got through an informer, perhaps? You often use informers, don't you?"

"Yes, we do."

"Will you give me an American cigarette, please?"

As the blue spiral of smoke drifts upwards, the red-head falls silent and observes the inspector. There is a barely controlled anxiety in her voice.

"Thanks. You people in the Social Brigade know something about my husband and don't want to tell me."

"What makes you think that?"

"I'm sure of it. You must have checked everything I objected to in the file, and I'm sure you know more by now."

After a moment's hesitation, the inspector admits he does have news, but claims he has not been authorized to tell her, and that anyway it is of no importance. It is in no sense bad news, he adds, so she should not worry. Víctor Bartra is still in an unknown hideout and is presumably in good health: that is all he can say on the subject.

"How do you know he's in good health?"

"We know where he's has been hiding these past few months. We are certain of it. And it's likely that he is fine."

"Where has he been? And why is he likely to be fine?"

The inspector takes a while to respond; when he does, he sounds sad and disgruntled.

"I can't say any more for now. I promise to tell you as soon as I can. I repeat, everything is fine, better than you could imagine . . . Now, if you'll allow me, I'd like to talk about something else . . ."

The two of them sit there by the low table, chatting in the weak evening light filtering in through the window, drinking coffee and smoking with an artificial, fragile sobriety agreed on in advance, a shared secret. It is as though in the encroaching gloom of this former medical consulting-room they are knowingly acting out a forbidden social rite, forms of co-existence and tolerance long since vanished: what I now know to be an illusory hope for the future, when neither of them has any future, and all around them their emotions are being betrayed. It is the hour of day when the last light of evening is fading, and long shadows creep into the homes of the district with a strange slowness, a precise, familiar sense of affliction, especially on Sundays.

The intense scarlet of Ma's lips and another cigarette between her fingers. She glances out of the corner of her eye at the inspector as he strikes another match. She leans forward to catch the flame, he does the same and I am sure his nostrils must fill with the scent of her freshly washed red hair, untidily scooped in a bun on the back of her neck.

"By the way," the inspector says, blowing out the match, "You haven't seen my lighter round here by any chance, have you?"

"You've lost it? No, not here. I would have seen it. When did you notice it was gone?"

"The day I took the dog away. It's really annoying. It could have fallen out anywhere, I often take my coat off and leave it around . . . I've looked everywhere for it, but I can't find it," he adds, a little bemusedly.

"If you had looked everywhere for it," Ma says in her slightly mocking tone, "it would have appeared by now. You say the funniest things, Inspector."

"Well, it wasn't me who was the schoolteacher, I don't have your skills. The fact is, I'm upset about losing my lighter because it was a present from my daughter."

"So you have a daughter?" Ma says, her voice neutral, elbows in the air as she gathers up a tuft of red hair that has escaped on her neck.

So it is that thanks to the missing lighter and the daughter the inspector has mentioned for the first time, she learns things about this man she never thought would concern her. She learns that the girl is called Pilar, that she is his only child and will soon be fifteen; a few moments later she also learns that the inspector's wife died five years earlier, that he has just turned forty-two and lives quite close to there, in Calle Miguel Sants, up above Plaza Sanllehy. And that before he became a policeman he was a wine expert.

"You don't say!"

"Are you surprised? I'll have you know it's a very respectable profession . . . Even as you see me now, I'd be able to judge the fluidity and consistency of a wine for you," he says, a flash of pride in his eyes, "just by tilting the glass then letting it settle."

"You could?"

"If it doesn't stick to the glass, it's what we call a light wine. If it slides back slowly like a teardrop, then it's a heavy wine . . ."

"Goodness," Ma says with a smile, "all that would have really interested my husband . . ." her voice trails off, then she raises her hand to her forehead, and closes her eyes. "Don't listen to me. Sometimes I feel like laughing at everything . . ."

"Are you feeling all right?"

"It's nothing," she says, taking a sip of coffee. "Go on, won't you?"

When he was studying all about wines, he explains, it was before he had joined the force, and he had a girlfriend, a girl from Algeciras who was a maid in the boarding-house where he was staying, in Madrid. He studied for a diploma in Oenology and Viticulture because he wanted to be a wine expert – his father had been foreman in some vineyards in Valdepeñas. He got married, and for a few years everything went well. Their daughter was born and they called her Pilar because that was the saint's day of her birth. But then the war came and all its evils with it; one day his father and elder brother set out for Burgos with the vineyard owner, but they ran into a patrol and none of them was ever heard of again. When peace finally arrived, he went back to Valdepeñas, but could not find any work, and he was soon a widower, on his own with a ten-year-old daughter, a lot of enemies and people he owed money to, a whole string of problems, that's life. Thanks to the recommendation of a colonel he had served under in the Information Bureau in Burgos, he applied for the Police Investigation and Surveillance Department, which soon became the Politico-Social Brigade. First he was stationed in Bilbao, then in Barcelona as part of the VIth Regional Brigade . . .

"I don't know why I'm telling you all this . . ."

"Give me another cigarette, would you?"

"This is your last. Don't even think of asking me for another, not today."

Shielded by the rising columns of blue cigarette smoke, she observes him curiously as he talks. On the side-table, next to her copy of *War and Peace* with the ashtray on it, and behind the cups and the china coffee pot, the yellow-shaded lamp competes with the twilight seeping in at the window, as the inspector's voice turns to a flat rasp, only occasionally taking on emphasis, and he sits there as stiff as ever from the inner tension he feels, perched on the edge of the chair as though ready to leave at the slightest hint. He must think the moment has arrived when she sighs, gets up wearily, and says: I'm going to get my pills. When she returns from the bedroom, she sits down again with such a tired gesture and such a resigned grimace of pain or discomfort that seeing her so suddenly defeated and vulnerable, yet beautiful despite it all, he no doubt thinks how alone, distressed and unhappy this poor woman must sometimes feel, but of course he cannot pluck up the courage to tell her so.

"As you can see," she says, as if guessing what he is thinking, "My husband could be right here with me now, and yet he isn't, and I don't have the faintest idea where he is. But, do you know something? When at night in dreams I feel for his arm to lean on, it's always there."

The inspector nods and mutters that everything will be all right, Señora, your bad luck will come to an end, feeling suddenly annoyed at himself for not being able to express himself more adequately, and secretly lamenting the harsh undertone to his voice. Perhaps for the first time ever, he feels as if the words rolling round his mouth were like distilling acid. He looks at the floor, and sees the red-head's sandals at an angle, as if they were still placed around the missing Chispa.

"By the way, you still haven't told me what happened after I took the dog away. How did your son take it?"

"You can't imagine – he was terribly upset. I knew it was going to affect him badly."

"That's understandable. Animals like that are easy to love. He'll get over it, don't you worry."

"He asked if you could return him the collar and lead. And he wants to know where you buried him."

"Well, I left everything to the vet. I think there's a municipal service that collects dead animals, in which case . . . I'll find out. They probably threw the collar and lead away. If he still has them, I'll get them back."

"David would really like to keep them."

"That shows the kid has feelings," he says, once again sensing the acid taste of the words in his mouth.

"Perhaps, but the fact is I think we were wrong, Inspector."

"What do you mean?"

"I shouldn't have listened to you. We've turned that poor mongrel into a victim. David can't get him out of his head."

"Whose victim? We're giving too much importance to something that doesn't really have any, Señora Bartra. It's only an animal, after all."

"As you know, victims, whether animals or people, stay in the memory and eventually become troublesome . . . don't you agree?"

The inspector appears not to have heard. He turns the matchbox over in his hand.

"The boy will forget it," he says, more convincingly this time. "It's a fact of life. He sees it as a tragedy, and I know why. It's because I was involved, because I helped you get rid of the animal. That's the reason for it," he says, falling silent again. He has forbidden himself to say out loud what he knows and thinks of David, at least for the moment. He is secretly proud of his discretion on this score, pleased with himself for the care he is taking not to inflict any more pain or embarrassment on the red-head. The cop feels as if he has discovered a new, previously unknown emotion. "We'll still have to be careful though," he resumes after a while, "we don't want his annoyance at the dog's death to lead him to do something stupid. You must agree with me that the boy is quite a handful, a bit wild, and his character is . . ."

"He's a good son. He doesn't forget his father, he earns his keep every week and gets my rations for me. He puts up with the queues, however long they are, and helps me with my household chores . . . what more could I ask?"

"Yes, that's all well and good. But a girl would have helped you more. I don't know what you were hoping for . . . I remember my wife, may she rest in peace, wanted a girl when she was pregnant. She always said it would be a girl, and it was."

"I didn't want anything. I was on my own," she says in an offhand way as she tries to straighten the battered lampshade.

Next to it, the tall empty purple glass vase has a tiny crack that runs down the whole length of it like a streak of lightning. The silent radio looks ugly, and the oilcloth on the table is worn. There is nothing in the surroundings that looks either special or worth pointing out; and yet the red-head's calm but firm and proprietary gaze bestows dignity on them all. She reaches behind her to move the cushion against her back, suddenly feels the tautness of the skin round her stomach, and groans. The inspector immediately gets up.

"Allow me," he says, already holding the cushion and patting it for her with poorly concealed haste.

If this man were only capable of expressing out loud the anxiety he feels each time he sees the slightest sign of suffering in Ma's face or voice, if he had revealed his feelings at all during one of these first evenings he spends with Ma, I am sure I would have taken pity on both of them and would have curled up nice and quiet in my corner so as not to disturb them. But now, for example, all he does is plump the cushion and arrange it behind her. She leans back slowly, gripping the arms of the chair, and says:

"I don't know if I'm being sensible spending so much time sitting up. The doctor told me to stay in bed. As if I could, with all the work I have . . . but it's true I'm scared of a hypertrophic pregnancy."

"I don't know what that is," says the inspector.

"It's when the foetus doesn't develop or come out. I know a woman who had an embryo inside her for fifteen years."

"Good Lord."

"That's the end of the coffee," she says, pouring what's left into the policeman's cup. Watching him out of the corner of her eye, she goes on: "Don't look at me like that, Inspector. I don't like people taking pity on me. I'm sure you're asking yourself how this woman, all on her own, pregnant and sick, can manage to bring up her son and reach the end of the month just by cutting and sewing skirts and blouses, sometimes by candlelight . . . well, the truth is, I myself don't know how I do it."

The inspector ponders what he is going to say for a few moments.

"Yes, but you have received some help, Señora Bartra. And I'm glad of it."

"Some help, me?"

"Yes, you, don't act surprised . . . I've had occasion to talk to the usher from the Delicias cinema, the one who was a friend of your husband's. He was very ill. He admitted that through him Víctor Bartra stayed in touch with you regularly. Apparently, your husband left or sent letters to this Augé's letterbox, and I suppose that's how you got your extra help."

"It's true," Ma says. "I used to get letters and occasionally some money, but Víctor never told me where he was. And it was never very much money."

"Do you know where he got it?"

"No, I don't."

"Do you want to know?"

"No . . . and besides, all that had finished long before you and your people arrested Señor Augé and carted him off to the Hospital del Mar."

"Yes, I know."

The red-head looks at the inspector in amazement, as if she cannot believe her ears.

"You've known this for a while, haven't you? You knew Víctor sent me money. Why did you never ask me about it?"

"I didn't regard it as important. I didn't even mention it in my reports," the inspector says, glancing down at his watch. "Anyway, as you yourself said, those contacts dried up some time ago. Although if I were you, I shouldn't worry, your husband is bound to find some other way of sending you news, and perhaps a bit of money as well."

"Hopefully, but I don't think so," Ma says drily, getting up rather tensely from her chair. "And even if he did, you wouldn't expect me to tell you, would you?"

"I wouldn't ask you to," says the inspector, also standing up. "You can set your mind at rest on that score, Señora Bartra. No harm will come to you or your son," he says, and this time his voice is a gruff smoker's growl that comes more from his chest than his throat. "Now I have to go. Please, I can find my own way out," he says, holding out his hand.

But she is already standing by the door, and shakes his hand with apparent reluctance while gazing down at her feet, overcome with sudden anxiety. He doesn't seem to be such a bad person, he really doesn't. As she opens the door to let him past, she feels the inspector's voice and breath very close to her.

"Thanks for the coffee," he says on the threshold. "And don't forget about my lighter."

"I'll look for it again, but I'm sure you didn't leave it here . . ."

"I'm sorry your son wasn't here. I'd like to have explained to him why getting rid of the dog was best for everyone. And that it didn't suffer."

"Some other day," the red-head suggests, still gazing at the ground.

"Yes," replies the inspector, moving away from her and finally crossing the threshold, "some other day."

Our dead-end street is like a withered, scaly arm cut off from the rest of the neighbourhood on its most easterly and least populated side; sometimes, when I am crossing it curled up in my bubble, coming and going from an appointment at the Maternity Hospital or from the market stalls, it seems as though even the cats have abandoned it. August is a month that has a scorched smell everywhere, I never liked it. The gang of kids sitting on the corner seem not to have moved the whole summer long, as they sit unravelling the same intricate small talk under the scarlet splendour of a bougainvillea bush. David does not live for or listen to this talk any more, he has moved on long ago, and now walks alone down the street, hands in pockets and a marguerite in his hair, always with that look of being numb with cold despite the heat, the appearance of a child lost in a wood, yet faithfully following a voice that guides him through the darkness. No-one would think he had a riot of crickets in his ears and a bloody cloud on the horizon; he walks on oblivious to the habitual gossip, but not to the voices; because beyond the tittle-tattle about the seamstress and the fugitive Señor Bartra there has always been the lament of shared defeat, the sad insistent beat of an affront many have felt: that is the only music he hears.

On Sundays there is more life in the street, and my brother hurries quickly by to avoid the loud-mouthed neighbours and their insidious questions, their well-worn excuses to start up a conversation and then wheedle things out of him with false flattery: hey handsome, you know you're soon going to have a little brother? Where has that father of yours got to? What does that tall, good-looking policeman want from your mother that he has to come up here so often? And what about you, pretty face, what do you want to be when you grow up?

Shirley Temple with her sluttish corkscrew curls.

They laugh out of the sides of their mouths at his joke. I don't want to say too much about all this: I cannot in fact, all I know are rumours – if my brother heard me, he would kill me – that is all I have to go on. I should have liked to talk about it with Ma, when her pulse beat together with mine, when she could only hear me with her heart. Since that was never possible, I prefer to keep quiet about what I think. All I will say is that when he wanted to be, David was sweet and affectionate, the best of friends. Ask the barber's apprentice, the fat boy with the maracas.

"It's true," Paulino says, his voice thick with snot and blood. "You're the only one who doesn't make fun of me. The only one."

"Yes, but I make fun of you in other ways. But they can say what they like, you don't look like a girl. That's nonsense, Pauli. So don't get your hopes up."

"Yes of course, with my head shaven like this . . . but you've got beautiful hair. Mar-vell-ous."

"Will you pay the cinema for me? I can't get in free any more, there's a new usher."

"If we catch a lizard, I'll pay for you. It's a horror film."

"So you've got money? How many did you shave today?"

"Thirteen."

"That's an unlucky number."

"Thirteen is better than twelve, sweetheart."

Squatting on his haunches with the maracas tucked in his belt, Paulino the fat kid brandishes his cut-throat razor. David motions to him. Even before the lizard appears to bask in the sun on the stones, even before it has come out of its hiding-place, David has heard its tiny claws scraping the ground, has seen its palpitating milky stomach and its eyes swivelling like ball-bearings in the scaly weight of its eyelids. Here it comes, he says, and when it appears and lies motionless in the sunlight, Paulino creeps up on it, catches it in his podgy hand, holds it still for a moment as he slices off its tail, then lets it go again.

"Lizard, how pretty you are, lizard," Paulino chants. "Nature was generous with you."

"What nonsense are you talking?"

"I read it in *The Jungle Book*."

As he watches the lizard tail wriggling in his friend's hand, David bends down to tie up a shoelace. It is then that he again clearly hears the shot and Chispa's last, despairing howl. It must be half a league, half a league upwards along this same riverbed, up beyond the market gardens. In less than a split second, the sequence flashes before his eyes: first he hears the shot, speeding down the river until it echoes softly here in the gully, then he sees the hole the bullet has made in his dog's head, the horror of the blood and the poor bag of bones collapsing to the ground, and finally he sees the tiny grave scooped out in the darkness, a heap of wet sand in the middle of the river. He cannot see exactly where the grave might be, but from that day onwards he cannot get the flame of the shot or the smell of cordite out of his mind. He straightens up as if he was on a spring, leaving his shoelace undone. Bastard son of a bitch, he says, searching for him with his furious eyes the colour of honey.

"What's the matter?" Paulino asks. "Seen your father's ghost again?"

David turns round slowly, leaving the door of dreams ajar.

"Who knows?" He can feel his presence close by, as he squats over by the reeds the wind combs on the river bank, tilting his elbow with his trousers down and two slits in his backside, one of them dripping blood that he tries to staunch with his handkerchief, the other letting out a great big turd. "He's shitting and settling scores with the past," he whispers, looking down at the ground. "It's terrible. He's washing his wound and his arsehole in the rushing water that is sweeping down, carrying everything away . . ."

"What a load of nonsense!" shouts Paulino. "It's been more than a long time since there's been any raging water here."

"That's what you think. I bet if you farted now, you'd see bubbles. I saw them coming out of Pa's arse. Dreadful, isn't it?" David spots a yellow-winged butterfly on a lavender bush. "Is that butterfly any good to you?"

"No," Paulino says. "Remember what that crazy guy in the Cottolengo said: yellow butterflies with a red spot on each wing."

"I've never seen any. Come on, that's enough hunting for today. Let's go to the Delicias."

"No, not now. Tomorrow, for the matinée. I have to be at my Uncle Ramón's house at eight, so we could meet outside the cinema at ten."

"When are you going to cut off the legionnaire's balls with that brilliant razor of yours?" David says. "When are you going to stop being such a coward, fatso?"

The red-head's busy arms are raised to the sky as she hangs out the washing, and her wet skin glistens in the bright morning light. Radiant mornings like these seem eternal, although I imagine I only felt them through the hopeful pressure of her belly, the beating of her blood, the secret quiver of her dormant sensuality, the buzz of bees all around her and the smell of bleach in the air. Nor can I forget the silent, expectant figure of the policeman, who always brings us something whenever he calls; no news yet about where Chispa's collar and lead might be, but instead a couple of tins of condensed milk, or a packet of 300 grammes of roast coffee beans, some Viennese rolls, or simply a long-stemmed white rose wrapped in tinfoil. Are you sure you want to accept the rose, Ma? Where are you going to put it so David doesn't see?

"Quiet, you," she says, sniffing at the rose.

"What was that?" asks the inspector.

"I'm talking to my son. I think the scent of roses goes to his head . . ."

I can see David jumping down into the gully, frozen for a moment in mid-air, his arms wrapped round his knees bent tight against his chest, also in the foetal position, but beneath a clear blue sky; I can see the lizard sleeping on the rotten, uprooted trunk of an oak the waters of another age have brought here; I can see the lines of ants and the moss growing green on a fold of rock, the bramble that scarred Pa's cheek, his sad slit buttock and the pale spits of sand lying untouched in the riverbed with their symmetric, parallel wave patterns.

In the brief patches of moonlight, the Wolf Man's hairy hunchback quivers as it pushes through the fog.

"You're shit-scared already," whispers David.

"You are, you mean," Paulino retorts in the darkness.

"I can't understand why you're so keen on horror movies, when you spend the whole time trembling with fear."

"It's not that. It's just that I can't bear all this blood I have to swallow from my nose, and I start coughing . . ."

"You went to give that brute of an uncle of yours a shave, and he ended up shaving the piles on your arse, is that it?"

"Hmm, what about moving further back?"

"Close your eyes, go on, here comes the full moon again. And try to hold in your cough, I can't hear a thing."

"What am I supposed to do?"

The horrible hairy back of the monster appears on the screen, and Paulino shudders from head to toe. He coughs and spits into his handkerchief.

"Just when things were looking up," moans David.

"What do you mean?" Paulino mutters thickly, as if his nose and throat were blocked with blood.

"Well just as the snake hissing in my ears was disappearing, or almost, because it never completely goes away, then you start with your cough. How am I supposed to follow the film?"

"I've got my nostrils full of blood, that's the problem."

Shrinking back in his seat, he squints at his friend with his big moist eyes. David always remembered those looks in the darkness of the Delicias, appealing for understanding and comfort for his fears, especially the most intimate and secret of all, not the one the moon on the screen arouses as it appears from behind scudding clouds, not the howls of the Wolf Man as he proclaims another ghastly crime in the foggy marshes, but the fear he has of himself whenever he picks up the cut-throat razor.

"You're trembling, fatso."

"Has he turned into a wolf yet? I can't bear to watch."

"You're such a baby! Close your eyes."

"What's happening now?"

"Mister Talbot has got lost in the marsh."

"I don't want to see it!"

His breathing is a frothy gurgle that threatens to drown out Mr Talbot's groans.

"Imagine a wheatfield full of worlizards and poppies," David says. "That's what I do before going to sleep."

"Who is that howling now?"

"Don't look yet."

Paulino's chest gives off a strong smell of liniment; a silver medallion glints dully at his open shirtneck. He leans over towards David.

"Can I hold your hand? Will you let me?"

"OK. But only a minute."

"Let me see your nails. Are they brown or yellow today . . . ? They're disgusting, look."

"Now keep your eyes tight shut if you don't want to die of fright," David sniffs at his friend, who has snuggled closer. He wrinkles his nose: "You smell like a footballer's legs."

"It's Sloan liniment. Don't you like it? My uncle puts bucketloads on after doing gymnastics," he says forlornly. "Today he slopped it all over my legs."

"Do you think that's going to cure you? Why do you let him do it, you idiot? The first time I saw your uncle I could see what he was like," growls David, remembering the man with the split lip and the white topee he saw one day with his great paw on Paulino's head, like someone stroking a child who is about to throw up. "You have to be careful. Go on, you can rest that stupid great head of yours on my shoulder if you like . . . but keep still. Is that better?"

"A bit."

"I'll tell you when you can open your eyes again, when the Wolf Man has changed back into Mister Talbot . . ."

"Yes, when it's all over."

"Or are you scared of Mister Talbot too?"

"No . . . but if you look carefully, that guy is almost as ugly as the Wolf Man," Paulino says, and joins in with his own nervous cackle when he hears David laugh. He starts coughing again: "I'm sorry, I'm not doing it on purpose."

"I know, fathead, I know."

The film stops and the lights come on. David takes advantage of the interval to go to the toilet.

"I'll come with you," Paulino says.

"No," David tells him, "you stay here in case someone comes and asks for me."

As he pees facing the wall with his feet treading in a sticky slime, he reads the anonymous graffiti drawn or carved on it, and suddenly gets the feeling that Chispa is watching him from somewhere, his tiny sad eyes peering out from behind a fringe of hair. He bursts into tears, then stands there for a good while, staring at the gouged wall and thinking of Chispa, his little prick hanging out, shaking it as he cries.

Out in the auditorium, the film starts up again to a whir of guttural voices and macabre music. David looks at his face in the speckled mirror, rubs his eyes as hard as he can with the back of his hands, then rejoins Paulino, who sinks down gratefully on his friend's shoulder, sniffing in the darkness. And what does David do, or let his friend do, while he is concentrating on the abominations Mr Talbot commits under the moon's baleful influence? His only reaction is from time to time to move his face away from the faint smell of sulphur coming from Paulino's shaven head, to avoid the mixture of bad breath, blood, and his barely stifled coughing fits. Then he feels his friend's hand touching his thigh, and hears his throaty voice:

"What smooth skin. Not a single spot or hair or anything. Un-for-gett-able."

"Get lost."

"What's this little bump?"

"What little bump?"

"Here, in your pocket."

"Ah, it's a lighter."

"Where did you get it? Can I see it?"

"It's a gold Dupont. I found it."

"Holy shit, what a stroke of luck! Where?"

David thinks for a moment.

"I'm not going to tell you."

"Why not, sweetheart?"

"Because you have to be careful. If you go around telling the truth, you get found out straightaway."

"Found out straightaway?"

"Anyway, it's not a real Dupont. It's fake, can't you see? Not that I care. Look, dummy!"

He flourishes the lighter in front of his friend's bloody nose and then, with a practised thumb movement, he lifts the lid, spins the wheel of the flint, and the flame spurts from the tinder. For a brief moment, holding the warm metal in his fist and seeing his friend squinting fascinated at the flame, David feels invincible, eternal. Then he pushes the lid down with the same thumb, clunk! and the flame vanishes. As it does so, a blue shadow slowly detaches itself from the silver light being projected on to the screen, and comes to a halt in the aisle beside him.

"Come with me, kid," the shadow whispers hoarsely.

A young man crammed into a greasy overall lays a hand on David's shoulder, grabs him by his shirt collar, pulls him from his seat, and leads him towards the exit. David glances at him out of the corner of his eye: it's the projectionist. Has he left the projection room and been replaced by someone, or is he working that night? As they reach the mouldy green entrance curtain, the man stops and takes a crumpled, sealed envelope out of his pocket.

"Hide it," he says, as he hands it over. "Do you know what it is?"

"Yes, sir."

David slips the envelope under his shirt as quickly and with the same secret emotion as when it was Señor Augé giving it him.

"From now on," the projectionist says, "I'll be the one. Understand, kid?"

"Yes, sir. What's going to happen to Señor Augé?"

"I don't know. Tell your mother I've taken his place for the handovers, but not for long. I've got other things to do. And don't come to the matinée. Come the first Saturday of the month."

"Señor Augé is going to die, isn't he?" says David. "That's why he gave me his dog."

"It's the best thing that could happen to him."

"To the dog?"

"To both of them. But I don't know anything. I don't want to know what's in the envelopes or where they come from. All I know is they're left at the box office for your mother. The same goes for you. Get it?"

"Yes, sir."

"I have to get back to the projection room. Don't forget: the first Saturday of the month. But don't look for me, don't come up to the room. I'll find you."

"Yes, sir."

David is confused – he is struggling to get out a whole jumble of questions. In the darkness he catches the gleam of the projectionist's pupils, his greasy hands and the tip of an equally oily handkerchief poking out from one of his overall pockets.

"You're Fermín, aren't you?"

"That's my name. But don't use it much."

"I wanted to ask you a favour. Señor Augé used to let me in for free, but the new usher doesn't know me."

"Tell him I've sent you and he'll let you in."

"Can I bring a friend?"

"Of course. Now be off with you, and make sure you don't lose the envelope."

"The film isn't over."

"OK, but afterwards, run home as fast as you can."

It was a friend of my father's, he tells Paulino as he sits down again. Once again the full moon slowly and fitfully crosses the night from one side of the screen to the other. Paulino shuts his eyes, shudders, and stretches his claws. They both laugh, and play at being brave in the darkness in spite of the film. Their laughter mingles with Mr Talbot's howls.

"It's true there is a lot of resentment nowadays: you can see it as soon as you go out in the street and talk to people, but that resentment comes from the fact that a lot of them are paying for past mistakes. What I mean to say is that almost everyone has something to hide . . . We live in a dreadful time, Señora Bartra. Just by telling the truth, you can ruin someone's life."

"When you talk about the truth," the red-head replies sarcastically, "you are of course referring to the truth as this regime sees it. But we all know what that truth means: everyone is guilty, everyone is a sinner, so everyone is worthy of being forgiven and of doing penance. That means there are no mistakes when it comes to handing out justice."

"You're thinking of your husband again."

"No, I'm not thinking of my husband," she replies, filling their coffee cups. "Two lumps?"

Still looking closely at her, Inspector Galván nods. As he stirs the sugar with his spoon, he puts on his gentlest, slightly artificial voice.

"Do you know that until recently, in the bar next to police headquarters, I never took sugar with my coffee? Not two or one or even half a lump of sugar – nothing at all. But you remember the first time you offered me a cup? You asked me if I took sugar, and I said I did: I still don't know why. I realized what I had said and I could have changed my mind, but I didn't and then you asked: one lump or two? and I said two, but I couldn't explain why I said that either . . . it was very odd, and I still wonder what made me do something like that."

After a silence, the red-head says:

"Well, that's your business."

"I suppose," the inspector says hesitantly, "I didn't want to upset you."

"What nonsense. Why would I get upset if you said you didn't take sugar, if that's how you like it?"

"I've told you, I can't explain it."

"Well, anyway, it's not important."

"Nothing like that had ever happened to me before," the inspector insists. "Never."

"Well, you must have had your mind on other things . . ."

"No, I wasn't thinking of anything else. It's very strange, isn't it?"

"Why does it seem so important to you?" she says, starting to feel uncomfortable.

"No, I know it isn't. But see, you think you know your own tastes, you're used to a series of things, your own habits and routines, no? And then one fine day . . . The fact is that ever since then I've drunk my coffee with two sugars, and not just here in your house, but in mine as well, and in bars."

"Goodness."

"And would you like to know something else? Before I met you I used to drink quite a lot."

"Yes? And now you don't?"

"No, I don't."

The red-head stares at her guest, somewhat taken aback.

"You changed the topic of conversation, Inspector. Why was that?"

The inspector considers what he is going to say, then speaks softly:

"Because you shouldn't get excited, Señora Bartra. Remember what the doctor says."

"How do you know what the doctor says?"

"I know you have to take pills. I've heard your neighbours say you've suffered from high blood pressure since the third month of your pregnancy . . ."

"I hope that's all you've heard," she says, smiling through the cigarette smoke and the aroma of coffee, the rim of the cup against her pink lower lip, protruding as though anxious for contact. Without taking her eyes off the inspector, she continues: "Well, let's hope that one day you do bring me a piece of good news. You know what I mean."

But for now what the inspector has brought, after she sets the tray with the freshly made coffee on the low table, is not exactly good news: the dog's collar and lead that David was so keen to get back have almost certainly been lost. The vet does not have them, and does not remember removing them, he's very sorry. As well as his usual gifts of a blue packet of roast coffee beans and a quarter of butter – thanks, you really shouldn't have bothered – this Saturday he has brought two bars of chocolate for David in the hope that they'll somehow make up for not getting the collar and lead back. But what was truly shocking was the fact that he arrived carrying a white rose. He held it casually behind his back, flower pointing downwards, wrapped in tinfoil. Here, put it somewhere, he mumbled with a hasty gesture, as if the tinfoil was burning his hand. The sister-in-law of a deputy inspector friend of mine has a florist's near here, whenever I pass by she's always insisting I take a rose . . . I only half believe you, Ma says with a barely disguised smile. Deep in her heart she feels a stab of gratitude, sadness and affection, the consequences of which she finds it hard to judge. She stares straight at the inspector, who shrugs and says hoarsely: Do what you like with it. There is another silence, and he adds: If you don't want it, throw it away . . . Why make such a fuss? Of course I want it, she says, the rose isn't to blame for anything.

It is a white, open rose. I can almost smell its perfume when the red-head lifts it to her nose. Now it is spreading its delicate fragrance from the vase on the side-table, between the lamp and the radio. Is it wise to accept it? I ask her heart. As she bends to sniff it again, I jerk my head and she whispers not now, please, behave yourself will you? and closes her eyes and bites her lip.

The policeman glances at her, concerned and serious.

"What did you say?"

"Nothing. This little devil just did a somersault, that's all . . . but let's talk about what interests you, inspector, what is supposed to be the reason for your visits. Look, I'll tell you once again: you know things about my husband you don't want me to hear."

The inspector looks sullenly down at his hands. He says nothing. Whatever the feeling may be that brings him to the house so often – a mixture of compassion and guilty conscience, together with that more secret desire he has experienced since his very first visit – if what he is trying to achieve is for his silences to seem more eloquent than any words he speaks, then today he has succeeded. Expectant, and still looking him in the face, Ma grasps the arm of the chair and straightens her back, unashamedly encircling her belly with her other hand as if trying to stop me falling, or at least prevent me giving her another untimely head-butt in the pelvis. Be still, darling, don't pester me. I'm watching over your dreams. An imperceptible smile lights up her pallid face and, her eyes still on the man sitting opposite her, she says out loud:

"You have to behave, because the inspector here has something important to tell us."

"Let's see," he says after a pause, his voice thick with smoke and saliva, "I'm not sure this is very wise. I don't want to add to your worries by revealing something which in reality is not that important . . . I'd prefer not to upset you."

"Why would it upset me? What's happened?"

"Nothing that can't be dealt with, I suppose," says the inspector. "But you're not used to this kind of procedure, so I don't know whether I'm doing the right thing . . . sometimes we get information from informers, but it's not always trustworthy. They lie out of self-interest, you see, so they get better treatment."

"Say it straight out for once, please."

The policeman ponders for a moment, then starts to speak slowly, still looking down at his hands.

"As I already told you, we know where your husband has been these past few months. As I also said, I didn't have the authority to tell you, but I reckoned as well that you wouldn't be too pleased to find out . . ."

"What has happened to Víctor?"

"It's all right, nothing has happened to him. He's fine, I'm sure, wherever he may be. What happened was that your husband was the indirect cause of a misunderstanding . . . but let's begin at the beginning." He clears his throat, raises the tips of his fingers to his lips as though he were praying, and goes on: "In mid-July, two months ago now, we arrested someone who had been an usher at the Metropol cinema. We found clandestine publications on him, and a diary where he had written the initials V.B. and the address of a villa in Sarría. Do you remember I asked whether you knew a certain Widow Vergés, and you told me you didn't . . ." – at this point, the red-head tries to butt in, but the inspector will not let her – "Well, you lied about that, but it's not important, let's forget it for now . . . OK. On the 20th of July, we carried out a surveillance operation on her villa, and by chance, just a few minutes after our two men took up their positions, a man came out of the house carrying a bulging briefcase. He had not gone more than five steps towards the garden railings when he took a hip flask out of his case, came to a halt and took a swig straight from it. He was tall and dark, the spitting image of Víctor Bartra. When he emerged from the garden he was intercepted, and he behaved so suspiciously that he was taken to headquarters for questioning. This individual maintained he was a door-to-door encyclopedia salesman, and knew nothing about the lady who owned the villa. He said he had shown her some pamphlets and a volume of the work, she had spent a few minutes talking to him, but had not placed an order. His briefcase was found to contain pamphlets and catalogues from a publishing house, and his papers seemed to be in order. However, there was something incorrect about his ration book, his signature or the date, and his behaviour still appeared suspicious, with the result that he was given a thorough interrogation."

"You mean he was beaten up."

"Please. There was a misunderstanding which the individual in question himself contributed to with his confused and contradictory statements; he became frightened and tried to escape, and the affair ended in an unfortunate accident. That's what happened. As a result, his presumed relationship with Señora Vergés and your husband remained unproven, but by no means ruled out . . ."

"What happened to the man?"

"He took advantage of a moment's inattention on the part of two policemen to jump out of a window. He's in the Clinic, in an irreversible coma, I think. It was a slip-up, an unfortunate accident," the inspector hesitates, "or perhaps an attempted suicide, who knows . . . Anyway, as I was saying, it proved impossible to reach your husband through him, so our investigation turned to the owner of the villa . . ."

"Don't go on, please . . . Just tell me what all this has got to do with Víctor?"

"Wait a moment," the inspector says. "I was coming to that. It so happened that the incident with the salesman only served to confirm our suspicions about the activities of the lady who owned the villa in Sarría. I thought she would deny any knowledge of Víctor Bartra, but quite the opposite happended. A remarkable woman, that Señora Vergés. She thought it was very funny we had confused a door-to-door salesman with Señor Bartra . . ."

"Oh she did, did she? Why did she think it was so funny?" the red-head says, keeping as tight a rein on her nerves as possible.

"Señora Vergés admitted she knew your husband well," the inspector goes on after draining his coffee cup. "Right from the start she had no problem admitting he had been, and still was, a close friend of hers."

Ma leans back in her chair and says nothing. Then she picks up the coffee pot.

"More coffee?"

"Yes, thanks."

"So that's Angelines the 'cocktail-shaker'," Ma says after a while, controlling her emotions. "That's what my husband's friends used to call her. The 'cocktail-shaker'. I hardly knew her, a drunk introduced me to her once in the doorway of the Bolero club, where I went with Víctor . . ."

"Are you sure we're talking about the same woman, Señora Bartra?" says the inspector. "A very smart, dark-haired woman about thirty years old and looking good on it, a rich widow with no children. She lives with her elderly mother-in-law and an unmarried sister-in-law."

He takes the pack of Lucky Strikes from his pocket and offers it to her. She pulls a cigarette out between her nails, and there is something both coquettish and mysterious about the way she flourishes it and leans towards his lighted match. The inspector pretends to look relaxed as he smells the perfume of her hair. Casually, he asks if his lighter has turned up by any chance. No, no sign of it.

"First of all, you should know that over these past months your husband was not hiding out anywhere in Penedés or in La Carroña or any other village down there, as he perhaps led you to believe . . ."

"Are you telling me he was in that villa the whole time? Is that what you're telling me, Inspector?" Ma says, screwing up her eyes in the cigarette smoke.

"We don't know for sure. My opinion is that he was," the inspector says in his usual flat monotone. "Of course, Señora Vergés flatly denied having offered help or shelter to Señor Bartra, and said she was unaware of any subversive activities he may have been involved in. You should have seen her. Cool as you like and without the slightest hesitation – taking advantage of the fact that she knows a lot of people in the city, including several in high-ranking positions – she alleged she was completely unaware of the fact that this man who had been a great friend of her husband's was now being pursued by justice. She said he turned up unexpectedly at her villa at midnight on the 7th of April, in a sorry state and the worse for drink, as if he had been in a fight. He told her he had had a row with his wife, and she believed him because she knew he was a very . . . how did she put it? a very impulsive man. From that point on, I didn't believe the half of what she said, Señora Bartra. She admitted having asked him in, and said they had dinner and talked together, and he had told her of his intention of leaving immediately for France on business. Early the next morning they said goodbye, and she never saw him again . . ."

"So? I wonder why you refuse to believe her explanation," Ma says calmly.

She is about to say something else, but the inspector anticipates her:

"I've found it very difficult to talk to you about this, Señora, and if you'll allow me, I'd like to get it over with as quickly as possible." He hesitates once more, then goes on: "For your own good, I would have preferred to talk about something else . . . Where was I? Ah, yes, I was saying that this, in general terms, was what Señora Vergés told us. However, we know she wasn't telling us the whole truth. It's true she put him up that night, and treated a small wound he had on his . . . here on his . . ."

"His arse."

"Yes, that's right. It's also true they dined together, and they probably did talk about his trip to France; but that wasn't the last evening they spent together, in fact it was the first of many, because the trip only happened much later . . . the lady being who she is, we have only been able to make discreet enquiries, and we've also talked to her mother-in-law and the servants. All three of them had been forewarned by the widow, but there were some contradictions in their stories. Well, I'd like to spare you the details, Señora Bartra . . . but we have reason to believe your husband spent three or four months hiding in this person's house," the inspector explains, crushing his cigarette end in the ashtray with unnecessary force. "From April to the beginning of July. In fact, he escaped by the skin of his teeth, he was very lucky. If we had been watching the villa a week earlier, he would have been caught."

"You don't seem too upset about it," Ma says with a forced smile. "Tell me, why are you so sure my husband hid in that woman's house?"

"Don't you believe it?"

"I'm inclined to agree; it's possible. But why are you so sure of it?"

"There is a report," the inspector says, then adds after a while: "the truth is often unpleasant. But there it is, Señora Bartra."

The red-head says nothing, squeezing the coffee cup between her fingers.

"The report," the inspector goes on, "was not included in his file because it was considered confidential. It seems this lady has got very good contacts, you see. But the facts are there . . . they were already friends, I suppose, and remember your husband was being pursued that first night. Let's say that he intended to stay the night, and ended up living with her for several months, because he felt safe there . . . Goodness, I don't blame him," the inspector adds in a falsely convivial tone, "I'm sure I would have done the same myself."

"Oh, sure."

"Look, I know you were hoping for good news about your husband, and believe me, I would have given anything to be able to bring you some, because

I appreciate the situation you are in. But if you think about it, that villa was no more than a temporary refuge. To someone on the run, everywhere is temporary . . ."

"It's getting late and my son is about to arrive," Ma says, her face pale as she leans on the table to help herself up.

As she straightens up, she grimaces with pain, and slips her hand under her swollen belly as if afraid once again that the placenta will become detached and I will tumble out on to the floor tiles. There is something both obscene and tender in her gesture that does not escape the cop's attention. He comes over to help, and I like to evoke him through these loving shadows because these are the only caresses of his that I can still feel on my skin. It's nothing, the red-head says. The inspector lays his hand gently on her shoulder. Do you need anything? Sit down – I'll get you a glass of water or your pills. She does as she is told, places her hand on top of his, and sits looking up at him. She is breathing heavily through her half-open, generous mouth, and her light eyes reflect the confusion that the inspector's consideration arouses in her. He quickly moves his other hand and places it on her forehead to feel her temperature. I don't think you have a fever, he says, keeping his hand where it is. For a few moments his fervent blood beats at the red-head's temples, and she surrenders to the unexpected balm of his hand. What a silent obsession it transmits. How the policeman suffers, how he feeds yet controls his desire. Ma lowers her sweating brow and looks down at her stomach, this child, she says. As she bites her lip and spreads her legs wider she imagines me, I know she is imagining me, that in her innermost fears she is picturing me and her hopes for a more intense, happier life than the one she has known. This child.

"I'm fine now," she says. "When I'm awake and get an attack like that, it's not a problem . . ."

"I don't understand. I'm worried about you, Señora Bartra, I think you don't look after yourself as you should."

"My nightmares are worse than this, you know. Sometimes I have a horrible dream that my son will be born with some deformity because of these pains . . . that something will go wrong."

"That's nonsense. I'm not even going to listen to you."

"I was thinking about it today, and I wanted to ask you something . . . I've thought it over a lot . . . you know that the only relative I have left is my sister Lola, and if anything were to happen to me, I'd like you to get in touch with her . . ."

"Nothing's going to happen to you."

"Let me finish, please. You have to promise me you'll get in touch with my sister. Promise me you will. You know she doesn't think much of me, but there's no-one else."

"All right, I promise. But let's not talk about it any more. Put the cushion behind you. No, not like that . . . sit up straight."

"But it feels more comfortable like this."

"No it isn't. Put the cushion behind your lower back, go on . . ."

"Whatever you say. But first, give me another cigarette. Go on, be kind."

"No, I won't. That's enough for today."

"Please," the red-head says, a mischievous glint in her eye. "Don't you think I deserve it?"

IX

The Gold Dupont

"Imagine my mother dressed in black from head to foot," Paulino says, stropping his razor on the belt hanging by its buckle from the dead fig tree's roots, "and blowing my Uncle Ramón's whistle for all she is worth. My poor sainted mother gets all of a flutter over traffic policemen. The white uniform, the topee, the leather straps, the whistle, she loves it all. And she can't stop bursting into tears . . . at table after lunch on Sunday her beloved brother – that is, my brute of an uncle – put his topee on her head and whistle in her mouth, so she was laughing and blowing it for ages. Christ! The din she made, and she reckoned she was doing it for me, to show me how wonderful it is to be a traffic policeman and have a whistle to blow. That's how stupid my mother is, David. She went on and on at me to try it, but I told her no, I said that the sound of traffic cops' whistles hurts my ears, that anyway it'd make me sick to put it in my mouth, and that she was being ridiculous. So then she started crying and Uncle Ramón smacked me round the head. And my father was sitting there with his cigar and his glass of aniseed, without even daring to open his mouth as usual . . . what a heap of shit!"

"I think you're laying it on a bit thick," says David.

"My father's chicken, but my mother is something else again . . . remember I told you Inspector Galván stopped my father in the street one day and warned him about us, told him to keep an eye on us, and that my father got scared as a rabbit and played dumb? Well, believe it or not, he went to see my mother as well."

The cop had come out of the florist's shop in Calle Cerdeña, and in his hand – you won't believe this either! he was carrying a rose. OK, that's nothing new, we already know he takes your mother roses, but you should have seen how he was holding it; not like you or I would do, straight up in the air trying not to break the stem; no, he held it downwards, he was swinging his arms and waving it about as if it was a stick or a twig he'd just found in the street, as if the rose had nothing to do with him. Some men are really crazy! The thing is, a cop feels ashamed to be seen carrying a rose in the street, David says, because he thinks he's too much of a man for that. Or perhaps the guy is just a bastard, says Paulino. That too. He's a bastard and a swine. Well, he was on his way to your house with the white rose, but as he was crossing Plaza Sanllehy he decided to drop in on us, it was on the way and he remembered the street and flat numbers: second floor at the front, no lift of course, welcome to the distinguished Bardolet Balbín mansion, barbers to elderly cripples and paralytics . . .

A woman in mourning opens the door. Her face is so thin and she has such a sad expression that the inspector hardly recognizes her – neither does yours truly sometimes, but she is my mother and as we all know, there is only one mother in this life of ours.

"Is the barber at home?" asks the inspector.

"What do you want?"

"Are you Paulino Bardolet's mother?" he says, flashing his police badge at her and keeping the rose hidden behind his back, he doesn't want her to think it's a present for her, now does he?

"Oh, my God, what's happened?"

"I'd like to talk to your husband, Señora. If you please."

"He's not at home."

"It's about your son."

"Paulino? What's he done, why have you come looking for him?"

"Calm down, no-one is looking for him. I just want to give you a piece of advice regarding him . . ."

"What's happened? Oh my God, if only they would listen to me!" Señora Bardolet suddenly bursts into tears. "If only my husband would listen to me instead of roving around all day! He always was a no-good . . . if only we'd handed the boy over to my brother, who used to be a legionnaire, perhaps you know him? He's the only one who looks after the boy properly, and besides, he's a traffic policeman now . . ."

"I know," the inspector says, intervening curtly, swinging the rose to and fro behind his back. "Look, I've come to warn you very seriously Señora. Your son has . . ."

"Wouldn't you like to come in?"

"No, this won't take long. Your son has a friend of the same age, you must know him, his name is David Bartra and it so happens his mother is a friend of mine. She is very worried. Those two rascals spend the whole time on the streets, out of control. David has missed his work several times and arrives home late at night, and Señora Bartra has made a complaint."

"I haven't heard anything about it."

"And in addition, your son sometimes has deviant tendencies, Señora, so . . ."

"Holy mother of God, don't say that!"

". . . so have a word with your husband and see what can be done . . . look, Señora, what can I say? We know your husband was against the regime. We won't bring that up again, but I want you to keep a close eye on your son if you don't want the authorities to get involved."

"Deviant! My poor son a deviant!"

"In short, he is to leave Señora Bartra's son alone, because she thinks their friendship is harmful. I don't know if I'm making myself clear. He is not to see him any more, because he's a bad influence on him. Do you understand?"

"Yes, sir, yes."

"It's nothing serious, but he should find other friends, understood, Señora?"

"I knew something like this would happen. But nobody listens to me in this house . . . how dreadful!"

"Come on now, don't cry. It's just a piece of advice . . . I told your husband the same not long ago."

"What can we do?" the woman asks, sobbing. "He . . . he's . . . no . . . not su . . . such a bad boy, he never gets into fights or does anyone any harm . . . he's reliable, and he likes music: his father and I often take him on Sundays to the Cristo Rey church, there's an organist there who teaches the kids music, and besides, his uncle wants him to join the Traffic Police when he's old enough . . ."

"Well then," the inspector interrupts her once more, anxious to be off, "so it's clear then, is it? I don't want to see your son with Señora Bartra's boy, or there'll be trouble."

"Whatever you say, sir, whatever you say. Oh my God, how awful!"

"Talk to your husband. You've both been warned, so goodbye for now."

She stammers a goodbye, her eyes lowered to the floor, and slowly starts to shut the door. At that moment, as he turns round, the inspector drops the rose. He bends to pick it up, and can feel the mournful, tear-stained eyes of this simple soul staring at the back of his head. He stands up, and turns back towards her, rose held high. He hesitates for a moment, looks at the rose, stretches his arm out and says:

"Here, put it somewhere," then turns on his heel again, and vanishes.

Early mornings with David lost in thought lying flat on his back on his bed, his eyes wide open in the darkness, clutching the hot, solid, chunky Dupont in his fist, waiting for his opportunity. Opposite him, Doctor P.J. Rosón-Ansio's ear seems to be listening closely to his thoughts, and to the chirupping of the crickets down in the gully, all the neighbourhood's night-time sounds as they filter in through the skylight. Sleepless and voracious, the huge pink hearing organ displays its multicoloured labyrinth of membranes, canals and passages, pierced by tiny arrows that refer back to names, scientific references and explanatory notes printed in the margins of the poster. David knows some of them by heart: "Cochlea or spiral canal. Contains the endolymphatic liquid which receives and transmits sounds from the external world and alerts the sensory cells which in turn activate the auditory nerve connected to the brain."

His gaze slides from the ear to the RAF pilot's incipient smile, and beside him the tense, open-mouthed German soldier shouting as he points his sub-machine-gun at him. He'll be the first to shoot, he thinks, and shortly afterwards he is not sure whether he is reading, dreaming with his eyes open or in his sleep when, exhausted by the heat of the night and the metallic whirring in his ears, naked on his sheet and still staring at the airman shot down and taken prisoner above and beyond time and legend, he suddenly hears the unmistakable scrabbling of Chispa's tiny claws on the floor tiles as he crosses the threshold into his room and approaches his bed. He does not want to look at him or treat him as though he were a ghost; he is not frightened or at all surprised that a dead dog is visiting him.

What do you want, Chispa? he whispers, and immediately realizes he is thinking out loud. What are you doing here? he asks, raising himself on one elbow. Didn't that bastard cop send you to the other side?

Still infirm and restless, but without the infinitely sad look in his eyes, the dog stops at the foot of the bed, sits on its hind legs, and looks up at his master, head tilted quizzically to one side. His head and part of his droopy ears are covered in a bandage with red cotton edging and a big pink stain in the middle.

Yes, I'm dead. But tonight they've let me out for a while.

Are you a soul in torment then?

No. I'm a basset hound and I feel fine.

That's not how it looks.

Some people are not how they seem, as you well know.

Is this where they gave you the German injection in your nut? David asks. He looks over at Doctor P.J. Rosón-Ansio's all-powerful ear and adds with controlled fury: was it so bad they had to put a bandage on it?

No, kid, no, says Chispa, it wasn't an injection.

Well then, don't tell me because I think I already know . . .

Careful, everything can be heard here.

The dog looks askance at the doctor's ear listening to them so openly it is almost obscene. He cocks his head and scratches the bandage with his back leg.

I'm feeling a bit giddy, he says.

Are you hungry? Would you like a sugar lump? We always have white sugar now, and tinned milk and coffee . . . they're gifts from the person who killed you. But don't imagine he brings us anything out of this world, and besides the swine pays himself back drinking the coffee all the time, and talking a load of ballyhoo.

He keeps her company, kid.

Yeah, company, do you think I don't know what that son of a bitch is really after? Oh, sorry, it's just an expression.

Yeah, I know, only an expression.

Listen, do you want some leftover rice and beans? I'd give you chocolate, but you know your belly aches afterwards.

No, not now. Now I can eat anything I like.

Would you like me to wash your eyes with thyme water?

No, I'm fine. I just came for you to scratch my belly a bit.

Climb up on the bed then and lie down on your back. That's right. Do you like it?

I liked it better when I was alive and full of fleas.

Tell me something, Chispa. Inspector Galván treated you badly, didn't he? And he shot you down in the gully, didn't he? You never reached the vet's, did you? Tell me the truth.

Walls have ears, the animal whispers, staring at the central spiral of the doctor's ear out of the corner of his eye, as if frightened of being sucked into the huge organ at any moment.

I reckon he did for you, and I want to know, David insists. Chispa puffs and blows, then growls. David says: louder, I can't hear you. I've got my ears full of fizzy pop tonight.

I was saying you should be careful not to make a mistake. As I told you, some people are not what they seem.

Yes, it's true, David admits, still scratching the dog's quivering, muddy belly with his fingernail. I know there are people who are not what they seem; but it's also true, daft dog, that there are people who do not seem to be what they are. For example, that swine of a flatfoot. And I'm going to show him up once and for all for what he really is, what he has always been, what he cannot help but be . . . Look, you wouldn't understand, because you're a good dog and you're sick and you've got a bullet in your brain.

Can I sleep a while curled up at your feet, like I used to? Your mother won't find out.

Go on then. Even if she did find out, she wouldn't believe it.

Later, the bubbles of fizzy pop give way to the persistent buzz of a saw, and then to the distant waters of the river roaring like underground thunder in God knows what night of time. Even so, David manages to reach a deeper level of sleep, still clutching the Dupont lighter in his fist. Now he sees a young man, the collar of his jacket turned up and a cigarette dangling from his lips, just like the one he saw once in the toilets at the Delicias cinema at the very moment he was loading a magazine into the butt of his gun with a sharp slap of the hand. It's our brother Juan, a good few years older. He no longer smells of musty gunpowder, there is no dust on his clothes now, and there is no splintered bone hanging at the end of his severed leg. He must have a wooden leg, and he looks so elegant now he's silver-haired at the temples and has a pistol, he looks just like an actor in a gangster movie.

What are you going to do with that lighter? he says before vanishing from David's sleep. Think carefully, brother.

At about two in the afternoons at weekends, an olive-skinned girl with dark eyes rides along the path at the top of the gully on a man's bike. She wears a yellow skirt with big green pockets, a saffron-coloured blouse and a red beret. She always pedals furiously in the direction of the market gardens, head down over the handlebars. The heat haze rising from the riverbed at that time of day distorts her silhouette hunched over the bicycle, making it float in the air and quiver as though it were a reflection in water, a shimmering mirage. Tied by two straps to the bike frame, a black violin case is visible between her legs as they pump the pedals.

"Did you see that, fatso?"

The red bike and her golden head of hair disappear behind the reed-bed like a flame flickering and going out in a mass of green-striped vegetation.

"Yeah, real cute," Paulino says, brushing sand from his trousers as he stands up.

David returns to the business at hand. Despite the beating sun, he opens an umbrella, and Paulino falls in beside him, hands down by his sides and head held stiffly erect. For some time, wretched but stubborn, the two of them stand to attention like soldiers on parade, sheltering under the black umbrella while the crickets chirrup all around, eyes fixed on the ground. It is not raining, but it will always rain on this tomb: the rain they conjure up in deepest summer is more real and lasting than the sun. It would be good to have a headstone with his name on it, David thinks, choking back his tears. Then the rain could wash his name from time to time, and in autumn a mantle of leaves would cover it . . . As if he can guess what his friend is thinking, Paulino says:

"Wouldn't you like to put up a cross with an inscription on it?"

"No," growls David. "It's just to know where he is."

"So you think this is where he is buried . . ."

"How am I supposed to know?"

Paulino considers it, still sheltering under the umbrella they share.

"Well, anyway, it would be a good idea," he says eventually. "On tombs in the desert there's always a cross with an inscription on it . . ."

"What inscription or cross or holy shit are you talking about, fatso? Do you want the flatfoot to find out?"

Paulino shrugs and says nothing. Whether it's true or a fantasy, a possibility or a magic spell, this is where Chispa is, beneath the innocent whiteness of the freshly heaped sand. All you have to do is look and believe, and that is exactly what Paulino does. After a while, still standing to attention, he whispers:

"Would you like me to recite a poem for him?"

"I can't hear you, I've still got fizzy pop in my ears."

"You could give me a drink!"

"You don't know what you're saying, fatso. Have you ever stopped to listen to the sound bubbles make when you pour some pop into a glass? It goes: psschuuss . . . ! That's the sound I've got in my ears, multiplied by a thousand."

"Jesus!"

So they stand shoulder-to-shoulder in the middle of the rocky riverbed, their feet on the trampled tip of a spit of sand, erect under the tattered, funereal umbrella, both of them sheltering not from the relentless sun but from a persistent imaginary rain, weather more in tune with the dark rage the seamstress's son has felt for the past month. He has a kind of bitter ash in his mouth, but he prefers to stay silent so that he can hear the murmur of the rain on the umbrella, the earth, and the small makeshift tomb he has built with Paulino's rapid and diligent aid, a small heap of spongy, wet sand they have just finished piling up. The spectre of his beloved dog will enjoy eternal rest beneath this unknown mound on the outskirts of the city.

His fingers stained with blood, Pa does up his flies on the river bank, staring with disbelief as his piss is absorbed and then swept away by the raging waters that have suddenly appeared once more. That's the way it is, son.

"If it rained a lot, really rained now," David says, "the torrent of water could come rushing down here again and take everything away with it, just as it did years ago; my father told me about it when I was very little. The rushing river carried everything away with it, even a sidecar with two soldiers in it, and a horsebox . . . Now the water would pour over Chispa's skeleton without touching it, at most it would strip him of his lead and collar: he must still be wearing them because the inspector didn't take them."

"A bit further up would be better, in the shade of a tree," Paulino says. "Why do you never listen to me?"

"No, here," says David, thinking to himself, this is the spot, in this obscure darkness beneath my feet. "This was where he killed him, I know it."

"Now you'll have to stand there and listen, because I want to recite a very pretty poem for your dog that I learnt in second year," Paulino says, clearing his throat and gazing down at the tomb. He begins: "If haughty Rome, on Numancia's fall, / thought courage and loyalty were no more, / the centuries showed their fault to all; / the fathers died, their sons sprang to the fore . . .'"

"Very pretty, dummy."

On the way back home, David asks him:

"Tell me something, fatso. Have you ever dreamed of a crime you committed?"

"What do you mean, I committed?"

"Did you ever dream you killed someone?"

"Why are you asking? Because of my uncle?"

"Have you dreamt it or not?"

"I never have dreams."

"You must dream something. Everyone does."

"I can't remember . . . oh, yes, I once dreamt that Errol Flynn was asking me if I had a sword handy. Quick, kid, give me a sword! he said, leaping in front of me. And then he took me to the Jorba Stores and bought me a lovely woollen scarf, for Christmas I remember . . . Errol Flynn himself! Weird, wasn't it? But I swear I've never dreamt I was killing anyone. I've thought about it, but never dreamt it."

"Well, I have," says David. "Not that I was actually killing a person, but I dreamt somebody told me I had killed someone, and I believed them and said: OK, so what? I took it for granted. It's not the same as killing someone, but it almost is, and it's a really odd sensation. Wouldn't the normal thing be for you to think: I'm a murderer, now I've become a murderer? But you don't, you don't suddenly think you're a bad person, or feel strange, or remorseful or unhappy or anything like that. Somebody says: listen, we know you killed so-and-so, and you believe them, it seems normal to you, and you're happy as could be. You're a murderer and yet you couldn't give a damn!"

"I don't like having dreams. I don't like it at all," Paulino stammers, overcome by a fit of hiccupping as David folds the umbrella to go inside. "'Bye, see you at the Delicias this afternoon."

Three hours later, Paulino very slowly eases his big behind into a stall seat at the cinema.

"The way you're sitting down, it looks as though you've got a thistle up your arse," David says, laughing. "The day you're least expecting it, that donkey'll shove a broomstick up there."

"I'm fine," whispers Paulino, but his hiccups are back and he is sobbing quietly. "This time he only beat me on the backside with the flyswat . . ."

"It was easy enough to see all this coming. So why do you keep going to his place, dumb-bell?"

"Because he gives me a good tip for shaving him, he buys me cakes, and lets me clean his gun for him . . . What can I do, David?"

"Fine then, let him beat you up. And let me watch the film."

After a while, Paulino stops snivelling, although he can't control the hiccups.

"What a lovely smell. It's your hands: they smell like Viennese rolls."

"It's the developing fluid," grunts David.

He leans back in his seat, puts his feet up on the row in front, and screws up his eyes to focus more closely on the cat-like grace of the young farmhand as he draws his gun from his holster.

"Who's playing Jesse James?"

"Tyrone Power," says Paulino. "He's the dark-haired guy. He's got a snub nose and a smile that really sends me . . ."

"He's too handsome to be a Wild West gunman."

"Nobody's ever too handsome, are they David?"

"I don't know. Who cares?"

"Don't you like the film?"

"Yes, it's not bad."

"What's wrong then? Are you sad because of what Uncle Ramón did to me?"

"Would you believe it? So Jesse James was a poor farmhand after all."

"Why are you surprised? In the Far West everybody was either a cowboy or a farmhand."

"Look at him. He's too good-looking. He's better when his kerchief hides half his face, and all you can see are his eyes."

"If you say so. Do you want some peanuts?"

"No."

"Some sherbert?"

"No."

"Would you stick your finger in, please?"

"What have you had to eat?"

"Green beans with bacon."

"No chance. After that my finger stinks of farts all day long."

"I'll give you an almost new bottle of Varón Dandy lotion I pinched from my uncle."

"Is it full?"

"Almost."

"OK. The Varón Dandy lotion and everything you've got on you right now."

"You really take advantage, don't you? You've no right."

"What have you got?"

"Seventy-five cents, a nail-clipper, the sherbert and a new nib I've got . . ."

"It's a deal. But I'm only putting it in and pulling it out."

"Twice."

"If I do it once, you come . . ."

"Good God, you're completely shameless."

"Take it or leave it."

The first Saturday in the month, at the Delicias cinema. The government newsreel, a film about the war against the Japanese, then a Western, then the newsreel again and then the war film starts again, and there they are sprawled in their seats, still waiting. No sign of Fermín with the envelope.

Follow me, says David. They go out into the foyer, slip past the attendant, climb up to the first floor and look for the projection room. David knocks on a small door that opens gently an inch or two as he does so. The whirring of the projector, the rattle of machine-guns on a beach in the Pacific, the howls of the Japanese as they are run through by bayonets or fall head-first out of palm trees, all combine to drown out his tapping. David is about to knock again more loudly, when they hear a soft and sticky woman's voice from inside – it's like she was talking eating a banana, Paulino says: a voice that sounds as though it's coming from the film. It must be one of the Guadalcanal soldiers' girlfriends, he adds in a whisper. What are you talking about, dummy: women don't eat bananas in a war film, David protests. It must be the projectionist's girlfriend then. Listen. Paulino grabs hold of his arm to stop him calling out. The fruity, glutinous voice rings out once more:

Before I suck it, show me the eight pesetas, sweetheart. Don't go thinking you've paid by giving me a milky coffee and half a sardine sandwich.

Later. Trust me.

Like hell, you swell. I'm giving you a discount anyway . . .

David and Paulino can smell the acetate and, peeping in through the crack in the door, they can make out part of the cabin, which is only about three metres by two altogether, with its pair of Erneman projectors and the floor littered with black corkscrews of film that the projectionist pushes away with his foot as he sits back on top of the canvas reel bag to finish his beer. He is wearing a vest, has a dirty bandage round one hand, a black eye and marks of being beaten on his arms. Opposite him on a low chair is a young black-haired woman smothered in lipstick, wearing a tight skirt and a low-necked blouse revealing a black brassiere. She is wolfing down a large chunk of bread with mortadella and balancing a plate and cup on her knees. She has taken off her high-heeled shoes and placed them beside her. Behind them, the grimy window opening on to the Travesera de Gracia lets in the screech of trams and the sound of car horns.

I've just changed the reel, sweetheart, Fermín says in a wheedling voice, so we've got twenty minutes. Go on, stop stuffing yourself, you'll end up fat as a cow . . .

There's no need to shout, or to be so rude.

But every fuck we have costs me an arm and a leg!

What about me keeping you company, big man? What about that?

I haven't seen you in two months, you liar! Aargh . . .

Take it slowly now, the woman laughs. You're so hot for it, one of these days we're going to set fire to all these films in here.

That bloody scar on your knee is redder than ever.

Want to know why, my little thief? Because as soon as I see you, I light up . . .

Oh yes, I really believe that. But it's an ugly scar.

Take a look at yourself, sweetheart! You look like Christ on the cross! What happened to your eye and hand?

Sticking my nose in where I shouldn't have, that's what, growls Fermín, then his voice is drowned out by the explosion of hand-grenades in a machine-gun post. David and Paulino see him turn round, and duck back out of sight. He has just noticed that the door is ajar, and kicks it to, but even so, as the sounds of battle on the beach and the dying, guttural cries of the Japanese fade away, they can still clearly hear the sweet-talk from inside:

But you're still as handsome as ever, so don't worry, she says, and Paulino believes that beyond the sounds of chewing and slurping he can detect a romantic note.

"It's his girlfriend," he says.

"What a dummy you are," David replies. "Just listen and shut up."

Take your bra off, go on, there's a honey . . .

Before I do, tell me who made such a mess of your eye.

I told you, I got it for doing a colleague a favour.

Tell me about it.

You wouldn't be friendly with any policeman, would you?

Who do you think I am, sweetie-pie? I don't want anything to do with the cops.

Do you still have one nipple bigger than the other, honey? Let me see it while you finish eating . . .

What trouble are you in with the authorities? I don't like the sound of that.

A stupid mess! On Monday morning while I was setting up the film two of Barcelona's finest came and asked me a whole lot of questions about old Señor Augé, an usher here – you must have seen him sometimes. I told them all I knew about him: that he had got ill, but that he was a good man. So then these guys get hold of me and frogmarch me off to headquarters in the Vía Layetana. They put me in a kind of cellar and right away started in with the third degree . . . do you know what that is, honey? When they interrogate you with everything. I didn't even understand half the questions . . . I only ever get about half of what's going on around me as it is, that's the way I am.

Yes, you are a bit slow on the uptake, Fermín. And pretty rough with it.

Well, anyway. I was simply trying to do someone a favour. A special favour, it's true. Nothing serious, just giving them news from a loved one . . . Come on, let me take your bra off, sweetie, so at least I can enjoy looking at you . . .

Take your big hairy paws off me.

Oh, so now you're the Queen of Sheba, are you? I have to put on silk gloves to touch you . . .

I might like that.

"They love each other passionately," murmurs Paulino.

"My arse! Will you be quiet?"

Another fusillade covers the projectionist's pleading voice, then shouts and orders to attack, followed by complete silence and the rustle of silk, the swish of waves on the shore of a beach littered with bodies beneath a Pacific moon.

"What's that? He's taking her stockings off," whispers David.

"She's not wearing stockings," Paulino says, "didn't you see? Anyway, girls don't let their boyfriends take their stockings off."

Don't touch me with that filthy bandage, she says. What did they do to your hand?

You won't believe it, Mercedes. First of all the pair of them tried to scare me – they were both deputy inspectors. I think. There was a brand-new pair of pliers on the table, with red handles, but they didn't use them. But one of them, the fat one, hit me with a wet piece of rope, here and here, look, and then in the eye. The pair of them were furious, and they were obsessed with one thing: they had found a key in my pocket and thought it was for a postbox where I picked up political propaganda and messages, like Señor Augé had done, that's what the son of a bitch said the whole time . . . I got tired of telling them it was only the key to the first-aid box here in the projection room – the one over there, look. They would have none of it. Then one of them said: listen, arsehole, we know you, we know you're the blue-eyed boy of the FAI, you used to go to a bar in La Cera street, a real anarchist rathole, and you get together with others from the Entertainment Union to distribute *Solidaridad Obrera* hidden in the sacks for film reels. So I said to him, what are you talking about, go and get stuffed, Deputy Inspector Bonehead, that's all water under the bridge, you're a heap of shit and I'm the blue-eyed boy who fucks your sister, I said it straight out . . .

You're crazy, sweetheart!

The thing is, when I'm pushed, I can't control myself, love, I'm capable of anything . . . but then the other cop took out his pistol – they had me sitting down with my hands in cuffs on a table top – so he takes out his gun and starts pounding with the butt on this hand here. I saw stars, Mercedes! But it's what happened next that you're not going to believe.

No, I'd rather not hear. See what happens when you get smart with them, and when you lie?

I didn't lie, the key is the one to the first-aid box. Go on, take your skirt off, that's right . . .

Hey, be careful, don't ruin the zip . . . you're very hot today, aren't you, sweetheart?

"It's his girlfriend, I'm sure of it. Can't you see she's crazy about him?"

"And you're so dumb it hurts, Pauli. Let me hear them, dammit!"

Well, if you weren't lying, why didn't you tell them to come and try the key here, then they'd have seen you were telling the truth and stopped beating you?

Mercedes, my love, that's not how it works. They wanted to frighten me so that I'd spill the beans about something else.

173

What else?

Hang on a minute, I don't know if this reel is rewinding properly . . . Yes, it is. It'll soon be finished, so get a move on, will you, sweetheart?

You might have had a bit of a wash, darling, you're going to get grease all over my cunt . . .

Then the door opened and another cop came in. This one was an inspector, and he looked familiar. I'd seen him once outside the front of the cinema talking to Señor Augé. He told the brutes to leave me alone, said hello in a friendly way, and offered me a cigarette . . . You know how in films there's always a good cop and a bad cop? Well he was the good one. He sat down beside me and said: You're friends with Señora Bartra, aren't you? I've only ever seen her once, I said, and it's true. Then he stared at me, and I thought he was going to ask me lots of questions, but he didn't. He stood up and said I'm sorry about these two, they're good officers just carrying out orders, like I am, like all of us here. He said he was very busy and couldn't spend much time on my case, which he was sorry for because he knew this pair, they're brutes whom nobody can control, so if you have anything to say you'd better tell me now . . . I'm not lying, I told him, this key is for the first-aid box in the projection room. I just kept repeating that over and over, until the guy grew tired and left.

Is that all?

Of course not! The two apes went on at me for another half hour, then set me free. They didn't even offer me a glass of water. Ah, and I was forgetting the worst thing that happened to me . . . Oh, but you're beautiful, sweetheart.

Weren't you dying for it? What are you waiting for?

Just a minute, love, while I put the next reel on.

What's that?

It's the ratchet that opens and shuts the film lens. Don't touch it . . . touch me instead, sweetie, get hold of it . . . no, wait, now comes the best bit. The last straw! We were still down in the basement, I was swearing my head off and my hand was smashed to a pulp, when all of a sudden the door opens again and in comes Inspector Galván, smoking a cigarette. When he sees me he says: what's he still doing here? I spoke to the boss and he's not interested, so let him go, will you? He himself took off the handcuffs, went to the door with me and held out his hand. Goodbye, he says, anyone can have a bad day, but in the future be careful, eh? so stay out of trouble . . . then he goes and turns over my damaged hand, which was hurting like hell, he turns it palm upwards and stares at it as if he were going to read the palm like a gypsy. That's what I thought, but I was wrong. Do you know what he did?

His ear pressed to the door, David imagines Fermín's crushed hand between the cop's paws: a lizard tail writhing in the bloody palm.

How on earth would I know?

You're not going to believe it. I thought he wanted to check whether they'd broken any bones, but what he did was take the cigarette from his mouth, flick off the ash . . . We don't have an ashtray, he said with a sad smile, as if he thought it was the best joke in the world . . . and then used my hand as his ashtray! And not content with flicking the ash on me, then he stubbed the thing out in my hand! Just like that!

What an evil bastard!

But I didn't say a word, I wouldn't give him that satisfaction.

Good heavens, my love, how could you bear the pain? Why did he do such a terrible thing to you?

I suppose it's just normal for those brutes. That's the way they are. You see one of them in the street and you think they're like you or me, but they're not. Anyway, come here, my little princess, I've got another little sardine to show you . . .

More landing craft roar through the waves and crash on to the beach at Guadalcanal. David can see every last detail of the scene. The Japanese machine-gun post has fallen silent.

I'm no hero, I'm just an ordinary guy, a soldier says, flat on his stomach on the beach. I'm only here because someone had to do it. I don't want any medals. All I want is to get the job done and go home.

Huddled together and weighed down with equipment, under their steel helmets the frightened faces of the Marines are splashed with foam and fears of death, but also the smell and taste of the lipstick on the mouths of girlfriends or whores, there is a photo in a dead soldier's wallet, and white thighs freed from a short skirt, the hand singed by the cigarette squeezing her buttock . . . David knocks more loudly, and this time they hear him.

"Who the hell is that?"

"It's me!"

"And who are you, dammit?"

"Señora Bartra's son!"

The whirring of the projector and shouted commands, curses, shots, and a woman's laugh that is not from the film. The door opens, and the projectionist's tousled head pokes out.

"How on earth did you get up here? Don't you know it's forbidden?"

"My mother wants to know what happened to this month's envelope," whispers David.

"It's finished. There won't be any more envelopes. At least not from me. Tell your mother so."

"What happened?"

"Nothing of any interest to you," Fermín grunts. "Tell her if she gets any news, it won't be through the same channel. And there's no need for you to come to the cinema."

"But you'll let us in free like before, won't you . . ."

"Yes, OK. Now scram! Go on, be off with you!"

They run out into the street and run arm in arm up Calle Escorial, eyes on the ground and hands in pockets. Paulino still has his doubts.

"Well I think she was his girlfriend."

Feeling giddy and with stabbing pains in her temples, Ma gets up from her Nogma sewing-machine after two hours of pedalling and lies on her bed for a while. David arrives soon afterwards, sits beside her and holds her hand. He tells her what the Delicias projectionist said, and also about the interrogation and the way the policemen roughed him up, and Inspector Galván's intervention. He does not mention the gratuitous violence of him stubbing out his cigarette on Fermín's hand.

"I thought something must have happened," Ma says.

"Now what are we going to do?" David asks.

"Wait and see," she says with a sigh, then goes on: "Just as well the inspector was there."

"Why just as well?"

"I think he always knew how we got the bit of money your father sent us: when and thanks to whom. Even though we couldn't have told him where it comes from, because I don't know either, he turned a blind eye. It was his way of helping us. That's why he let Fermín go as well."

"Why would that flatfoot want to help us?"

"Because deep down he's not a bad person . . ."

"Yes, he is! He feels a bit sorry for us, that's all, especially for you, because you're sick and pregnant and have to work so much; that's the only reason," David mutters, lowering his gaze. Then he adopts his sweetest voice and adds: "Do you want to know what he did to Fermín before he let him go? He stubbed out his cigarette on his hand."

"What's that? Someone must have been joking at your expense, son. It can't be true."

"Yes it can. I heard Fermín telling his girlfriend."

"His girlfriend?"

"She was with him in the projection room."

"Ah, well I expect he was showing off a bit in front of her . . . That'll be it. He wanted to impress her. I can't believe the inspector would do anything like that . . . It must be Fermín boasting. Your father could tell you about those youngsters in the Libertarian Youth, they're very enthusiastic and generous, but they're a bit wild and unreliable. Like your father himself, in fact. So he invites his girlfriend up to the projection room, does he? That Fermín has got some cheek. What's she like?"

David thinks for a while before replying. Before he answers, he has another question.

"Why don't you want to believe me, Ma?"

"Of course I believe you, son! Fermín is the one I don't believe . . . Anyway, what's his girlfriend like?"

"She's blonde and blue-eyed, very elegant and sweet, but a bit slow . . . Paulino is crazy about her. He says she has a voice like a banana."

"He said that? What strange things your friend comes out with."

"Yes, very strange. He's such an idiot."

"David, listen."

"What's up, fatso?"

"Have you ever dreamed you were flying with your arms outstretched?"

"Of course. Thousands of times."

"I was thinking. What if you and I hadn't seen each other for ages, and one day we met when we were both flying and we hugged each other with our eyes closed . . ."

"Why closed?"

"Just because, don't butt in. If we hugged like that with our eyes closed, what exactly would be the first thing that came into your head to remind you of me? A smell, a song, a film, a flower, a stiff prick, a dream, a poem . . . ?"

"How should I know? What crap you do talk!"

"Go on, think about it!"

"Don't start with your nonsense, Pauli."

"Please!"

"Can you hear the wind whistling in the electricity cables? That's exactly the sound I've got in my ears. So count me out, kid."

"Please."

A few moments later, David admits defeat and growls:

"A flower."

"What colour flower?"

"White. A white rose. Is that OK, dummy?"

"Yes, that's nice." Paulino switches his razor from one hand to the other, and goes on: "Those aren't electricity cables, they're telephone wires. And it isn't the wind whistling in them, it's the voices of frightened people calling each other from far away, trying to get in touch . . . Listen!"

X

Paulino's Razor

Bam! It's now or never, kid: you're not going to be a dummy all your life, I thought all of a sudden, bam! and I could even swear I shot out the word while he was washing the blood from his neck with a towel, Paulino says. My uncle had gone into the bathroom and was standing naked in front of the mirror, scratching his armpit. He felt for the towel, and I said to myself: it's now or never. Bam!

"Why was it that moment you decided?" asks David. "Or had you already made up your mind?"

"I wish I knew."

"They say it was an accident, that the gun went off by mistake . . ."

"I wish I knew, I tell you."

He describes what happened as if he was sleep-walking, as if it had nothing to do with him. It was after he had given his uncle a shave in his bachelor apartment in Calle Rabassa and they had eaten mussels and mayonnaise for lunch (the kid eats nothin', he's disgustin', according to Uncle Ramón) and the two of them were there in the dining-room with the scorching sun and the stench of boiled cabbage and Floyd massage oil. Now's the time, he thought, you don't even have to put your trousers and shirt back on, nobody's going to see you. What are you waiting for, put an end to this nightmare of beatings and cursing and licking and biting, of stifled cries and the eternal refrain of "I'll make a man of you, nephew, by these balls of mine I'll make a man of you."

Bam.

"But what happened, Pauli? What a scandal you've caused. They say they're going to put you in a reform school."

"They're taking me straight to the Asilo Durán. Thank God!"

"But what happened?"

He tells the story as if it were a dream. The ex-legionnaire had threatened yet again to kill him if he said anything at home, then went into the bathroom, leaving the door open and looking at himself in the mirror, hairy arms on his hips, waggling his ears with pleasure. From where he was sitting at the dining-room table, Paulino could see the corner of the corridor and the bathroom, his uncle's back even hairier than his arms, and the disgusting tattoo on his high, dark arse. His topee, uniform and the always immaculate white straps and harness were hanging from the back of a chair, the only things in the line of fire between the barrel of the 9mm gun and the ghastly mermaid. Paulino, head on the table that had been pushed into the corner by the recent violent thrusting, still with its cloth and dirty plates and the razor, the brush and the bowl of soapy water, none of which he will use again for a long time, the next time they'll shave you in hell, picks up the Star automatic in his limp hand. His uncle is in front of the mirror drying his foul-smelling armpits on the towel. He has a smiling mermaid tattooed on his buttock, a souvenir of his time in the Legion. His prick is a corkscrew like a pig's, silent and damp as a snake. You bastard traffic policeman with your white topee and your white harness, you've ruined my life. What else can you do, I told myself, how else can you escape from all this shit, there's no other way out, Paulino, butterfly wings and lizard or worlizard tails are no use any more, however many David catches with his penknife, he's so eager to help, you can't imagine how much I thank you for that, how much I appreciate you, but the fact is that all that crap never did anything for my piles, it's no use lying to myself any more, no use begging my uncle to stop, no use crying, it's all over, no-one can cure me, I can't take any more. So it's now or never.

The shadow on the wall shows a hand seizing the gun, then slowly turning back on itself like a snake's head until it is pointing at the boy's forehead.

"Did you really want to shoot yourself, dummy?"

"I wanted to see the flame spout from the gun barrel."

"Did you really think you could see the flash before the bullet shot out? You can't really see it, Pauli, especially not if the sun's in your eyes. You never understood how these things work."

"But I did see it. I saw the flash even before I pulled the trigger, and even before that I saw the tiny spark of the detonator go off, but by then I wasn't aiming at my own head, I had the gun firmly in both hands and I was aiming at the mermaid on his arse, I think."

You think? What happened? Don't cry. We only want to know the truth.

I don't know.

Why fire two shots?

I lost control . . .

What were you aiming at?

I don't know officer, sir.

You're only making it a whole lot harder on yourself. What were you aiming at?

At a lot of places, a lot of things . . . First I aimed at a calendar, then a photo of Uncle Ramón tacked to the wall, then a pestle he shoved up me once, then the topee hanging from the back of the chair, then my own head . . .

Did you really want to shoot yourself, you nincompoop?

No, sir. I only thought about it. First I tried aiming at myself, to see what it was like . . . I wanted to know how it felt with the gun barrel between my eyes.

And you didn't take the magazine out.

No I didn't, sir. I had to do it with the magazine in, and the safety catch off. Everything had to be for real. All make-believe, but for real anyway, with real gunpowder and real bullets . . . everything except the tears, that is.

You'll have all the time in the world to cry in reform school. So don't start again.

All right. I'm fine.

When did you start crying, before or after you fired?

Before. But they weren't tears of rage, that's why I couldn't really tell what I was doing. I was crying for myself, for all my bad luck, sir. That was why everything went wrong.

So why did you fire a second time, if you say the first was an accident? It's obvious you intended to kill him. Why?

"It was an accident, David, that's why things went wrong. He turned towards me, and the second bullet could have killed him . . ."

"If you'd made up your mind, why didn't you do it earlier, when you were shaving him?" says David, his voice as quiet and soothing as a balm. "You couldn't have had a better opportunity. One slice of the razor across his jugular, and that would have been an end to it. No-one would have suspected a thing – nothing more than a silly accident by a barber's apprentice."

"I did think of it. More than once. But there I was, aiming at his arse . . ."

"Yeah. Bam . . . at the smiling mermaid you'd had stuffed in your face so many times . . . I'm sorry, I didn't mean to remind you of all that."

"It doesn't matter."

"Tell me something, Pauli. Did you really miss?"

"I don't know. I was aiming at the mermaid, like I'd done before. But I didn't mean to pull the trigger, at least I don't think I did . . ."

"You don't think you did. And you missed."

"I hit him in the other buttock."

"But they think you hit what you were aiming for."

"Yes."

"Well let them think that, because that's what you should have done: hit what you were aiming at."

Bam. The first bullet hits the gluteus and penetrates some five inches in, slowing up in the mangled flesh and blood. The second smashes into the washbasin. You spent so long cleaning and oiling the gun with those soft and eager hands of yours, you raised the gun so often and aimed it at the traffic cop's hairy arsehole, you perfected your aim so stealthily, so furtively, slathered over it, savoured it. And then you missed, you poor dummy. Unbelievable.

"Well, next time."

Among all the sounds that afflict David's tortured hearing day and night, the whine of the mortally wounded Spitfire still acts as a soothing ointment.

Achtung! Hände hoch!

He opens his eyes suddenly and lifts himself up in the bed on one elbow. He is relieved to find he is still clutching the inspector's lighter in his right hand. Shot down by the German batteries, the Spitfire's engines are still throbbing. The column of smoke rising from its fuselage is thinner and blacker now, and the two soldiers pointing their guns at him seem even angrier. David cups his chin in his hand and screws up his eyes, searching for the pilot's defiant gaze among the flashes.

Why are you smiling, Flight Lieutenant?

What else can I do in a photograph?

Aren't you afraid they're going to shoot?

I couldn't care less. You can't imagine how boring it is being in a photo and not doing a thing. Or what's worse, simply being propaganda for the Third Reich on a magazine cover, as if I were a trophy. I'll climb down for a while and stretch my legs.

Wearily but nonchalantly, Flight Lieutenant Bryan O'Flynn drops his stiff arms and pummels his thighs. He takes his helmet and goggles off, loosens the scarf round his neck, uses it to rub a bump on his forehead, then sits on the end of the bed and crosses his legs. In his charred hand he is carrying a white rose.

Bueno, let's see what's so important for your father to tell me. The Flight

Lieutenant smells the rose and smiles. O Rose, thou art sick! I've brought it just to annoy him.

Is my father coming? David hears himself say.

It won't be long before you see him sitting on this very bed, breathing that chloroform breath of his all over us. But before he gets here, and ruins your sheet with his blessed haemorrhage, I'd like to talk to you.

Good.

I'd like to know what *la pelirroja* told you about me.

Who?

The red-head! Your mother!

David is doubtful, and screws his eyes even tighter. The outline of the white rose disappears.

What she told me about you? Nothing.

Your father then.

I can hardly remember. It wasn't much, and it was so long ago . . . He said he brought you across the mountains from France four or five years ago after you were shot down the first time, and that you were here at home while the British Consulate fixed papers for you to get to Gibraltar, because you had to hand over a suitcase with a part from a German submarine.

Fantastico! You could say, *chico,* like the poet did: Once a dream did weave a shade O'er my Angel-guarded bed. But . . .

Go get fucked, Bryan O'Flynn, Pa's ruined voice roars under Doctor P.J. Rosón-Ansio's huge ear.

. . . But what your father didn't tell you – and we'll see why in a moment – is that when I left for Gibraltar, I didn't take the suitcase with me. That day I told your father that as the Franco police were keeping a close watch on me, for security reasons it was better for the case and its precious submarine part to stay here. Someone, possibly even myself, would come and collect it later on, I said. What your father didn't know is that when I left this house, the part was no longer in the case . . . *Bueno,* in fact it had never been there.

David has to close his eyes even tighter if he is to see and understand. There is nobody now under the doctor's ear. In the pilot's smouldering hand, the perfume of the rose mingles with the smell of burnt nails, confusing David. But only momentarily:

That part never existed, did it, Flight Lieutenant?

It's true, it was a kind of joke. *Mira,* it all began with a lie I told your father as we were crossing the Pyrenees, when I saw how he liked to *empinar el codo.* Boy, he really liked to drink! In the suitcase I had documents and two bottles of the best French wine, Château d'Yquem. They were a gift from a lady and I wasn't prepared to share them with anyone, least of all this walking sponge who had already downed two bottles of brandy. I was very grateful to your *padre* for helping me cross the frontier, but everyone is faithful to their fondest memories in their own way, *lo siento*. So I invented the part from the *submarino alemán* made from a new metal that would be of tremendous interest to the Admiralty, in order to make sure nobody opened the suitcase . . .

Is that all? David asks, disappointed.

There is something else. The fact is . . . I was looking for an excuse to come back to Barcelona.

So that was why you left the case with the bottles of wine in our house?

There weren't any bottles in it by then either. Your mother and I drank one of them one night over dinner, when your father wasn't there. I drank the other *solito* the next day, because I felt sad. Since I intended to leave the case here, I substituted the bottles and the documents for two iron bars, a couple of rusty bike rods I found among the rubbish in the gully . . . like I told you, I needed an excuse to come back.

What did you want to come back for, Lieutenant O'Flynn?

The pilot lets the question float off in the darkness. David peers at his long freckled face, hovering indistinctly in the air as though disappearing into a cloud, then re-emerging. Beneath it, the blackened hand holding the white rose looks like a forlorn claw.

Why did you need an excuse to come back? David insists.

Bueno, I suppose you are owed an explanation. Flight Lieutenant O'Flynn sniffs the rose before continuing. Because that way your father, who had to go back to Toulouse on other business, would not be suspicious if he found out. The idea was that I was coming to get the suitcase, *entiendes*? That and nothing else. Let's just say it was rather underhand of me, but I did it for the sake of your *valiente padre*, so as not to cause him more problems than he already had . . . he faced a lot of danger both in Spain and in France, which is why we should forgive him if he drank a bit too much or often flew into a rage over nothing. All I wanted to do was to say hello to your mother: we'd become great friends. I suppose you ought to know that as well . . . anyway, what happened then was I couldn't pilot a Spitfire any more – just look at my hands – so I was given other missions, and the war went on and on, and it was a long time before I could get back here. I had a good opportunity at the start of June last year, a few days before the Normandy landings, but in the end it proved impossible, and I had to wait until only a few . . .

Why don't you damned well shut up for once, you heroic fighter pilot? The other voice roars again, exploding like a banshee in the darkness. Loud-mouth! While you're at it, you could add that after you left you wrote Rosa countless letters. You could tell the boy that as well, after all, he had them in his hand before he burnt them on the red-head's instructions – she'd already torn them into a thousand pieces anyway . . . go on, tell him that too!

Pa is perched on one buttock at the other end of the bed, the bottle squeezed between his thighs. Curiously for him, he looks meek and vulnerable, and is busy lighting the stub of his cigarette without taking his eyes off the Flight Lieutenant sitting opposite him. By now there is no way he looks dignified or presentable. The features in his puffy face look disjointed, as if like all the things in Ma's kitchen they had swapped places: not only are his teeth not in properly, but his nose does not seem to be in the right spot, nor the manly lines on his cheeks, nor his penetrating gaze or the look of humorous disdain that always characterized his high, thick brows. The only thing that seems to be in the right place is the slit on his backside. It's hard for David to compare his wretched appearance with that of the Irish pilot of his dreams, but he bites his tongue and says nothing, simply wishing that his father might at least have a wound in some other part of his body, could be wearing a bandage round his head for example, or be using his scarf as a sling for an injured arm, or have a black leather patch over one eye . . . anything that looked a little more decorous.

Or isn't it true? Pa says, tossing the lighted match over his shoulder. Go on, spill it all for the seamstress's boy.

It's true, O'Flynn admits with a shy smile, scratching the back of his neck. They were naïve letters, full of poetry, clouds and tigers and worms, dark impulses and lonely flights that ended in nose-dives, the terrible symmetric spiral. The blame for it all, he says, seeking out David's sleepy face with his piercing blue eyes, masked by the clouds of smoke, is down to my private passion for poetry and my public weakness for red-heads, not necessarily Irish in origin . . .

Go get fucked, Bryan, invincible ally!

Roger. Message received. *Gracias.*

Don't go on with your nonsense, or you'll have me to answer to! Pa insists. Why did you have to tell the kid all about your little tricks and your poetic clap-trap, you RAF dandy?

Weren't you planning to tell him one day? Aren't you a *padre responsable*? Doesn't the boy have a right to the truth?

As he replies, Pa is staring at the golden Dupont in David's hand: you have to deserve the truth. That's something my son is learning for himself, and in the best possible way.

Best possible for who?

For the fatherland, of course! Pa exclaims, folding the bloody handkerchief over and once more pressing it with great care against his raised buttock. His rolling tongue propels the disgusting cigarette butt from one end of his mocking lips to the other. Your problem, Allied warrior and honoured arsehole pilot, is that you're stuck in your own legend and you're unable to return to this country for what really matters! Like so many other invincible heroes of your sort, you've forgotten the cause you risked your skin for so many times in your pretty little Spitfire . . .

Bryan O'Flynn raises his hand to be heard.

Un momento, por favor. You're talking about the cause, our common sacred cause? Just take a look at yourself, Víctor my friend, and tell me what you see, take a look at your blessed bottle, your ghostly, unshaven face and your slit backside, your pathetic disguise as a loser on the run, take a good look and tell me what that cause means to you.

To me it's what it has always been: everything that didn't come out how you expected it to. A rice stew, for example! And anyway, don't imagine I've changed all that much. I'll always spit on the words and the faces of the powerful, because they are the ones who carpet their path to glory and their trumpeted love of the fatherland with dead bodies.

What things you say, Pa.

How wonderful and how boring your heroic pilot is becoming! Can't you see he's a complete bonehead? The difference between your father and this guy is that I am trying to think of a different, more worthy way of life, whereas this R.A.F. rosebud still thinks he's a winner. And you can't imagine the horror that's going to bring us!

So you don't celebrate our great victory over fascism, O'Flynn says.

I never raise my cup until someone's filled it for me.

David lets his father's resonant voice die away in the darkness, then looks at Flight Lieutenant O'Flynn. He pauses, thinking of all the questions he has never had answers to:

So how many days did you spend in our house the second time you were here?

One night, just one night, the lieutenant says.

Why don't you stick your tongue up your own arse, Bryan O'Flynn? Pa's disarticulated voice resounds again. Or would you prefer me to shove the whole of the nose of your famous Spitfire up there?

You can say what you like, you won't rile me. I have *una vida excitante*, I come and go from horizons of fire and emerald, over the rainbow, *mi amigo*, I'm a fighter pilot, a dreamer. I'm romantic, enchanting, intrepid. I slide through the air like a worm slides through rose petals, because a lonely desire for pleasure brought me to this tumult in the clouds, to this immaculate silk . . .

Victory is nothing more than an illusion dreamt up by stupid, conceited men, Pa growls, staring at David. And in my opinion showing off like this scoundrel does is disgusting. The true victory is that clump of marguerites your mother has managed to grow outside the door . . . But I'm not your mother. She always wanted to live by a moral code, and that's why some of her memories trouble her so much now. So don't try all this shit on, O'Flynn.

The lieutenant silently shakes his head. He looks sceptically down at his blackened nails, at his fine dark hands, and says:

Tell me something, Víctor. What is this bitterness you're spewing all over this kid here? What is it that so disturbs and obsesses you? The fact that I offered his mother a few dreams, at a time when she was in such despair, so crushed by loneliness and disillusionment, or the fact that you have to assume your role as a defeated man for all to see?

My role as a troublemaking Red! Pa's unhinged voice cuts in. Some part I have to play!

So, the Flight Lieutenant insists, what hurts you most: betrayal or defeat?

Lying on the bed, his chin cupped in his hands, David awaits his father's reply.

Damned pilot. That's the most pertinent and difficult question I've been asked since I escaped from home, Pa mutters, his voice spraying the air as he sighs deeply and sets his badly fitted dentures chattering. Tick-tock-tick-tock, I've no idea, Bryan, no idea . . .Tick-tock-tick-tock . . .

Your dentures are falling out, Pa, David moans, tears spurting in his eyes.

. . . I don't know. Until a short while ago, I was a man branded by defeat – even the youngest kids in the neighbourhood know that – but now I don't know. Misfortune has taken its toll of me, but it's because I never knew how to fight either in the skies or on the ground. At any rate, the best thing to do would be to make a bonfire of all that shit, like David did with the letters. I'm too full of pain and despair, and above all of the infinite horrors I've seen – including the ones I myself have brought about – to want the memory of any trace of that to remain. It was worth having hopes and fighting for them, yes: both gave me moments when life was full, and I wouldn't change them for anything. But they're over and done with.

That's where you're wrong, *cariño*, Flight Lieutenant O'Flynn says, flicking back a lock of blond hair with his charred, claw-like hand. Listen: if you lose the memory of a single one of those details, then they'll all be lost, and us along with them, and the whole universe along with us. Either all of us are saved with everything, or nothing and no-one is saved.

Don't preach to me, Bryan!

Bueno, you always did like to wallow in the pestilent mud of defeat, with your beloved bottle and your arse open to the skies and your blood tainted by ideas of the fatherland and all that nonsense, *bueno*, I understand how you feel, *pero* I've never seen you like this, my brave friend, so viscerally against everything, so rabidly avoiding everything. No, I see you as a living metaphor of civilian dignity, oh, *sí!* And in spite of everything, in spite of your fall in the gully, of the way you stink of brandy and your slit backside, you still have the respect and love of your Rosa. You've won your victory. You're a hero whether you like it or not. The same as me.

A war hero is nothing more than a blood-stained accident! And I'm not that, Lieutenant.

What I'd like to know, David says interrupting and sitting up in the middle of the bed, what I'd like to know is this. The fighter pilot Bryan O'Flynn visits the house a second time, and brings Ma a rose. Where were you, Pa?

I'd escaped down the gully three nights earlier. But I wasn't there any more either.

What about me? Where was I, Pa?

Let me think . . .

If you were clever you'd shut up right now, O'Flynn warns Pa under his breath.

It must have been towards the end of March, in Easter Week, so you were in your grandmother's house, at the beach.

Yes, David says, exactly a year after I saw the B-26 bomber crash into the sea. You told me Flight Lieutenant O'Flynn had died burnt or drowned in that plane.

Me? An RAF bomber crashing into the sea? There was nothing in the papers about any bomber crashing off Mataró, remember . . .

Ya veo, the Flight Lieutenant growls. He told you that because he wanted me dead.

I thought you were dead. It's not the same thing.

David is beginning to hear the bedlam of crickets starting up again inside his head.

Who's telling the truth?

Keep your ears pricked, son, Pa growls. The truth is a question of listening.

Exactamente, says Bryan O'Flynn, standing up at the foot of the bed. Well said. He ties the silk scarf under his prominent Adam's apple, adjusts his flying jacket, puts on his helmet with the goggles still on his forehead and, before he vanishes, smiles his lopsided smile at David, touches two burnt fingers to the side of his head in a mock military salute. *Buena suerte.*

As he climbs calmly back alongside his ruined fighter to face the Boches once more: "Please, not the flying jacket", in the far distance behind him high above the devastated fields, flecks of pink clouds outlined in the twilight drift gently down to night. Pa's faint voice also says farewell.

Don't let it worry you, son, put it out of your mind. That's one lizard tail you'll never cut off.

Waking with a start in the early morning in this miserable room means you are at the mercy of eyes staring at you in the darkness, almost always from the black depths of the half-open wardrobe. But David feels the panic lessen when he clenches the chunky, persuasive outline of the Dupont in his hand, warm from sleep and clutched firmly under the sheet as if it were a weapon, the urgent pulse of revenge.

He whistles in the dark, but Inspector Galván's steely eyes not only follow him still, but wink at him obscenely and evilly. David jumps off the bed and opens the wardrobe door wide. He rummages among the winter clothes, his father's threadbare overcoat and a few of his mother's dresses she can no longer fit in to because of her pregnancy. He verifies that of course the inspector is not in there, but keeps on whistling to face his fear. Then he stands on tiptoe to reach two shoe boxes hidden on top of the wardrobe, and takes out the saffron-coloured blouse, the yellow skirt with its green pockets and a pair of pink girl's knickers. Angrily and with chattering teeth, he puts all this on. He opens the other box and takes out the red beret and the red plastic handbag with its long strap, puts it on his shoulder and holds it firmly against his hip, then sneaks across the dark room again holding his breath, and collapses stiff as a board on to the bed. The red beret is tilted over one eye, and he is still holding firmly on to the gold Dupont.

Are you still spying on me, you bastard? Keep right on, I couldn't give a damn, I'm going to get you anyway. Swine. Butcher. Arsehole cop.

David leaps out of the reeds and stands in the middle of the path, blocking the bicycle. Taken by surprise, the girl brakes sharply, and puts her feet on the ground.

"That's a brilliant bike you've got," David says huskily. He's wearing a bandage round his head, with tincture of iodine stains, and has an aura of secret heroism about him. "Is it your father's?"

She stares back at him with hard eyes and says nothing. Standing more firmly on the track, she gently pushes her stomach forward and lifts her behind off the seat. She sits with one leg dangling over the bike frame, but keeps a firm hold on the handlebars. Now that he can see her so close up, David notices the transfer of a butterfly with red and black wings beneath the vaccine mark on her right arm.

"What's your name?" David asks. He gets no reply this time either, so he turns his attention to the violin case strapped to the bike frame. It's an old scruffy case, with battered corners. "Do you study music, then?"

He thinks he notices a mocking gleam in her eye, and suddenly realizes that although it is a violin case, it does not necessarily contain a violin: it could be her lunch, or some crochet work, or even kilos of rice or beans.

"What's this?" David insists. "Cat got your tongue?"

She does not even blink. Still staring at him, she calmly brushes an insect from her face. She is wearing a pair of small silver earrings.

"Don't you know you can't go beyond here without saying the password?" David will not give up. "The password is Zapastra. You have to say the word Zapastra, and then I'll see if I let you through. Go on, say it: say Zapastra!"

She moves the bike as if trying to get round him, but does not insist. She is more curious than scared, and soon stands still again, staring silently at him.

"Don't worry, I'm not going to do anything to you," says David, snapping off a reed and starting to peel it. He thrusts his hip out challengingly. "But the fact is you're in trouble, girl. If you refuse to say the password, you have to pay a forfeit . . . I live back there, in that villa. See this great lighter I've got?" he takes the Dupont out of his pocket. "A gentleman friend of my mother's lost it down in the gully while he was burying a dog. He's in the house now with her. If you go and give him back the lighter, telling him you found it in the riverbed where he buried the dog, I'll let you pass through."

By now the girl is suspicious of him. She straightens the bicycle, sits back on the seat, and lifts the pedal with her instep.

"Wait," David says hastily. "What's it to you? All you have to do is tell him that one day while you were going past you saw him digging a hole with a hoe, and that's why you thought the lighter must be his. That's all. If you don't, I'll make you show me your knickers right here, and if they are white or pink, too bad for you, because the forfeit for not saying Zapastra is that you have to come with me into the reeds, and I'll gag you and tie you up, and I won't let you out till nightfall, and I might just pinch your bike as well . . ."

All he has time to see are her blonde curls flying in the wind, because her first push off on the pedals makes the bike rear up, leaving her flailing along, skirt in the air and knees pumping furiously as she tries to control the bucking machine.

"It was a joke, silly, I won't do anything to you!" David shouts, jumping out of the way just in time to avoid being knocked down. As he watches her speeding off beyond the reed-bed, he complains bitterly to himself: "I couldn't care less what colour your knickers are anyway, I've already seen them. You're a real idiot, you know that? What skin off your nose was it to give me a helping hand? If you only knew what they did to my poor Chispa, I'm sure you would have helped me. Sure you would."

He climbs down to the riverbed, and spends more than an hour penknife in hand searching for lizards for Paulino. He sees two or three but does not manage to catch any, and finally gives up. It's not my day today.

As the daylight fades, an uncertain breeze from the outskirts of the city reaches the poor areas up on the hills, bringing with it the smell of burning hooves. Dark, hunched tramps shuffle along the street walls like shadows. A small man striding past treads in some dog dirt and says what the holy shit was that, it shouldn't be allowed. Deep in thought, David avoids everyone and crosses Plaza Sanllehy muttering words of farewell. Hiya fatso, I've come to say goodbye.

He has just come out of the dark-room where he has been developing photos of a third-rate wedding and of soldiers and maids feeding the pigeons in Plaza Cataluña, and he wants to see Paulino before he goes home. He throws a pebble up at the window-pane, and before long Paulino is next to him on a bench in the square. They sit there for a while without saying a word.

"I only came to say goodbye, I have to be off," says David, pulling a rolled-up piece of paper out of his pocket.

"Fine."

"I've brought you this coloured programme of Sabu. It's the film we saw at the Delicias, remember?"

"Of course. Thanks," says Paulino. They have already shaved his head again, and he looks like a jailbird, with his big sad eyes close to his nose, and the lined face that makes him look like an aged child. "They're coming to get me in a minute as well. I'll be in the reform school within half an hour, so . . ."

David clicks his tongue.

"I'm in a bad way too. It's like it was raining stones in my ears, but if you look, there isn't a cloud in the sky."

"Do you want me to play the maracas as loud as I can for you?"

"No, I couldn't bear it today." Then, after a long pause, David adds: "They really caught you with your pants down, didn't they?"

"If I don't say anything, nothing will happen to me."

David thought Paulino would be more tearful and scared than ever, but he is not. He is wearing his best clothes: long trousers with a proper crease, and a blue sailor's top, open across his chest with the cord undone. His maracas are in a cardboard box.

"Will you keep them for me till I get back?"

"Of course."

"I'm taking my razor with me. They say I can go on practising in there."

"Will you be locked up long?"

"It's not a prison, you know. The Asilo Durán is like a school . . . OK so it's full of boys who've gone off the rails and immigrant kids with no parents, but it's not a prison."

David nods silently. Then he says:

"I came here thinking they wouldn't let you out of your house."

"Why not? I'm not a criminal. They don't guard me. As my uncle told everybody, it was simply an unfortunate accident."

"And the cops swallowed that?"

"I don't know."

"You might fire one shot by mistake, but two . . . ? Why didn't you tell them the truth? They'd have put the son of a bitch straight into clink."

"You think it'd have been better to talk? Even with a hole in one buttock and when he was bleeding like a pig all over the bathroom floor, my uncle was still shouting he'd kill me if I said a word. However bad the reform school is, it can't be that bad, can it?"

David falls silent again, head on chest. The buzzing in his ears increases. Zzzzz . . . Paulino looks across at him.

"What are you thinking about?"

"Nothing." But then he immediately adds: "Did you really not want that bully to die?"

"No," Paulino says, and with a voice that is already different, stronger, he goes on: "The one I would have loved to kill is my father, he's such a chicken. Before I go I'd really like to leave four white feathers in his razor pouch . . ."

They are sitting about a yard apart on a wooden bench close to the fountain, with the maracas in their box between them. Paulino sits very correctly, his back straight and hands on his knees pressed together. He glances at his friend's rebellious profile, as David stares defiantly down at the ground between his sprawling legs.

"Are you scared, Pauli?"

"Yes, a bit . . ."

"I'll come and visit you on Sundays."

"But they're not going to beat me there, because I'll do everything right."

"What do you mean?"

It is Paulino's turn to say nothing for a while.

"Everything they ask me to do," he says, between clenched teeth. "If they ask me in the proper way. I've had it up to here with people being rude and abusive."

Another silence, which David breaks, speaking quickly, stumbling over the words:

"I'll go on looking for worlizards for you. If I catch one, I'll keep the tail . . ."

"What stupid tails are you talking about? I'm never going to need that crap again. When I get out in a couple of years, I'll be cured and no-one will remember a thing."

A dark gun clutched in trembling hands, above a soapy shaving mug. The festering buttock of an ex-legionnaire tattooed with a blue mermaid cupping her breasts and smiling obscenely. And no-one is going to remember a thing? David turns and faces his friend with bloodless lips and a frightened look, scarcely containing his anger, as if he were aware of the fate in store for both him and Paulino, a fate that time would confirm in due course. He does not say it, but thinks: what's going to happen to you when you come out of reform school in a couple of years, or even before, is already settled, Pauli: you'll be back shaving old goats again the whole damned day, at the Cottolengo and the hospital, you'll be warming towels and lathering soap and stropping razors for your father, and above all you'll be back shaving the traffic policeman at his place, because the bastard will be waiting for you, so when you get out you'll be as fucked as you ever were, kid, until one fine day, one sunny Sunday morning after he's been to fetch you from the Asilo Durán so that you can spend the day with him – you know, he comes every other Sunday, you shave him and he takes you to the pictures or the dodgems in the Vía Augusta, then drops you back in your hole – one day as you are hurrying to finish his shave on the roof terrace, all of a sudden you'll shudder with fear and zip! you slit his throat with one slice from ear to ear, and there's an end to it . . .

Paulino's changing voice puts a stop to these sombre premonitions:

"I'll be a new man when I get out, you'll see. That'll be the end of it."

"Whatever happens," David says, looking away from him, "you've really shown you've got guts. I always thought you didn't have it in you. That of the two of us it was me who was the tough one. But no."

"You hesitate too much," Paulino says.

David shrugs and falls silent for a moment.

"I wanted you to do me a favour before you left, but there's no time now," he says eventually, then explains his idea: to appear at home when Ma's policeman friend is there, and give him back the Dupont, saying he found it in the riverbed, on the spot where someone said they saw the cop digging a hole, etc.

"My mother would have believed you," he goes on. "What a shame."

"But the inspector would have grilled me, and then what?" says Paulino. "Do you really think he'd swallow that nonsense?"

"It's not nonsense. Besides, I'm not worried about what he does, the important thing is that my mother believes you. Well, I'll think of something else," David says, picking up the cardboard box. "I'm off. 'Bye."

"Wait," says Paulino, feeling in his trouser pocket. "I've written you a poem."

"Don't be so wet."

"You'll have to hear it before you go, whether you like it or not."

"By all the shit in the sea, Pauli, you really are a dummy."

"It's very short. Listen. 'Plucking the petals from a marguerite, I thought how sweet, is this best friend of mine.' Do you like it?"

"A whole lot."

"I wrote it just like that."

"You have to be a real chump to spout stuff like that . . ."

"Have it your own way," says Paulino, then, seeing the bulge of David's fist in his trouser pocket, adds: "Anyway, what are you going to do with the inspector's lighter?"

"I've already told you."

"You should give it back to him without any fuss . . ."

"'Bye, fatso," David interrupts him. "Good luck."

He does not take the Avenida to get home, but walks up the dirt tracks beyond the square and then out across the wasteland, where he meets only starving cats and stray dogs. He climbs up the low hillside on the near side of the gully, passing by the broom bushes where the day's laundry is still draped. The girl's clothes he admired so much are there, their bright colours shining now they are dry. He quickly snatches two or three of them, hides them under his shirt, then continues on his way, the maracas still in their box under his arm.

He walks past crumbling back garden walls, shacks, market gardens and faint traces of old country paths. He walks along the top of the gully, then crosses it much higher up than his house, coming to a halt in the middle of the riverbed, at the small mound of sand under which the ghost of Chispa lies. From the river bank he hears the song of a thrush and the murmur of water rushing over polished stones. Standing there in the rocky gully he can feel the tug of dead waters roaring by as they have done since the beginning of time. Some strange force, an energy field he is unaware of has brought him and the gold Dupont to this tiny dune in the river. Wherever the dog may be – here, he tells himself again, it was here he was shot and here he was buried – all that's left of him now must be pure skeleton, the arch of his ribs opening beneath the earth, his eye sockets silted up with sand, his collar and lead perishing beside him. What bad luck you had, Chispa. Did nobody see what they did to you? Did nobody go past just at that moment?

A young girl on a bike went past, says Chispa, sitting stiffly on top of his own tomb, his forehead still swathed in bandages. I saw her.

A blonde girl riding a man's bike, David agrees.

Yes. Do you know what she's called?

Amanda.

Christ! What a lovely name!

And you say that girl saw you, you and the inspector?

I don't know about that.

She must have done. When she rode past, the inspector was still dragging you along by the lead . . .

No, it was later.

Was it when that bastard pulled his gun out?

Let's not confuse things. I didn't see any gun.

Of course, you didn't even have time for that, poor Chispa.

Well, I was scared to death, kid, what do you expect?

So then, David calculates to himself, the girl must have ridden past when the guy was already digging the grave. Even though the lighter was half-buried in the sand, it must have glinted in the last rays of the sun, and Amanda saw the glint from her bike when she came back an hour later, so she got off and went to pick it up . . . try to remember, Chispa!

Hey, you really do want it served on a platter, don't you? the dog howls, shaking sand and maggots off his back. What happens when something happens that you happened to think of because it was bound to happen, but who knows if it did happen?

Chispa sneezes and sits still again, ears drooping and with his usual sad look beneath the bloody bandage. You want everything cut and dried, but that's not possible! The cop could have just gone off and tossed me aside, like a cigarette end . . .

For Pauli and me to find you with a hole in your skull? No, I bet he dug a grave straightaway. He got a hoe from one of the shacks or gardens, and dug a hole, David concludes, sinking down, legs crossed, on the spit of sand.

Sitting there opposite the tomb and thinking again about Chispa's last walk with Inspector Galván must be like staring at the riverbed after it has rained, waiting for something to happen; like reading the name of Chispa's murderer on a tombstone the rain washed clean of dead leaves or rotten flowers. Here it is. This is how it must have happened. But David's thoughts are not gloomy this time: according to his calculations, the inspector dragged the dog along, tugging pitilessly on the lead until they crossed the riverbed, which must have been like a furnace at that time of day. They could not have gone very far, because Chispa was out of breath and exhausted, and it was impossible to imagine the inspector picking him up and carrying him in his arms to the Guardia Civil barracks in La Travesera to hand him over to the vet . . . this dog is so old and suffers so much, he must have thought, he's like a dead animal walking, he will never even make it alive to the strychnine pellet, so the best thing will be, and so on. They would not go any further, that is why they would climb the riverbed until they almost reached the lonely spot of the market gardens, with the cop very nervous and fed up with having to tug on the lead the whole time, and Chispa already half strangled and with his tongue hanging out; I can see the yellow froth spilling out of his mouth, I can really see it and it drives me crazy. He cannot go any further, and flops on his belly on a strip of sand. This is as far as we are going, flatfoot, not a step further. But probably even before they reached this extreme, resigned to the implacable destiny of tugs and jerks, dragging along his bald back legs like rags, before his sight clouds over and his heart stops beating, his soul has already died of sadness. It also might have been, David thinks, that the inspector got mad and decided to end it all there and then, not because of the dreadful heat and Chispa's stubborn refusal either to carry on or to lie down and die, but for other reasons, who knows, a cop is always bound to be a bastard, and this one in particular is capable of anything . . .

David has imagined the way the death took place so often and with such emotional intensity that even its cruellest details are fixed in his memory with overwhelming certainty. He knows for a fact, for example, that at the last moment Chispa tried to scratch the inspector, because he was a dog who had a fierce cat's soul, and that a few seconds before he was shot, the poor creature raised his eyes and gazed reproachfully at his executioner and then without a sound, except perhaps for a sly meow, laid his head down and said goodbye to this world.

The shot and its echo still resound in the shell of my ears, competing with the usual buzzing. Or were there two shots, Chispa? Neither, you fibber. Yes there were. I'll tell you . . . I was far away, up above Plaza Sanllehy. I bent down to tie up my shoelace, I could see close up the bits of dry weed the wind was blowing at the side of the road, so the wind was coming in my direction, right? I had just handed over some wedding photos to a family in Carmelo: the bride and groom were so poor they only kept two, one of them at the altar, the other in the church doorway, the groom was stiff as a board, all smiles, as ugly as sin, and anyway Paulino was with me and he says he heard nothing (or perhaps he did: it was an airgun someone fired to scare off the pigeons. No it wasn't. Have it your own way, sweetheart, whatever you say), but even if I had been further from the gully and had the wind against me that day, I would still have heard the echo of the shot, because I heard it before the inspector pointed his gun, a long time before he even took it out of his shoulder holster and put two bullets in the chamber. I raised my head all of a sudden, as if the first bullet had gone through my skull too, I felt the recoil of the gun after the shot. The echo spread out from here and almost at once filled my damaged ears like balls of cotton-wool, one after the other. And before it died away I could smell the cordite too. Cross my heart.

The echo from this fantastic shot mingles with the sound of a bicycle bell, and David turns his head quickly as he stands up. He hears the wind rustling through the reeds after he has seen it ruffle the young girl's hair.

With her feet on the ground as she sits astride the bike frame with the violin case, she is staring at him from about fifty metres away on the path along the top of the gully. Her eyes are hard, and her bad-tempered mouth appears to be saying something. Can she be thinking this cheat has just stolen a skirt and blouse of mine? Can she have seen me? But why would a boy want to steal girl's clothing? She shakes her head, sits back on the seat and starts to pedal hard. As she rides away with her flaming blonde head erect and the violin between her legs, David suddenly grasps the intimate link between the gold Dupont he is clutching in his hand and her fiery mane as it vanishes behind the reeds, between the tense determinism of revenge and the laws of chance. It is nothing more than the pure intuition that has always directed his dreams, the fierce opportunity to wreak revenge that he has been looking for: he opens his hand and the lighter falls to his feet at the bottom of the mound, lying there on its side, half-buried in the sand.

It's true, son, don't think any more about it; that girl came past on her bike and stopped to see what was going on, I saw her too, he hears the anaesthetized voice say behind him. But I don't like what you're plotting . . .

Pa is coming towards him, hands dirty but head held high, the cigarette stub wobbling in the corner of his mouth, the brandy bottle he is clutching by the neck wobbling too; he walks as if he is struggling against the wind of a curse or of a dream determined to keep him here, in this stagnant pool of history. In contrast to his voice, his body is not the least bit insubstantial, intangible or gaseous: it also has a pretty nasty smell.

Inspector Galván is hiding the truth, Pa. He's a con man. Now he brings her a white rose whenever he comes, he no longer says dreadful things about me, and he claims he wants to help us. It's all lies.

Your mother's going to need all the help she can get.

You must know he visits us almost every day. He always brings something: chocolate, a bag of beans, sugar cubes . . . when I get back from the photographer's, I find the two of them seated round the side-table, Ma serves him coffee and he lights her cigarettes for her: you should see them chatting away so relaxed, the rose is in a vase Ma puts in between the lit lamp and the cop, so that when he's sitting in his chair its shadow falls across his face while he's talking and sometimes in the darkness his eyes gleam . . . Do you know what he said to her the other day? He said I wonder, Rosa, sometimes I really wonder if your husband was a true libertarian or simply a womanizer. Imagine that.

What does it matter, son? The important thing is to pass the time.

I never understood your jokes, Pa. You're another one who plays with marked cards.

It wasn't me who marked them. It's a very old pack, it's been played with more often than Señora Vergés' backside, but for now it's the only one we've got.

Who is Señora Vergés?

Don't ask.

David drops his head on his chest and waits, staring down at the calligraphy traced by lizards or rats in the sand round his feet. He is beginning to miss the sound of Paulino's maracas in the box under his arm: their soft sandy tropical shuffle always drowned out the buzzing and voices in his ears. The shadows of evening are lengthening across the riverbed, and the trickle of water is submerged in darkness, but the half-buried fake Dupont still gives off its feeble golden glow. All at once David bends down, picks it up and stares at it thoughtfully. There are grains of sand stuck in its joints, and he is careful not to dislodge them.

Am I allowed to know what you're doing? says Chispa, brushing away a blowfly.

Can't you see? I found the cop's lighter, look.

Oh yes? Goodness, kid, what a stroke of luck!

It was right here. It must have fallen out of his pocket when he was digging the hole to bury you in.

You know that's a lie, says Pa. And no matter how often you repeat it, you won't turn it into the truth.

We'll see about that.

I reckon you haven't switched on, kid. Have you forgotten your father fought against that kind of deceit all his life?

Speaking in police terms, Chispa butts in with his sad white smile, which I would be the first to admit neither my pedigree nor my race exactly qualify me to do, speaking in police terms, what the kid is doing is using false evidence to frame a suspect he knows is guilty.

I know that kind of game, grunts Pa, as he clutches the bottle between his legs and uses both hands to press the filthy handkerchief against his backside. You're furious and I'll tell you why, son. You say that loud-mouth killed your dog in an underhand way, and you see that as a fact. But for now, it is not so much a fact as a supposition. That's what makes you so angry. You're in a false position, and that's dangerous, I've suffered that myself. I know it's not that you're lying to conceal the truth, you're trying to do the exact opposite, but in any case, you're lying . . . He grabs the bottle again and takes a long swig, then stares into space with a weary, resigned look on his face. There are people who think that reality is one thing and truth is another, and you're one of those. You're dangerous, son . . . Well, anyway, I'm off. He stares down at the city with dull eyes, still firmly clutching the neck of the bottle, his shoulders drooping and defeated. You should go and hide somewhere far from here, David thinks or says. No, Pa replies, this spot is exactly right for me, here in this wound in the earth that won't close, this stinking, deceitful gully . . . I wonder how a man can get it wrong so often in life. If I have to change hiding-places, I'll leave a bit of paper with, written on it: here Víctor Bartra got it wrong yet again. As you can see, I've got nothing left except for this cigarette end. You've got the lighter, and the least you could do is light my cigarette for me and then give it back to the inspector.

He'll get it back, but not through me. He wouldn't believe me, says David.

What wouldn't he believe?

That I found it right here, on the spot where he killed Chispa. He thinks I'm a liar, and so does Ma . . . Somebody else has to tell him. That's it, someone else.

Pa whirls round, waving the bottle above his head as if it were a stick of dynamite, then hurls it at a rock. Before it shatters, while it is still flying through the air, David has already seen the shards of glass scattered across the riverbed; before the brandy is spilt, even before the bottle containing it has smashed, he sees the wet earth avidly sucking up the alcohol. Then, standing upright in the middle of the riverbed, with Paulino's maracas under his arm and the Dupont in the other hand, he thinks that's it, I've waited long enough, and sets off resolutely for home.

At the night-time door, it looks as though Inspector Galván is saying goodbye for today. The red-head has her back against the doorframe, and stands with her hands behind her and her head to one side, a dreamy or perhaps slightly mocking look on her face. She's wearing the faded grey housecoat and has her hair up in an untidy plume. The inspector is talking to her, hands thrust in his pockets and staring down at his shoes. He is very close to her, and there is a tension in his shoulders; although neither of them seeks out the other's eyes, it is as though all they are doing is looking at each other.

David stands by the ferns on the river bank and decides to wait a while longer. Ma has lifted a hand to one of the grips holding the mass of red hair, then all of a sudden brings it to the front of her neck, and her head falls even further to one side. She closes her eyes, and her entire body seems on the point of sliding to the floor. Without moving from the doorframe, she puts out her hand to the inspector's shoulder for support, and almost at once she is in his arms, her forehead resting on his chest. Even though in David's retina all these images seem to follow each other in slow motion, in fact it has all happened so quickly in the indistinct evening light that he has no way of knowing whether she has fainted again, or simply fallen forward clumsily, the result of an attempt to show her friendship and gratitude for his kindness that suddenly becomes a gesture which might not have been so out of place or clumsy as expected . . . the inspector puts his arm round her waist and with his other hand gently lifts her chin to get a good look at her face. Her eyes are still shut, her arms hang loose by her side. Both of them move so sparingly it is hard to discover their intentions. They soon pull apart, but she is still giddy, so he touches her elbow and shepherds her back inside the house. The door closes.

The riverbed in the gully is a furnace, and from the cracked clay an enormous, black-skinned, aged lizard peeps out. It has no tail, but its head is alert above its front feet, and its tiny eyes glow like red-hot pellets of shot. It could be the famous worlizard of Ibiza he used to fool Paulino with, except that it does not exist. David puffs at it, and the creature scurries away. Lucky you, tail-less lizard living in the cracks on the bottom of this void, this non-place between my house and the world, between the silence of the river and my father's voice. As he squats on his haunches and stares up at the house with a pang of longing, he has the feeling he is still being observed, as though a pair of eyes were staring at the back of his neck in ghostly reproach, but he no longer feels lost or despairing, and no longer seems to want the roar of ancient waters, to feel swept far away from here on the current. His face is screwed up with determination, the girl's clothes he has stolen are under his shirt and his vengeful hand is still wrapped round the lighter in his pocket. All on his own, deep in thought, he is guardian of the truth built from lies, and will wait there for as long as need be. The weighty, angular shape of the lighter in his hand gives him a sense of security: something tells him that to be clutching that fake Dupont is like having the policeman's heart in his hand. He remembers what a Red Indian said in a film he once saw: the skill of a good tracker is to find something out of place. As for his father, his spectral, oxygenated presence has left a wake of chloroform and tincture of iodine, a sense of suffering flesh, and David lowers his gaze. Near his feet, a double line of shining white pebbles lined up by chance among all the debris suggests a set of false teeth protruding from the depths of the earth. David again senses he is being watched, and turns his head. There are eyes that stare at us long after they have vanished.

XI

Adventures in Another Part of Town

"Great holy shit, Tejada, the amount of stuff that goes on you never get to hear about. Did you know Galván was mixed up in illegal gambling, and that four years ago he was reprimanded in Bilbao for threatening an inspector with his gun?"

"You don't say. Who would fucking believe it? Hey, Mario, a siphon with some gas in it over here! And another plate of tripe and a red wine for Quintanilla!"

A bar that cops frequent in Vía Layetana, near Police Headquarters. At the far end of the counter, two deputy inspectors are shouting for a soda siphon that works. They are over forty, thick-necked but well-dressed, both of them with high-coloured faces: red the fatter of the two, green the other man. Lined up on the bar in front of them are a dozen plates with fried birds on them, heads stripped bare, guts hanging out. There have been some terrible stories heard within these walls, and the one I am about to tell is yet another. And these are not imagined memories, supposedly dreamt up in the red-head's warm placenta: I can see these two bloodhounds with my own eyes, exactly as my brother will see them in a few minutes, shortly after midday on this warm sunny day at the end of September.

One of the deputy inspectors is short and puny-looking; the other is pot-bellied with florid red cheeks. He is sitting casually on a high stool, wears glasses with a metal frame held together with dirty sticking plaster; one of the buttons of his flies is undone. He sticks a toothpick into an olive, puts it in his mouth and grimaces with distaste. The first finger of his right hand is bound up with lots of gauze and covered with a leather pouch tied to his wrist by a piece of elastic. They are drinking wine and vermouth as they flick through the morning newspapers: Europe in ruins is spread across every page, the Nuremberg thing looks like a farce concocted by the Allies. You're right there, Quintanilla. So Basora scored three goals? So what? The best winger Spain has ever seen was Gorostiza, whatever they say about him, and I know his nickname is 'The Red Bullet', there must be a reason for that. It's true, his companion agrees, he's the best, with apologies to Gainza.

Then they get to talking about the unfortunate episode Galván was involved in at the end of May. The fat man does not know all the details of the case, like, for example, as the little guy explains, that the man arrested, the door-to-door encyclopedia salesman, did not have his papers in order.

"That was enough to haul him in," the fat cop says, trying another fizzy olive.

"Yes, but that was what led to the mistake," the other man says. "That and the fact he turned out to be a bit of a tough nut. They mistook him for someone else, and even after two weeks of the treatment he still stuck to the same story and denied everything. And you should have seen what they did to his feet! Holy mother of God! And they put twelve studs in his skull and burned him all over with cigarettes."

"Did you see him?"

"I saw him afterwards, when Serrano had taken over. He hit him too hard once, and smashed one of his balls. That Serrano is nothing but a brute and an animal. He's got his own blackjack for things like that, hasn't he? But no sir, he had to use my cane, and he knows how much it cost me, you should see how the ivory handle was ruined by all the blood and gore from the guy's feet . . ."

"OK, but in any case that bastard was about to cock a snook at Serrano and all the rest of you, I saw it with my own eyes. He might have been in a bad way, but when they weren't looking he almost got out of that window looking on to the interior courtyard, he had one leg out and was about to jump. I think he would have done it, and if he had I'm sure he would have killed himself, but we'll never know for sure . . ."

"Shit, don't complicate things, Tejada," the fat guy says. "I don't know if he was thinking of killing himself, but he was thinking of another life."

"What the fuck do you mean by that?" the other one says, frowning. "God, Quintanilla, are you out of your mind? Are you suggesting that a Communist bastard like him was thinking of going to heaven?"

"No you cunt, how stupid can you get? What I mean is the guy was thinking he must have a better chance if he could only get out of there, compared to the shit you were giving him. But that was a real miscalculation, as it turned out."

"I had nothing to do with any of that. The guy was astride the windowsill, with one foot on the other side as they say, so Galván had no time to think, and besides, he was annoyed as hell anyway, his arm was in a sling and his collarbone was killing him, if you remember, he'd broken it on the stairs at the Horta police station, and then that miserable son of a bitch had withstood the interrogation, so this was the last straw, don't move or I'll shoot he said, then he completely lost his head, just imagine, a man like Galván, who knows how to get a confession out of the most difficult suspect, someone who's always so patient and cool: all of sudden he loses control and runs over to the window and pushes the guy out, go on show us how you can fly, arsehole, he shouted. I had nothing to do with it . . ."

"The fact is, it was like pushing a dead body anyway. A suicide asking you to give him the final shove – that's how the commissioner explained it later."

"Yes, because whatever happened, the guy would have thrown himself out," the thin cop agrees.

"I don't know," the fat one responds. "I'm not so sure of that."

"Because you weren't there. Look at it this way: the window was his only means of escape. I think I'd have gone for it too."

"The one who really messed up was Montero," the fat cop says. "He pulled out his gun and fired at him when there was no need. Two bullets in his back, to help him on his way down."

"It was the fall that did for him, not the bullets," the other one replies.

"So what?" his colleague puffs, shrugging his shoulders. "It can happen to anyone. What did they do with the body?"

"Put it in the morgue at the Clinic," the thin one grumbles, busying himself with the newspapers once more. "They had to think something up on the spot, to find someone who could identify him as a different person, a tramp with no relatives nobody would come and claim . . ."

"What a way to waste everyone's time and make life more complicated than need be!" the fat man says.

"You're right there. But you know Portela likes to do these things by the book. What time is it, by the way?"

"Twenty to one."

"You're five minutes slow," a voice behind him says. It belongs to a smiling young girl who is consulting her bright plastic fairground wristwatch. "It's a quarter to one."

Heading down Vía Layetana, on the right-hand pavement under the scorching sun, and there on the corner, in the midst of the weary confusion of exhausted people, stands this little girl. All the day's colours and reflections seem focused in this one figure as she comes to a halt for a moment and consults her little plastic watch with its yellow numbers and painted metallic hands. Its dial is sky-blue, and the strap round her wrist is a clear purple with yellow edges. Why are you staring at it, brother, when you know full well the hands are painted on and will always show the same time, a quarter to one? Are you looking at this cheap imitation watch to pretend you are busy, someone in a hurry to get to an important meeting? The plastic hands of your watch say it is a quarter to one, and I like to believe that by a twist of fate that is precisely the time all the other watches show as well, the same exact time on Inspector Galván's real watch as he quickly leaves the Sky Bar to catch the metro at Jaime I station to meet his daughter out of her convent school, at the same moment as the passers-by see this adolescent girl with long dark-skinned legs striding gawkily down the avenue, leaning slightly backwards and smiling to herself, as if a head wind were pushing her back, and she was enjoying it.

I am speaking from a kind of moral slit-trench in time which allows me to cancel out any nostalgia, as well of course as the rejection, amusement or simple astonishment this brave young girl must have aroused that day. It is likely that if even I had come across her, I would not have recognized her. There she goes, looking for all the world like an oblivious little whore with the insistent buzzing in her ears, brilliant scarlet lips, and hips swaying like Paulino's maracas. She is wearing her green skirt with big green patch pockets, the sleeveless saffron blouse printed with faded wheatears and poppies, the red plastic handbag hanging from her shoulder, her page-boy haircut tied up in an elastic band, white-framed sunglasses, rebellious fringe hiding her brow, and the red beret pushed back over her ears. On her right arm, just under the vaccination mark, there is the transfer of a butterfly with black wings and red spots. The sad knees and slender ankles shine in the sunlight, the ivory-coloured rubber sandals leave the dancing, sensual pink insteps of her agile feet open to the air. The calm purposefulness of her chin and its defiant tilt are the only things that could belie her cheerful, elegant appearance, but how her eyes shine as she defies the hustle and bustle, how intense is the emotion that grips her amid the lies and deceit all around her! How happy and trusting her eyes look as they reflect the daylight, how much this girl smiling unashamedly at the passers-by seems to love life!

This apparently natural glance at her plastic, useless watch seems to me now like an irrepressible nod in the direction of her characterization, or perhaps it is no more than a reflex produced by the imposture my brother is acting out, the conventional true detail that this contrived disguise requires. It is dedicated not so much at the gallery – the man who lights a cigar and stares at her out of the corner of his eye as she goes past – as at himself: a nervous reaction to the intuitive tension he has always experienced, especially whenever confronted by his personal illusions – those which one day will seal his fate.

By now she has reached the policemen's bar. She goes in cautiously. Slowly, with one hand on hip and carefully placing one foot in front of the other, she makes her way to the far end of the bar counter. It must be those two, she thinks; all she needed was a whiff of their sweaty armpits. She asks for a lemonade, pays, and spends some time sipping it through a straw and listening to their whispered commentaries about the beaten-up body whose identity had to be disguised, and why all the fuss anyway, and so on and so forth. When she has heard enough – she has not come here to listen to the idle gossip of barfly cops, and she is anxious to get on with what has brought her here – she moves silently behind the two of them, glass in hand and still sipping on the straw. She pulls down the hem of her yellow skirt and clears her throat.

"Excuse me. Do you know an inspector by the name of Galván?"

"He's just left," the skinny deputy inspector says, spearing another olive and looking amused when he sees who is talking to him. "What's it about?"

"What do you want to see the inspector for?" the fat man insists, turning slowly on his bar-stool. He does not appear to believe his own eyes, and points his bandaged finger at the girl as if she were something in a zoo. "What have we got here, Tejada?"

"I'm looking for Inspector Galván. You know him, don't you? Could you give him a message from me?"

"What message?" the smaller cop says, but instead of waiting for a reply, he turns back to the bar, folds up the newspaper and orders a plate of anchovies in vinegar from the waiter: quickly, these stuffed olives are off, Mario, where have you been keeping them, in your granny's cunt? He spits on the floor then turns to look at the girl again. "Well then, who are you?"

"I know this tart from somewhere," says the fat cop. "Take a look at those anchovy lips, Tejada. I've seen you somewhere . . . Didn't you used to sell carnations in the Chinese Quarter?"

"No, sir."

"But you live down there, I could swear I've seen you."

"Well, yes . . ."

"What's your name?"

"Amanda Espinosa de los Monteros, at your service."

"Are you making fun of me, you snot-nosed brat?"

"What's wrong? That's my name."

"All right," the other cop interrupts, "what do you want with Inspector Galván?"

"I found this lovely cigarette lighter, and I think it's his." She takes it out of her bag. "Look."

"Yes, it does look like his," the fat man says, inspecting the lighter, which still has grains of sand in its joints.

"I found it in a dry riverbed up in Guinardó, in a spot where hardly anyone ever goes," Amanda says, chewing on the straw.

"And how did you know it belongs to Inspector Galván?"

"I'll tell you: I was going along minding my own . . ."

"What were you doing in Guinardó anyway? That's a long way from the Chinese Quarter, isn't it?"

"My grandparents live there, so I go every summer. I've got a bike and I take violin lessons . . . So I was riding along minding my own business up above the house David lives in – he's a boy I met this summer – when I saw this tall man digging a hole with a big hoe. He had taken his jacket off and folded it on the ground next to a dead dog that had blood on its head, and on top of the jacket was a pack of Luckies and this lighter – I noticed it because it looked as though it was made of gold, it was gleaming in the sunlight . . . I didn't stop to watch him bury the dog, because I was upset when I recognized it, it belonged to my friend. So I carried on, and then an hour later when I passed by the same spot on my way home, I got off my bike and looked round, but I couldn't find the dog's grave. I looked round everywhere, and all of a sudden I spotted the lighter on the ground . . ."

"So why have you taken so long to hand it back? I bet you thought you'd keep it, didn't you?"

"No, sir," she opens her plastic handbag again and rummages inside it, but takes nothing out. "Goodness! I left my powder puff at home," she says, pushing her body as if innocently up against the plump knee of the deputy inspector sitting on the stool with his legs splayed open. "I had no intention of keeping it, but what could I do if I didn't know who the dog-burier was . . ."

"Did you hear that, Tejada?" the fat man says, without taking his eyes off the girl for a second. "What do you mean, dog-burier, dammit? What are you talking about?"

"I'll tell you, sir. I was cycling past the reeds in the riverbed when I saw something sticking up out of the sand. I said to myself: it's one of the dog's paws, perhaps it went rigid under the ground – that happens sometimes, you know, I saw my own grandmother raise her hand when she was in her coffin. She leans forward over the bar and absent-mindedly lays her hand on the policeman's podgy thigh, while with the other she reaches for an olive. She pops it in her mouth, commenting: "They're not so bad. You two are very fussy . . . As I was saying, the dog's paw made a sign as if calling to me. Has either of you ever seen the paw of a dog that's been hastily buried poking out of the ground? It gives you the shivers, I can tell you. Well, anyway, I got off my bike and went closer, and then I saw I was wrong, it wasn't a dog's paw sticking up at all, it's just that I'm an impressionable girl, it was the branch of a pine tree half-buried in the sand. Then I saw this lovely lighter. The inspector must have dropped it when he picked his coat up . . ."

"So he's burying dogs now, is he?" the fat cop interrupts her. "That's odd. Inspector Galván burying dogs. Why would he do that?"

"Because it was dead, sir. He was the one who killed it."

"You don't say. Did you hear that, Tejada? And why did he kill it?"

"Because it was very old and sick, so he must have thought it wasn't worth taking it all the way to the vet's to get rid of . . ."

"Do you hear what she's saying, Tejada? Since when has that been our line of work? Do you think he got paid extra for killing a dog?" the fat cop laughs, looking at his colleague, and then turns to face the girl once more: "What shitty dead dog are you talking about anyway?"

"I've already told you, it was my friend David's dog," she says, and then pauses thoughtfully, her fingers drumming on the stuffed sausage of a leg, while the cop observes her with half a smile.

"What did you say your name was, sweetheart?"

"Amanda, at your service. So as I was saying, there I was not knowing what to do with the lighter until David told me one day he knew the inspector. I'll give it him, he said, but right from the start I didn't believe him. You see, I don't know him very well, but I've heard he's a bit of a thief and a trickster. And this lighter is wonderful and very valuable – it looks as if it's solid gold. I'm sure he would have pinched it. Anyway, I told him no, look, tell me the inspector's name and where I can find him, and I'll give it back to him myself, who knows, he might give me a reward. So I went to Headquarters and they told me I'd catch him here . . . So that's that, and now I have to go. You give the inspector his lighter, and please don't forget to tell him how and where I found it; and that it caught my attention because while he was digging the hole, there was blood pouring from a hole in the dead dog's head . . ."

"Oh, yes? And why do we have to explain all this nonsense to Inspector Galván?" the thin one interrupts her.

Amanda takes a few moments to respond. She settles the sunglasses on her nose, clasps her handbag more firmly and says:

"Because it's the truth, sir."

"Hey, do they know at home you paint those gorgeous lips of yours?" says the fat cop.

"It's my natural colour," gurgles Amanda.

"Don't tell lies, or your nose will grow. Another glass of red for me, and a Cinzano for Tejada, Mario! Do you know something, sweetie? One of these days I'm going to crush someone's balls."

"What's that got to do with me?" asks Amanda.

The fat man stares at her as if her face was a hieroglyph, and says nothing. For some time now, he has been looking at her in a very different way. Amanda leaves her glass of lemonade on the bar.

"Well, I've told you what happened. I have to go now."

Without taking his eyes from her, the fat cop reaches for the toothpicks. With the bandaged finger of his other hand, he strokes his trouser front.

"Wait. Why on earth do you keep looking at the time on that cardboard watch of yours?"

"Because I'm in a hurry."

"How come they let you out looking like a parrot?" the cop stabs an anchovy with his toothpick, and all at once he is disgusted at being so close to this insolent excuse for a woman, her voice and the way she perspires. "Have you taken a look at yourself in the mirror, rosebud?"

Amanda was on her way out, but hearing this she turns back to face him, one hand on hip.

"You think you can speak to me like that because I'm uneducated, a girl from a poor neighbourhood who hasn't been to a proper school and who doesn't have an education or fine friends, or connections or good taste. But look here, these sunglasses, for example, are wonderful, they're exactly like the ones Ginger Rogers wears. And don't tell me Ginger Rogers doesn't have good taste, because that means you're not only blind but dumb too . . ."

"You tell him girl! That's the spirit!" the thin cop guffaws. "Did you hear that, Quintanilla?"

"Just listen to our little parrot," the other man says, staring at the impudent girl's fingers gripping her bag. The blackened nails seem out of place in such a haughty and presumptuous young woman. "Tell me something, since you're so smart. Have you ever had problems with the authorities?"

"No, never, sir."

"Well I reckon you soon will. And I'm sure I have seen you somewhere before . . . do you know what you look like, godammit?" he squirts soda into his glass of wine and goes on, laughing: "You look like a little doll who's escaped from the cat-house!"

"Come on Quintanilla, that's enough," his colleague tells him, still immersed in his newspaper. "Tell her to get lost, and you keep the lighter. Next season, Coruña are in the second division. It's a disgrace. Acuña is good . . . Go on, get out of here, girl."

Again she turns on her heel to leave, but the fat cop grabs her handbag strap.

"Just a moment, will you? I know who you are now! You're that tart who used to go round the Chinese Quarter selling cigarettes and matches."

"No, sir, you've got it wrong . . ."

The cop's eyes narrow behind his pebble glasses, as he insists:

"Aren't you the whore they call 'Sucksie Suzy'?" He turns to his colleague and asks him: "Have you ever met her, Tejada? Do you know who I'm talking about?"

"They dress and behave the same way, but this isn't her. You're making a mistake Quintanilla, be careful."

"Look at those lips of hers. It's her: I can't remember where I saw her once, a real low-life dive in Calle Robadors or San Ramón, and she was wearing the same skirt and the red bag, just like a little whore . . ."

"What are you saying!"

"Come here, my treasure, don't be angry. Come to your Quintanilla. Go on, take your glasses off and look me in the face and tell me you're not 'Sucksie', I dare you."

"It's not me, I tell you. I'm Amanda!"

"That's enough, don't rile me! I know who you are, kid. You've cured a good few guys' heart problems with a good suck, haven't you? Yes, you're 'Sucksie Suzy' all right! The boys in Calle San Ramón know you well. Your mother works in the cloakroom at the La Maña club, and that's where you peddle your wares too, selling American cigarettes and matches and whatever, and you offer more besides to anyone who buys something from you: you were once caught in a doorway with a baker's dick in your mouth, or so I've heard . . . Stand still, don't go!"

"No, Quintanilla, this is shit. It's not her," the other cop says, looking at the girl over his shoulder with a mixture of sympathy and scorn. "It's not."

"Balls to you, Tejada. I tell you it is."

"And I tell you it isn't!"

"Look at that sweet anchovy mouth of hers," the fat man insists, grabbing her by the arm. "I bet she sucks a treat, and for only fifty cents."

"You're off your head. How many times do I have to tell you, it's not her!"

"We'll soon see," the other cop growls. He turns on his stool and lifts his sheathed finger to Amanda's face. "See this poor finger of mine? I can't do anything with it. Can't pick my nose, squeeze the trigger, or scratch my little balls, ha, ha! Why, I can't even undo my flies to have a piss. And I really need to piss right now."

Amanda looks and listens, standing stiffly with her knees pressed together, her mouth caked in scarlet lipstick, a faintly disdainful gleam in her eyes behind the tinted plastic of her cheap sunglasses. I have to take whatever this guy gives me, she thinks, put up with everything. We always knew there would be risks, so now there's no hiding, no going back. I'm ready for whatever you want to throw at me, arsehole. She adjusts the glasses on the bridge of her nose and clears her throat.

"Do you really need to piss?" she says huskily, arching her hip.

"That's what I said. How about you offering to help me? But I don't want there to be any misunderstanding about this, OK? So we're going to have it all agreed and out in the open, in front of my colleague here. Listen to what I say, then repeat it for me: By chance I noticed that Deputy Inspector Quintanilla, attached to the Fourth Division of the Sixth Brigade, had a fractured index finger on his right hand . . . Go on, repeat it."

"By chance I noticed that Deputy Inspector Quintanilla had broken the index finger of his right hand . . ."

"And seeing that he urgently needed to urinate and could not undo his trouser buttons . . ."

"And couldn't open his flies . . ."

"No. He urgently needed to urinate and could not . . ."

"And could not undo his trouser buttons because of his broken finger."

"That's good. So I felt sorry for him and spontaneously offered to accompany him to the toilets in the bar and help him. Come on, girl, say it!"

"I felt sorry for the poor man and accompanied him to the toilets to help him to . . ."

"To relieve himself."

"To wash his hands . . ."

"No, dammit! To help him undo his flies so he could relieve himself."

"OK then, to relieve himself."

"And I performed this charitable act without anyone forcing me to do it, and without any ulterior motive, without any wish to take advantage of or poke fun at the authorities in any way . . ."

"You're going too far," the skinny cop says. "Be careful, for Christ's sake."

"You be quiet, Tejada."

"But what are you trying to do?"

"First name and family names!"

"You're way out of line, Quintanilla. What's that about?"

"Shit, I'm sorry, I got carried away!" the other man laughs, one hand still on his flies. Then he insists again: "Did you take down everything she said?"

"Come off it! I'm having nothing to do with it!" his companion says, ordering one of the cooked birds from the barman.

Amanda thrusts her hands into the big patch pockets of her skirt and observes the two men. The fat one slides off his stool and clutches her wrist, where the pulse has started to beat wildly.

"Come on, rosebud, repeat after me . . ."

"Bla bla bla . . . all signed and sealed," Amanda gurgles, one hand on her hip and a defiant look in her eyes, even though she already has the taste of ashes in her mouth. If this is the price I have to pay, then I'll pay it, you bastards. "But you won't hurt me, will you, sir?"

"Come with me, little girl. You're going to perform a charitable act."

Out of breath, swaying a little on his big feet, and with a sudden brutish, vacant look on his face, Quintanilla leads her by the hand to the toilets at the back of the bar. His colleague watches him go without leaving his stool. He shakes his head and buries himself in his paper once more, listening to the girl's running commentary die away as she follows his colleague: I don't mind helping you, but please treat me properly, officer, please don't push me around. Even though you don't believe it, I'm a good, sweet girl, and from today on I promise to be more obedient and loving towards my mother and brother, even though we have no news of Pa at all, you know; listen Lieutenant Faversham we should light more bonfires to scare the vultures off the dead bodies and burn everything and paint the bike a different colour . . . I'm just a poor little orphan who has no father, my mother's about to bring us another baby brother, I only hope she has a good birth and nothing happens to her, and the boy is born healthy and strong and that he won't some day feel ashamed of his sister and can overcome all the obstacles with a cheerful smile and a wonderful flying jacket, like the brave gentleman of the skies . . ."

"What crap are you going on about?" the fat cop says, pushing his way into the toilet. "Undo my flies and get it out, I can't manage." Without a moment's hesitation, the girl obeys with nimble fingers. The policeman lowers the toilet seat lid. "Now sit down."

Whatever happens, I won't give in, she tells herself over and over. In the foul-smelling darkness she suspends all her senses – the sense of touch and smell that threaten to overwhelm her – and keeps her eyes fixed on the image of a white butterfly fluttering let's say between her heart and Ma's clump of marguerites. Afterwards, she throws up all the lemonade.

Toothpick in mouth, Deputy Inspector Tejada saunters to the toilets and pokes his head round the door. He says nothing, and returns to his seat at the bar – a few moments later, the girl appears behind him. She is tense and silent, but as light as an angel or devil. She orders a bottle of fizzy pop and gargles with it, spitting it out into her glass. She stands up thoughtfully, boiling with rage and resentment, but immediately steadies herself and carries on gargling and spitting out the pop. A short, bald man who has sat down beside her and ordered an aniseed drink turns and takes her to task:

"You should do that kind of thing at home."

Deputy Inspector Tejada lifts his head from his paper and spits out the mashed toothpick.

"What's the matter with you? Don't you think people should wash their mouths out?"

"I wasn't talking to you . . ."

"Well I was talking to you, arsehole. Go on, tell me what's wrong with a bit of hygiene, whether it's gargling or anything else. Come on, explain yourself . . ."

"I don't think this is quite the place for it . . ."

"Ah, no? So, Mister Smart Alec, what would be the right place?"

The man catches a glance from the barman warning him to drop it, and he does so. He gulps down his aniseed, while out of the corner of his eye he notices the girl is about to pay for her drink. The deputy inspector nods his head discreetly for the barman not to accept it, so she puts her money away, claws at her fringe to tidy it, flicks her hair back disdainfully, peers down again at her wristwatch with its phosphorescent dial and painted metal numbers, then says goodbye in a loud, clear voice.

"It's late," she says, and then, looking at no-one in particular: "Give Inspector Galván the lighter from me, please. Don't forget. Please."

A work trip to Zaragoza prevents Inspector Galván from turning up at the house for five days. When he appears again he brings a kilo of beans, two tins of condensed milk, a pair of purple slippers with gold decorations on them for Ma, and a china sugar bowl with a view of the River Ebro and the Pilar basilica on it. And that same day the cigarette lighter is where David was hoping to see it, on the side-table in our tiny living- and dining-room, between the two coffee cups and the new bowl filled to overflowing with sugar cubes.

David arrives at the decisive moment, after spending the afternoon running errands for the photographer. He has come in through the night-time door, crossed the doctor's ghostly consulting-room, taking care to avoid pieces of furniture rotting away under their yellow dustsheets and mirrors shedding all their silver, unevenly reflecting dead hares and partridges laid out among bunches of grapes and sliced water-melons, run down the dark corridor to reach the green dividing curtain, then crept to the table with its two empty wicker chairs under a window framing a vivid late September sunset. The first thing he spots is the lighter, standing upright on the white tablecloth and shining with its fake golden glow; then he notices the inspector's jacket hanging from the back of one of the chairs, the half-open bedroom door, and finally, on the floor in front of the chair Ma usually sits in, the basin with water, and the brand-new pair of slippers.

The frosted-glass door to the bedroom yields easily to a push from David's fingers. The red-head is lying on the bed, wearing her housecoat with the faded poppies on it, and a grey cardigan. She is barefoot and has one hand on her pregnant belly. Sitting by the bed, the inspector is lifting her head with one hand, offering her a glass of water. She takes a sip, and closes her eyes; he takes his hand away gently, and neither of them says a word.

"What's wrong, Ma?"

"Hello son," she says with a faint smile. "It's nothing . . . Would you bring me my cup of coffee? It's in on the side-table."

Glass in hand, the inspector stands up.

"Don't listen to her," he says. "What you should do is tell the doctor."

"I'm fine, son, don't worry," she says, struggling up and plumping the pillow behind her. "As soon as I drink a bit of coffee, it'll pass."

"No more coffee," the inspector insists. "Not for now."

David cups his hand behind his back, as if he were already clutching the Dupont.

"I'll be right back, Ma."

"No, kid, stay where you are," says the cop.

David pays no attention, turns on his heel and goes back into the dining-room.

He picks up the cup and saucer, and while he is there recovers the lighter as well – or rather, he grips it as if it were a gun. As he is going back to the bedroom, he stands for a moment in the doorway, listening and wondering about the strange silence in the room, his mother in bed and the inspector standing there with the glass of water in his hand, attentive to her needs and watching over her, controlling his rash impulses. The silence conveys an unease that only serves to increase the buzzing in his ears. Why are they so silent, above all her?

Since Pa left us, she has never shared this kind of silence with any man. Their relationship did not used to be like this. Whenever during the many afternoons they spent together, sitting at the low table drinking coffee, she had agreed at his insistence to talk about herself – only so as not to seem rude or ungrateful for all his gifts and kindness, she had said at first – telling him about her work as a seamstress, for example, or her pregnancy and its problems, or whatever else it might have been, provided he would then allow her to discuss the topic of Víctor Bartra and his eternal fight with justice, there had always been a moment when, due perhaps to a lull in the conversation, she would suddenly fall quiet and there would be a growing silence between them: who knows what sense of danger, or forewarning of disaster or death led her to stop speaking. But this silence in the bedroom, David correctly realizes, is not the embarrassed silence of two people who suddenly find they have nothing to say to each other; on the contrary, it suggests the embarrassment of two people who have so much to tell each other they do not know where to start.

He goes into the room and walks over to his mother. He hands her the cup of coffee and then, clenching the Dupont as if it was a talisman, turns to the inspector. His furtive adventure is reaching its climax, and he knows it. Armed only with a fake cigarette lighter and his capacity to bluff, but convinced he is right and knows the real truth, here he is at last, about to give the cop the final push without the slightest hesitation or sense of shame, without showing any trace of the fatalism and despair that would lead to his own tragic demise six years later.

"I see your lighter finally turned up," he says. "Where was it?" His brown-stained fingernails reveal the Dupont in the palm of his hand. He grips it, lifts the top and with his thumb turns the flintwheel; the flame shoots up, he stares at it for a moment and then clicks the lid back down with his finger. Clunk. In some way, he thinks obscurely a second time, lifting the lid with his finger is like pulling a trigger. He drops the lighter on the bedside table and says: "That was a bit of luck. Where was it? Here in the house?"

A sudden tension – which does not escape Ma's notice – distorts the inspector's usually imperturbable features.

"We can talk about that later, if you don't mind. Your mother isn't feeling well."

"Do you want to tell her what happened, or shall I?"

"What's the matter, son?" she says, faintly but briskly. "The inspector never thought you'd kept it . . . He's just told me about it. He left it in a bar, and a friend of his found it there."

"Is that what he said? Well, it so happens I know the person who really found it, and she told me a very different story." Smiling mischievously and glancing at the cop out of the corner of his eye, he starts to outline his fantasy. "He lost the lighter in the riverbed the day he took Chispa away. A girl saw him as she was riding past on her bike."

"Saw what exactly?" with her head lolling back against the headboard, Ma clasps the coffee cup in both hands, as if scared it might be taken from her. "What are you talking about, David?"

"The bwana knows what I'm talking about. Listen," he says, not taking his eyes off the inspector, "Didn't that cop friend of yours tell you who found the lighter? Didn't he say it was a girl who was in the Sky Bar a week ago? She went to try and find you. Didn't that fat guy with the broken finger explain? Or the other cop, the skinny one . . . ?"

One of those two bastards, David is sure, must have given him the lighter and told him who found it and where and when, shortly after seeing him bury a dog with a bullet hole in its head – it was very important they had repeated that – although it was too much to expect they had mentioned the dirty trick they had played on the girl who gave them the Dupont.

While David is speaking, the inspector watches him without saying a word. He is still smiling, a mixture of curiosity and contempt on his face.

"Yes, Deputy Inspector Tejada explained it to me," he says eventually. "But how do you know all this?"

"The girl told me."

"As far as I can tell, she was talking complete nonsense. She doesn't know me from Adam."

"Oh no? Well, how did she know the lighter she found was yours, if she didn't know you from Adam? And why did she go and look for you in that bar – I mean, how did she know you were a cop and that she'd find you in a cops' bar . . . ?"

"David, please . . ." Ma cuts in.

David has been asking these last questions looking not at the inspector but at his mother, hands on hips and studying her face to judge her reaction.

"The fact is, when she showed me the Dupont," David continues, "I told her: I know the man who lost it, he's a friend of my mother's and he works at the Police Headquarters in Vía Layetana. Give it me and I'll return it to him. But she didn't want to, she didn't trust me. That's when she told me how she found it in the riverbed . . . I know her because I've seen her riding past on her bike, Ma. She says she saw the inspector digging a hole . . ."

"What's this, David? What are you trying to tell us?" Ma interrupts, looking sadly at him. "Come here and lend me a hand, I want to get up."

"You shouldn't. Rest a while longer," says the inspector.

"I'm feeling a lot better . . ."

"Will you let me tell you or not, Ma?" David implores her.

She stares for a few moments at the inspector, who is standing at the foot of the bed with his hands in his pockets, glowering, and then at David. She leans back against the bed again, and drops her hands back on to her body, still holding the coffee cup but seeming more relaxed.

"All right," she says, "I'm listening."

And David tells her more or less what Amanda told the deputy inspectors in the bar: that the girl on the bike heard the shot and saw the inspector in the riverbed with the hoe and the dead dog beside him, that when she came back that way he had gone, and that was when she found the lighter; that our Chispa never reached the vet's, dead or alive . . . I'm not saying he intended to kill him when he took him from here, Ma, but seeing the poor creature couldn't even walk, and refused to be pulled along by his lead, the inspector lost patience and decided to shoot him there and then; he probably thought he was going to die anyway, so why go to any more trouble. Even before David finishes saying all this, he is wondering why the inspector has not interrupted him, why he has not reacted; he had been expecting an angry outburst and a string of questions of the sort: where on earth did that little liar get her story and what have you got to do with her? where can I get my hands on her? what's she trying to do with these lies? why don't you bring her here and we'll see if she has the guts to repeat it all in front of me? and so on. But to his surprise the inspector says nothing, and lets him finish speaking. He stands there, immobile at the foot of the bed, one hand on the edge of the sewing table, the other in his trouser pocket, while his steely eyes scrutinize David and his muscular mouth twists in an almost imperceptible smile.

"This is the limit," is all he mutters. The smile crosses his lips like a sliding worm. Anger must be piling up deep in his throat, but all his eyes show is a scornful disdain. "What's wrong, kid, I've heard you make up much better lies," then looking at her, he adds: "You surely don't believe all this nonsense, do you?"

Still staring at David, Ma takes a sip of coffee. She has been paying more attention to David's extravagant tale than to the inspector's reply, as he runs his hand through his hair and starts pacing to and fro.

"You'd save your mother a lot of worry if you stopped right there," he growls. "Do you get me?"

"I want to speak to you right now, David," says Ma. "Bring me my slippers," she says, and adds for the inspector's benefit: "As for you, please go and fetch me a towel from the bathroom. My feet are frozen. And while you're at it, take the basin away and throw the water out . . ."

The inspector gently takes the coffee cup from Ma's hands and, before leaving the room, turns in the doorway to stare at David. There is no rancour in his gaze, only a hint of complicity. When he has gone, Ma moves to sit on the edge of the bed, puts her feet down on the worn mat and, taking off her cardigan, gestures to David to come over.

"Now explain everything you said and where it's leading," she says, dropping her hands on to her lap again as though willing herself to be patient and calm. "Another of your messes, I suppose."

"Why don't you ask him?"

"I'm asking you."

David meets her gaze, but takes a while to respond.

"I only told you what that girl told me. If you want me to go and find her . . ."

"That's not what I asked you."

"Then you have to believe me. It's true!" David insists. "He killed my dog in that lousy, underhand way."

She takes his hand and looks at him for a while, eyes flashing. Eventually she says:

"How could you think that of Inspector Galván? Why would he do that?"

"Just because. You've no idea . . ." David starts in a whisper, then trails off.

"No idea what? Come on, tell your mother."

"You don't realize. He brings us nice things, and keeps you company, and you like him — you like him a lot, don't you? but even so, he's not a good person. He only seems like one when he comes here and sits with you drinking coffee and looks at you and asks how are you feeling today, and tells you not to smoke so much, or not to do this or that, and gives you your medicine or brings you roses." Then he adds in an even lower, silkier tone of voice: "He seems like a good person, but he isn't, Ma. He isn't."

There is an air of entreaty in David's eyes and voice that Ma perceives and interprets on an emotional level, as ever. Somehow she can scent the truth, even though the facts are untrue. And she is right. Now I realize that it was having to live alone and poor for years, and putting up with the situation without complaint, that forged my mother's sensibility, her secret harmony with the world, even her romantic daydreams and her restless sexuality; whenever the mysteries of life leave me feeling defenceless and lonely, I think of her, and the thought brings me the miraculous consolation of her vulnerability and her strength. In his own way, David also accepted this contradiction: as if he knew the truth does not exist, only the wish to discover it, he fought not against truth itself, but against the fragility of its appearance.

"Very well," Ma says, letting go of his hand. "Bring me my slippers, then go out into the street for a while."

"Into the street? Why?"

"Because the inspector and I have to talk. Do as I say."

When the flatfoot comes back into the room with the towel, he finds her sitting at the sewing table strewn with patterns and scraps of material. She has hairpins in her mouth, and her arms are raised as she tries to control the flaming red mass of her hair. That is how David left her, reluctantly letting himself out of the night-time door – because that is the one the inspector normally uses, and he wants to see him leave. He dawdles at the edge of the gully, where the evening bats have already begun to fly; he crosses the riverbed back and forth. He thinks of the lizards asleep under the warm stones, safe from anyone's razor, and this evokes Paulino's crossed eyes and their silent patience, his piles bleeding on to some miserable straw mattress in the Asilo Durán; then he can feel Chispa's cold nose licking his bruised ankles, keeping himself alive, sniffing at his scratches and tincture of iodine. Be still, brave dog, all we have to do is wait, he whispers, his eyes fixed on the villa door, searching for shadows. We've got him, we've got him . . .

It is almost an hour before the door opens and the inspector emerges, unusually for him carrying his jacket crumpled in one hand. This time, the red-head has not come out to say goodbye and shut the door behind him, so he does so and, still rooted to the spot, pulls the brandy flask out of his back trouser pocket, takes a swig, and stows it away again. Putting his jacket on, he starts down the three steps, and comes to a halt once more, his eyes on the ground. He scratches his head as though he is bemused at being hit by some object or other. As David tells it, the look on his face as he stands there on the steps is utterly inscrutable; he slowly finishes doing his jacket up and sets off again, gradually disappearing down the track along the top of the gully, hands in pockets, back straight and alert as ever.

That night, the next day and the one after, Ma refuses to tell David what she and the inspector talked about, so that what my brother was so impatiently waiting for on the gully's edge, what for three months had been his dearest wish, the chance to see the cop unmasked and ejected from the house and his mother's life, the chance to show him for what he really is, a hypocritical liar and a brute of a cop, remains only half-fulfilled, although the consequences of his action could not be more dreadful.

Saddened and with no wish to talk about it, Ma sits sewing by the light of a candle because of the power restrictions. The only thing she lets slip, more to stop David asking any more questions and to get him off to bed than for any other reason, is that Inspector Galván will not be coming back to the house for now.

"What do you mean by 'for now'?"

"Well, just that: he won't be coming for a while at least."

"How long a while?"

"We'll see."

"Was it you who decided that?"

"Yes."

"So what happens now? Won't he be bringing you any more things?"

"That doesn't matter," she says, staring at him. Then she adds: "You're the one I'm worried about."

"You have to think about what I told you . . ."

"I'm thinking of lots of things, son. But most of all, about you."

And Inspector Galván does not appear again until the first week of November, when he turns up unexpectedly and in a state that even David comes to bitterly regret. In the days following David's accusation, not only does he not come near the house, but he disappears from the neighbourhood altogether for three or four weeks, before eventually he starts frequenting local bars and hanging around in them longer than he should. He hardly ever speaks to anybody, and when he does it is to talk about his former job in the wine trade, which often raises laughs at his expense, and occasionally ends in arguments. He quickly starts to go downhill for all to see, and soon seems like a different person. Even today I cannot imagine why he did absolutely nothing to counteract David's slanderous lies, and try to regain the red-head's respect and affection. Everything points to the fact that he is neglecting his professional duties more and more each day, and his superiors in the Brigade must have taken steps, because a representative of law and order who cannot command respect – I'm sorry to have to say this, my girl – the voice is that of the florist in her shop on Calle Cerdeña, as she hugs a tearful young girl who must be none other than the inspector's daughter – a police officer who sets a bad example in bars and cannot even behave properly in his own home, well, someone like that, however much they are suffering, and whatever hopes they may have had crushed, because I know what's wrong with that man, he's had his heart broken yet again, I know, may the Lord have pity on him . . .

Is that what they're saying? may the Lord have pity on him, the red-head wonders, without expecting any reply, without taking her feet from the sewing-machine pedal, patiently cutting and stitching her own patchwork of loneliness; shoeless and with the thick white pair of socks cutting into her swollen ankles, her feet in constant motion, like two doves that can never co-ordinate their flight. If David were at home she could ask him, he must have heard what people are saying, but David has just gone to Señor Marimón's studio, because today he has to develop photos from two baptisms and a wedding, and he will be back late.

At more or less the same time, half past two or three in the afternoon of this misty, cold Wednesday in November, Inspector Galván is propping up the bar in a tavern not far from the house, repeating for the umpteenth time to anyone who cares to listen that it is time he visited Señora Bartra again.

"Give me a coffee and tell me how much I owe you. I'm leaving here right away, do you hear me? I've waited long enough . . . I should have gone there a week ago now."

"That'll be seven pesetas and fifty cents, with the coffee," the barman says, totting up the drinks. "Here you are," he says, pushing the coffee towards him with a sugar cube in the saucer. Before he can withdraw his hand, the inspector grips his wrist like a bird of prey swooping on its victim.

"Two lumps, Amadeo, two! Don't you know that by now, or are you just completely tight-fisted?" says the inspector, still pinioning his hand. "I always have two lumps with my coffee, try to remember that!"

"I'm sorry, I didn't realize, Don Manuel . . ." says the barman, who suddenly senses in the other man's burning hand, in the fury that the rushing blood conveys, something of the private hell he must be going through. But the inspector is no troublemaker: he never has been, and is not one now. "I forgot. Here are your two lumps, it's all fixed."

"Fine, fine . . . What time is it? Almost three? I'm off, someone's waiting for me . . ."

But the afternoon goes by with him saying he is going, and then it is evening and he is still there, alternating wine and coffee, and when he finally makes up his mind he does not tell anyone, he simply puts his hand on the top of his glass, as if he were trying to keep it quiet, pays with the other hand, and strides determinedly out of the tavern. His back to the sunset, he sees the first street lamps going on in Plaza Sanllehy, hears the whir of bicycle wheels as they come flying down the hill, the voices and happy chatter of girls coming out of a pharmaceutical laboratory, then the dark gully once more, with its pulsing web of bats, and almost at once the door to the villa with its imposing knocker. His feet unsteadily mount the crumbling three steps. The door which never used to be locked is now tight shut, so he has to go out and up along the track again, then turn into the dead-end street and walk down to the day-time door still guarded by its clump of cut back, faded marguerites. The light from the living-room flickers on and off, as though the bulb is badly connected. He strides up to the door, but a few seconds before he reaches it, he is overwhelmed by the certainty that it is too late. He tramples down the marguerites and gazes in at the window. The red-head is lying slumped on the floor next to the sewing-machine. She has her housecoat on, and one hand is outstretched, holding a slipper. She is not moving, but the inspector can see that her hand is trembling convulsively, so he launches himself at the door and presses as hard as he can on the bell, although he already suspects David is not at home. He beats at the door with his fists, and tries in vain to open the window. As quickly as possible, he smashes the pane with his elbow, feels inside and opens the window. He drops his trenchcoat and jumps into the room. He kneels beside her and tries to bring her round by slapping her cheek and calling her name; the convulsions cease, but her swollen eyes and lips frighten him so much he stops, picks her up and rushes out into the street. He runs along with her in his arms, shouting for a car or taxi. A few of the neighbours come out, in time to see him suddenly turn a corner in the direction of the Avenida, where he stops a private car, shows them his police badge, and orders the terrified driver to take them to the Maternity Clinic as fast as he can. At one point, Ma appears to recover consciousness, but then the convulsions start again and by the time she is taken into the operating theatre fifteen minutes later, she is virtually in a coma.

I have not yet been born, and already I am dying. More than once throughout my life I have regretted the fact that she did not take me with her that night, still snug and warm in the secret romantic hopes of a former schoolteacher barred from her profession, the naïve daydream I represented for her during those seven months, a shadow in her womb already with pen in hand. Come out and tell the story, she would have said had she been able to. At his birth, the stars had told my mother that David was a portent of the terrible masquerade to come; I though, she thought, would bear witness to a bright and truthful future. The fact is that seeing me arrive in this world in such a ghastly, moribund way, seeing her losing blood and slipping inexorably from us in that dilapidated, ill-equipped hospital theatre, nobody would have agreed with her. I was born prematurely, blue from cyanosis and weighing less than a mosquito, with a cerebral lesion that will keep me in bed for heaven knows how many years, and with the look of a wolf-child that curdles milk. For three months, my tender claws are wrapped in cotton wool.

"I'll look after the baby, if it survives, and his brother too; you will sleep at my house tonight, David," Aunt Lola decides as soon as the doctor has explained what has happened. She has been unable to get a word out of the inspector, thanks to whom she was sent for and told to come.

Everything took place so quickly. The red-head is still lying covered with a sheet in the operating theatre. In the corridor outside, a yard in front of Uncle Pau, who is silent and obviously upset, still crammed into his uniform and carrying his tram conductor's satchel over his shoulder, it is Aunt Lola who deals with all the sad details and takes all the necessary decisions, doleful and uningratiating as ever, but resolute and without shedding a single tear. She has been standing at the operating theatre door since she arrived, in her old-fashioned, grey-lapelled coat and carrying her black velvet bag with its gold clasp that sounds like a gunshot, listening to the surgeon's explanations – the diagnosis was hopeless even before we went into theatre, Señora Ribas – and considering the suggestions a priest is making about the religious service in the chapel, and all the while observing close at hand the collapse of the distraught man sitting on a bench in the corridor, the same man who some time ago had questioned her about the whereabouts of her brother-in-law Víctor. She had heard rumours of a policeman's strange obsession with her sister: rumours which only served to confirm her impression of what she called Rosa's libertarian nonsense and the unhappiness and misfortune she was letting herself in for as a result of her disastrous marriage, but now she prefers not to get involved, to avoid any kind of familiarity with this gentleman.

Making a great effort to appear calm and in control, the inspector asks a nurse if he can go into the operating theatre, but she says not now please. Lola and her husband are sorting out more details in some office or other. In the otherwise deserted corridor, David is waiting, leaning back against the wall as he weeps without a sound; on a bench opposite him, totally oblivious to his grief, the inspector sits, head in hands, staring at the floor-tiles. A good while later, he turns to look at David with a mixture of despair and contained contempt, as a single word whirling obsessively through his mind.

When David first hears it, the word means nothing to him: eclampsia. In that stubborn fatalist way of his, it is not until a long while later that he accepts there is a direct relation between my birth and her death; and even then he cannot shake off the bitterness of guilt, cannot help but think that Ma was all alone in the house when she had the attack, and that if Inspector Galván could have been with her as he had so often been, chatting and drinking coffee with his two lumps of sugar and the American cigarettes he sometimes denied her, with his gold Dupont and his famous white rose, if the two of them had been able to carry on talking about Pa or the war or her problems with the pregnancy, about anything or nothing, simply if this man had been able to appear at the villa at the time he used to come, if David had not sought so viciously to blame him for everything, then the red-head would have got medical help in time and would still be alive. That is the plain truth. Nobody, not even Inspector Galván, could imagine how much this affected David, and many years and many empty trams had to go by – as Pa used to say – before I myself became aware of it.

David raises his head, and realizes that the inspector is still sitting on the bench. He sees his hand groping for the hip flask in his back pocket; with nimble, surprisingly quick fingers, the inspector unscrews the top and lifts the flask to his lips, then all of a sudden stops and puts it down again. David looks away and a few seconds later when he turns back towards the policeman, the bench where he had been sitting is empty and next to him the flapping doors of the operating theatre come slowly to rest, without ever meeting.

XII

Return to the Gully

Now I have to take a leap back in the blurred memory of my blood, a kind of backward somersault. It's not another of my bits of supine mischief inside the womb, whose aim was always to get a better vantage point for myself in the placenta of this story: no, this time I want to paint a picture of myself years later, the child chosen by destiny, living in a poor household near the bridge in Vallcarca, laid up in bed and still trying to cope with the consequences of a premature birth. I am barely six years old, and spend most of my time still curled up like a foetus, surrounded by photos of trams and scrawling short-sightedly with a black pencil in old school exercise books. Lucía, Aunt Lola's youngest child, is two and is playing at the foot of my bed with a rag doll. I am looked after by my aunt and uncle, by my cousin Fátima, but above all by David, who will soon be twenty and now works full-time for Marimón the portrait photographer, who has done well over the years and has a studio and shop in the Rambla del Prat.

For three years after the red-head's death, nobody can control David, who runs a real risk of joining his friend Paulino in the reform school. A trouble-maker and a loner, he is always involved in any disturbances in the town. For a long while he is good for nothing, and manages to keep his job only thanks to Aunt Lola's good offices and her determination to straighten him out. In addition, Cousin Fátima's gentle complicity in his first fumbling attempts at romance succeed in calming him considerably, at least for a while. But nobody could have imagined that what would really save him from his own furies would be work.

In the photographic studio, David learns the art of retouching portraits to enhance the sitter. According to Señor Marimón himself, he is very good at this: he knows how to make brides' smiles broader and more attractive on their wedding days; how to emphasize the innocent look of boys and girls all dressed up for First Communion, how to make their eyelashes seem longer and silkier; how to soften the skins or straighten the noses of unfortunate young women. After a while though, this kind of work starts to pall: he becomes more interested in photo-reportage, in capturing the reality of the streets with his own second-hand Voigtländer, then developing it without any embellishment, without having to retouch the negative with his sharpened pencil. Cousin Fátima, who was always more or less in love with him, reckons that David discovered his true vocation by taking photos of her, after a short but enthusiastic phase devoted to artistic photography, a solitary and somewhat ridiculous activity whose most noteworthy results were a dozen shots of her on the beach or here at home – Fátima sitting naked on my bed, smelling a white rose, a photo I keep between the pages of one of my books – and above all, the ones he took one morning up in Guinardó, after spending hours wandering the streets with his camera slung round his neck in a naïve search for the unexpected.

It was a quiet, close Sunday in September. It occurred to him to return to the gully and take photos of the villa with its bricked-up windows, of the small consulting-room door, and the riverbed, by now even more ravaged and stony. The last rains had left tiny new banks of fine white sand on the riverbed, and various bits of debris were sticking up out of the mud. David photographed them from the most elaborate and unusual angles: a soldier's boot grimaces through a mouthful of twisted nails, the bald and battered head of an eyeless doll staring up at the sky as a potato might do, a leash or belt coiled up on itself, and so eaten away by the damp that it looked more like a snake's skin, the stiff legs of a half-buried bird scrabbling at the sky, half the face of a wall clock with a snail crawling across its hours . . . in each and every one of these discarded objects, the eye of the camera investigates their hidden identity in close-up and redefines it, seizes hold of it and rethinks it, re-creating it above and beyond the specific history its decay and abandonment might suggest. Photos of the gully, of the little that remains of its crumbling sides and childhood sense of daring, photos covered in a layer of time, a reflection of the light that is not so distant from my own observations here in the hollow of my pillow. There is not a single voice among all those I have noted here, not a single word scribbled in these old school notebooks – endless symmetrical waves that seem like a parody of a cripple's illegible handwriting, according to some – which does not have its origin in that crumbling, fetid riverbed my memory keeps from oblivion. My pencil rushes across the squared pages only to preserve the memory of it alive and untouched.

And so against all the odds – since he was not chosen by destiny – David is launched on the path to becoming a scrupulous seeker after the truth, an artist. A few months later, at the start of March 1951, he frees himself from the well-worn techniques and the retouching he has become such an expert in, and starts out as a photo-journalist. That is when it all happens. I am in bed and my Uncle Pau sits beaming and silent beside me. He has just brought me my breakfast, and has a bandage on his forehead that makes his tram conductor's peaked cap sit awry. He watches me eat while he buttons up his uniform before heading off to the tram depot for his shift. Yesterday a stone shattered his tram's back window, and a splinter of glass gave him a sizeable cut on the forehead. From somewhere in the house Aunt Lola's voice can be heard: I don't know why you have to go in after what they've done to you, stay at home and let them kill each other, they're going to burn your trams, don't go, don't be so stupid . . . but my uncle sits there buttoning up his jacket and watching me eat my tuna sandwich with that vacant smile of his on his lips, shakes a few crumbs off the bedcover and whispers yes, they got me right on the nut, yes, smiling at me again, and those transparent eyes of his, such patience he has looking after the poorly kid, so silent and easily attainable all that he wants from life – from tram to bar, bar to home, home to tram – it was yesterday afternoon in Plaza Cataluña, he tells me, whispering as though it were a secret, they gave us a good stoning, so my aunt won't hear, even though the tram was completely empty, we hadn't had a passenger all day, and they throw stones at us and insult us . . .

The strike by tram users, caused by a steep fare increase, has kept the city in suspense for two days already. Señor Marimón, who is linked to a clandestine union which has been very active since the start of this popular protest, is deter-mined to get a photographic record of what is going on in the streets of Barcelona so he can send it abroad for publication. Knowing how interested David has become in reportage, he suggests the idea to him, and asks him to take photos of trams travelling empty. It's a bit risky, he says, but if you get a good photo you could become famous.

On the next day, Saturday, David goes out into the streets with his Voigtländer and joins the demonstrators, running the gauntlet of the mounted police and more than once narrowly avoiding having his camera snatched from him. Until now he has shown little interest in what was going on, and has not sided with anyone or anything. As taciturn and aloof as ever, neither at home or at work has he been heard to express an opinion for or against the strike and the street protests; their success or failure seem to be all the same to him. Coolly, moving about cleverly and stealthily and hiding his camera under his raincoat, he manages to shoot an entire roll, which he develops that same night. All the photos show trams travelling empty, with only the driver and conductor on board, but the framing and the focus are inadequate, and they do not convey the sense of movement and veracity he is looking for.

On the afternoon of Sunday the 4th, he shoots off another roll outside the Las Corts football stadium, among the crowds leaving the Barça-Santander game. Despite the pouring rain, not a single person gets on any of the numerous trams that the civilian-military authorities have laid on for them, aware that large numbers of fans will be going to the match. David takes his last photo in a downpour, standing firmly in the middle of the tram tracks on a bend, as the last light of day is fading, raincoat draped over his head to protect his camera. For a split second, the noise of the rain all around him drowns out the coffee-pot hissing permanently installed by now in his ears, and something tells him this time he has got the perfect photo. And he has, it's in my hand right now: lit by a ghostly light from its windows, twisted and ominous, the tram charges round the bend at you on its rails, the curtain of water giving it a spiky halo. All around it you can see the indifferent, hunched-up crowd, a sea of heads ignoring its presence, men shrinking from the dreadful weather, some of them seeking refuge under umbrellas, others using newspapers, all the rest at the mercy of the rain. Lit up in the midst of this crowd, the tram looks like a spectre rising from the depths of the rainstorm.

But when David examines the negative closely before he starts developing it that same night, he spots a small blurry white cloud in one of the tram's side windows. When he develops it, the blur becomes clear: it is the black silhouette of a passenger sitting there with his hat on and the lapels of his jacket turned up. He must be the only person in the entire city who dared to take a tram that evening. Rotten luck. David wants to throw the photo away, but when Señor Marimón sees it, he says it is so good they ought to use it, and suggests David removes the human shape by retouching the photo as only he knows how. He thinks David's work is an excellent example of the photo-journalism he aspires to, and congratulates him on it. At first, David refuses to manipulate the photo: he can get better shots than that without any need for tricks or special effects, he says. Señor Marimón does not understand his scruples, he gets impatient and orders him to do it so that he can have prints ready the next morning. Reluctantly, David obeys; he returns to the negative and, using his sharpest pencil, carefully blocks out the white shadow. This time when he develops the photo, the untimely passenger – a blackleg perhaps, or a policeman? – has disappeared without trace.

He explains all this to cousin Fátima, sitting on my bed. He shows her the retouched photo he has not yet handed over to Señor Marimón. In fact he has no intention of doing so, I can see it in his face when he tosses it into my lap for me to look at and amuse myself with, to tear up if I wish. That child stammering and smiling as he looks at his brother, then at the photo, then again at his brother, is me. I am lying there in the helpless state from which I conjure up my visions and my wanderings, surrounded by coloured pencils, breadcrumbs and books; I can see David as he pulls away for a moment from our cousin's welcoming mouth, to look across at me and pretend I am saying to him: I don't like it brother, you're up to your old tricks, you've cheated.

I know what you're thinking, you sad foetus, his eyes say to me. But however much you think about it and insist, don't imagine you're going to make me feel any worse than I do already.

I'm not blaming you for anything.

Stop playing the victim, hairy monkey, I can do that for both of us.

Anyway, I like that photo.

Keep it then.

"David, listen," says our cousin, sitting next to me on the bed, opening the book where patiently every afternoon she points out the letters of the alphabet to me and tells me the names of things. "If it's empty trams you want, go with Pa to the depot at Sants, you'll have all the time in the world to take photos of as many as you like there . . . Look, Víctor: Do-ve. Say it slowly: Do-ve."

"No," growls David, rubbing his lips with the back of his hand. "It has to be a tram that's really travelling in the city."

"Ap-ple. Bir-die. Bi-g-ki-ss. Say it slowly: bi-g-ki-ss," our cousin says with a smile, but David's expression turns sombre and he draws even further away from her. "What's wrong with you? You've got a wonderful photo, isn't that enough? Señor Marimón will be really angry with you, he'll sack you if you don't take it to him . . ."

"I couldn't care less, cousin. It's for Víctor. I think he likes it – look, he won't let go of it. I'll get a better one. One that's as it should be."

On Monday the 14th, when popular discontent on the streets has turned into an attempted general strike that goes far beyond the tram dispute, David goes to meet his appointment with destiny at a lonely intersection in Gracia. He is walking through Bailén on his way to the demonstration in Plaza Cataluña, watching out for empty trams on routes 30 and 38, taking photos from behind a tree. Each time he clicks the shutter he feels that the pure and simple truth he is now searching for flashes in his eye like a luminous ray. He is taking a bite from an apple he had in his pocket when at the intersection with Calle Santa

Eulalia he runs into two armed policemen. They demand he hand over the camera and identify himself. One of them grabs him by the arm while the other tries to seize the camera, but he manages to save it.

"All right, but give it to me," the cop says.

"No, bwana. I'm a photographer, and Inspector Galván of the Social Brigade has given me permission . . ."

"OK. Give me the camera and behave, come on," the cop says, pulling out his blackjack.

"Call the inspector and you'll see I'm not lying," says David, stepping back and flailing his arms to keep them off.

"I don't want to have to get violent . . ."

Some of the photos he has already taken must be very good, and he knows it, otherwise he would never have done what he does now: he sticks his finger in one of the cop's eye, trips the other up, and sets off running towards the tram that is roaring down the hill, its pole sending sparks from the overhead cable. In order to avoid being caught again, he wants to reach the platform on the far side of the tram, but it is travelling too quickly and slams into him. The impact throws him into the air, and before the tram can slow to a halt it has crushed him beneath the iron steps of the front platform, dragging him along for several yards.

The first of the two policemen to reach him does not dare touch him. David opens his eyes and looks around as if he does not know where he is.

"Goodness. Are my legs buried in sand?"

"Your neck's broken, dammit," the cop growls.

The second policeman also bends down, stares at him, then jumps up quickly and asks an onlooker where he can find a telephone. The conductor is sitting on the tram steps, head in hands. David clutches the camera to his chest, and with the other strokes the cold, wet cobblestones.

"My hands are burning," he says faintly. "I bet you've never seen a leather flying jacket like this one, have you . . . ?"

"Don't try to move, kid," the cop says. "We'll get you out of there."

"Nobody will ever get me out of here."

"Don't look down at your chest."

"No holes in my jacket, please . . ."

"Don't talk, stay still. Do as I say."

The policeman straightens up when he sees his colleague arriving with help. David looks away from him, and picks a piece of apple skin from between his teeth. As he does so, he senses the roaring in his ears slowly receding, and lays his head on the ground without any sign of pain, as if he was bending over a river to hear its murmur, or resting it on a pillow as he curls up to sleep.

Nobody ever returned his Voigtländer to us, or the last film he shot that afternoon, the one which perhaps contained his favourite photo, luminous and emblematic, bathed in that glow of truth that comes from persistence, the one whose negative he wanted to develop without any retouching. I don't know if he took such a photo, we will never know, but the one I do have, the one he took a few days earlier of the ghost-like tram in the rain, surrounded by a crowd of cowed yet obstinate people, with frayed raincoats on wretched backs and soaked newspapers over their heads, that photo he had manipulated with his sharpened pencil in the solitude of the developing room, is still the most relevant and moving image of all the ones David took, the fullest and truest testimony of an event that, many years ago, shook this city.

Now someone has opened windows and shutters, under my pillow I can feel my pencil and my exercise books filled with scribbles like waves chasing each other in a boundless sea. Soon Lucía will be here with another glass of milk and my medicine, and then I'll want to read for a while from the only novel I have of the red-head's, and I'll say to Lucía: pass me *War and Peace*, will you? I'll have to repeat it several times though, because even though I make a great effort, what comes out of my mouth sounds like assmewarapis.

The fact is, I still find it hard to make myself understood.